"*The Secret Swan* by Shana Abé is a delightful novel that should not be missed! Ms. Abé has crafted a tale that is sure to grip readers and never let go. Once you start reading this tale of love, you won't be able to stop until you turn the last page—it's that good! Ms. Abé delivers an exciting and beautifully woven tale with a rich and fascinating plot which is layered with plenty of intrigue. *The Secret Swan* boasts excellent narration and engaging dialogue. Ms. Abé has definitely penned a winner! Readers of historical romance are sure to claim this book for their keepers shelf!" —*Reader to Reader*

# INTIMATE ENEMIES

"Shana Abé has created an unforgettable pair of star-crossed lovers caught in an age-old feud, while beautifully evoking the misty isle and the historical backdrop. She truly makes us believe we are part of this wondrous tale."
—*Romantic Times*

"Historical romance at its finest!"
—Jill Marie Landis

"Ms. Abé has written another winner."
—*Affaire de Coeur*

"Ms. Abé's expert writing transports the reader to medieval Scotland, where they become enthralled in an emotional romance complete with passion, drama, danger and adventure." —*Rendezvous*

## Also by Shana Abé

QUEEN OF DRAGONS

THE DREAM THIEF

THE SMOKE THIEF

THE SECRET SWAN

INTIMATE ENEMIES

A KISS AT MIDNIGHT

THE TRUELOVE BRIDE

THE PROMISE OF RAIN

A ROSE IN WINTER

# The
# LAST
# MERMAID

## Shana Abé

BANTAM BOOKS

THE LAST MERMAID
A Bantam Book

PUBLISHING HISTORY
Bantam mass market edition published June 2004
Bantam reissue / May 2008

Published by Bantam Dell
A Division of Random House, Inc.
New York, New York

This is a work of fiction. Names, characters, places, and incidents
either are the product of the author's imagination or are used
fictitiously. Any resemblance to actual persons, living or dead,
events, or locales is entirely coincidental.

Bantam Books and the rooster colophon are registered trademarks of
Random House, Inc.

ISBN 978-0-553-59186-6

Printed in the United States of America

www.bantamdell.com

OPM 10 9 8 7 6 5 4 3 2 1

For Darren, who loves me.

And for Wendy McCurdy, who saw the promise of three love stories in just a few rough sentences.

*Mucho aprecio* also to Annelise Robey and Andrea Cirillo, and to the family, of course, because they always get a thanks.

# The
# LAST
# MERMAID

# Book One:

# The Legend

# · PROLOGUE ·

Once there was an island. . . .

For a thousand, thousand years it lay untouched, well apart from man, a place of myth and magic, enduring every dawn, every lavender twilight in sparkling isolation. No ship dared brave its waters, no human stepped its shores. Sailors who knew of it swore it was home to the sea gods, forbidden to mortals. They offered unearthly proof, silvered songs swept over the waters, distant laughter, sinful sweet. Wild storms whipped up should a ship come too near, blinding mists, an angry sea. Others still swore that to try to reach it was to sail along forever, the promise of perfection hanging always just out of reach.

So while the world constantly roiled and changed, the island remained pure and calm, a shining pearl suspended in blue, blue waters.

Sometimes the sea winds smiled, and the mists would lift and glow. Those few who glimpsed its

wonder never forgot the sight: a lost lush land, bliss-
ful poison, both dulcet and deadly; an enchanted isle
so dazzling a man would sell his soul to claim it.

And, in time, one man did.

No one ever knew his full name. He lived before
such records were kept, before even the lessons of
the fields were written in scrolls, or ancient fables
sung from father to son. The man was known only
as Kell, and he gave his name to the island he settled
as much as he gave his life.

He was a lone fisherman, lost at sea, dying. In the
rapture of his death he dreamed of a woman beside
him, crooning a song that seemed to cut loose his
pain until he floated beside her, bespelled.

She was not a woman, of course. Like her island,
she was that which no man could claim: a mermaid,
with hair of spun gold and eyes of blue storm and
skin that gleamed rarest ivory. In her bewitching
voice she offered the fisherman a bargain, and he
grabbed at it—his life for his soul, and a marriage to
her.

Far and wide she had haunted the seas, the last of
her kind, doomed by her very nature to live and die
alone unless she gained the willing soul of a mortal
man. In marriage she vowed to keep safe the fisherman's soul, to honor and serve him as well as any
land-bound maiden could do. He would have riches
beyond his dreams, a castle, a family, a home. He
would be forever loved.

Now, as the legend was told, Kell was neither
heathen nor fool. He knew what he risked but he did
it anyway, for by then he had lost his reason in the
siren's blue storm eyes. Moreover, he had seen the
island she declared would be their own. It was green

forest and glittering streams, sanded beaches and hidden grottoes, deer and owls and night creatures stirring, and all the secret wealth the earth and sea together could offer.

So there on the sunswept sea he gave the mermaid his soul, and reckless more. He pledged to love her in return, to let her swim the waters and walk the land, and to never doubt her wild, wild heart.

On her enchanted island they lived a very long time, longer than any man could count. The mermaid wife bore him many children; everything she promised turned true. For a while, Kell was content.

Yet time changes all men, and fisherman Kell was no different. Although he had lost his soul he still had his own wild heart, and in it lived a tiny, tiny seed of doubt. Over the years it grew, slowly, quietly, until he came to regret his bargain, despite his charmed life. He began to resent the island and his sea-born family. He spoke of returning to his old home, a place of plows and furrows and plain men, far from enchantment.

But the mermaid would not release him. She kept his soul locked tight near her heart in a locket of shining silver, on a necklace she never removed.

Finally, one moonless night, Kell could abide it no longer. While his merwife slept, he crept close and snatched the silver chain from her neck, opening the talisman locket. It waked her instantly, and she reached up to him and cried out:

*My beloved, my fool! You have forsaken us both!*

For all the while she had kept it close, the soul stayed captive near her heart, enslaved but safe. But when the fisherman opened the locket, his soul fled free to the stars.

Old Kell died in that very moment, forsaken as the mermaid had said. And that night she returned to the sea, wounded and forlorn, vowing in her pain to curse love, to keep her island and her children safe from faithless mortals.

From the starswept grottoes she sang her siren song, fair warning to all who passed by:

> *An island charmed, the world full scorned;*
> *An ocean rough, rash sailors mourned.*
> *Here is my curse, born of true love's lie:*
> *Leave off this place, leave off or die.*
>
> *Dare come and long you'll stay,*
> *Trapped in heart, night and day.*
> *Leave again and the price is steep:*
> *Plea not to spare; 'tis death you'll meet.*
>
> *Three spins my curse I give,*
> *The will to change, the hope to live.*
> *Six lives shall come to be,*
> *To end this spell, to set me free:*
>
> *King's kiss to siren death, a soul retrieved;*
> *Child of the sea unveiled, belov'd of his enemy;*
> *Twin spirits lost, returned, to complete this destiny.*
>
> *So say I. So mote it be.*

And still the island lingers just beyond reach, dazzling, seductive. And still the sailors whisper: Beware the siren and her children. Beware the sweet poison of Kell.

# CHAPTER ONE

❧

## Kingdom of the Isles, 512 A.D.

The sea was fitful tonight, and the creaking and moaning of the ship kept Aedan awake long after his parents and sister had drifted to their dreams. He lay there in the almost-dark, watching the last narrow flame of the hanging lamps with drowsy distraction.

The ship rose and fell. Aedan's stomach lurched with it.

The royal quarters were fine but very close, smelling of musky furs and rushes and the ocean. Always the ocean. If he closed his eyes he could imagine it past the hull: black and chopped and slick with moonlight, silver caps over endless waves.

He would not close his eyes. That made his stomach worse.

He would defeat this. He would not succumb. That was the way of kings. True, he was not yet a king, but someday—

The ship plowed high and hung, suspended; Aedan pressed his head back into his pillow and grabbed the edge of his pallet, swallowing hard. With a mighty groan the prow slammed down again, sending shudders through the floor.

He sat up, breathing through his mouth. The lamp swayed in place with sickening gaiety, back and forth and back . . . he could smell it now too . . . hot metal and oil, greasy, cloying.

He staggered from his pallet and to the door, groping for the latch.

A soft voice, just behind him. "Aedan?"

So Callese was not asleep, but he didn't have time to talk to her. He tugged open the door and made it to the stairs, gulping fresh air, then somehow managed to find his way up them, his hands flattened to the walls, fighting the roll of the sea.

It was dark out, black as his imagination, but it was some time before Aedan noticed. He was entwined with the lower deck railing. He was holding on for his life, his eyes squeezed shut, until the cold wind on his face began to bite. Gradually, cautiously, he opened his eyes. A writhing sea, a cloudless night. A figure in white huddled near—his little sister, seated with easy balance on the treacherous deck, her nightgown fluttering, staring up at him with great blue eyes.

"How is it?" she asked.

"It's nothing." He turned back to the wind.

Aedan loathed this weakness within him. It shamed him, more than he could say, that his body was so flawed. He worried it was a sign of some deeper fault, that he was secretly craven, or stupid, or weak. He was a prince, Lord of the Woods, heir to the High Throne. He could not have faults. What would people—*his* people—say if his private fears were true, if he failed them? He was twelve now, old enough to control his stomach *and* his flaws. He would learn to control them.

Callese scooted closer, until her gown blew over them both and she could wrap her hands around his upper arm. They sat there together, side by side, and watched the ocean bounce by.

"You should go back down," Aedan said, quiet, because there would be a sailor nearby. "You're freezing."

"I'm not."

"You're not allowed here without a guard, Callese."

"Neither are you," she answered, reasonable. He glanced down at her, stubborn and skinny, her profile hidden by a wildly waving mop of flaxen hair. She was small for her age, five years younger than he, the most precious thing in his world. If he was flawed then Callese was his opposite in every way: brisk and brash and truly fearless; as she stretched her bare feet between the rails, he wound his arm around her shoulders to pull her back.

"Callese, go down."

"Come with me."

He tested the thought of that—cramped chamber, hot metal, musk—and had to take a great breath of air again.

"Not yet. You go. I'll be down soon."

She didn't even bother to reply, only nestled closer, her head against his ribs. She would not go without a fuss, and Aedan knew, wholeheartedly, that he did not want a fuss. The last thing he wanted was to have to explain why the two of them were out here, at the forbidden edge of the ship, in late, late night all alone.

Very well. He settled back on his hands, enjoying the warmth of her at his side. It wasn't so bad out here, really. He didn't *hate* the sea—after all, one day he would rule it, just as he would rule all the isles that made up the kingdom. He rather liked it now, Aedan decided. Aye, right now, in this moment, even with the sharp cresting waves, it was almost . . . peaceful.

Callese raised her arm and pointed silently to the east. A wisp of green flared to life on the horizon: eerie, distant, like faerie fire lit above the water. Out of habit Aedan turned his head and searched the other direction, looking for markers that would tell him how far they were still from home. There was an island, just coming into view . . . he couldn't tell yet which it was . . . not very large, so not Bealou, or Alis. Not Griflet, with its distinctive cove . . .

Aedan frowned. He should know this. He knew all the islands, better than his own heart—

He realized the truth just as Callese gasped and stiffened. They said it together:

"Kell."

Just the name pricked the hairs on the back of his neck. They were looking at Kell! The one island no one, not even the king, ever touched. Aedan knew it by whispers and legends, all that was left of the untamed earth, a cursed place with the souls of countless sailors trapped upon its shores. It was dangerous, profane. Prohibited.

Aedan scrambled to his feet to see it better. Callese was already up, leaning over the railing. He leaned with her.

He had glimpsed it from a distance before, but never this close. Ships weren't even allowed to come this close, he thought—perhaps the wind had blown them off course. . . .

Rough hills above the waves, faint at first, catching the barest hint of green dawn. A beach, sand and the ruffled line of trees. Cliffs, very tall. Faerie light, soot shadows. Lost ships all wrong in the water, broken and torn, menacing, toothsome with jagged timber—and then finally—

"The castle," Callese breathed. "Oh, Aedan, look." She

was enthralled beside him, nearly trembling. Aedan let out his own breath, astonishment and awe and still a twinge of disbelief, even as he stared.

A castle—or what might have been one once, with stone walls tucked behind trees, and a pointed roof, and pillars. It was very difficult to see, small and blurred, as if a mist lurked between them and it. It was the castle, surely—or more cliffs? No, no, that had to be cut stone; why else would it glow, why else would it gleam?

The siren castle of Kell. Aye.

Callese sighed. "Why . . . it looks like—"

"Sanctuary," finished Aedan softly. "It looks like sanctuary."

"Yes."

Their ship was moving very quickly, angling away from the isle as if the captain only now realized how close to danger they had come. Above them the sails cracked with the new direction; men shouted and the ship bucked, protesting the heavy waves. Without warning, Callese hurried off, running down the deck toward the vanishing isle.

"Callese!"

He darted after her, his own gaze still drawn to the shore, that teasing flash of castle behind trees. They would be caught—Father would be so angry—but it was *Kell.* . . .

She stopped at the stern, slanted against the short railing there, a little girl on her toes with too much hair and not enough weight, silhouetted against the open sky. Somehow, in the dark nightmare part of him, Aedan realized what was about to happen. He knew it and could not move any faster, his feet too slow, the wind too strong. He had her name on his lips and his hands outstretched—

—but the ship heaved, sending him stumbling, and his sister dipped and fell, quite gracefully, over the side.

A wordless howl escaped him. He was sliding across the slippery wood, clawing his way to her. He was at the railing, half over it himself, searching for her, calling for help as the ocean streaked by in blue and black and faerie green.

One hand, one slim and pinched hand, had stopped her fall, clutching the very bottom of a post. She dangled there, her mouth wide open, maybe screaming—he couldn't hear her—the ocean, the wind—

He bent over the rail, grabbed her wrist, braced his feet, and pulled. She wasn't heavy—he knew she wasn't— why couldn't he lift her up? His hands were too wet from the deck, they were slipping from her wrist to her palm, her fingers—no, no, he had to do it, he had to. . . .

Her other hand slapped at the top of the railing. He grabbed that one too, hissing with effort. Where were the others? Why didn't they come?

Her head came into view, her hair floating, pale yellow across her face. He had never seen her so frightened—she could not be half as scared as he. She tried to hook her elbow over the railing and missed; he leaned out, clutched a handful of gown, stretching the material taut. She was nearly there, nearly there. . . .

Callese *was* screaming. It was his name, over and over, high-pitched and frantic. A faraway commotion was building, pounding footsteps, men yelling. But he had her now—

She was stuck halfway across the railing with nothing left to hold, her legs kicking over the sea. Aedan reached out even farther, caught her ankle. For an appalling moment they teetered there together; he had a very clear view of the water below. Oh, God, he had thought it nauseating before. . . .

Callese kicked again, clipping him in the jaw, hard enough to draw blood. He lost his grip on her leg.

*Don't let go, don't let go, don't let go!*

He had leaned too far. They began to slide the wrong way. Callese's screams choked thin, barely a squeak as they started to fall. They were going to die; it was his fault for not watching her, his fault, his—

Something deep within Aedan awoke, a fervor he did not recognize, gathering swift, gathering strong. He felt it rising through him, a voice, a will, a command:

He would not die like this. He would not let her die.

With a full-throated cry, Aedan wrenched them both back, tumbling them onto the deck. He landed on his elbow and then his shoulder, rolling with his sister, right into the skidding feet of the captain and his men.

They were lifted apart. He was standing, stunned, shaking. There were hands on his shoulders, clapping his back. A jostling crowd engulfed them; all he could see were tunics and beards. The sailors were shouting over one another—*Mother Mary, what a feat*—*he caught her, Holy Jesus, did you see the lad go*—and in the middle of the confusion Callese wobbled over and threw her arms around him, breaking into sobs against his chest.

He held her and let her weep as the feeling seeped back into his limbs. Slowly the buzzing in his ears receded, and the men's praise began to filter through.

He had done it. He had saved her.

Aedan looked up at the rough faces surrounding them and grinned.

# CHAPTER TWO

❧

## 531 A.D., nineteen years later

"Are the men prepared?"

"Aye, my lord."

"Good." Crouching in mud, covered in leaves and dye, the commander surveyed the scene below him, the line of riders and horses that snaked along the mountain path. "There," he whispered, his lips barely moving. "There he is, in the lead. The great prince himself."

"I see him, my lord."

"Tell the men. He is the one."

"Aye."

Down below, riding ever closer, the black-haired warrior at the head of the party scanned the trees and grass, tall on his mount, moments from his undoing.

The commander raised one finger, his signal to the others, pointed to the warrior, and let his arm fall.

It was a damned inconvenient place for an ambush.

They were near the very end of the journey. It had

been a long, arduous ordeal from the start, and Aedan was finally beginning to relax, to contemplate the pleasures of home. The summer clouds that had skirted the horizon all day were at last beginning to rise and thicken and rush the sky. Their edges had swollen barbarous black, rolling closer as the sun began to set. They promised a monster storm, but Aedan and his people would be well inside the fortress before it let loose.

He had already sent the outriders ahead to Kelmere, to announce their arrival in the style his father would appreciate. He had had no choice in it; this was a royal entourage, and the fact that there were merely twelve of them, battered and weary, was a thing that could not be helped. His father would expect the outriders. What the king demanded, the king received.

The king, no doubt, had not anticipated an insult such as this, a massacre at his very gate.

It was an upland trail, one of the many secret ribbons of dirt that laced through these hills. At times the path seemed to vanish entirely, leaving only a suggestion of itself winding along fields of feathered grass and pink heather. This close to the fortress it wound delicately around the rim of the mountain, vertical thick woods on one side and a dizzying drop down the other. They rode single file here; again, a thing that could not be helped.

But then, help could not have reached them in time anyway.

Aedan was warned first by the silence, the utter and absolute lack of sound, aside from the tired clip of the horses and the thin, lonely ballad of the wind.

No birdsong. No crickets. No animals in the woods.

It was twilight; blue glow and sliding shadows, the space between worlds, as Mòrag would say, and in that strange void of quiet Aedan realized, all at once, that he and his group were riding straight into a trap.

Even as he raised his arm in warning, it was too late. They came from the woods, pouring down the side of the hill—savage men, cloaked in leaves and dirt and forest moss, with shrieks and swords and eyes that burned even in the soft evening light.

His mount reacted to the sudden fury, bounding back, panicked. It was the third such attack in a sennight, and the stallion was beyond his limits.

"To arms!" Aedan shouted, but his words were lost beneath the battle cries of the Picts swarming over them, locusts erupting from the earth. He drew his own sword and plunged it into the man nearest him, dodging the lance of the next, trying to turn both himself and the stallion in the impossible confines of the path.

Two Picts launched themselves at him at once, managing to unseat him. Aedan landed with a stunning *whump*, blinded by dust and hooves, his shield tumbling away. Instinctively he deflected a blow, rolled over, and found his feet.

There was an unholy noise shaking the sky; it was their howls and his own, the unmistakable din of war. Surely the sound reached Kelmere; surely the sentries would hear—

He managed to bring down one of his attackers, but the second was bigger, wilier, dashing just out of range, lunging close to stab at him again. The savage was laughing. He was grinning madly, blood flowing down his face to stain his teeth a terrible red.

Aedan's men were fighting as they could, but the pathway hindered them all. From the corner of his eye he saw his second in command fall from his steed, a Pict dagger in his throat. He saw the steed itself stumble, lose its footing and not recover, sliding down the mountain with a ghastly, piercing squeal. Another man fell, and another. By all the gods—

The Pict he had just killed lurched back to life, rising up beyond him. Muddied hair, a lumbering step. A cudgel, upraised.

A woman, screaming.

*No. Damn it, no!*

The Pict was running for the princess.

She carried no weapon, Aedan knew. A desperate glance showed him the flare of her blond hair, her saffron gown; her mount was spinning in tight circles, a frantic dance amid the chaos. Her guards had already fallen. In the swift, frenzied moment before his death, Aedan had a clear view of the expression on her face: pure astonishment. She had thought them as safe as he had, this close to the king's home.

"Callese!" he roared, still fighting. "Get the hell behind me!"

Again, too late.

The grinning man had taken advantage of his distraction. Aedan barely saw the sword swing at him; he leapt and turned, but the Pict had aimed high, and Aedan had not ducked. The flat of the blade caught him across the temple, a vicious blow that sent the world slurring and stole the ground from beneath his feet.

He was lying on the road, staring up into the circling clouds. Amazingly he felt no pain, only hot blood pouring down his cheek. But he could not move, not even when his horse screamed and reared and landed on his leg.

Still, no pain. He marveled at that, at the faraway

voices and the cry of his sister and the sweet, sweet stars just beginning to wink at him from the center of heaven.

The sky faded dark. The stars winked: *goode-nyte*.


Motion.

Endless motion, a sickly, violent sort of rocking that kept him lost in his mind, his body gone, the whole of the world gone, no stars or Picts or horses, only his bare thoughts remaining, and this awful, infinite swaying.

It was black and black and merciless. Aedan did not know this place, this utter lack of everything. But then, in his dazed and reeling haze, he realized he did know it. It was death, and it was quick and rough and swaying, swaying . . .

" . . . to shore . . . time . . ."

" . . . there, ahead. See there. . . ."

He could not see. He could not feel. Was he breathing still? Did the dead breathe?

"Damned rain . . . how . . . supposed to . . ."

Salt. He smelled it. He tasted it. He had no lips or nose or tongue, but he tasted salt.

" . . . cursed! I say we turn back now."

"Nay. You know the orders."

Was it blood? The sea? Aye, the sea. Sea salt, strong and pungent. He felt it now too. It filled him, every corner of him. He would burst with it, the salt, the spinning dark.

" . . . never get close to those shores! You know it as well as I! This storm will tear us apart if we don't turn back. . . . I say we drop him *here*, and let the fates decide. . . ."

Wetness, stinging. Rainfall pelting him, a brutal wind.

"The hull is leaking! We must—go—back—"

Wicked thunder; crackling, quaking, unhinging his very bones.

". . . our throats cut. If it's known—if it's discovered—"

"No one will know! We cannot go nearer. Here, now! Help me."

And suddenly past the salt and rain and thunder came the pain, screeching through him. He was *not* dead, not yet. Aedan found his voice—he thought it was his—a smothered sound, inhuman. New words engulfed it, reduced it to the mere pathetic groan that it was:

*No one will ever know. . . .*

It was the last thing he heard. He was lifted, rolled, bruises and blood, his entire being convulsed. With an eager surge the ocean took him in and there were no more voices, no more rocking. There was only the cold ruin of the sea embracing him, dragging him down, squeezing the air from his lungs until at last he surrendered to it, and took a long, deep breath.

He was sinking, sinking. . . .

There was the sense of something rushing by him, something warm, weightless. Aedan came to understand it was he himself, his own soul departing, leaving his mind behind him, a suffering—a punishment for his inadequacy, for the loss of his honor, his family and his domain.

He tried to move and could not. He tried to breathe, and could not. He could only experience this moment, confounded, and wonder at why he felt so calm.

He realized that his eyes were open, that he was still beneath the water. That there was more than just the ocean around him, his billowing tunic, his drifting hair. . . .

But it was not his hair.

Between the ocean darkness and a faint, curling whisper of blood, he glimpsed a new face before him, pale and ghostly—a woman, with silken hair that weaved all around, flowing fire, beckoning. Her eyes were cast away from him, long lashes and skin smooth like silver, or stone—like the rain or the storm, elements beyond his understanding.

She glanced back at him. Before he could think, before he could reason, the sea swept black again.

*"Hush. Do not speak."*

*She leaned over him, spoke against his lips, her own soft and warm on his, sweet as life, as honeyed dreams. Her kiss was brief, a teasing contact, her tongue, the fleeting brush of her breasts against his bare chest. When she pulled back he reached up for her, incomplete. She was a goddess above him, cool marble yet burning flame, a living contrast of bright hope and deep, dark desire.*

*He could not look away from her. He wanted never to look away.*

*Long locks fell across her shoulders, her arms. She was perfection in the moonlight, magical colors, red hair and white skin, eyes of indigo dusk. His fingers threaded through the tumbled strands, bringing her back to him. She smiled as she surrendered to his silent command: a knowing smile, seductive and alluring. Her head dipped down to his once more. He lost his breath with the taste of her.*

*She was the ocean. The swelling waves, the wind-whipped mist.*

*He stroked her, craving more of what was already offered, her firm breasts, taut nipples pushing against his palms. Each breath she took filled his hands, sent a ripple of pure, erotic lust through him. He squeezed her, gently, and felt a moan build in his throat. She lifted her chin* and arched her back, still with her beguiling smile. Moonlight favored the column of her neck, glinted off the silver chain she wore, the scrolled locket. Her skin was luminous pearl; she was sleek and strong and radiant, a merging of woman and the mysterious divine.

His hands skimmed lower, to the junction of her thighs. She crouched above him with her legs spread, rubbing against him, her long hair swaying as he caressed her, as he felt her, so wet and hot. When he slipped a finger inside her, she gasped and closed her eyes and he could not wait any longer, he could not hold back. He pulled her to him, rougher now, demanding. No words were needed; she took hold of him and sank down deep. And then it was he who gasped.

He had never felt this before. He had never known such rapture, such an aching pleasure as the heat of her wrapped around him, and he wanted more of her, more of this moment. He wanted all of her body on him, he wanted to claim every bit of her, every mouthful, full breasts and soft belly and the wild, wild heart of her—

She sucked at his lips, panting; he kissed her back, hard, as hard as his body was pumping into hers, and they shared the same air and danced the same dance, and her red hair flowed and her lithe, beautiful body held him, kept him tight. His hands slid to her waist, down to her hips, his fingers pressed into her, urging her faster, deeper, yes, yes, like that—

He cried out with his release, felt hers light through him as well, and he nearly died from it, nearly wanted to die as he flooded her with himself, and she arched over him again, taking it all in with delicious, shuddering greed.

The linnet was singing in her cage.

Aedan scowled, turning his head, reaching for a pillow to cover his ears. He had been having the most amazing dream, the most wonderfully intense, carnal dream, and he did not want to leave it. . . .

That damned bird, always singing so sadly, a weeping cascade of notes, night and day. He had already given it to Callese, he thought—she had taken it to her own quarters, hadn't she? It had seemed such a pretty gift at the time, the fair little bird, the woven wicker cage.

The damned singing, trilling in his head. If he had known that it was never going to stop—

"Enough," he said, and opened his eyes.

This was not his chamber. Worse, this was not even Kelmere.

Aedan lifted himself up from the bed—not his pallet—and took in his surroundings, caught in the uneasy sensation of waking to a dream—*not* the one he had hoped.

He was in a chamber of stone, with three arched, hollow windows and a ceiling that showed blue sky peeking past crumbled mortar.

The room was larger than his own back at his father's keep, a master chamber, perhaps, filled with things both bizarre and beautiful. There were couches without cushions; chests without hinges; a cupboard, grand and imposing, layered gilt peeling away from the edges in metallic curls. There was a table of shining black granite, a scattering of pebbles across the top. Strips of cloth—some tattered, others whole—draped the walls in gauzy colors: silver and white and darkest purple.

There was a blackbird perched atop a high-backed chair. It fell silent at last, watching him.

Aedan stared back, still cupped in his dream. Without

warning, the bird took flight, a fluent dip in the air, sweeping up and out of one of the open windows.

And that was when he saw the Roman helmets, bare and empty as skulls, lined up in sinister procession against the wall across from him. Each had been set carefully atop an X of rusting swords embedded in the rubble of the floor.

No dream. He would not dream of this. So where was he?

*Picts. Twilight.*

Wherever he was, someone was doing a damnable job of either guarding him or watching over him. The chamber appeared to be deserted. He heard no voices, no sound of man or beast, only a distant rumble, familiar, constant. A door was set back behind him but was buried in shadow; he could not even tell if it was open.

He had to leave. He had to find his people, his soldiers. He had to understand what had happened.

Aedan sat up too quickly, wincing at the sudden agony in his body, an arc of fire from his head to his left leg—

—*the Pict lunging*—*his black horse against the stars*—

—and beneath the blankets he discovered he had no clothes, not even leggings or bandages. He raised his hands to his head and felt the wound there: undressed, tender skin and a thin, straight cut from his temple to the edge of his cheekbone. He took his hands away and saw no blood. The gash had been cleaned. That was good. His leg, however, was a problem. Also clean, but the skin from his ankle to his knee was swollen shiny and tight, vividly colored. Two long wooden planks braced either side of it, tied firmly in place.

His leg was fractured. Someone had gone to the trouble of setting it but hadn't bothered with much else. There was no hint of medicine on him, no poultice to draw out the swelling or reduce the pain. And he had no memory of any of it, not of being found, or taken, or put in this place. Where the hell *was* he?

*Surprise attack, the gleam of his sword, Callese's face—*

Callese was in danger. Kelmere itself was in danger; aye, there had been an ambush, a Pict raid, and who knew what had come of it, what they had done with his people, his king—

Aedan set his teeth and dragged himself from the bed, balancing on his good leg. When the dizziness grew bearable, he began to hobble over to the line of helmets and swords. He did not bother to be quiet about it. Whoever had done this to him knew that he lived, had placed him here with deliberation. If they wanted to stop him, they were welcome to come and try. He'd be delighted to hit someone right about now.

He passed a pile of salt-stained rags and realized it was his own tunic, his cloak, cast off and crumpled. Aedan did not slow.

The wood splints fixed to his leg were too long for proper walking; they caught on loose stones and knocked agony all the way up his spine. It took an eternity to cross the chamber. But he did it.

With a grunt he lifted the closest of the helmets, a monstrous thing of bronze and tarnished silver, and slung it aside, sending it clanging across the floor. One sword of the crossed pair was useless, oddly bent, the tip of the blade snapped off. The other was more promising, clearly ancient, broad and plain and etched with rust, but it still had the cracked leather grip of its hilt, and the blade still sang true when he slapped it against the wall. With its heft in his hand he felt slightly better and managed, by a series of awkward, staggering steps, to reach the window nearby.

Nude, lamed, but well-armed, Prince Aedan of Kelmere looked out upon the view before him. In one disastrous instant he understood that he was not going to make it home to his king or his people, not ever again.

# CHAPTER THREE

A man on her island.
A man in her home.

Ione frowned and bit her lip, drawing loops with one finger in the sand by her feet. She was seated, tucked and silent, in the shadow of her castle, letting the wind tangle her hair into her lashes. Above her the sky shone pristine blue, inviting her to sea, but Io did not stir. With her back against the stone she fancied herself unseen, even by the clouds.

She had done a dangerous thing, a terrible thing, and did not know how to undo it. She did not know even if she wanted to.

A mortal man, asleep in her bed, his scent on her sheets, his cheek on her pillow. And his face, oh, his face . . .

She had seen him first by storm light, tossed by waves, dark and lovely even as he drowned before her.

It had been a night of nights, lightning and the angry roar of the ocean, the currents as deep and strong as Ione had ever felt. It was a treacherous night, even for her, yet she had gone out anyway, drawn to the water in a way she had never felt before. And once out she was lost, as much a victim of the ocean as that little boat had been, tossed herself, searching frantically for what held her in the squall.

It was he. Io felt it all the way through her, an invisible tug that turned ferocious at her first sight of him: the doomed, flowing grace of a man being pulled to the bottom of the sea.

He had been heavy in her arms, a deadweight, and she honestly thought she had come too late. A cloud of crimson blood swirled up from his head, ominous. Yet even in death he was the fairest human she had ever seen, with hair that gleamed blue ebony beneath the water, and a face both classic and cold, a study of nature's chance harmony—straight nose, strong jaw, curving lips that suggested splendor to her, masculine and sensual. Closed eyes with elegant black lashes, matched to the slash of his brows.

His eyes had opened. They were silvered gray, starlight over storm.

Above the waves again he lost none of his beauty, and when he took a ragged breath she felt an unexpected relief. He would live. For reasons beyond her understanding, she had saved him, and he would live.

Because she didn't know what else to do, Ione took him to her home, a sacred place, hidden and protected. She had never done such a thing before, never even considered it. To bring a man to Kell was to invite the wrath of the curse . . . but he was hurt, and he was bleeding. He had eyes of silver. Amid the colossal waves, all other shores seemed suddenly much too far.

So Io had granted him shelter, and her bed, where he slept and slept and she could study him at her leisure.

Now, at least, she knew why she had done what she did. She understood the lure of him, why she had chanced so much for merely one mortal man, however fair he was.

Three days had passed. Three nights.

Today was bright and glistening, the pull of the ocean sweet. The wind sang of whales and dolphins and velvet clouds, of sunlight breaking over long, laughing waters.

Ione looked up at the flash of movement in the tower window, dark hair, a face. The man was awake. In the square of light he was lean and sharp, a lone wolf trapped in stone; he stared, frozen, at the view she loved, gripping the edge of the window with curled fingers.

A swell of something uncomfortably close to regret took her. Io stood and slipped deeper into shadow, then turned and ran the other way, following the seawall until it ended in the froth of the surf.

She needed to think. She would return home again soon.


The door to his chamber was open after all.

Aedan lingered there silently, surveying the shadowed hall before him. His own shadow was nearly swallowed by the gloom: a tall crippled man in a ruined tunic, the line of the sword he carried, the length of the javelin he used as a cane.

Like the other wonders of this place, the javelin was unfamiliar to him, a weighty rod of reddish-black wood, sinew and bone wound around the top, a string of what once might have been feathers tied by a leather cord. He had found it pitched askew against one of the walls, like his clothing, flung aside and forgotten. The shaft was both polished and scarred, well-used but more recently damaged. Aedan did not have to guess at its history—it had come from the ocean, this strange weapon. Everything around him had been hurled from the sea, from the massive graveyard of ships piled upon the reef beyond his chamber windows.

He was on an island. Not one of his father's chain; there was nothing of an official kingdom here. Yet Aedan knew, with deep, stark certainty, exactly where he was.

He was on Kell.

Impossible, unbelievable—but, aye, Kell.

There were no torches lit, no lamps or braziers, but the hallway was not quite empty. From the edge of the doorway he could see broken furniture lining the walls, smashed wood, shattered pottery. The floor itself seemed almost to glimmer, even without the light. He took a small step forward, puzzled. There were *coins* spread across the stones as far as he could see, countless little suns and moons, discs of gold and silver and the rough green of old bronze.

Sweet Mary. A fortune thrown down before him, gathering dust.

*Kell, Kell, an island lost, a sailor's hell.*

"Hail," Aedan called, lifting the sword. The echo of his greeting faded to cold nothing. He inhaled deeply, fighting the way the corners of his vision threatened black, then limped—barefoot and splinted—out into the corridor, upon that path of coins.

He had not yet found his boots.

*Kell, Kell* . . . land of myth, of oblivion. Aedan had grown up on its fable, the legend of the mermaid and the fisherman, their ill-fated love. None but the most superstitious believed the story any longer. Kell *was* an island, but only that. It had been in plain view for as long as any could remember. And for just as long, Kell had been utterly avoided. A very real danger outweighed the myth: No ship could approach, it had been proven time and again. His own brush with the island as a boy was as close as anyone had come in his lifetime—and lived.

The currents here flowed savage and deep. No one ever survived them.

*Not quite,* whispered a sly, inner voice. *One man has. One maimed, desperate man, stranded on a haunted isle. . . .*

And so, of course, no one would come to rescue him. No one would even think of it.

The javelin clinked and thunked against the coin floor; the wood splints scraped. Aedan concentrated on keeping the sword aloft, pulling himself grimly forward, ignoring the heady pain, that voice.

There *was* someone else here—a *real* person, no siren or ghost, a survivor of one of those wrecks, most likely. Aedan was going to find him and get some answers, even if he had to take this place apart stone by stone.

*Clink, thunk. Clink, thunk.* One step at a time. One more. One more.

He paused at each doorway, catching his breath. The other chambers proved much like his own, crumbling and crowded with riches, odd shapes, amazing discoveries. Amphorae, carved screens, a pile of glazed crockery in astonishing clear colors, blue and white. Enormous seashells, scattered bits of jewelry. Fishing nets with their glass floats still secured, gleaming and whole. Statues of men and gods, foreign faces, lustrous stone.

One room held nothing but weaponry. At last Aedan did more than pause. There was enough armament here to equip nearly all of Kelmere. He took up an elaborate curved dagger, the blade of it keen. It sliced the air with a deadly hiss, but he would have to abandon the sword to take it. He had no scabbard to secure it, not even the simplicity of a belt.

Aedan put it back. He was very good with a dagger. He was lethal with a sword.

The black corners stalking him were creeping ever closer; he thought it might be hunger, combined with the problem of his leg. His head. He took care to fill his lungs in slow, measured breaths and limped on.

At the end of the hallway he was forced to stop. A line of stairs stretched below him, wide and steep, dropping down into the depths of the castle.

He closed his eyes in frustration, leaning back against the wall. He hadn't even realized he wasn't on the ground floor.

Stairs, more coins, teasing shadows. Aedan knew, abruptly, that he could not do it. He could not confront those stairs, not now. He was exhausted, shaking. His body throbbed with hurt, his vision blurred.

But the javelin moved down one step. His good leg followed, balance, exquisite torture. His left leg dragged behind, and he bit back the scream that wanted to come, his entire body bathed in sweat.

There. The first step conquered.

The javelin moved down again.

The fourth step was uneven. The javelin slipped, and he staggered. His swollen ankle struck the stair behind him; Aedan was blinded with pain, instantly, fatally. He dropped the sword and pitched to his knees, but it was not enough to save him. After three full rolls he almost caught himself, but his fingers skidded over the stones and he plunged down the stairs again.

\* \* \*

The two men hung from the rigging with practiced ease, allowing their bodies to sway with the pitch of the galley, their eyes narrowed against the salt wind. They had spent untold time here together atop the high mast, day and night, fair weather or foul. They were sailors, merchants, pirates when need be, but today they were merely ship-mates, out to sea on the first leg of a three-month journey that would send them south and east and finally north once more.

The men worked quickly, threading a rope back and forth between them above the great sheet of white that was the sail.

"What was the king's illness, did you hear?" shouted the younger sailor to his companion over the wind.

"Fever," called back the other. "Demons in his blood. The court is in turmoil."

"Turmoil?" The younger caught the heavy rope, tied it into a looping knot. "You mean because the prince is dead?"

"The king is bereft." The elder man gave his end of the rope a pull. "We have lost our champion, but he has lost his son—and our land its heir. The king remains bedrid-den. They say he will not survive this fever."

"He mourns the prince."

"Aye."

The wind shuddered hard around them; both held tight to the rope as the sail groaned and engorged below. But it was a fair day overall, and soon the gust began to ebb. The sailors resumed their work.

"The Picts grow bolder," noted the younger man. "I heard there were hundreds of them. I heard they slew nearly all but Callese."

"Aye."

"But she lives. The king should celebrate that."

"Aye."

Again the wind changed; again they paused, letting it bluster and bellow and gradually calm. By the time it died, neither man felt the need for further conversation. They worked in rhythm, concentrating on their job. When the last knot was tied, they lingered a moment longer in agreeable silence, gazing out into the vast cobalt that was both the sky and the ocean, the whole of their world.

The younger gave a start.

"Look—look there! Did you see?"

"What? Where?"

"There! There! She's there again—do you see her?"

"What the devil are you—"

The elder broke off, staring at the sea.

"Mother Mary," the younger breathed. "She's . . . she's beautiful!"

The elder jerked back, nearly losing his hold on the ropes, his face waxen. "Don't look! Don't look at her, I say! Turn away, lad! By your soul, turn away!"

And he grabbed his companion by the arm, pulling him toward him, and the two of them scurried down the web of ropes, hand over hand, bungling, not quite falling, seeking the shelter of the deck below.

Out in the water the mermaid watched them drop, agile as spiders. When they were no longer in sight, she dipped beneath the white-capped waves, long red hair and fins of silvered green, splashing the water neatly behind her.

Far and wide she swam the seas, the same paths her ancestors knew, following fish and canyons and sweeping currents. There were few ships passing today. For the most part Ione was content to watch them from a distance, their great, hulking black shapes bobbing against the horizon.

There were sailors on those ships, she knew. Ships were never empty of sailors, not even after disease, or storm, or weeks away from their beloved land. Mankind, like this-tles, survived no matter what manner of disaster at-tempted to flatten them.

She floated a moment longer, considering the galley before her, then pushed her hair out of her eyes and slipped back down beneath the water.

It was a separate world from above, entirely beautiful. She passed eels drifting by in black spirals, beds of kelp alive with fish, delicate shrimp that danced between her fingers. Deeper still were forests of plants, brazen colors, rippling fronds. Mansions of coral mazed the seafloor; crabs scuttled past them in fleet solitude, leaving faint crooked tracks against the sand.

She swam slowly, lazily, delaying the inevitable as long as she could.

Ione had been born here in these waters. She lived here and would die here. She knew the sea in all its moods, ac-cepted each one with the steady patience of kinship. But she enjoyed the ocean best like this, with sunlight filter-ing through it, shining across her in radiant lines. She loved the warmth the sun spread near the cresting waves, the way coolness sank lower, lower, until near the bottom of the sea all was hushed and dim, a vivid sapphire dark-ness that helped mask the sand and plants and creatures sheltered there.

She approached the place where her mother had been killed and circled wide to avoid it, swimming deeper, em-bracing shadows.

Yet she could not swim forever. The man awaited her on Kell, and before long Ione was in view of her island, her pearl amid blue waters. Past the secret grottoes that domed beneath the castle, past the wild reef with its necklace of splintered ships, past the sharp-edged rocks that lined the southern shore was a beach, a simple beach of simple sand, and it was here that Io headed. When she was near enough, she broke the surface and smoothed back her hair again, exchanging water for air, an easy thing, primal and unthinking.

At the very edge of the shore she paused, still in the foam of the surf, as close as she could come in her true form. She looked up at the tower window: empty now, only shade to greet her.

Perhaps he had ventured out. Perhaps he was searching for her. A nervous thrill took her; she quelled it, closed her eyes and concentrated, feeling the sand beneath her palms, the warm firmness of it beneath her body. . . .

And the transformation came, here in this place between the ocean and the land. It washed over her with the sea spray, a burning, stinging sensation, but finer than that—a feeling of *change*, of endless, tiny bubbles sparkling in her veins, rising, rising, until in a flowering of short, splendid pain Ione herself was transformed, and where her magnificent tail used to be was something new and earthly, a figure shaped for land, not sea.

She stood from the sand and walked up the beach, the ocean kissing her feet farewell.

Her palla was where she had left it, a span of jade-green wool pinned to the ground with fist-size stones, the breeze tugging at its edges. She freed it, let the cloth blow across her body, snapping folds that dusted her with sand. Dressing was a human practice but it suited her, especially now. She tied the palla around her impatiently, approaching the stairs to the entrance of her castle.

All the while she swam, Ione had thought of the man.

All the while she had remembered him, his sable black hair, his striking clear eyes. His touch. His taste.

The shape of his lips, the growth of new beard that darkened his cheeks. The calluses on his palms, how they dragged rough against her skin.

Io walked a little faster.

*He dreamed of her again. Kisses, stroking, penetration. Breathless, brilliant pleasure, and the end that consumed him until there was nothing left, nothing but her and him and their long, tempered aftermath. Her indigo eyes, her seductive smile.*

Aedan awoke to the drifting scent of incense. He knew it was incense, although he had encountered its smoky sweetness only once before, in the camp of an Angle prince. The prince had captured it in a bloody raid and burned it to banish the ghosts of the dead.

His head hurt. Ah, God, his entire body hurt.

The smoke glided over him, pale wisps of gray against the ceiling, dissolving into dark air.

He turned his head, slowly. Not his room. Not his castle. Not even his room in this castle.

He was on the floor, near the bottom of a sweep of stairs. Aye, he remembered that. Searching, falling. And then—

Aedan sat up, a hand to his forehead, trying to will away the pain. He had been sprawled across a very hard floor, with what felt like fragments of stone biting into his back. Both legs were straight before him; apparently the splints had held up to his tumble. Although his shin was a rather ghoulish green and black, it did not ache nearly as much as he probably deserved.

He glanced down at his hand; his palm was wet with blood. The cut down his brow had reopened.

He came to comprehend, gradually, that the dull spark of colors on the floor beside him was more than just the endless coins of before. There was a large chalice by his thigh, brimming with what might have been water.

Aedan lowered his hand, staring, then dipped one finger into the liquid. He examined the drop that hung from his nail.

Water.

He brought the drop to his lips. Fresh water, clean and pure. Suddenly he realized how thirsty he was, how incredibly parched, as if he hadn't had water for years, for a lifetime. Lifting the chalice with both hands, he drained it, and he had never tasted anything so wonderful in his life.

When he finished he set the chalice carefully down— opals and amethysts and polished silver—and looked around this new chamber.

It was a great hall, impressive and tall, soft shadows, empty hearths. Sunlight fell in long columns across the floor, breaking in past windows above, past gaps in the roof. There were tables laid out but no benches, only chairs, and only a few of those. The grandest of these was more throne than chair, large and cushioned. A slanted sunbeam managed just to encompass it, a halo of light, illuminating the golden-red hair of the woman seated there, watching him silently.

# CHAPTER FOUR

❧

O nce, as a small boy, Aedan had chased a dragonfly across a meadow, following the burning blue thread of it into the woods where it was said the faeries lived.

He had chased it with the joy of youth, with leaps and skips and clapping hands, until a hidden root had felled him, and his head struck the ground.

In his dreams then the wood faeries had come to him, winged, golden, smiling. He had awoken and recovered and told no one of them; even as a boy Aedan knew what it meant to be touched by the faeries. He would be held apart from his people, both worshiped and feared. He kept the secret of them buried deep in his heart. Yet in the many years that had passed since that spring day—perhaps as punishment for his silence—the faeries returned to him at their whim, haunting him in sly and shifting dreams.

He had thought his fantasy woman an echo of those

faeries. She held the same sort of fey resplendence, the same shining eyes and cool touch.

But now in this great hall Aedan could only stare and wonder, for here she was once more—a faerie and yet not, for the woman in the chair had no wings, and her hair definitely gleamed more red than gold, with ropes of pearls twined through it, and jeweled cuffs about her wrists. She wore a gown of green in a style he did not recognize, wrapped loose around her—so loose it draped only her right shoulder, leaving one perfect breast exposed in the sunlight, alabaster tipped with rose. A locket of silver lay suspended at her throat, glinting.

Aedan closed his eyes. Opened them.

She was still there.

He wanted to look at her face and found he could not. He wanted to look into her eyes—they would be indigo dusk—and, again, could not.

She was real—but how? By heavens, he had just now dreamed of her—

"Hail," the woman said, finding his greeting of long ago, giving it back to him in a voice of dulcet sin.

Aedan did not reply. Instead he tried to stand, bracing himself against the wall beside him. In his struggle the chalice was knocked aside; it rolled away with a reproachful chime.

The woman showed no alarm, no fear at his sudden movement—nor should she, he thought with a measure of black humor. She was far and his leg was useless. Clearly he was no threat. The injuries that seemed so muted before were flaring back to life, relentless. But it felt better to stand, even with the wall supporting him, and once he was on his feet Aedan forced himself to turn to her, to examine her face.

She was just as he remembered: perfection, pale skin

and a bewitching gaze, lips of ruby, the barest blush across her cheeks. He had been correct in thinking her fey; her beauty was almost unsettling, like the flame of her hair and the dark of her eyes.

No wonder he had dreamed of her. *She* was the one who had saved him, he knew it. *She* was the one he had been seeking, this woman, the other survivor on the isle.

It seemed so unlikely, he glanced around them both—surely there was someone else here, a stranded sailor, a fisherman. She could not be alone. How could a woman alone survive Kell?

The lady in the chair lifted one winged brow—amusement or curiosity, he couldn't tell. She spoke again, this time in a fluid language he did not understand, and then paused, expectant.

"Hail," Aedan responded, at last finding his voice.

"Ah." She slipped back into his own tongue. "A Scot. I thought as much."

Her accent was not quite pure. There was something of a lilt to it, a faint note of song, elusive. Or perhaps he was imagining that. Christ, he felt so strange, as if the dream had never ended and he was trapped inside it, uncertain of what to do.

*Wake up,* chided his mind. *Wake up. You are the leader of armies. Lives depend upon you. Assess. Command.*

"Who are you?" he asked, keeping his voice gentle, although she still showed no sign of fear.

"The keeper of this isle," the lady replied.

"Keeper?"

"Aye."

He looked around again at the tables and chairs, two tall braziers glowing subtly behind her, the incense he had smelled before coiling up past black iron. "How long have you been here?"

Her lips curved, a slight smile. "Forever."

"On what ship," he asked distinctly, "did you come?"

"On no ship."

"You were born here?" He did not bother to hide his disbelief.

"No." And her smile grew wider.

She was enjoying this. Aedan felt a surge of anger that she would toy with him with their circumstances so obviously dire, after the hallway and the stairs and his broken leg pulsing with pain. To mask the anger he turned away, searching for the javelin. It had come to rest against one of the tables, not too distant. He hobbled over, picked it up. The sword was nowhere in sight.

All the while she watched, silent once more upon her grand throne.

Aedan of Kelmere had led twenty-two battles since the age of sixteen and lost only one. He had bled and wept and suffered for his people, for their greater good and the will of his father. He had witnessed both enemies and friends die in his name. He was a warrior, a hunter, a prince. He would not stoop to game with this woman, no matter the color of her eyes.

"How did I get here?" he demanded, firmer than before. "Where are my men?"

"I know not."

Using the javelin, he began to thump his way toward her, winding through the labyrinth of tables. "It was you, wasn't it—the chalice of water. The splints on my leg. You must know something of what happened to me."

"I know that you were lost, and I found you. I know that you were given to the sea, and so to me."

"What—" Nausea took him, sudden and fierce. He had to pause to master it, gripping the javelin with his knuckles pressed white. "What do you mean, given to the sea?"

"You were thrown overboard. Do you not remember, Scot?"

"I was—on a ship?"

"A boat," she corrected him. "A small one for such a squall. Perhaps you were not the only sacrifice to the sea that night."

And without warning, he *did* remember—the bitter rain, the taste of salt in his mouth. Voices, casually debating his life. And a face in the water . . . *her* face. How could that be?

"You rescued me," Aedan said, and then shook his head. "But how did I get to the boat? Who were those men? How did you find me in the storm?"

"I know nothing more of the boat or the other men. I know only you."

And, by God, he knew her too.

Aedan fought that image; it did not help him now, to dwell on illusions of her, his fevered dreams centered upon a stranger. He needed reality, not fantasies. He needed answers.

He had washed ashore. She had found him. That had to be what happened. But he frowned at her, trying to remember as the nausea grew stronger, lodging in his throat.

*Dark sea, violent storm turning him, turning turning—her arms around him, long hair whirling—*

Aedan broke away from the memory, dizzy with it, fighting the urge to give in and fall to his knees and retch. He would not disgrace himself in front of her—he would defeat this. He gritted his teeth and stared up at the ceiling, counting stones, counting holes, until his body was his own again and he could speak.

"Who *are* you?"

"Ione."

"Ione. Are you alone here?"

"No," she said gravely. "You are here as well."

Was she mocking him? There was no hint of jest about her, only that sober blue gaze, bound in smoke and light.

"There's no one else? Only you and I on the whole of this island?"

"There are birds. There are seals. There are many fish—"

"People," he interrupted, still past clenched teeth. "Are there other *people*?"

"Oh. People," she said softly. "No."

He wanted badly to sit but didn't trust his leg to get him up again. He ran a hand down his face, forgot about the Pict's cut, grimaced as he drew blood. Damn it all.

There was a chair near her, just within her splash of light. Aedan made his way to it, folded his arms over the back. She watched his progress with unwavering interest. He kept his focus on her face, ignoring the fact of her sun-lit body, her gleaming bare breast . . . the scent of her, heated with the sun and so very, very feminine. . . .

He would not look away. He would not be distracted by the loose gown of green, her ivory skin. He had questions still, he had plans to make. . . .

Her chest rose and fell, rhythmic, serene. Perfection, like the rest of her. Aedan remembered his dreams, the satin of her hair. Her nipples, hardened against his palms.

"Do you have pain, man?"

"What?" He wrenched his gaze back up to hers.

"Pain." The woman—Ione—leaned forward, somehow allowing the gown to fall open further. "Your leg. Does it hurt?"

"It is broken," he ground out. He would not, would *not* look down. "What do you think?"

"I think," she said, "that you ought not be out of bed."

Perhaps it was the incense clouding his senses, or the

heat of sun upon his head. He was not thinking clearly. She said the word *bed* and his entire body leapt *yes*.

Io settled back in her chair, allowing the sunlight to bathe her better. She knew how she looked to him: alight as a lone spark in the night, bright colors and unspoken desire. In his silver pale eyes she saw herself reflected—and liked what she saw.

He wanted her, past the stoic suffering, past the confusion. He wanted her. That frozen dismay she had glimpsed upon him in the tower window was gone.

Good.

"Shall we go up?" she asked.

He frowned down at her, her comely dark man, not answering, and something about him then moved her; perhaps the way he used the chair to conceal his pain, or how he tried so hard to fight her brightness—or even just the fine, troubled furrow of his brow as he took her in. Oh, it could not have been an easy thing, drowning, dying, waking to her and to Kell.

Ione reached out, placing her hand on his arm. "Are you unwell?"

He looked down at her hand. "Aye," he answered slowly. "I am . . . unwell."

She rose from her chair. He did not withdraw from her, not even when the nest of starlings rustled in the beams above, sending a whirl of dust motes spinning down around them, an elfin storm in the sun.

His muscles were tense, hot. Her fingers glided over his tunic in the barest stroke.

"Do not fear. The sickness will pass; Kell will help you mend. It is my home. But you are welcome here."

He did nothing to acknowledge either her words or her touch; only his lashes swept down, hiding his thoughts.

"Scots," she sighed. "A Roman would have thanked me."

The man raised his face toward the sky, toward the sun and those restless birds. The lines around his mouth began to loosen, allowing a smile to come. It was a handsome smile, faint as it was, a smile that reminded her of splendid starred nights, and of her own ambitions.

The smile turned into hushed laughter. "I think I must be still asleep."

"Come," she urged, still touching him. "Come with me, Scot."

"My name is Aedan," he said. But he allowed her to help him back up the stairs.

# CHAPTER FIVE

ar sweeter than the candid taking of a man was
the seduction of one, Ione's mother had told her.
It was why Io wore the open palla, why she bothered with the pearls and the cuffs—although the locket,
of course, was always a part of her. She was never without
the locket.

The Scot noticed such things, and more: the way she
moved beneath the palla, the swell of her hips, the flash of
her legs. She had planned it all carefully, down to the
color of the jewels set into the golden cuffs. Aye, Io was
learned, well-studied in the ways of mankind, but more
than that she was a creature of honed instinct. The Scot
was wounded but strong. If she did not take care, her
grasp of him would slip and he would fly. She would not
risk that.

So she half-carried him back to the room she had chosen for him, making certain that his arm rested upon her
unclad shoulder, that the loosened mass of her hair
brushed his collar, his chest. They walked the hallway to-

gether, their halting steps matched, two sets of bare feet pressing into coins and stone.

They found the bed and she eased him into it. He lay back, watching her, the black of his hair very dark against the pillows. Twin narrow plaits framed his face, bound with beads of onyx and quartz.

"Sleep," Ione said. "Sleep, and when you awaken I will be here."

"That's rather what I feared."

She smiled at him, amused. "You never answered my question. Does your leg pain you?"

"No," he said, but did not close his eyes.

Io knelt beside the bed, pushing aside the blankets. His injured leg was propped atop a pile of furs; she evened them out, molded them around the splints for better support. Despite what he had said, the bone was not broken but badly splintered, doubly painful. She started at his thigh, allowing her fingertips to skim the length of it, following curves of solid muscle.

She had touched him before, of course. He fascinated her, rough where she was smooth, firm where she was soft. Such interesting sensations, her skin against his, a delicious contact. He was so warm. She loved that he was warm. Were all men warm like this?

He shifted and she glanced up at him. His gaze was silver-hard, intense; it sent a shiver through her.

Io took a deep breath, exhaled, and began to stroke his bruised shin.

Peace and peace and peace . . . she kept her touch light, her thoughts focused, and drew the pain from him up into her fingers, let it spread across her hand. In him the ache was a gripping beast, but in Io it paled, grew thin and weak until the man's lie became truth, and it was nothing indeed.

"You're healing me," he whispered.

"No." She did not look up from her task. "I do not have the power to heal. Only to cease the pain."

"Are you a witch?"

She smiled again. "No." Without meeting his eyes she shifted, coming closer to examine the cut that slashed down his face.

It had sealed already, the blood dried to flakes. She brushed at it, thoughtful, distracted by his stillness, his absolute quiet at her touch.

He was warm and he smelled of man and earth, and his lashes were ebony, and his hands were strong and lean, pressed flat against the covers of the bed.

"You will carry a scar here," she told him, very soft.

"But I'll live." There was a question beneath his words.

"Oh, yes. You will live." She hoped it was true.

"Thank you."

And then he looked up at her, just as she looked down at him. The shiver returned, potent, compelling. It was Ione who broke the moment, closing her eyes, searching again for her inner focus. This was not the time for his hungry look—that would come later. After tonight.

With her eyes still closed she traced the terrible cut. Despite the dried blood she feared this was the more serious injury. The pain went deep, so deep it was nearly hidden. But she did what she could for him, finding it, wrestling with it until it, too, was vanquished.

When it was done they were both breathing heavily. Io drew back, wiping her hands down her skirts.

"Listen to me, Scot. You feel better now, but it will not last. Do not rise from this bed. You must believe me when I tell you this is safe haven for you. I will care for you, I promise."

"Ione." He made her name beautiful, even in the little

daze she had given him. "I confess, I'm not much inclined to rise at this moment."

"Excellent." She stood and studied him, the slumberous gray of his eyes still fixed on her.

"Ione of Kell. Have you anything to eat?"

"What?"

"Food. I'm afraid . . ." His voice faded; his very essence seemed to dim, slowly recover. ". . . afraid I won't be leaving this bed ever again without any."

Of course, of course. She had not thought of it—he would need to eat. She knew that. She knew, and had forgotten.

"Await me," she said, and left the chamber.

By the time she returned to him the sun had settled low in the sky, sending a warm glow across the room, the last of the sunset painted against the far wall. Aedan watched the colors turn, yellow to amber to orange, and knew that outside this room, outside this strange castle, the island shadows would be long and deep and the ocean would glitter.

At Kelmere, so near and so impossibly far, the tips of the mountains would be catching the end of the day, tapering violet into the dark of the sky.

His father would be in council with his advisers, his sister supervising the kitchens. He thought of what they might have for supper: bread, of course, thick, soft bread. Roasted meat with salt, lamb or perhaps boar. A dish of fowl or hare, whatever Callese had captured with her beloved osprey. Nuts, fruits. Warm stew, to ward off the chill of the coming night. . . .

Or perhaps not. Perhaps there would be no supper, because Callese was no more, and their father was no more, and Kelmere itself . . . no more. Perhaps the Picts had won. They had certainly been tenacious enough in their attacks. Perhaps this time, after all these years, they had succeeded instead of failed, and taken over the mighty fortress and made it their own.

He should be worried. He should be thinking of ways to reach his people . . . pondering boats, sea tides, battle strategies. But all these concerns seemed to belong to someone else; they were the complications of another man's life, a faraway prince . . . not Aedan himself, so empty now, so calm.

He had a vision of Callese's osprey set free, roaming the clouds unfettered. Soaring.

The painted wall turned from orange to rose. The ocean churned and churned.

He felt so relaxed. He felt he might never move again, actually, and that would be fine. That would be just . . . fine.

"Aedan."

The sound of her voice jolted him from his contemplation of the wall. Somehow he expected to find Callese before him, but it was not his sister. It was the sorceress . . . what was her name? Ione. She carried a tray in her hands.

Not boar nor hare nor fowl but fat cod, three of them, still steaming from the fire. She knelt beside him again, and he noticed only distantly that what he thought was a tray was actually a platter of solid gold, round as a breast-plate, almost as big. She set it down easily, then lifted one of the cooked cod—still whole—and pulled it apart with her fingers, not even flinching at the heat.

"Eat." She brought the fish to his lips. That was what finally woke him from his stupor, the pressure of her fingers against him, how she leaned so close and looked so serious.

He sat up. She did not retreat, only waited, still holding the cod.

Cautious, he scooped it from her hand into his. For all he could tell she had merely charred the fish on a fire until the skin burned black. It was unsalted, unspiced, and, by heavens, ambrosia on his tongue.

She handed him more.

"Bread?" he asked, hopeful.

"I have none."

It didn't matter. Halfway through the third fish he finally took note of her scrutiny, how she sat patiently on the floor with the empty platter at her side. Aedan looked down at the food in his hand, then back up at her. "What of you? Did you eat?"

"No."

"No?" Guilt turned his voice sharp. "Why the hell didn't you say something? Here, take this."

She pushed back the cod he offered. "I do not eat fish."

"Don't be so noble. You have to eat."

"I don't eat fish," she repeated firmly. "But you do. These are for you."

He hesitated, searching for the familiar signs—hollow cheeks, glazed eyes, sallow skin—but she showed none of them. She looked as fit and healthy as any woman—*sorceress*, his mind whispered—he had ever seen.

She held his gaze, inscrutable. "Go on. I have said I will not eat it."

The soldier in him would not waste food. Aedan finished the makeshift meal in silence. When he was done she nodded her approval, handing him a cloth to wipe his fingers clean, as formal as any hostess of his clan.

He eased back upon the pillows, and this time the haze that settled over him was one of satisfied exhaustion. His stomach was full, his pain subdued. In the half light of the room his situation began to seem . . . not entirely impossible. Aye, he thought, with a sleepy sort of acceptance, not impossible at all. Indeed, in the near-dark even his sorceress became almost normal, her beauty less distinct, the unique color of her eyes disguised.

He found himself puzzling over her yet again, how a maiden who seemed so ethereal had survived in such a place, magic or no. How she had come to be stranded here, how she managed to live. What she did every day, where she walked. Where she slept.

"Will you lie here, with me?" he wondered, and then realized he had said it aloud.

"Not tonight." She seemed unoffended, her voice practical. "Tonight another storm comes."

"Ah," he said, as though this made sense to him.

She rose, taking up the platter in her arms; shadows melted it into the color of her hair, flame and gold combined. "But you will see me on the morrow, Aedan. Be wise and remember what I said. Do not leave the bed again."

And she left his darkened chamber.

It was too late for the ship.

She had done her best for them, tried to lure them away from the storm, from the deadly reef that ringed her island. They saw her. She knew that. But as sometimes happened, they raced away from her, not toward her, and by the time she got in front of them again the storm had them, and then the reef.

The ship broke into pieces quite neatly, as if it had been waiting for the moment when it could. The rain and the sea drove the men frantic; they dropped into the waves and swiftly vanished, consumed by the frenzied currents. Ione knew the pattern all too well. The sailors would not be able to think, or swim, or breathe—the ocean sucked at them, and what the ocean truly wanted, even Io could not save.

None of these men would outlive the storm, no matter how she tried to help. They had come too close to the island, and now the curse held them fast.

So she fought those same currents and did what she was made to do. She found the luckless sailors as they sank, caught them in her arms, one by one, and began to sing. As they drowned she sang to them, songs of the world beneath the sea, of sunken palaces and fine gardens of coral. She looked into their eyes and knew that each man looking back at her saw a different face: his wife, his sweetheart, his daughter, clasping him close, taking away the pain and the fear.

Ione sang and sang, letting the currents work their will, until in the end there was only her siren song left, soothing the sailors to endless slumber beneath the waves.

By flashes of fitful lightning Aedan watched the ship shatter, ignoring the rain that blew in past the chamber window, drenching him. It was a fearsome sight even from this distance, the towering black waves, the tilted masts, white sails that shredded in the wind.

He couldn't make out the name on the prow; perhaps that was a blessing. He thought of his father, who loved to sail, and of the fishermen and traders who traversed the seas, the lifeblood of the kingdom. He thought of how many lives were lost each year to storms just like this one.

Thunder raged. Lightning spat devil forks across the sky.

He squinted against the rain but found no sign of life on that ship. No sailors fought against its sinking ruin. Perhaps it had been a ghost ship.

He could hope so. If it wasn't before, it certainly was now.

Aedan watched until the wind drove him back to his bed, where he lay bleakly awake, listening to the thunder and the rainwater dripping, dripping through the many gaps in the roof.

He did not see the lone, red-haired figure swim ashore. He did not see her climb onto the empty beach and then remain there, windblown, staring out at the baleful sea.

# CHAPTER SIX

❧

He would insist upon leaving his room, even though she told him at least three more times this morning that he was not healed, that he needed to rest. He only looked at her askance from those silver bright eyes and limped on anyway, determined to explore her tiny world.

So at last Ione surrendered and found him a cane, a true cane, and not the heavy African spear he had been using. The cane was a Greek thing, a shaft of sturdy oak, a head of carved ivory, crackled with age. The ivory carving was of a Hydra. The Scot did not seem to mind it.

"All these treasures," he said, gesturing to one of the chambers he passed. "Did you put them here?"

"Some of them," she said, from her place just behind him in the hallway.

"They washed ashore from the ships?"

"Some of them," she said again.

"But not the statues." He turned and looked at her, scowling, as if her coming answer already displeased him.

She had exchanged the palla for a sheath of sheer linen, creamy white, narrowly pleated. It hung from her shoulders by two golden brooches and four golden chains. The linen reached as high as her ribs and hugged the rest of her figure closely, falling all the way to her feet. After one long, astonished look at her this morning, the Scot had not lowered his gaze below her chin since.

"No, not the statues," Io agreed, leaning past him to see into the room. The gods lived in there, loosely placed, facing each other, the windows, the walls. It pleased her to keep them together, the Greeks and Romans and Celts, a few Norse, fewer still Persian and Egyptian. They stared at one another in eternal silence, standing or seated, blank stone eyes. Her favorite was Circe, with one sandaled foot set delicately upon the head of a peacock.

"How did they get here?" Aedan asked. "Who put them here?"

"I did. I, and others."

"You said there are no others on the island."

"There aren't. Not any longer."

"But there were before?"

"Of course," she said lightly, stepping back from the doorway, giving him room to turn. "My parents were here before, and my grandparents, and so forth."

He did not move. "Your parents?"

"Aye."

He seemed to weigh that, still facing the chamber. After a long while he spoke, his voice level. "Is anything you say true, Ione?"

"It is all true, Scot."

From their corners the gods almost watched them, smiling their frozen stone smiles. She knew the name of each, from Jupiter to Vesta to Set. She knew every marble vein, every polished curve, because she had studied them so well and for so long. They had been her only company for more time than she could count. She had spent perhaps years in here with them, stroking their hard arms, offering flowers to pedestals of jasper and malachite. Io had come to think of them as a perfect union of the old and new: the best of her kind and of mortals, images of man but still beyond man, ancient powers and cunning beauty.

"It's cold in here," Aedan said abruptly, pulling back. "I want to go outside. How do I get outside?"

"I will take you," Io replied.

But he did not wait for her to lead, moving past her down the hall.

The storm of last night was gone but for a smudge of clouds to the west, hovering over far waters. It had left the island littered with debris; damp leaves turned the outside stairs slick, and the man was forced to lean on her as they descended them. She wrapped her arm around his waist and felt the firm weight of him, how he tried to hold himself rigid, as much apart from her as he could. Io grasped him more tightly. The beads of his braid tapped gently against her cheek, matching their slow rhythm.

He wore a belt today, a scabbard for the sword he carried. He had found those for himself.

At the bottom of the stairs was the little beach, the sand drying in streaks of amber and bleached gold. He released her quickly and stood looking around them as the wind tossed his hair and turned her sheath to gossamer. Behind them, behind the castle, the forest shone emerald green, scented of rain and wet earth.

"There was a ship out there last night." Aedan pointed to the distant reef.

"I know."

"Did you see it? Were there survivors?"

"No."

"No," he echoed, grim. "Of course not." He lifted a hand to his eyes, blocking out the sun. "We'll search anyway. We have to try. Someone might have made it. Someone—"

She cut him off. "You must again accept my word. No one survived that ship."

He glared at the surf, speechless, then took up the cane and began to struggle down the beach. She walked after him.

"Perhaps you should stay away from the shore, at least for now. Perhaps it would be wiser to return to the castle."

He ignored her, grappling with the sand. The cane sank deep with every step. He jerked it back up again angrily.

"Perhaps there will be—things out here you do not wish to see," Io said.

He stopped, finally looking at her: a stern, distrustful gaze, as if finding suddenly a foe where a friend once stood. Ione edged back, an unexpected guilt in her chest, and then from the guilt came something else, something warm and bittersweet.

She knew his looks were pleasing. Like the afterglow of stars, his features were etched into her memory. But now she realized that the castle light—even the sea light—had hardly revealed him. Out here in the bold yellow sun the Scot was truly glorious, even with his new scar. Yet his expression stayed troubled and dark.

"How did those statues really get into that room?"

"I told you."

"Aye, you told me. You did it. Others." He laughed, but it was a cutting sound, also angry. "You, Ione of Kell, lifted a statue of solid stone taller than yourself—taller than I— and carried it up those stairs, into the castle, then up the stairs again to that chamber. Was it magic, sorceress?"

"No. It was only me."

"Naturally," he muttered, caustic. "Only you."

She reached out and snatched the cane from him, holding it in front of her with a hand at either end. With her eyes steady on his, she brought her hands together and snapped it cleanly in two.

"Only me." She dropped the pieces in the sand and walked away before she shocked him further.

She had not meant to lose her temper. She had meant to bring them together, not drive them further apart—but he was so *difficult!* She was used to silence and gratitude from men, not this brooding, surly choler that seemed to threaten each time she neared. She liked him better asleep. She liked him much, much better at night, when he did not speak, or pull away.

To hell with him. She would leave him to his misery and doubts. There were other things to do today than wait upon an ungrateful man.

Aedan watched her go, her red hair swinging, the translucent slip of cloth that barely covered her stretching tight across her legs. She rounded a copse of trees and did not return.

He lowered himself to the sand and took up the parted cane, examining the fresh break of each half. The wood was not soft or rotted; the heart of the oak barely flattened at all beneath the pressure of his thumbnail. He held up one of the pieces as she had, testing his strength against it. It would not yield.

Yet she had snapped it so easily, as a child might the bone of a chicken, or a giant the arm of an enemy.

He did not know giants. He did not know who could do this, what Ione had just done, split a shaft of hard oak without pause or doubt.

He did not know. He did not understand. He looked out at the waves and tried not to consider the new and awful idea that came to him.

* * *

The king's private chamber smelled of death. It was stifling dark, the windows shuttered, no trace of perilous sun or wind allowed inside. The figure on the royal bed was gaunt beneath the covers, nearly lost behind vibrant stitched quilts and heavy furs. Distant torchlight revealed the bones of his face, the wasted curve of his shoulders. He had been a tall man in his prime, a powerful man who maintained his leadership throughout his final days, even from this bed. Even as the sickness ate at him, and turned his yellow hair to white and his beard to grizzled gray. He was beloved, respected. His people knew him best as a father to all, a man who had led and protected them, who watched over them for decades with the silver sharp eyes of a wolf.

But those eyes had closed, and they would not open again. The king left his storied life without even a sigh, and it took his daughter's desperate wail to summon the physicians back to his side, the priests chanting prayers and blessings as they pried her fingers from his.

"The king is dead," announced the elder of the king's council, in a voice of solemn ceremony. "Honor the queen!"

All eyes turned to the young woman who still knelt beside her father, her head next to his upon the pillows, her soft sobs filling the room.

"Honor the queen," came the murmured response, but the new queen did not cease her weeping.

Aedan built the first signal fire that afternoon.

He searched for a place where there might have been one before—surely *someone* had done this before him, in all these years—but there was only smooth beach and knotted trees. No hint of a fire pit. No ash, no coals.

So he dug his own, using his hands at first and then the remains of an oar he found buried in pebbles in the sweep of a cove. The oar made his work easier, but by the time he was satisfied, his back was burning and his skin was raw. He took breaks at the edge of the shore, holding his palms in the stinging salt of the sea.

Ione did not reappear.

He managed a decent enough blaze. There was driftwood everywhere, and in the sand from his pit he discovered a true blessing: a shard of thick clear glass, plain and very sharp. In the full sun it devised an excellent thorn of light, a small smoldering, smoke, smoke . . . and then finally the first flame.

He sat back, encrusted with sand and sweat. His fire spread in long, beautiful licks, flickering hope against the blue sea. If a ship passed near . . . aye, if luck was with him, and if anyone was looking . . .

God knew what they would think. That the ghosts of Kell were rising. That the mermaids danced by firelight. That, please fortune, there were people here, lost people who had to return home before it was too late.

A curious gull circled by, tangled with the smoke and left, squawking.

A pair of crabs wrestled on a rock to the left, waving fat claws. Aedan sat up straighter, watching their slow, menacing dance, then stood, following their descent to the other side.

More blessings: It seemed Kell had tide pools, a wealth of them. He had found his dinner.

He was not unskilled at cooking. Long campaigns away from Kelmere meant he learned the basics to survive. He knew that the brown mussels were edible but the red ones were not, that the blue crab was faster than its green cousin. That if he had a net, even the smallest net, he might have had fish as well. But there was no net, and his tunic was already in use, holding the mussels and crabs.

He crept between the pools, and his leg hindered him, and the sun beat down, and the terns wheeled and scolded. But Aedan would eat.

Growing up on the islands had prepared him well; he recognized the tough, slippery seaweed that clung to the rocks. It would add flavor to whatever he cooked, so he stuffed a bit of that into his tunic too. With the help of a crooked staff of driftwood, he made it back to the keep, losing only one crab in the process, which dropped from his tunic and scurried furiously away.

He left the cane for the sea to take, rolling with the surf.

The castle kitchen was light, spare, nearly eerie in its cleanness. He knew the kitchens of Kelmere, of course. As a child he had stolen sweets from hot trays, and as a lad brought out the king's meals himself. He knew sooty hearths, bustling women, the richness of warm spices rising in the air. But here the hearths were scrubbed down to pale stone, and the air smelled only of the sea. Clearly this place had not been used in a very long while.

Yet there was a cauldron already set in the fireplace. It was as clean as everything else, without a trace of rust. Another contradiction, here in Ione's castle.

Thank God there was a cistern of rainwater just past the door. He had dreaded the thought of having to search for a well.

He emptied his tunic into the cauldron, added water from the cistern, then realized there was no wood.

Aedan traveled outside again.

The driftwood in the hearth burned slowly, moist from the rain, and the flames seemed to cast colors at him, pale pink and green and gold, sizzling with salt. Smoke billowed up and around, blinding, but he stayed where he was, minding the fire, the stew, stirring it slowly with a slender rod of birch.

And still Ione did not come.

He ate from a bowl of hard-glazed clay, stacked with a score of others in a corner cupboard. He made certain to leave half of what he cooked, embers of the fire now settled to a cherry simmer. The sky outside began to change. He took his crooked stick and went out to watch the sunset, his second waking one upon the isle.

Still no Ione.

He tended his signal fire, gradually adding wood for the night, feeding the flames, searching the waters. No points of light winked back at him; if there were ships out there, they stayed as dark as the dusk.

He stood alone in the light.

Where was she?

Finally, he gave up waiting. Aedan finished the stew and rinsed out the cauldron, tossing seaweed and shells past the kitchen steps. He followed winding corridors until he reached the great hall again, then toiled up those main stairs, pausing on every step, managing the pain. The full moon guided him, allowing scattered light within the keep, a vague frosted glow. At the doorway to his chamber Aedan stopped once more, wiping the sweat from his brow, then finished his journey, all the way over to the elaborate wooden bed where Ione now slept, curled on her side beneath the blankets, an arm tucked under her head and her remarkable hair for a pillow.

He looked down at her and felt something inside him begin to splinter. She slept so sweetly, her face utterly calm, utterly pure. And perfect—no woman was truly perfect, he had lived enough to realize that. But somehow, in some miraculous way, this woman was. This woman, who lived alone, as far as he could tell, on an enchanted isle, lived without flaw or friend. He had come so far to find her, and now that he had he could only watch her sleep, his tongue tied into silence. Everything he believed as a man shied away from this moment. But his beliefs had turned and turned until he found himself here, facing down childhood myths, simple faerie tales.

She had saved his life, deep in the ocean. He could think of only one way how.

The scrolled silver locket had slipped on its chain to the hollow of her shoulder. It gleamed at him like the moon hanging above.

Ione opened her eyes. She showed no consternation at finding him standing over her, no astonishment. Without speaking she sat up, folding the covers aside. The locket swung back above her heart; she wore no clothing at all.

"Come," she invited him, when he did not move. "I have forgiven you."

"I saw you when I was in the water," he said to her, abrupt, still standing. "There was blood between us, and above us was the surface."

She pushed back her hair, listening. Waiting.

"Above us," Aedan said again, for emphasis. "We were together beneath the waves, beneath the storm."

"It was safer there."

"I saw—I saw—" He laughed at his own words, could not even finish the sentence.

She rose from the bed with natural grace, as unconcerned about her nudity as the children who frolicked in the streams back home or the Druids in their pagan rites. He took the hand she offered and stared down at it, smooth lines, supple strength. Her skin, pale as mist; and his own, burned by the sun.

"I've brought you food," she said.

"Bread," she added, at his continued quiet. "Cured meat. Most of it was still good."

He did not release her hand. "Where did you get it?"

"From the ship of last night."

"How?"

"I swam out."

"To the reef."

"Aye."

It occurred to him then that he had been asking her the wrong questions—all the wrong questions, because there was only one that actually mattered. He knew that now.

Her eyes were so dark a blue they took on the night, shining black before him, brilliant. What he saw in them made his mouth go dry, and his voice, when it came, was pained and rough.

"Ione—what are you?"

She looked surprised, then perplexed. Her fingers closed over his.

"But I thought you knew. I am the siren of Kell."

# CHAPTER SEVEN

T he what?" the Scot inquired, in a softly chilled sort of way.

"Siren," Io repeated, less certain now. "Haven't you—don't you know about Kell?"

It seemed impossible that he didn't. Kell was of the ages, and so was the curse. She thought all humans knew of it. She thought—oh, God, she thought he knew.

All her life Io had imagined the lands beyond her island. She had not far to imagine their shores; on balmy nights she swam close enough to taste the smoke of the fishing villages, to hear the boasting of the men as they cleaned their catches, to peer into cottage windows and espy wives and widows and clamoring children.

Dogs barked at her and the winds whistled them gone, allowing her private musings in inland lagoons. She did not understand humans and so she had sought them out whenever she could, much to her mother's dismay.

*Stay far*, Mama had warned. *Stay far, stay silent. Do*

*not let them see you in return, Ione. You will not be welcomed, only feared.*

And it had always seemed the oddest irony to her that those who feared her were the very ones she caught at their deaths, to chase away the fears.

So Io swam and swam but never garnered a lasting glimpse of human life. To her they lived in a world of laughter and light, a forbidden place ripe with mystery. Harvests. Dancing. Courtship. Love.

*Love.*

She took from them what she could. Eager for all things human, she learned their songs, their words. She watched them court and couple, eat and drink and sleep. She climbed the ropes of midnight ships and listened in secret to the mariners' tales, stories of her kind and others, of monsters and families and speculation on the supply of mead. She took care never to be seen, as her mother had instructed.

But it was not enough. She didn't learn enough to satisfy the ache within her. She didn't learn what magic the people off Kell had that Kell had not. She would never understand why her father had left the isle.

Men, she supposed, never flourished in one place very long. But Ione was determined to try with hers.

Tonight's moon sculpted his features; he was lovely enough to be one of her own kin, with his jet-black hair and silver clear eyes. His face shone hard as stone, his brows drawn up into an expression of elegant reproof. With his beads and braids he was exotic, dark, and wondrous comely. He might have been one of the gods, posed in place with his palm on hers. A stone god, but so warm.

The Scot took a single step back. Just one step, but it was enough to cut her to the bone. She kept her hand in his; their arms stretched out between them.

"How could you not know?" Ione asked, baffled. "You saw me in the water. You said it yourself."

"I thought you an illusion." There was a terrible twist to his lips, not a smile. "I thought I had died."

"You would have. I saved you."

Very gently, very precisely, Aedan unloosed their hands. His fingers betrayed the faintest tremor; he closed them to a fist. The stone set of his face had deepened to something distant and taut; he looked sharply away from her, off to shadows. It was an expression she well recognized, and it filled her with gloom.

"Do you fear me now, Scot?"

"I don't fear you. I fear—" The line of his lips grew thinner, a sullen downward curl. "God help me. I must be mad."

The despair in him took her aback. Io thought of the mortal men she had trailed, how they never looked past the bottomless waves, never ventured too far from firm land. She glanced at the strip of driftwood the Scot used for support and felt a flush of shame.

"Not mad," she said. "And tomorrow I will prove it to you. But tonight the waters are wild, and it's not safe to go out. Tonight we'll sleep. Tomorrow you'll be sane again."

"I'll not sleep," he said, almost a snarl.

"Very well. You need not."

The bed was soft and pleasant. She slipped beneath the blankets and lay back, one hand lifted to him.

"What are you doing?" he asked stiffly.

"You did not wish to sleep. So, come."

"I'm not—I'll not . . ." He seemed to lose the end of his thoughts, staring down at her.

"We won't be sleeping," she said, exasperated.

"My God." He took another step away. The driftwood made a sharp *clack* against the floor. "That was *real*? The dreams of you—of us together—"

"Your mind does not fail you." She gave him a consoling smile and kept her hand steady. "Do come. You will enjoy it, I promise you. I am no dream."

"No. You're not, are you? None of this is."

His voice was pitched low, nearly too low to hear. He leaned against his makeshift cane, his hair tousled, his knuckles clenched white against her. For a moment, awash in moonlight, he looked almost more beast than man— a wolf bedecked in onyx and quartz, fierce and shining danger.

Then he moved out of the light. Io felt her heart tear, just a little, and sat up again.

"Aedan?"

He began to limp past her, circling wide to avoid the bed.

"Aedan—"

"No."

"Don't go," she said. "Please."

At the three-legged divan he halted but did not look back at her.

She spread her hands, helpless. "Is this not what people do?"

"What?"

"Mate. Man and woman, in bed, in the woods—I know it is. I have seen it."

Now he turned. "You have?"

"Aye. And I thought—you enjoyed it before, Scot."

"I was senseless," he said harshly. "You should not have lain with me."

"I liked it." She dropped her eyes, smoothed her palms over the covers. "So did you."

He said nothing, but she heard his exhalation, long and hard.

"You do not wish to sleep, or eat," she said quietly.

"You do not wish to be with me. I am mystified. What *do* you wish?"

He lifted his head from his study of the floor, where the honed end of the driftwood rested, and threw her a hot silver glance.

"I don't know." He sounded sullen again. "I don't know yet."

"You should stay here. You know that."

"No."

"Where else is there to go, then? What else is there to do? There is only the castle, and the island. There are creatures outside these walls, creatures it would be best not to meet at night."

He rolled the driftwood in his hands so that it turned a grinding circle against the stones.

"I think you're lying," she said. "I think you do want to stay."

His head had angled slightly toward her. She could just see the slant of his cheekbone, the rigid flex of his arm revealed beneath the tunic.

"Don't you?" Io stole to the end of the bed, extending one leg, then the other over the edge. A sheet of crumpled silk bunched behind her; she gathered it up, draped it over her shoulders.

"Don't you?"

She left the bed and the silk floated behind her, a scant swelling curve. He watched her approach from the corner of his eye, immobile, caught between his will and hers. Already she felt the heat of him, an incensed desire, a rising need. She slipped behind him and wrapped her arms around his chest, still holding the sheet. The silk settled over them both, loose binding, soft as a breeze.

"Don't you?" Ione whispered, and with slow deliberation pressed her body into his, resting her cheek against his shoulder blade. He made a sound deep in his throat, pure masculine hunger; it shimmered all the way through her.

She let one corner of the silk drift free, drawing her hand up and down his torso, a languid rhythm, finding the shape of him, warm contours, spiraling tension. She lifted herself to her toes, using him as her anchor, and kissed the column of his neck.

He moved at last, so swift she had only a glimpse of his face, savage, beast again, before he took her lips. The driftwood clattered to the floor; his hands twisted sharp in her hair as his mouth ground against hers.

The suddenness of it checked her. She hung there, a prisoner in his embrace, feeling him as she might a living flame: a fevered shock across her skin, a welcome burning that spread far and deep.

He was force and movement, driving them across the room until together they stumbled into the bed with the silk sheet trailing behind. She fell with barely a sound and then he was there again, an ungentle man with lovely lines and hard muscles spread over her, covering her.

Her arms came up around him.

"Don't let me," he rasped, his body straining against hers, pushing her legs apart.

"Yes," she said, not a proper answer, but it was true and clear and what she wanted.

"Yes," she said again, and kissed him back, his lips, his chin, the salty rise of his shoulder. He groaned, a rumble that shook them both, and pressed his face into her hair. His breath blew ragged against her throat.

She tugged at him, restless beneath him. "Aedan, don't stop."

But he had. There was a new tension in him now, a deep shivering hush that pressed heavy upon her until she was still as well, until they were both panting in the shadows.

"Please don't stop," Ione whispered, forlorn.

"Tell me this." His voice was thick; he did not raise his head. "Have you—have there been others?"

"What?" He made no sense to her, none of this did—why had he stopped? He wanted her, she wanted him; Io tried to stretch against him and felt his arms clench tighter.

"Before me," he grated, insistent. "You said you'd seen people—the woods, in bed. Have you been with another man, like that?"

"Mating?"

"*Aye.*" The word was an explosion of sound.

"No," she said. "Only you."

"God." He held her harder, a brief, impassioned squeeze, then lifted himself up. He rose from the bed, his arousal in full evidence, and moved away.

"Why does it matter?" Io sat up in the bed. "Aedan?"

He could barely think, barely see, or even stand. He heard her voice like water over stones, a sweet murmur, even with the note of hurt beneath it.

He had wounded her. He had not meant to.

She was innocent—she had been. And he had lain with her, and used her, and loved her with a freedom and passion that stunned him still, that even now had the power to cloud his mind and send him back to her, back into her arms and her bed and her luscious, luscious body.

He had used her. And she didn't even realize it. Not yet.

Whatever else she was—siren or maiden, he hardly knew what to think—he could not forgive himself that. He'd always fought so hard for his honor, wanted so much to prove himself worthy of the title to which he had been born. And now, here, he had done a thing he could never repair.

*A prince indeed,* he thought, acrid.

Part of him had realized the truth, that no dream could be as real as she, no fantasy so tangible. He had known it—aye, his heart had sounded recognition—the moment he laid eyes on her in the great hall.

Innocent. Alone.

The way she dressed, the way she spoke—he should have seen it sooner. She'd never been among people before; she'd never done any of the ordinary things he had taken for granted every day: talking with friends, riding in the hills, chess by candlelight, minstrels, feasts . . . all the hallmarks of civilization. All missing on Kell.

And worse, he'd lashed out at her when the fault was his. Another mark against him, another point of disgrace.

He felt her touch on his arm, light and sliding, and turned. She looked up at him pensively. Moonlight sparkled in her hair.

Even if she *had* been with another, with a hundred others, he still had no right to claim her. No right at all.

"I'm going to sleep elsewhere," Aedan said, and was surprised to hear his voice so firm. "Don't follow me. Stay here, Ione."

"I have offended you," she said, somber.

"No." He took her hand and kissed her fingers. Desire surged back, instant and absolute; he had to force himself to let her go. "No. I have offended myself."

He limped out of the room.

The coronation took place that very night.

The queen rode a majestic black stallion to the church. It was her brother's horse, not her own; small and slender upon its back, she rode it as a tribute to his bravery, and the people of Kelmere sounded their approval as she passed. The queen greeted their cries and well wishes with solemn nods, keeping her eyes fixed on either the lane before her or else well above, to the darkening sky.

The coronation was to be an evening event. All agreed it was another homage to Prince Aedan, who had died at twilight to save his sister.

Lining the lane to the church were a hundred lit torches, their flames more brilliant than the dusk, than the stars that were just beginning to rise. Callese kept the stallion to a walk, and the copper coins tied to her saddle jingled with every step, and the white ribands in the stallion's mane bounced and flared. She wore her father's colors, his emblem patterned across her skirts, so that all would see she honored his ways as well.

Around her were her father's wise men—now her own—warriors and councillors and bishops, everyone in their finest raiment, watching the crowd that pressed close, watching their queen.

At the church door were more people, countless more, and inside, Callese knew, even more still. Royalty awaited her within—not as many as could have been here had she bided a day or so more for her crown, but still stalwart rulers, blooded princes and Highland chieftains, even the Lady of the Woods. Everyone waited.

She dismounted with the aid of a wide-eyed lad, stepping from his hands to the ground. She turned and waved to her people and as one they released their favor, roaring back at her, an enormous clamor. The torch flames trembled and sparked.

The stallion took a fitful step and Callese reached back to catch the reins. She drew her hand down his nose, and the horse stilled and then dipped his head to hers, as if in solace. It was a pretty sight, the fair young queen with a garland of lilies in her hair; the mighty stallion, rook dark against her.

The priest standing next to her observed the moment. With great stateliness he leaned close, addressing her under his breath.

"The prince is now in a better place, my queen."

Callese lifted her head. For the first time in days she smiled; a dazzling, joyful smile that quite took the priest's breath away.

"Good father," she replied. "I do know it."


That night, as his sister was crowned High Queen of the Isles, Aedan did not dream at all.


Ione found him at dawn, asleep in the chamber her father had preferred, filled with human things set about, he once told her, in the human way. Three chairs around a table inlaid with colored glass; a cupboard for practical things, maps and scrolls and inkwells, a bowl of fine sand; two chests of clothing, sealed against the light; a tapestry of a castle, smaller than her own, with farmers walking below it, scattering seed to the earth.

Aedan slept slouched in one of the chairs, his legs thrust out before him, his chin to his chest. He did not look very comfortable. No doubt he would have done better in the bed.

Io took one of the empty chairs and settled into it quietly, waiting for him to rouse. She did not count the time that passed. She only watched, admiring the blush of new light across him, admiring his form, his crossed arms, his very breath.

Yes, she decided. She liked him *much* better asleep.

In sleep his fierceness gentled; he looked younger than before, lines of worry eased. No longer a statue of stone beauty, he was flesh again, plain human, tanned and scarred and stubbled with beard that cast his cheeks blue.

She found herself contemplating his hands, strong fingers cupped at his elbows, marred with scratches but elegant still. Capable hands; he held a broadsword or a chalice with equal grace.

She remembered how they felt on her body. She remembered the heat of his lips, how he kissed her as though she were midsummer dew, bright and delicious.

Ione rested her cheek on her fist, holding back a sigh. She wanted that kiss again.

How was it possible, she mused, to feel such things for a man she hardly knew? He was mystery to her yet; she had had no glimpse of him beyond Kell. It almost seemed he had sprung to full life in the ocean—much as she had, long ago—and all else before paled and dimmed to today. But it was not so. He was mortal. He had been born to mortal parents somewhere, grew up on mortal land. Learned and lived perhaps in one of those mortal villages she haunted.

How was it possible that her heart was so filled with him?

Io had no explanation. She had only looked into his eyes and was caught, enchanted, by the spirit there, the hard, pure honesty of his soul. Trouble might come from her choice. She had always made decisions quickly—rashly, her mother claimed. But Ione would not regret taking this man into her arms and home.

No matter what came.

She wondered, idly, if this had been what it had been like for that first siren and her lost fisherman. This sweet, hot hope in her chest.

Still asleep, Aedan turned his head, sending one rough

braid sliding along his cheekbone. He was mussed, in dire need of a comb and a bath.

She leaned forward, brushed back the braid. His beard was pleasantly strange beneath her fingers.

When finally he woke, she did not move, unwilling to startle him. He scowled blearily at the room, easing up into the chair with a groan, kneading his neck. Still she waited, and when his gaze eventually landed on her, Io only nodded at her father's table.

"I've brought you food to break your fast."

Hard bread and salted meat, set out on a platter. A cup of bitter ale, salvaged from an unbroken barrel.

She hoped it was what he liked. She hoped it was seemly; people ate different foods at different times, she knew that. But she could not quite recall what foods went when, and there was never much variety on the ships Kell claimed, anyway. The ale had been a stroke of luck, the barrel floating trapped between two walls of the sunken hull. She had taken a chance collecting it. The waves were brutal, but she had managed to secure it, imagining his face when he saw it. Imagining his pleasure at familiar drink.

A breeze swept in. It touched the Scot, appeared to brace him a bit; he rubbed his eyes, sat up straighter, near dwarfing the little chair. He stayed there, staring down at her tribute, making no move to touch it.

After a moment, Ione said, hesitant, "If it does not please you, I will slay you more fish."

"No." He maneuvered his leg so he could sit closer to the table, still avoiding her eyes. "It's fine."

Aedan focused on the food. It was simple and plain, the sustenance of sailors and practical men. It was the sort of fare he might find anywhere, at home or at the hearth of strangers, traveling the lands of his people or abroad, aboard one of his father's ships.

But he was in none of those places. He was in a place no man dared travel, next to a creature no man dared fathom. She was the opposite of the repast she offered, he realized, in every way possible—by her own word nothing ordinary at all, but fable and sorcery, a woman who was not a woman, yet so much more.

Aye, he knew well how much more.

In that moment, with sun just beginning to pinkly rise, there in the drafty, sandy chamber of an ancient castle on an ancient isle, Aedan began his slide into acceptance. He had no choice in it; it was either accept his fate or rail madly against it. Useless to battle fate—his father had told him that once long ago, his gaze falling upon Aedan's mother, the queen, with her long black hair and flashing quick grin.

She had been of the Old Ways. Everyone knew it; no one spoke of it. In secret she had worshiped the moon and praised the sun, had cut mandrake for spells and mistletoe for luck. As a child Aedan had followed her; as a man he had merely loved her, accepting her quiet difference from his father and the men of the church. When she died just after his seventeenth birthday, Aedan alone had slipped back into her tomb in the dark of night to offer her one last ceremony of smoke and moonlight and myrrh.

He thought, not without humor, that his mother would have approved of his unlikely savior—if not his own behavior.

Aedan lifted his cup to Ione, who watched with her usual deep blue interest. Then he started to eat.

The food was damned awful, the bread stiff as wood, the meat so tough he nearly could not chew it. Only the ale was decent, and he suspected that was mostly because it sufficed to wash the salt out of his mouth.

"Is it savory?" she asked, as he gnawed at another bite.

"Yes," he lied, and was glad he had when she smiled.

As before, she ate none of it. He devoured every scrap.

"You have finished," announced Ione, in the manner of a grand occasion as he set down the empty cup. "Let us depart."

"Where?"

"I told you that I would prove to you your sanity. I am ready."

She sat forward in her chair, flushed and pretty, almost a normal girl. Her hair fell free this morning, no strings of pearls looped though it, no ornaments that he could see. It slid forward over her shoulders in locks of a hue he could not even name, red and gold, spun fire and sun. She wore a cloak edged in carnelian, fastened with silver clasps. It ended at her ankles, crossed demurely beneath the chair.

She took note of his examination; one brow lifted, an expression he well remembered.

"That is, if you're prepared to face the truth, Scot."

"Fine," he said, standing. "I'm ready too."

She nodded and went to a pair of chests he hadn't noted last night. "You'll need something warmer than that tunic. It's cold in the caves."

*Caves?* he almost said, but stopped in time.

From across the room she tossed a bundle of material at him. He caught it easily, shaking it out to find a fresh tunic the color of sandstone, heavy, finely woven.

"Leggings?" he asked. She threw a doubtful glance at his splints.

"Boots," he persisted, stubborn, and she turned, rummaging until she found a pair.

Aedan sat again, working with the boots while she

stood and offered no assistance, staring from him to the window and back. He deliberately took his time, loosening the laces, maneuvering his foot inside, the splints awkward, the deerskin soles still holding the shape of their last owner. Finally the blood to his head was too much to abide. He tied the second boot more quickly, then sat up, blinking away the spots in his vision.

The tunic lay across his lap. He looked at Ione. She looked back at him.

"Well?"

"Step out," he said.

"Why?"

"Because I wish you to," he replied, clipped.

She raised both brows this time, but she left.

The sandstone cloth was soft as well as heavy; it was a vast improvement over his old tunic, which was not only tattered but smelled distinctly of last night's supper. He thought at first it might be too small—he was one of the largest men in his clan, as the seamstresses at Kelmere endlessly exclaimed—but the new tunic apparently had been made for someone big, so that was fine. There was a line of dancing brown horses stitched along the sleeves, foreign but appealing. He wondered at the origins of the unusual design . . . at the woman who had sewn it, and the man who had worn it, at least for a time.

Ione waited in the hallway, her head bent, her face shielded by her hair. At his appearance she walked away, not looking back to see if he followed.

He was slower than she; his leg was already stinging, and the driftwood was truly too short for proper use. She outpaced him quickly, gliding down the sunless corridor. A third of the way down the main stairs she turned impatiently, climbing back up to him, crouching. She ran her hands over his leg and then his head, her touch as temperate as her face was not. Aedan stood still and allowed it, silent, basking in the relief that flowed like cool water through his veins.

They moved on together.

The great hall was dim, the sun not yet high enough to pierce the ruin of the roof. Ione guided him now, past the barren tables to an arched doorway nearly concealed in a corner. It led to more stairs, a sharp descent, but with her arm around him it was not as difficult as he first thought. She did not speak and neither did he; it seemed natural not to, to let just the sound of their passage take up the air, echoing in the narrow stairwell.

It grew darker, then lighter, then—surprisingly—light. A curious light, pale and cool and stained with turquoise. The stairs ended in a worn platform of marble, damp with moisture. Beyond the platform was the sea—rather, the seawater trapped beneath the castle, beneath the island itself, for they were in caves after all.

Aedan stared, taking in the hollowed space, the slick cavern walls studded with crystals, the lapping blue water. There was no exit to the outside from here, no glimpse of sky. As far as he could tell, all the light was coming from below the water, from what must be a submerged opening leading out to the daylit sea.

Ione released him. She moved to the lip of the platform and unfastened the cloak, letting it settle to her feet. She was nude again, painted Otherworld colors, her skin the palest blue, her hair nearly violet. Without looking back at him she raised her arms above her head, her fingers meeting in a steeple; with one smooth, powerful leap she dove into the radiant water.

# CHAPTER EIGHT

❦

The first moments were always like a blessing. Wonderful relief, a feeling of rightness surrounding her, saltwater cleansing away all impurities. Io felt the pain of transformation take her and she yielded to it, even enjoying it, the bubbles peaking through her, the change coming, coming—*yes*—and in an instant, her legs were gone and her true form was back, and she was splendid once more.

From her head to her hips she stayed the same, with arms and breasts and flowing long hair. But below her waist began the magic: a mermaid tail of shimmering green, wondrous perfect, each scale etched in silver as if layered by glinting frost.

She turned a loop of joy, breathing the water, stretching the long spines of her fins. Io felt them as naturally as she felt her toes on land, knew instinctively how to move them, how to press the water to send her where she wished to go. She was daring and grace, queen of the seas. This was her realm, undisputed. Let the man doubt her now.

Io rose to the surface, where the Scot stood watching. He was stone again, no expression. The driftwood slanted a precipitous angle from his body.

"I am the last," she said, floating in place. "There are no more of us."

"I believe I've heard this tale before." She caught no emotion from him, no judgment on his face, other than those carefully empty eyes.

"So you *do* know the story?"

"Story?" He laughed; it echoed around them. "Aye. I know it."

"Then you know me," she said, pleased. "I am the child of the child of the child of that first siren."

"Certainly you are. It is perfectly reasonable."

She swam a little toward him, never taking her gaze from his face. "Would you like to come in with me?"

"No," he said, very polite. "I would not."

"You don't like the ocean?"

"No."

"You would enjoy it."

"I don't think so."

"You would." Beaded water on her lashes gave him rainbows; she rubbed the surface of the sea, letting it slip between her fingers, back and forth. "It's not cold."

"The devil it isn't."

"Not *that* cold," she amended. "And with me beside you, you won't note it."

"That I can believe." His voice was tight. Despite his size he seemed strangely brittle, a tall, grown man of warm muscle, a beating heart—yet Io fancied if she tapped him she would open a hidden fissure; he would shatter into countless sharp pieces.

She could not allow that to happen.

She swam closer, and her hair floated ahead of her, and the ocean pushed at her back.

"Come in with me, Aedan."

"No."

A battle of wills again. She would win this round, she had to.

*"Come in,"* she beckoned, singsong, and watched his resolution falter. He took one reluctant step toward her, his foot dragging. Another.

They met at the edge of the platform. She held it with both hands, her face upturned.

"You're so beautiful," he said, but he sounded angry.

"I know." She touched his cane of twisted wood, the grain of it worn bare from the sea. "You won't need that down here."

He sat and looked at her with black-lashed eyes; the driftwood rolled silently away. The beard on his cheeks gave him a faintly wicked air, wary and darkly focused. She smiled at him, reaching for his hand now, drawing him ever closer.

"Down here," Io promised softly, "you can fly."

Something in his face changed. He was still angry, still wary—but there was more. Awareness. His eyes flicked down, taking in her bare shoulders, the tips of her breasts just visible beneath the water. She felt that look; fire thrummed to slow life in her blood, a tight tingle began in her belly. Her smile faded. For a long moment all they did was stare at each other.

Then he moved. Fully clothed, still wearing the deer-skin boots, Aedan put his feet into the water and dropped, splashing down beneath the surface calm. Ione blinked and shook her head, then followed.

She had not asked if he could swim. She meant to protect him, to keep him safe in her grotto, so it hardly seemed to matter. But she saw that even with his bad leg he had the way of it, strong, quick movements that feathered the water against her skin. He studied her and then the grotto floor, then her again, hovering before him. Their hair tangled lazily with the currents.

Ione took his hands. She placed one on her shoulder, so that he did not have to swim, and the other on her waist, inviting his exploration. She kept them both steady and it was just as she had said: He floated as a bird in the sky, weightless.

His touch was restrained at first, his fingers barely grazing her. But as the water gently rocked them he grew bolder, shaping his palm to her, up her waist, her ribs. The back of his hand brushed the curve of one breast, sending her senses spinning, but his hand only drifted again, down to the thrust of her hip . . . and then lower, to where the smallest scales began, uniform and fine.

With languorous arms of seaweed waving around them, with starfish and crabs and a school of glassy fish in witness, Aedan stroked his hand down her tail.

And then, wonderfully, wonderfully—he smiled.

Ione kissed his comely smile, his lips tight beneath hers. Before he could react, she took him in her arms and propelled them both upward, back to the chill cavern air.

He broke the surface gasping, shaking his hair from his face. She found his hand and locked their fingers together.

"Would you like to see more?"

"Aye," he said, his eyes clear and blue-bright.

She pulled him back down with her to the grotto floor.

There was treasure here, though not the sort found in ships and castles. There were giant pillars of rock, home to sea horses and limpets, striped scallops and darting black minnows. There were great branched fans of coral, purple and red and orange. There were mollusks in inky blue pods, gray mullets, a young shark hiding in bladder wrack. She took the Scot past these things and more, all the way over to the luminant circle of the open sea, pushing in past the cavern portal.

His hand was tight in hers. With rising ease they were swept out of the grotto, into light and warmer waters. She brought them up to the air again, and this time when Aedan filled his lungs the ocean foamed white into his hair, and sea spray rose above them in prismed mist. He turned in place, taking in the cliffs of Kell high above them, flecked with grass and brush, then the other way, out to the spreading sea.

"There," he said, pointing to a line of waves breaking in *V*s. "Take me there."

So she did, farther out to the southern sky, where the currents converged and crossed each other like the weave of a basket, buffeting them from both sides.

Aedan kicked with his good foot and let the other lag, still managing to hold himself in place as he surveyed the wind and water. Kell was a green sanctuary from here, the only land in sight, appearing to rise and fall beyond the ocean's edge. The line of doubled waves he examined led straight back to it, telling.

This was the path to take home then.

He was breathing more laboriously now. Ione frowned. "Enough," she said, and without warning wrapped both arms around him, dragging him down beneath the surface. He choked but could not move; he did not want to move, for she was moving them both so swiftly he barely registered the passing sea. There was pressure against him, tremendous pressure, and her arms were very hard and her form very close. He kept his eyes open, even as his vision began to dim and the rush of sound in his ears was more from his straining heartbeat than the water.

When he could bear it no longer, when his chest screamed for relief and his head jerked against her, there was suddenly land beneath him and wind on his face.

Aedan collapsed on his side in the surf, panting, letting the waves push and pull at him. He did not see Ione, only damp mellow sand, and in the distance an inquisitive seal, watching with sloe-black eyes.

A pair of legs blocked the seal. They were shapely legs, leading up to shapely thighs and shapely hips, but at that point Aedan closed his eyes, coughing, and rolled over onto his back.

He heard her settle beside him, the sizzle of the sand and foam between them.

"I am sorry," Ione said, matter-of-fact. "I swim faster underwater. I thought you had taken sufficient air."

He managed to stifle a groan, throwing one arm over his eyes. The sun was a distant warming, the beach a soft cradle. He sank deeper into it with each surge of the surf but did not care to raise himself up at all.

"You will burn," said the siren. She didn't sound worried.

He moved his arm and found her seated on her legs with her knees pressed together, her hands clasped on her lap: a properly modest pose foiled only by her complete nudity. Her hair clung to her in suggestive tendrils, threads of gold in darkened red. Sea bubbles frothed a skirt around her, there and gone and there again. Her eyes were a thousand blues deeper than the sky.

Of course she was a mermaid. Of course.

And even here—with the ocean beating at him, too spent to turn from the sun—his craving for her remained brilliant, a living ache pulsing just beneath his skin. Aedan swallowed and looked away.

"How long have I been on Kell?" he asked, when he could speak.

"Nearly a sennight," she said promptly.

A sennight. Not so long a time, ordinarily—but king-doms had fallen in the turn of a day, he knew. A sennight might be an eternity for Kelmere.

"Is it true that no ship ever survived this island?"

"It is true."

"Not even beyond the reef?"

"Close enough to see the reef is the end of any ship," Ione said, and the wind played circles with her drying hair.

"But beyond that?"

"Beyond that—you mean out in the ocean itself?"

"Aye."

She did not answer. Her eyes narrowed; she lifted a hand to her hair, distracted, holding it out of her face.

"Where we were just now," Aedan continued, "out there, far out. Is it safe there?"

"Is that what you were thinking when you asked me to take you there? Of ships that might survive Kell?"

"No." He sat up at last, dripping. "I am thinking of ships that might *leave* Kell."

"Leave?" she echoed, hollow. "Why would you want to leave?"

He had too many answers to that . . . the king and Callese, Picts and the fortress and the many hundred crofters and farmers and fishermen who needed him. Mòrag and the untamed woods and the great herds of sheep and cattle of his people, Saxons and Angles and ambushes.

The two men who had stolen him by boat, and left him to die at sea.

"If I had a vessel of some sort—one of those from the

reef, perhaps—could you guide me out to safe waters? Could you guide me even to one of the other islands?"

She pulled away from him, rising, and the sun slanted behind her so that he could not see her face.

"Why should I do that?" she asked coldly.

"Because I can't do it alone." He stood as well, cautious, finding his balance in the sly sand.

"No, you can't. And I won't leave Kell, Scot. Put these thoughts from your head. You will remain here."

He had managed to provoke her. She stalked away from him, back toward the water. The ocean welcomed her with sparkling white waves, and the seal snorted and barked and flapped after her, both of them disappearing from his view without a trace.

When he went to feed his signal fire, Aedan found it kicked dry, sand coating every stick of wood. Not a sliver of flame survived.

Doggedly, he brushed off the sand, gathered new wood. Built up his beacon again.

It was days before she returned—five of them, to be exact, enough to consume a pale mountain of driftwood. Aedan used the hours as best he could, maintaining the fire, exploring the castle and the land, staggering along in his slow hobbled way with yet another cane, thorough if not fleet.

He wasn't used to being alone for days at a time; at Kelmere he was constantly surrounded, constantly questioned, counseled, a prince both directed and directing. The quiet of Kell pulled at him, reminded him of the winter hunt he had taken ten years past, a lone quest into the frozen heart of his territory. It was a rite of passage of his people that had conquered more than a few young men—yet that Aedan had conquered in just over a month.

And like that bygone quest, there could be no noble ending now but one.

Kelmere would not survive without an heir. The islands were prosperous and the people largely scattered. The Kingdom of the Isles was rich with diversity; unlike most realms, all men were welcome, as long as they worked for their sustenance and pledged fealty to the king. There were spats still, local disagreements, petty irritations that without royal intervention had the potential to grow into serious unrest.

Worse were the outside threats, invading forces determined to steal what was not theirs. In his warrior's heart Aedan understood them completely; were he a Pict, a Saxon or an Angle, he might do the same. Land was for taking. Home was for defending.

It was what he did—had done, until now—so very well.

Without him the very fate of the kingdom would be thrown into question. He supposed Callese might be named heir to the throne. It was not unheard of for a woman to lead. Aye, in Olden times it had been common enough. There was a chance the council would allow her to succeed, even if only in name. . . .

Either way, suitors would descend. Her hand, already so sought, would become the most valuable boon in five kingdoms. Allies would be forged in the choice of her husband. Enemies. And Kelmere had already so many enemies.

The people needed a strong ruler to bind them to the throne and to one another. In Aedan's father they had found such a man. But Prince Aedan was privileged to know what most did not—the king was mortal ill. He would not survive the winter.

Whenever Aedan thought of it, a smothering blanket seemed to enwrap him, a terrible thick sense of suffocation. It was imperative he return to the fortress before his father died. For Kelmere. For himself.

He had to say farewell.

Each day, he scanned the ocean, searching for ships. Each day, he saw only barren sea.

He decided to conserve the sailors' food and foraged for his meals instead, making use of an old fishing net to capture what he could from the tide pools. He learned the kitchen of Kell, where to find useful stacks of pots, flasks, crockery—even the location of the well. He came across a storeroom pungent with herbs and oils, and made use of both for his suppers. He explored the unused spaces of the keep, traced his fingers along the fitted stones, and considered who had cut them, who had set the mortar.

He went back down to the turquoise grotto—empty— and then out to the beaches—emptier still. He discovered the remains of a formal garden, with trellises and windflowers and roses spreading wild.

He shaved off his beard with water and a hard Celtic blade, using a scrap of polished tin to guide him.

He found a lamp to light his way at night, a thin yellow heat to banish the gloom.

And in the end, he scoured the shores for unfortunate wreckage and began, piece by piece, to gather what he could for his journey home.

Sometimes the seal watched him work—the same seal or another, Aedan couldn't tell. He thought it was the same, spotted and curious, a sleek head against the waves, long whiskers shining. It never came too close to land, only observed him as he sweated and strained and dragged hulls and oars and rigging across the sand. Whenever Aedan paused to rest, the seal seemed to nod at him, splashing away once more.

Never Ione, only the seal.

In his daytime vigilance his palms became blistered, his eyes scorched. But at night, by the glow of his tarnished brass lamp, all his vigilance seemed for naught.

He tossed and burned and dreamed of her. He was haunted by her touch, her smile. He remembered her in the water, her sun-polished hair, the bounce of her breasts. The whisper of her fins—*fins*—over his skin, teasing, the sensation of a slow, maddening seduction.

And he wanted her. He did.

He tried to summon his reason, his scruples. If this were a game, she was winning already; by her very absence he was forced to think of her, to damn her white skin and her soft body, her willing hands and mouth.

*Stop, stop, sweet God, stop.*

As the days slipped by, Aedan resorted to tricks to push her from his mind: categorize the many duties awaiting him, count the number of steps from the stables to the motte, describe the exact dimensions of the carved cross hanging in the great hall . . . but they were only tricks, easily devoured by this stronger, darker force within him.

Gradually his good intentions crumbled. He invoked Kelmere but could see only Kell. He pressed his fists over his eyes and thought sternly of battles he had fought, concentrating so hard on his memories that the smell of burning fields filled him and the dull metallic gleam of swords sparked behind his lids. He thought desperately of rain, of snow, of tracking deer through the woods. He thought of the fox pups born near the end of every winter and the autumn leaves of the aspen grove just past the fortress walls. He thought, he focused, he remembered his home.

But always, always, he *dreamed* of Ione.

He had to leave Kell, and it had to be soon. She would not retreat long. If he wasn't prepared to go when she next came to him, he truly feared she would be able to persuade him to stay. He would forget his father, his kingdom, forget it all happily, lost in her arms. Aye, she had every advantage over him, magic and desire, indigo eyes, sweet tempting flesh . . .

He imagined making love to her, spreading her legs and burying himself in her as he had before, losing himself, over and over, until it no longer mattered where he lived or died. It would be an easy thing, so easy that even daydreaming about it occupied him for hours, and he would catch himself staring hotly at walls or trees, seeing Ione, feeling her, his body aflame and his mind adrift.

He had to leave.

But then on the sixth day she returned, and Aedan began to understand that it was too late for him after all.

# CHAPTER NINE

❧

The far side of Kell stayed crowned with mist. There were mountains here, high and sheer, with forests that spilled down their slopes to dapple the rest of the isle. In the wood lived bears and rabbits and boars; wildflowers bloomed in lavish colors, dewdrops bending their stems into shepherd's crooks. Streams nourished moss and fish and fed waterfalls, smoothing the stones in their beds to even pebbles. It was a heady place, scented of pine trees and clouds.

Ione knew all of it. She had explored the woodland time and again, never so far from the sea that she could not feel it, yet enjoying her own dab of lush green earth.

Her mother taught her of the sea, but her father had taught her of the land, and so it was here that she came to contemplate the Scot, to consider what best to do with him.

He was unhappy. She didn't know why; she couldn't pretend to understand it. She supposed he missed his human ways, taverns and roads and tall ships, villages built without magic. She could never offer such comforts. But,

Io had thought, she could give him something far better. She could—if she were bolder, braver—offer him her heart. In truth, she was afraid she already had.

But he wanted to leave.

She lay down in the ferns and scowled at the sky. What was wrong with him, to spurn her so thoroughly? Was she wicked? Was she a hag, a sea witch who captured wishes and granted them in the most terrible of ways? No. She was merely . . . herself. Fair, she had thought, to mortal eyes, but perhaps not to his. No hag or witch, no empty lures.

But he wanted to leave her. He would leave, and she could never follow.

God forgive her. Perhaps she had doomed them both.

It was weakness that had made her bring him here. Weakness, her own loneliness, that made her reach out and take what should never have been hers. . . .

Years and years she had spent alone on Kell. How lovely it had been, for even this short while, to have a companion. To speak aloud and hear another voice. To see footprints in the sand that were not her own. To be warm at night, at last warm.

What would she do if he left?

Io dashed away an unwelcome tear. She would not weep for him. She disliked weeping intensely.

She rolled to her side, her head on her arm, running her fingers across the brown dirt. To leave or stay had to be his choice. No siren could keep a man against his will, or the curse would come crashing down on them both.

Fine, then. Let him try to leave. If he was blind and stupid, if he was foolish enough to want to go, he didn't deserve her, or Kell. He could return to his ridiculous, dull mortal land and live his ridiculous, dull mortal life and forget all about her, just as she would forget about him—unless the curse killed him first.

She scooped up a handful of earth and sent it scattering over the ferns. Aye. Lackwitted man. Ungrateful, thickheaded Scot.

Let him leave.

But inside her, buried deep and away, was a flame of obstinate hope, extremely irritating. It burned no matter how she reasoned it gone.

Hope whispered, *There must be a way to make him want to stay.*

Io turned to the sky again and pressed her palms over her heart, holding back the ache.

Days slipped by. At last she went home.

She found him asleep in the castle garden, stretched out atop a bench of chipped alabaster. He lay in the shade of a bryony vine; sunlight sifted through the leaves above him, a mosaic of light and shadow across his form.

As she approached, his eyes opened. He pinned her in place with a silvered glare.

He appeared both better and worse for her absence. The beard was gone, revealing once more the strong jaw, the sensual lips she knew—but his skin was reddened, his black hair disheveled, his tunic torn. The binding around his splints badly needed to be retied.

"Ione." He sat up, glowering. "Where the hell have you been?"

"I do not owe my time to you," she responded, but kept her tone tranquil.

He stood, taking up a new cane, she noticed, one of ash. "I've been—" He stopped, cleared his throat. "I was concerned for you. That's all."

"No need." She lifted her hand. "I've brought you a gift."

He looked at the plain little pot she carried as if it might contain an asp; his expression made her smile, and then laugh.

"Don't worry, Scot. I do you no harm. I've made a salve for your skin, to better heal you. To protect you from the sun."

He said nothing, still glowering.

"You need it," she added bluntly. "Without protection the sun will poison your blood, addle your mind."

"Perhaps it already has," he muttered.

"Perhaps," she agreed, blithe. "Sit down. Let me help you."

She had taken the time to find clothing again, this time a gown of deceptive austerity, purple as the heart of a cockleshell, regal and deep. Her hair was pulled back into a single plait that fell past her waist, knotted with pearls. She meant to set him at ease, to have him think not of her but of what she offered. At least for now.

Aedan eased back against the bench, not quite relaxed, watchful. Io handed him the clay pot, let him remove the cork.

"A simple oil, you see?" She knelt before him, taking back the pot, tilting it so that a drop fell into her palm. "Sweet almond, essence of roses, marigold, lavender. The scarlet petals of poppies, for warmth." She raised her palm to her lips, licked off the drop. "Safe enough to drink. Naught to fear."

"I don't fear you, Ione."

"Excellent."

He took hold of her wrist. "I don't fear you," he repeated, intent. "You need to know that."

He was so close she could make out the faint fanning lines around his eyes; they held hers, steady and sharp, like light off a sword.

"Well," she said finally. "I'm pleased."

"What I feel for you—could never be called that."

A strand of black hair lifted with the breeze, brushed against her nose. Io pulled away, flustered, afraid somehow that her thoughts and hopes were laid bare to him.

"Here." She gave him the pot again, standing. "You shouldn't wait to use it."

"Thank you."

She shrugged, walking away from the bench to face the mass of twisting green bryony. She reached out a finger and let a threading coil encircle it. She did not think Aedan had moved behind her.

"I will not look," she said to the leaves.

There was a rustling, the barest sound of cloth, of feet shifting on gravel. She felt a sweet pressure build in her chest, delicate as the bryony vine, just as strong.

"It smells . . . nice," said Aedan.

"Roses," she reminded him. "They grow plentiful here."

"I've seen them."

She gazed past the leaves to the haze of blue sky. A pair of wrens flew by, heading for the woods.

"Does it please you?" Io asked.

"What?" He sounded cautious.

"The salve."

"Aye. It does."

She tugged at the vine. "Are you finished?"

"Nearly."

"Then let me put it on your back," Ione said, "where you cannot reach."

The silence that followed was long and heavy. Finally he said, "Very well," in a flat, peculiar voice. She turned to him in a slow sweep of purple skirts, her braid swinging behind.

He was wearing the tunic still, but the drawstring was loosened, showing her the broad expanse of his shoulders and chest, now gleaming with oil. The sword, belt, and scabbard lay beside him on the bench. He was seated, staring down at the rounded pot in his hands; lowered lashes turned his eyes to slate. For the first time she noticed his braids were undone, the beads missing.

Perhaps she would do them up again for him later.

Her feet made no sound upon the path. She stood before him and extended her hand. Aedan gave her the pot.

She poured a measure of oil into the cup of her palm, admiring the clean buttery sheen of it, then set the little pot beside his sword. Instead of going to the other side of the bench, Io stepped between his legs and, before he could object, leaned over and rubbed her hands down the hard slope of his shoulders. She felt the tension in him resist her; instead of relaxing, he stiffened more—but did not push her away.

Up and down went her hands, spreading the salve in fine layers, exploring the sculpted muscles of his back, smooth all over except for a single scar by his right shoulder blade. The scar was a crescent moon, pale with age, arcing just around the bone. A few inches farther and he might have lost use of his arm.

"How did you get this?"

"Battle," he said distantly, from down by her waist. "Battle with . . . Britons, I think it was."

"Ah. Britons."

She paused to pour more oil. When she leaned over him again, the pressure of her hands increased beyond the gentle stroking of before. With her fingers slick she massaged his taut muscles, working her way around the crescent scar in small, kneading moves. He made a sound, deep and almost wistful, and allowed her to delve further beneath the tunic.

She was resting against him now as she worked, her body embracing his with every stroke, every motion, feeling the solid strength of him, his head at her side, his arms clenched, rigid, to the bench. He was a sturdy support, unyielding, all man and leashed need. Her belly was against his shoulder, her thighs to his chest, and the sweet pressure in Io was unfurling, expanding, ever potent. When she could endure it no longer she straightened, dragging her palms up and around his shoulders, sinking to her knees before him, her fingers splayed against his chest.

He stared down at her, his face fierce with longing: a hard, handsome face, so dark and wicked and fine. Slowly Io's hands slid lower, finding his heartbeat, living thunder in the flexed curves of him.

His own hand came up—not to capture hers, as she thought. With an unexpected tenderness he brushed the pad of his thumb across her chin. His touch was light, a calm restraint belied by the tempest in his eyes.

"It is not honorable," Aedan whispered, almost to himself. But his gaze was on her lips.

"What is honor here?" Ione countered, just as soft. "I don't ask that you harm anyone. I don't ask that you suffer. We are alone on Kell, and always shall be. That honor you speak of lives far away." She laid her palm to his cheek. "But you live here, with me."

He shook his head. She leaned forward and caught the corner of his lips with hers, a slanting, sideways kiss that sent him deep into stillness.

Ione shifted, following him to complete the kiss. He did not resist; he did not respond. The breeze returned and ruffled his hair, soft as silk against her. She put her hand to it, letting it glide between her fingers, then traced her kiss downward, across his jaw, lower, until she touched her tongue to the base of his throat.

Aedan moaned, a low tortured *hum* against her lips.

"Ione, I can't—"

She smiled against him. "But I know that you can."

He drew back at last, catching her shoulders in a painful grip. "Listen to me." His eyes were a silver glitter. "I have nothing to offer you—not a home, not a kingdom. I can't even give you my name."

"I don't want your name, and I don't want a kingdom. I want your heart. Your body."

He gave a harsh laugh. "My soul?"

"Aye," she said, relentless. "That as well. And I swear that I will care for these parts of you as no other could."

The secret of the purple gown was that with the release of a hidden tie the bodice came loose, slipping from her shoulders to her waist with marvelous ease. She raised her arms and it slithered all the way down her body, until she knelt before him in a puddle of skirts, the air cool on her skin.

Aedan no longer seemed to be breathing at all.

"You grant me these parts of you," she said quietly, "and I grant you everything I am in return." She cupped her breasts, lifting, rubbing the oil in provocative circles. "Everything, Aedan."

It was what broke him, the sight of her offering: erotic, deliberate, her hands glossy with scented oil, her fingers teasing her nipples to hard peaks. He felt himself falling, falling into the promise of her, his body restrained by only a bare ribbon of will. He wanted what she offered, wanted it so badly he felt it shaking through him like the earth in seizure, or lightning striking from the sky, and he was lit, burned, illumed with desire.

She paused. He heard his name pronounced in a soft,

questioning tone, uncertain, as though she might rise again and leave.

Aedan shoved off the bench and took hold of her in one move, driving them both to the ground. His arms were poor shield against the gravel, but she did not seem to mind; Ione bent with him, following his will with her head thrown back and her throat bared in white welcome. He covered her impatiently, no subtle lovemaking, no courtly grace. They were beyond such limits, he and she, lovers familiar with the other, from face to form to most intimate touch. He stretched over her and felt the lightning turn to flame.

His lips dragged down her skin, tasting her, until he found the firm tip of one breast and suckled hard. She clasped him to her with an eager sound, her hands in his hair, an artless grasp that held him close. Her back arched, her legs opened. The gravel scraped his palms, his knees; it didn't matter, it was another part of his conquest of her, ache and fury and fierce, deep pleasure.

Behind them the pot of oil tipped and rolled, dropped to the base of the bench. Their feet tangled together in the folds of her gown. He kicked at it, freeing them both, wanting nothing left between them.

She was pulling at his tunic, her hands insistent. When he rose to remove it she quickly rent it in two, and he laughed against her lips, her perfect lips, her gleaming skin. Ione laughed with him, breathless.

Then Aedan kissed her—a long, carnal kiss, tongue and taste and roses, his body slippery and hot, throbbing for her.

He felt something cool on his back. She had found the salve, was pouring it over him, over her, reaching, rubbing. He sat up, taking her with him. Bright with oil, she shone like a star, resplendent, a wonder of colors and delight and a sweet, stunning smile. It touched him—actually stilled him—held him in a deeper place, his heart constricted, his soul bedazzled.

"Ione, I . . ."

But Aedan didn't know what he wanted to say, how to express what he felt. Words were not enough to encompass the need inside him now.

*Beautiful, blinding glory, want you, want you, beloved—*

She tilted her head and kept her sweet smile, her hands reaching, stroking. She found his shaft and pressed her palms around him in a slow, exquisite squeezing. He took her by the wrists—in his daze of passion he hardly knew if he meant to stop her or encourage her—and she did it again, leaning closer, sliding her body along his in luscious agony.

"Kiss me," she said, and he did, winding her braid around his fist, drawing her to him. The string of pearls snapped, milky beads scattering around them with the patter of raindrops.

"Touch me," she demanded, and he did that as well, finding the cleft between her legs, the moist folds ready for him, slick with oil, with her. He caressed and teased and stretched her until she was panting, pushing back at his hand with soft, urgent whimpers, and Aedan thought he would die.

"Do it," she commanded, throaty. "Come inside me."

And he did.

It was rough and raw and violent, glorious. He thrust into her without tact, using her for his release, letting her use him. They bucked and rocked together; he pinned her arms above her head, she pressed her teeth into his neck. The pearls rolled against them, the gravel scored, and he pushed at her harder, harder, with her thighs open and her hair spread wild beneath her. She writhed and gasped, her lips bruised, her eyes lost. He released her wrists to slide his hands beneath her hips, lifting her, grinding, and Ione cried out and climaxed around him, pulling his own from deep within him, an exhaustive, aching flow.

Time passed. Io could not say how much time, only that the sun drifted across the sky and the bench of alabaster caught the changing light with snowy illumination.

She lay on her back beside Aedan, feeling an absurdly happy sense of relief, hard stones beneath her and a plume of white clouds above. She was no longer alone. She would never be lonely, not ever again.

"You never eat," he said suddenly, as if finishing a conversation of long ago.

"I do," she replied. "But not like you."

"No fish?" he asked.

"No."

"No meat."

"No."

"Then what?"

"Little things," she said, considering. "A drop of rain. A leaf of wintergreen. Things of the island."

He leaned up on his elbow, surveying her. "And this sustains you?"

"Aye. It does here."

"But elsewhere?"

"There is no elsewhere," she said peacefully. "All we ever need is on Kell."

He appeared to ponder that, framed with trees and sky. He was gleaming yet, her Scot, his hair long and tousled, the curve of his lips serious. Oil burnished his skin to bronze, made his eyes even paler than before. They moved from her face to her throat, paused at the locket, the chain now loose against her.

A wolf at rest, she thought. Her wolf.

She could still taste his kisses. She could still feel his breath against her cheek.

"Have there been many others for you?" Ione asked.

He looked up again sharply.

"Mating," she said. "You asked me before. And I wondered . . . have there been others, like me?"

A most unusual expression crossed his face, a hard sort of closure, his lips compressed. In time he said, "No. There has never been another like you."

"Oh." She turned her face away to hide her pleasure.

A bee buzzed between them, reeling with the fragrance of almonds and roses. Io lifted her hand. The bee landed on her fingers, began a drunken walk.

"Listen." She turned her hand as it went, keeping the bee upright. "She says tonight will be calm."

"A bee has no language."

Io smiled. "Of course she does. You are not listening."

"Forgive me." His voice was very dry. "I suppose I don't know how."

"You could learn," she suggested shyly.

He didn't answer; instead he sat up and the bee swayed into the air again, off to a trellis of vibrant pink eglantine missing half its slats. They watched it vanish amid petals and thorns. Three more bees came and went before Aedan sighed and ran his hands through his hair—mussing it even further—and finally spoke, a note of frustration buried in his tone.

"Did you plant this garden?"

"My father did. He planted nearly everything here."

He glanced back, dark, unreadable. Pink flowers beyond him clustered to form a halo about his head. She fought the return of her smile.

"He was a navigator. A man of the sea who came to

love the land." Io indicated the flowers, the vines and brush and sleepy noontime herbs. "Much of this is his work."

"What was his name?"

"Allectus."

"So he wasn't . . . like you?"

"Hair of red?" she asked, mock-serious. "Two hands, two ears, a nose? Aye, he was."

His look did not lighten; if anything his mouth drew flatter, his eyes more severe. "Like you. Siren."

"No," she said at last. "He was mortal."

*Like you.*

"It is the way of us," Io tried. "How we are. Siren and mortal come together. It's how we live, how we"—*love*, she almost said, but changed it to: "survive."

He was staring at the ground now, at the pearls nestled between gravel and dirt. "What became of him?"

She stretched beneath the sun. "He left the island, and he died."

"The siren curse," Aedan said slowly.

"Aye."

" 'Dare come and long you'll stay, trapped . . .' " He trailed off, frowning. " 'Trapped . . .' "

" 'In heart, night and day,' " she finished for him, soft.

He flicked a pearl with one finger. "I don't believe in curses."

"Don't you?" she asked, and his lashes lowered. He found another pearl, rolled it against his thumb as though the surface held some profound meaning.

"Will you die, Ione?"

"Aye. I will die too."

He looked at her with almost ire, his eyes turned to smoke. "Here? Alone?"

Io's precious relief began to dim; she sat up as well. "Perhaps."

"And then what will happen to you?"

She opened her hands to the sky. "What happens to any of us? Does God watch, and wait for us to come to Him? I shall fly, then, Scot, up to the stars. Up to God."

"With my soul," he remarked, in that dry voice again.

"Cradled in my heart," she said, earnest. "Beloved straight to God."

He studied her, then the locket. She thought he was going to speak—but instead he leaned close, brought his hands to her face, and kissed her. Io caught her balance by his shoulders, surprise and pleasure blooming through her. She returned his kiss and more, her fingers in his hair, his name on her lips. He touched her ardently, feverishly, as though he never had before. Hands and hearts and bodies matched; together they eased back down to the oil-darkened earth, exploring the wonders of each other beneath the massing clouds.

# CHAPTER TEN

*

He needed new clothing. Again.

As fortune would have it, Kell had trunks and trunks of clothes, enough to last the Scot the whole of his life, a wardrobe of emperors or soldiers or sailors, whatever he wished. Io showed him the trunks, let him browse from among the jumbled outfits within. She watched him hold up tunics, togas, palliums, enjoying the range of expressions on his face, bewilderment to satisfaction, wry amazement at a ruby-lined mantle of cloth-of-gold. He put that back with the togas.

Io leaned against the wall as he searched, remembering with no small amount of her own satisfaction the reason why he needed new clothes. Clouded sunlight from the window adorned her lover in softened lines, falling into the loosely tied folds of the sheet he wore from the bed, where they had taken their lovemaking after the garden's delight.

He looked very good in the sheet, relaxed, his body shown lean and gleaming, just like the sculpture of

Apollo in the chamber nearby. In fact, she preferred he wear only the sheet—or nothing at all—but Aedan had refused.

Ione toyed with her locket. Well, let him dress. Let him have what he desired, as she did. He would undress again soon.

He settled upon a tunic much like the old one, green as sage, unadorned. He chose leggings to go with it, kept the same boots. When he finished and turned back to her, he was a man once more—albeit a striking handsome one—done up in men's things, leaning against his cane.

"Dinner," Aedan said, emphatic.

"Downstairs," she replied, and pushed off the wall to walk with him.

He dined on dried meat and bread, fresh fruit from the garden. She fed him sliced pear, one crisp sliver at a time, and he licked the juice from her fingers, his tongue velvet on her skin. Their eyes met; Io leaned closer, drawn into silver depths.

When they kissed he tasted of summer, of nectar and bliss. She dropped the last of the pear back to the table.

"Not again," Aedan said, and pressed his face to her neck. "Not yet, Ione. You'll kill me."

"Never," she vowed, and settled into his embrace, her cheek against his hair.

She thought then that her heart was full, truly full, and hardly even started when he said, "I have to go now."

He straightened, slipping out of her hands. The warmth of his body was replaced with the faint, constant chill of the keep.

"Where?" Io asked.

"To the beach."

"I'll come with you."

He sent her a slanted look. "As you wish."

The mountain clouds had spent the day creeping down the isle while they played, settling with ghostly vigor into glens and dells. By the time Aedan and Io reached the shore it was well veiled, which is why she didn't see the collection of broken wood, spread out in pieces across the sand, until they were nearly upon it.

Not broken wood—no, not merely that. Broken boats. Rudders, ropes, oars, pegs, the long shell of a rowboat or a skiff. All of it laid out in painstaking detail, the outline of what could be an entire vessel diced into sections.

Aedan moved away from her, found a place to sit. He took up a fractured oar and began to bind it with the rope.

"What are you doing?" Io asked, but she knew—oh, she knew.

He was silent, wreathed in white. He worked slowly, methodically, and in his movements she saw the skills of a lifetime, how he handled the wood, the tight wrap of the rope, the careful knots. She felt a sinking, terrible weight in her stomach, watching his hands, the top of his bowed head. She felt mute and wild and then betrayed, outraged at him, at herself. She shouldn't have trusted him. Why had she ever trusted him?

"You would leave," Io heard herself say. "You would leave, even now."

"Aye." He did not look up.

She could not seem to move. She could not think beyond one simple, devastating realization: *He's leaving, he can't leave, he is.*

"You could come with me."

The words were low, half muffled with fog. She thought she had not heard him correctly until he lifted his eyes, meeting her look.

"You could come with me," he said again, clearer.

"No. You cannot go. You'll stay on Kell, with me."

Slowly he shook his head at her, his expression set. She took a step toward him.

"You will!"

"No, Ione."

"Yes," she cried, frantic. "You must stay."

He stood, tossing the oar aside, a show of temper at last. "You don't govern me, siren. I'm going home."

"There is nothing for you there that you won't find here!"

"Nothing for me . . . ?" He laughed, disbelieving, and gave a sharp gesture to the sea. "Beyond Kell, beyond these shores, there is a *war* taking place! The Picts, the Angles, the Saxons and Britons—the Scots and all the tribes—all desire the same thing. To win. The Romans have left and the world is open for the taking."

"What has that to do with us?"

"Everything! It has everything to do with *me*. I am needed, Ione."

"You're needed so badly you'll risk *death*? To fight the reef, the dangers of the sea, one man alone?"

"Yes," he said.

She made a sound of disgust, kicking at the sand. Through the mounting haze Aedan watched her, stone patience and bone-deep resolve. She would not move him, not like this.

"Don't you understand? You've come to the island, Scot. You've walked its shores. Kell won't release you now; you belong to her, just as I do. The curse has you fast. If you leave here—if you try to go, you will die."

"I know the story. I'll take the risks."

"You will die," she repeated, despairing.

His face gentled. "Ione . . . my people are of the islands, much like yours. We want no enemies but have them anyway—and any one of them would steal our homes from us if they could. They try, nearly every day. It's what happened to me, how I came here. I was attacked and left for dead."

"Then perhaps you are meant to stay dead. Let the others fight your war."

For some reason that won her a smile, a faint lift of his mouth, mirthless.

"I am a prince. I don't think I ever told you that, but it is so."

"A prince," she echoed, frowning.

"It means ruler. One who commands."

"I know the term, Scot."

"Then you know my responsibilities as well. My father leads now, but he is old and—weary. My home is called Kelmere, my kingdom the chain of islands around your own. I gave my oath to protect it with my life. I will not forsake my word. I truly would rather be dead than that."

"Truly you *shall* be. The curse will kill you before you ever reach your war."

"Then so be it."

She crossed to him, stepping over the oar. "Let this place be your home. Let *this* place "—she took his hand, placed it over her heart—"be home."

"Ione." It was not her imagination, the hollow hunger behind her name. He gazed down at her, tangled black hair and eyes that matched the day, his palm a hard warmth against the chill.

"Please stay," she whispered.

His fingers curled around hers. For an instant hope flared through her . . . but his eyes held a different answer, stalwart, stubborn silver.

Io pushed away.

"You'll never survive in that." She pointed to his rubble of wood. "The keel is warped. The rudder is cracked. Half the hull is rotted."

He did not rise to her spite. "Then help me," he said, still composed. "Help me make it right."

She backed into the coiling mist. "I think not. Sink if you will, Scot. I do not help fools."

"My people need me, Ione."

"*I* need you."

"You?" His smile returned, even bleaker than before. "I can't imagine that you need anyone. I've never met a more capable creature than you." He turned to face the sea, reduced to a distant rushing past the fog. She barely heard his next words, they were so hushed.

"But *they* will be lost without me."

The surf swelled and fell. The sky had gone pewter, a weeping sad gray.

"I will not help you leave," she said. "I will not help you destroy yourself."

"Fine," replied Aedan, in that dispassionate way. "Then don't. I'll manage the boat alone."

He sat again, taking up the oar, the rope, his head bowed once more over his work.


Fog shrouded the Kingdom of the Isles a full week, a thick, choking fog that rolled and sank across the lands, blinding chieftains and goosegirls alike. At Kelmere the torches were lit day and night, and still horses stumbled into gullies, and two children were lost to the swift-moving river. Men cursed and carried on; the sheep in their pens cried out in mournful *baas*, missing fresh grass and clover. Even the fortress was not immune to the mist. It crept past windows and doors, stole through shutters and crevices and battered thatch. It raveled the chambers and corridors, vanishing only in the very bowels of the keep, where darkness never retreated.

Ships were late to port. Journeys were postponed.

Every journey but one, it seemed.

Across the flagstones of the bailey came the unmistakable sound of a soldiers' march, the restless steps of horses and the creak of boiled leather. By the turn of the granary wall, a weaving woman wrapped her arms around her young daughter, keeping them both in the safe white dark, pressing back against the stone.

"What is it, Mama?" the girl asked, trying to peer past the fog.

"Saxons," said her mother, and then did something she never had before: She spat on the ground. "The queen has brought Saxons to us."

"Why?"

A new woman answered, close behind them, her voice a scratching murmur.

"Revenge, little one. Revenge on the Picts, for the death of our prince."

And the other woman spat as well.


He would take her with him. Aedan wasn't certain yet how to convince her, but his need to leave Kell was equaled only by his desire to be with Ione, two immediate, opposing demands that each clamored for satisfaction. They gnawed and plucked at him, ever present in his turning thoughts. How could he take her? How could he not?

How to explain her to Mòrag, to his father and Callese—hell, how to explain her to anyone?

He was drunk with her, with desire for her, and admiration, and need. He looked into her eyes and saw his life spread out before him, what could be.

What might be.

It was crazed, it was irrational; he did not try to make sense of it. Part of him knew he had been lonely too long. Days and nights voyaging, in battle or in peace, visiting farms and villages and the farthest nests of the kingdom—days and nights that had slipped so easily into years. He hadn't realized it until he found her, how empty he had become, a man formed of duty, of honor and war but little else.

All his life before Kell seemed blanched to gray. Ione alone was vivid bright, a rainbow before him, just out of reach.

He would not leave her behind. Aedan would not allow that, no matter what she said. He would find a way to manage it, to soothe her temper and win her to his side, to defeat the curse and woo the siren out to dry land. Aye, somehow . . . he would find a way.

He thought he might be bespelled. He thought the island clouds had spun themselves into invisible threads, binding him to her, binding his mind, his heart, his soul to her.

And for all his past glory and infamy, Prince Aedan had no means to break those threads. He was bound fast, as surely as a spindle to a spinning wheel, his fate tied to hers so tightly he would never, never be free again.

He did not want to be free again.


She could destroy his boat. It would be effortless, really—flimsy planking, tattered hemp, wooden pegs flung far and wide. She could render it to pieces once more, so many pieces he could never puzzle them together, and he would stay and stay and stay, just as she desired. Ione envisioned it as a mad game they could play forever; each day he would build, each night she would destroy. And between times . . . in between they would meet in truce, and come together, and love.

She could do that, she knew.

But instead Io left Aedan to his toy, swimming ferociously as he worked, diving and surfacing, turning and twisting, trying to outpace her anguish. She swam until she could swim no longer, and each evening she dragged herself to shore, to his bed, where he took her in his arms and caressed and savored her until the sea salt melted away beneath their passion. Until she could sink, exhausted, into mindless oblivion.

Every morning, he went out to the beach again, and she to sea. And thus a week went past. Two.

Three.

The trees began to turn from green to speckled scarlet. Aedan removed his splints and kept them off, managing now with just the cane. And his wretched little boat grew sounder and sounder, and the gulf between them wider and wider. Io felt as if she watched it all from a very great distance, a man on an island, determined to leave. A siren drowning in heartache, who had no words to keep him.

Indeed, in these final days, she had no words at all. She could not speak to him. He did not seem to mind or even notice. At night, in the dusk, all he said was her name and his same demand of before, *come with me, come, come.*

Io could only close her eyes, shake her head, awash in impossible thoughts.

Yet he kept trying.

Too often she would wake to find him standing at the window, gazing out at the waves and his imagined home. When he turned back to her his face was always the same: lined and stark, a dear-held memory in his eyes.

He was not with her then. He was already back in his

kingdom, living a life she could never touch. She mourned a man who was already gone.

The day came when the boat was finished. She knew without asking that it was done; he was different when she went to him that night. He was cool, detached, even as he drew her to him. When he touched her she felt bruised— an illusion, of course, but a telling one. They struggled together in the cushioned bed, a silent battle of kisses, stolen gasps, formidable desire. He moved to conquer her and she resisted, pinned beneath him, fighting until he had no choice but to fight back, to take what he wanted. She didn't care if she hurt him, or if he hurt her. She welcomed it, forced it to a head, and then sobbed his name at last as he entered her, the dam in her heart breaking.

Afterward they lay in the rucked sheets, panting, limp. Outside the ocean roared.

"Tomorrow," Aedan said, without looking at her.

"I know."

He stirred. "Ione—"

"Don't ask me again."

"I'm no longer asking. I'm commanding. You will come with me."

"Commanding?" she repeated in a dangerous voice.

He leaned up to see her. He'd taken to keeping a lamp near the bed, a wan flutter of light that danced across him now, sliding gold along his face. Beneath hooded lids his eyes burned still and deep, contrast to the wavering flame.

"I'm prince of these islands, I've told you that. All these islands, including Kell. That means you are my vassal." Deliberately he placed a hand on her breast—a firm, possessive move. "I'm certain you know that law."

"Man's laws," she sneered, very soft. But she did not pull away from his touch.

"The law of man and nature. There is a hierarchy, Ione. You belong to it as surely as the rest of us."

"You presume too much, Scot."

"You have no idea what I presume, siren." He slipped over her, his body covering hers, heavy, dominating. "If anyone belongs to nature, it's you. Nature has rules; man only copied them." He bent his head to kiss her—ruthless as before, almost painful, his teeth finding her lips, nipping. "I want you to come with me. I bid it. You obey."

Another kiss, his knee forcing her legs apart. The heat of him gathered in her blood.

"Obey me," he whispered, and his hands enmeshed in her hair, pulling back her head to expose her throat. He traced his tongue down her neck, below her ear, tasting, sucking. The air waned too thin; it had her searching for breath. She tried to turn away but he caught her with his fingers fanned against her jaw and continued his gentle torture.

"Obey," she heard him breathe, imprisoning her with his words, his touch. "Obey me, siren." And he claimed her lips just as he came into her again, a slow, potent thrust.

Ione found her wits. She caught him by his shoulders, pushed at him until she could see his face.

"I will not leave. I cannot leave. I will die if I leave."

"What's this?" he murmured, moving over her in that hot hungry way. "The curse again? Ione, my heart—"

"No," she said, sulky. "Not the curse."

"Then—"

"By all the heavens," she exclaimed, vexed, "haven't you guessed? I was born before your people ever knew these isles, much less called them a kingdom! I've already lived a dozen of your lifetimes, Scot."

The hooded look vanished. He was motionless inside her. "What?"

"If I leave Kell, I leave my strength. I leave the hope for my child." Io turned her head, unable suddenly to bear his look. "Our child," she finished quietly, to the embroidered pillows.

He nearly leapt from the bed, sending the lamplight to bow blue with his passing. Io sat up, pulling the blankets to her chin.

"Is that why you . . ." His voice choked, hoarse. "Is that why? A baby?"

She shrugged to cover her dismay. "Are you so amazed? Did you never think of what might happen between you and a woman?"

"You are no woman!"

"No," she agreed. "But you are a man. And it may happen anyway."

"You want to bring a child into this place!"

"Yes, as I was brought."

He looked at her with a sort of baffled shock, then placed a hand over his eyes, gold and night around him.

She lost her nerve and dropped her gaze to the quilting, feeling a petulant tug at her lips.

Cowardly man, to claim he wanted her just before he fled. Typical man, to run away from the truth, to abandon her on Kell.

Foolish, foolish Ione, to wish that he would not.

Her lashes lifted. Let him say it to her face then.

"Are you?" Aedan asked, into the dreadful hush. He glanced down at her stomach, hidden behind blankets, then up again.

"If I were, would you stay?"

Oh, his hesitation was so slight. "I would."

She looked away. "Then you are fortunate, Scot. I am not with child. You are free to leave."

He came nearer; his shadow lapped the stones.

"Are you certain?"

"Aye," she said, and bit her lip to stop its tremble.

Slowly he approached, standing close beside the bed. His face was taut and edged with darkness, slanted black brows, moonlit eyes . . . a true prince of the night. Of another world.

What a reckless dream she had let kindle in her heart.

He raised his hand a fraction, let it drop. "Ah, God—Ione."

It tore her apart, swiftly, completely. In the syllables of her name she heard all she knew of him, pride and rough longing, a hopeless hope. Without looking back she rolled away from him, wrapping the covers over her, facing the wall.

He came onto the bed after all, fitting himself behind her, his arm around her waist. He was longer and wider than she; he nearly engulfed her, one leg thrown over both of hers. But he did not attempt to remove the blankets, and he did not kiss her again.

The little lamp flame flickered and finally began to die.

When Aedan awoke at dawn, he was alone. He searched for her with a sinking heart, knowing that she would not be found, that she had taken him at his word and decided to leave him first.

But he searched anyway, all the morning he searched, calling her name. Only the terns replied.

He came across his signal fire, still burning, a funnel of smoke twisting up into the sky. Aedan smothered it with sand. He didn't want ships to see Kell now. He didn't want anyone discovering her here by herself. It would be small protection until he returned; small but better than none.

He found his boat suspended in the rising tide, tethered

with the last good rope to a stubborn sapling. He could wait no longer. His food was still there, his water and spare clothes, all of it stored the night before. But atop the stowed oars lay something new: her necklace, the chain neatly coiled around its oval locket, a bright reproach against the weathered wood.

He lifted it, scanning the waters, seeing only whitecaps and waves.

Aedan released the clasp and placed the chain around his neck, a tight but tolerable fit. Then he untied the rope, sending the boat into a drifting spin.

"Ione," he shouted, one last time. "I will come back for you!"

He pushed his cobbled vessel out into the wild blue water.

# CHAPTER ELEVEN

*❧*

Io had lied to him. He had asked what would become of her when she died, and because she was afraid, she had told him only her hopes, and not her fears.

After the death of old Kell, his wife had slid into sorrow, into wrath. She spent her days and nights in seclusion, abandoning even her family in her madness, until at last she died as well. One by one her progeny left the island, seeking passion and adventure. But true love eluded them all. One by one they perished, thrown to ill fate by their own imprudent hearts.

A siren loves but once, Io's mother told her—and that love is infinite. But men could trifle and play with love; to them it was no more precious than a sunny sky, a cloudless day, a smooth and placid sea. To risk love with a mortal, then, was to risk everything, for they lied and laughed and pledged their hearts as children did, without thought of tomorrows.

But to deny that risk was to pay an even greater price.

A siren's fate was always linked to love. Without that

bond, without a true pledge of a mortal heart, at the end of her life she would simply . . . vanish.

Io had never thought to gamble her heart; she did not like to lose, not in sport or game or chance. But then he had come. And she had lost anyway.

From the ocean bed she followed the shadow of Aedan's boat. It passed over her no larger than a splinter, high above, thin and vulnerable. Spindling oars dipped and stroked, fighting the deadly currents. He was clearly struggling, losing his course. Perhaps the wind blew too hard, or the waves rushed too tall. She watched him find his path and lose it again, the oars beating more frantic. Inevitably the boat turned and washed, sideways, into the jagged, rising reef.

She could suffer it no longer. Io swam up, fitting herself just beneath the hull, where he could not see. And so she guided the Scot out of this particular danger, steered him straight until the coral was well past, sloping away to sand and sunken ships. With the waters tamer she released his hull, dropping down once more.

The little craft grew even smaller, became nothing more than a speck against the surface, and then not even that.

She had torn her fins on the reef. Ione examined the wound, blood seeping, diaphanous silver green now ragged.

Blood drew predators. She released her tail and headed back to Kell.


Leaves crackled ahead of him.

There should be no reason for that; by all rights Aedan should be alone in these woods. Ancient and thick, they belonged to the king, were protected by royal decree. He knew that as well as anyone. Aedan had hunted here nearly all his life. It had been sanctuary to him, the one place on the main island he could go without explanation, without undue fuss.

But there was someone unseen in the green up ahead. Not an animal; there was no grace in this shuffle, no stealth. A person.

*Picts,* he thought instantly. A poacher, if he were lucky.

Silently he slipped his sword from its sheath, then stood alert, listening, as every nerve in his body hummed *danger.*

He was home at last. The question was, who else claimed it home now?

It was determination more than skill that had landed him ashore. He knew the way back to Kelmere. He knew how to navigate by the wind and stars; once past Kell's reef he had set his course and held to it. If he had not the true talent of a sailor, at least he had the luck of one. By the second day he had scouted the far mountains of Kelmere. Skipped and flung across the water, fighting and damning the blood that slicked the oars, he slid into the rough edge of the island, crashing into a shore more boulders than sand.

The boat had shattered. Aedan had staggered to land and gone to his knees on it, blessing the surf, blessing the woods and the clouds and the soft, steady earth.

In time he found his senses again. He recognized the black thrust of rock that cradled this cove; there were no villages, no piers on this part of the isle. The nearest people were due south, at least half a day. Aedan had started walking.

By his reckon he was still hours from civilization when he heard that first stir of leaves. Hours from anyone else rightfully near.

He held fixed in the forest calm, his sword ready, and turned his mind outward.

At first there was only his breathing, the familiar beat of his heart. Soon a little stream came clear, the quiet plash of running water. He smelled earth and ripe autumn, the promise of frost hanging near. Somewhere above, a bird murmured and stretched its wings.

His Roman blade was speckled with rust; he was glad of that now, that no stray gleam of light would betray him.

Aedan closed his eyes, listening, listening.

*There*—there, to the right. It came again, behind a thicket of copper beech. A shape lumbered past branches and leaves—a man, certainly, moving with open deliberation, a man making no attempt to hide.

*Gamekeeper*, Aedan thought. Warden.

But the *danger* whipping through him did not abate.

He crept on, silent as the shadows. Trunk to trunk, as mindful of the brittle leaves as the other was not, instinct and years of training quickening his blood. The stranger—invader—never even glanced past the trees; he was pacing back and forth, finally crouching, so that all Aedan could see was the dusty brown crop of his hair.

There came a new sound, metal striking stone. On the third strike the man reared back, cursing, and stalked away. Aedan caught the faint perfume of smoke. A fire had been lit.

He moved more quickly, stopped again in the dark masking of an oak.

A camp spread out before him, a small one, the sort set up for day hunts, for entertaining nobles and ladies after the chase. There were tables laid with cold fare, fruits and meats, hard cheese, flagons of wine; no sign of the cursing man. Five tents had been pitched in a half circle, the last much grander than the rest, white with a flutter of gold edging.

He knew that tent—of course he did! Aedan took a step forward, out of the shadows, just as the dusty brown man emerged from the tent, speaking to someone behind him.

". . . prepared. I don't see why it has to be us. We've done all she asked."

"And so we shall again."

A new man appeared. Aedan was frozen, mid-step. Those voices—

"Every day, something more. Every day, a new concession, and they gain more and more power, and she less."

"She pays in gold," said the second man. "We follow her orders."

*You know the orders. . . .*

"I tell you, we should leave. We're the only ones who know what happened—God's wounds, do you think that keeps us safe? I can't sleep at night any longer. I see that bastard's eyes everywhere. I say we go now."

*I say we drop him here. . . .*

"Go where?" The second man laughed. "If he wants you, he will find you. Better close to a false friend than far."

"Better alive than dead! He could kill us here, today— do you think she'd stop him? Do you think anyone would ever know?"

*No one will ever know. . . .*

Aye, he knew these fellows: men of nightmares, of sick motion and blinding pain. It was not likely he'd ever forget. Here, dropped in his lap, were the first two verses of the riddle he'd sworn to resolve.

Aedan had no shield, no armor, no leather guard save his boots. He had only the speckled sword and a slow fury blooming in his chest.

"Let us fly!" pleaded the dusty man.

"Enough."

"We should not *be* here," the other hissed.

"No," Aedan agreed, moving full into the dappled light. "You should not."

They jumped, both of them, and skittered and turned, their mouths dropping open at the sight of him. He walked forward into their elegant camp, bared his teeth at their blanched white fear.

"And yet," he continued, "here you are. I find myself as astonished as you." His smile narrowed. "Well. Perhaps not *quite* as astonished."

He recognized them now, or thought he did, armsmen of the second guard, adequate in battle, no better or worse than the majority of young men he commanded. He had supervised them in the field himself; Prince Aedan had overseen all of his men.

But these two were no longer his.

The first made a sound like a croak, his lips moving. Words began to tumble forth, cracked and rushed. "Lord Jesus protect us. God save me, Jesus, Mary Jesus save me God—"

"Who paid you to betray me?" Aedan inquired in a voice of iced civility.

"Jesus-Jesus-Mary-helpmeplease—"

"You were mine once." He stepped closer, a pace for each of theirs that backed away. "And now mine again. You know what I may do to you. Tell me the name, and perhaps you'll live."

"MaryMaryMary—"

"The name," he insisted, although he did not truly need it. Mother Mary indeed—he did not think he needed it—

With a cry the second man drew, rushing forward. Aedan parried and lunged, the fury now burning hot in him, and the speckled sword held, bearing hard upon the other blade, pressing back, back. The man shouted something and swung out again, a rash move, undisciplined. Aedan blocked it and swept in, snarling, felt the connection slam all the way up his arm. They held there together, face to face, as his enemy drained of blood and his mouth grew slack.

Aedan stepped back, pulling free his blade from the man's neck. The body toppled to the dirt.

He looked to the other guard, cringing by the white tent.

"The name," Aedan said, soft as silk.

The man turned and fled.

Aedan sprinted after him, following the dull flap of his tunic through the trees, dodging branches and fallen logs. He would win this; he knew in his bones he would win this because he was right, because he was wronged, because he already knew the name of his nemesis—

The man vanished past a wall of gray nettles. Aedan crashed after him, smashing through the thorns, directly into a clearing that held a pack of mounted hunters, large men all in leather. Several of the horses took offense to the intrusion, snorting and prancing aside, but Aedan's prey paid them no mind, flying straight to the black stallion in the lead, falling flat to the ground before it.

The lead rider was not one person but two: a woman seated in front of a man, her legs across his lap in the casual way of peasants, or lovers. The lady had turned to observe the commotion, just as did everyone else, her hand still cupped against her companion's cheek. Her hair blew fair against his chest.

She was no peasant.

The dusted man was wheezing, clutching the straw grass in his fists.

"My lady, my lady, my liege—"

Aedan stood still. The sword tilted from his loose fingers.

Callese looked back at him with growing incredulity, but it was not his sister who emptied his heart so swiftly. It was the man she embraced, yellow-haired and grinning—the Pict who had slain him in ambush not two months before.

"Take him," said the Pict, and the hunters on their steeds rushed forth, rolling thunder through the ground from the many hooves.

Days went by, long, empty days of clouds and wind and rain. Ione didn't bother to venture from her castle, from the glum safety of her keep. Her wound was slow to mend; she limped now on land as Aedan had done—still did, no doubt—but shunned the help of a cane until one morning she found the spear he had once used. Io carried that instead.

Storms came, blistering the sky, heralding winter. She watched them from her chamber, feeling no desire to swim amid them any longer. Even the gods held no pleasure for her. They seemed mocking now, blank but laughing, and finally one day she dropped smirking Apollo from her window, letting him smash to slivers on the rocks below. That helped. For a while.

But in the end, Ione surrendered to the call of her heart. She scoured the trunks of clothing and took what she thought she should, bundled it in sealskin. On a day of brisk breezes she left her castle, left Kell itself, and set out to sea.

\* \* \*

It was an island, dark and immense. Not the closest to Kell—not at all—but the largest of all the ones nearby. She had been here before, of course, but did not know its name, or even if it had one when she last visited. It seemed a good place to start her search. If Aedan's Kelmere was a kingdom, surely it flourished here. And if not here, she would discover where.

There was an inland sea-loch, brackish water filled with ships and reeds. Io glided among them unnoticed, silent, alert. The harbor was clogged with men; another good sign.

She waited until nightfall to leave the water, limping out to a muddy shore and then the woods beyond.


The woman walked into their camp with perfect confidence, startling the sentinels, who were gathered around the fire to finish the last of their supper. They jumped to their feet as she emerged from the forest, bread and charred venison scattering. More than a few had their swords drawn and raised before they realized that she was alone.

And so very, very lovely.

With calm interest she surveyed them in return. Her hair was autumn red, loose and curling, her skin luminous, her eyes alight. She wore a long gown of pleated gold, bejeweled in cuffs and pearls and a wide sapphired belt—such finery they had not seen on even the queen. In one hand she carried what appeared to be a pike, dark polished wood that thumped the ground with each step.

At the fire's brink she halted and smiled at them.

It was as though, one rugged old soldier later told his son, he had never seen a smile before, never felt his heart skip at the radiance of a woman, never known awe, or fear, or happiness until that moment.

"Good eve and well met," said the woman, in a voice that seemed to melt at the edges, impossibly sweet. "I seek your prince."

Kelmere was less than she had expected and at the same time more. No Roman grandeur here: These people were Celts of the hills, and it showed. They dressed in wool and felt and leather, thick, warm clothing in shades that mimicked nature, sky blue and ivy green, robin red and the smoky orange of sunset. Io had the uneasy sense that her own garments were far too fine—she had had only Aedan's old tunic and cloak to judge by—but that was before she was taken to the great hall of their fortress.

It was truly a place of the earth, spiked wood, carved slate, corridors and timbered walls stuffed with moss and peat. The keep had been set high upon a hill; windows were rare, unglazed, showing only the shimmer of stars over snow-peaked mountains. Torch smoke filled the chamber, spilling upward to cloud the ceiling.

Yet for all its rustic appearance, there was wealth here too. She saw it in the flashing gold of the Scots' brooches, the rich blended silver of rings and torques, bronze flagons on the tables, and a large gilded cross hanging at the end of the hall.

In the world of men, wealth meant power, Io knew. And power could mean any number of unpleasant things for the unwary. This hold was far from her domain. Never had she felt it more keenly than in this moment.

Cold air, cold breath, cold stares. It seemed inconceivable that Aedan, her lover of warmed silver and stone, had come from such a place.

People lined the walls—scores of them, hundreds. She had never seen so many mortals gathered in one place. They inspected her and she them, hiding the ache of her torn leg, walking her slow walk down the narrow aisle before her, toward that ornate cross.

She did not see Aedan. She saw only a crowd of leery strangers, too many to count, too many to fool long, bristling with weapons.

The soldiers she had charmed flanked her now, not quite a guard but assuredly an escort. They carried her spear with them, two men holding it between them with something close to reverence. Io had decided to enter Aedan's home unaided, even though her leg was not healed. Even though it felt as though she walked atop a carpet of endless prickling knives.

The magic of Kell was already fading, and with it the certainty that had led her so far. She was tired. She was in pain. Let him be here, so that she might rest.

But it was not Aedan on the dais at the end of the hall. Not Aedan . . . not even a man, but a solitary woman—hardly more than a girl—who watched her approach with a cool, curious gaze, her face composed, her hands very slim and pale on the arms of her carved chair. Standing men fanned out behind her; they were older, burly, swathed in shadow.

Steps away from the dais Ione paused, then deftly unwound one jeweled cuff from her wrist.

"A gift, oh queen," she said, and went to one knee. "From my people to you."

The girl-woman's gaze flicked to the studded cuff Ione offered, then back to her face, her gown, the rich folds of it pooled on the floor.

"Who are you?" she asked, unmoving.

Good fortune, to guess at her title. If a king ruled this

realm, surely he would be beside her. If a prince ruled—surely he would be here as well. But there was only this slight, wintry blonde on the dais, a fillet of braided gold across her brow.

"A traveler," Io answered, still kneeling. "A stranger to your land, who has heard tales of wonder of this place."

The queen's eyes were the palest blue, her lashes the color of honey. After a moment she leaned down from her great chair and plucked the cuff from Io's palm.

"And your people?"

"Sea folk," Io said. "From afar."

"Sweet mercy," drawled the queen, with a small, chilly smile, and held up the gleaming cuff. "Are there such gems to be harvested from the sea? Perhaps I should turn my warriors into fishermen."

A rumble of laughter took the hall, winding its way back to the corners. Ione bowed her head, silent.

"Are you a spy?" demanded the winter queen abruptly.

"No, lady."

"A stray princess, I suppose, wandered into my realm?"

Io ignored her sarcasm, lifting her face. "Of sorts."

"Where are your servants?"

"Lost. There were brigands in the woods, days past. They stole upon us as we slept. I was sent ahead by my guard—I had hoped to find them safely here."

"Brigands. Indeed." The queen turned her head. "Fergus. Have you news of strangers arriving? Of this woman's men come to Kelmere?"

One of the men came forward, gray-haired, bowing low. "Nay, my queen. No strangers have come, save she."

The girl glanced back at Io, a measuring look. There was something beyond speculation in her pale eyes. There was intelligence. There was doubt.

"Perhaps they scattered," said Ione softly.

"The woods are always a danger." The queen drummed her fingers against her chair. "What is your name? You *do* have one?"

Another ripple of laughter from the people.

"I am called Ione."

"Princess *Aye-oh-nay*." The girl-woman considered the cuff again, turning it before her to catch the light, then slipped it on, pushing back bangles with a soft lay of chimes. "Well enough. You come alone before me, unarmed. Our laws dictate we bid you welcome. But pray remember that here in Kelmere you are not a princess, but a guest." Their eyes met, blue on blue. The queen gave the barest nod. "Albeit a noble guest, to be sure."

Ione rose. "I had come to send greetings to a man—we thought a king ruled this court."

"Did you?"

The girl's tone grew more frosted, but several of the men in the shadows had started at Io's words, exchanging glances.

"A wise and venerable king," Ione continued, careful not to watch the men.

"Alas," said the queen. "My father. He has died."

"But there was a son. Your . . . brother? Aedan, we thought his name."

A bitter bow took the other's mouth. "Aye, and he is dead as well."

Io blinked and lost her delicate balance, taking a step back. One of the sentinels caught her from behind, let her go.

She could not seem to see. She was blinded. The smoke—the light—she could not see—

The queen and all her court only waited, countless avid mortals caught in winter ice.

"Forgive me," Ione said at last, swallowing the telling stammer in her throat, "I—we—we did not know."

Someone new spoke, one of the shadowed men. "It was a Pict attack. Prince Aedan was murdered protecting his home."

The queen had finally stood, sharply focused, her face pinched. "You knew him, didn't you?"

It was almost an accusation. Io didn't bother to deny it.

"Aye," she replied, hopeless. "I knew him."

And without warning, the queen's composure dissolved. Perhaps no one else could see her as Ione did: She aged in an instant, her youthful beauty marked with strain. Her eyes grew bright and glimmering, tears threatening to spill, and to hide it she turned her face away so that the torchlight fell only in her hair. She brought up one hand, very swiftly, and brushed at her cheek.

One of the shadow men stepped forward, blond as she, done up in battle gear, hard leather bossed with silver. Without looking at him the queen extended her hand. The man took it, standing mute beside her.

Ione watched the girl gather herself, square her shoulders. When she spoke again, the frost was gone. There was only grief in her voice, true sorrow.

"How?"

Io stared up at the gilded cross, trying to think.

"Please," said Aedan's sister, very quiet. "Please tell me. I miss him so."

"It was an accident of fate. We met at sea."

"At sea?" She wiped once more at her cheeks. "But—Aedan hated the sea."

"I know."

Silence; the queen seemed to study her anew.

"You were his friend." It was not a question.

Io nodded, her throat closed, unable to find words for what she truly was to him.

In modest steps the young queen descended her dais, halting before Ione. No one else shifted. Suddenly the girl embraced her, a rushed, impulsive move, her body soft, her grasp firm. She felt as fragile as a butterfly's wings in Ione's arms, fragrant with flowers, her plaited hair against Io's cheek. Very gently Io hugged her in return, closing her eyes.

"Come," said the queen, with new warmth. "Dine with me. Tell me what you knew of him. I am honored to break bread with anyone who called my brother friend."

Io inclined her head. "As you wish, oh queen."

Not Picts. He knew that now.

Aedan did not speak the language of the Picts, but he knew the sounds of it, guttural and throat-deep, plus a few simple words learned afield: *stop, drink, hunt, moon.*

The Pict on his stallion—the Pict holding his sister—had used other words, a command, and Aedan had understood it.

*Take him,* the Pict had said, in a language both smooth and clipped. So it was not Picts at all. It was Saxons.

Saxons, pretending to be Picts.

Aedan considered that, alone in the frigid dark. He had little else to do, chained and bleeding in the cell they had given him.

He thought he might have a head wound; he could not reach his hands high enough to tell. But it seemed so. This muddled, wretched dizziness that plagued him could be from little else.

Perhaps poison.

Perhaps insanity. Truth enough, he could not tell what

was sane and what was not any longer. Surely only a madman would have these thoughts. Surely a sane man, a man not trapped in a cell, would be able to stop the images that Aedan could not.

In the circle of his memory he kept reliving that moment in the glen, the blond man with his arms around Callese. He saw afresh her hand against the man's bearded cheek, so small and trusting, a soft little hand on a killer's face.

And then his mind would turn again, he was back on the island, back with Ione on Kell, in sun and sand and a gracious bed. Forbidden thoughts, unbearable loss.

Ione, of the lucid eyes and brilliant smile. Ione, who had held him to her heart and begged him to stay.

He should not wish that he had. But he did.

Had she even been real? He was thirsty and cold; he was short-shackled and maimed. He did not know if she had been real, and somehow that enraged him more than all the rest.

His life whirled on, slurred memories, his father's face, his mother's voice. Battle cries and blood on the earth, pain and suffering and sacrifice in the name of the kingdom. For the honor of his people, his home.

All that, lost to one small hand on a cheek.

He thought of all the times he had cheated death and wondered if fate had kept count. This was his reckoning, he supposed, all those deaths saved up and sent back to him, wrapped ruinous and pretty in the guise of his own sister.

Perhaps it was the siren's curse, after all. It made him laugh, the thought of that, great silent fits of laughter that turned into gasps in the black, black gloom, until he could not breathe or feel beyond the pain in his chest.

Alone in his cell, Aedan dazed and dreamed. He

weighed the risk of poison; it was a coward's ending, and he would not yield to that.

He drank nothing, ate nothing. He kicked over the pail of water they tried to give him, let rats steal the bread.

In his brief, clearheaded moments, Aedan wondered if they would dare to kill him outright, and hoped it would be soon.

If it was soon he would have strength enough, he thought, to take one or two of them with him when the time came.

He would damned well die trying.

# CHAPTER TWELVE

֍

I o moved quickly, favoring her damaged leg as silently as she could, no cane or spear to help her. It was the black marrow of night and the darkness was dense, unrelieved by torches or lamps. Ione did not need firelight to see; she traversed the passageways from the chamber assigned to her with the supple surety of a cat— a wounded cat, still limping.

She had eaten the queen's food. She had tasted the queen's mead. Her body was already reacting to the mortal fare, slowing, wearying. But Io pressed on, past doors both opened and closed, past shuttered windows and hounds that watched her with red-glow eyes.

At one point she came across a hallway lined with sleeping men, laid out in neat rows. The queen's guard, she judged, aligned to protect the lone door in the corridor; a mighty force for a woman so small.

The queen did not sleep easy, it seemed, even in her own home. Io thought she knew why. If she was wrong, she would be gone before anyone grew the wiser.

But if she was right . . .

She picked her way among the guard, a step here, a stretch there, bearing the agony of her weight upon her leg, her lips pulled back in a grimace.

She did not enjoy feeling aged. She did not enjoy persistent pain. She missed Kell, and her locket. She missed the smooth cool strength of her true self.

A careful foot between two men, another below an arm. On her toes past an unkempt head, and another man, and another.

One let out a snore just as she moved over him. He yawned and turned, his hand glancing off her leg, subsiding.

She waited, tensed over him, her heart in her throat, but he did not awaken. Io stole on.

It took an aeon to reach the center of the keep. She was following her instincts and the subtle, sour smell of decay, which grew stronger with every turn. Finally she found the place: a rough-hewn door squat against the ground, clearly locked, a narrow barred window set within.

Beyond the window was another man, a flight of downward stairs just past him. He sat on a stool with his eyes half closed, his chin layered in fat. A single torch burned dim above him.

Io rapped her knuckles across the bars. He started, tipped on the stool, caught himself, and settled upright again.

"Hail, gatekeeper," Ione whispered, her face against the bars. "The lady queen has sent me."

"Eh? The queen?" The man rubbed his eyes, coming close to the grille. He was bearded and swarthy, his cheeks mapped with veins.

Ione smiled. "I am to see the prisoner."

"Prisoner?" he echoed, gruff.

"Aye. You know the one."

The guard hesitated.

"Do not force me to speak his name," Io hissed. "This a matter of kingdoms! Your queen has agreed. I will see him." She held his eyes and said the words again, this time with faint song. "*I will see him.*"

"Aye," agreed the guard, with that faraway, lost look she knew. "You . . . will see him."

With much rattling of keys he opened the door, allowing her to stoop and enter. Then he unhooked the torch and walked down the stairs, toward the growing stench of the lower dark.

Io caught her breath and moved to follow.

It was a crude, cramped stairwell, with miserly little steps designed, certainly, for discomfort—and in Io's case, burning pain. She clutched her gown with both hands, unwilling to even graze the walls unless she had to.

The gatekeeper ambled before her, slow, nearly drowsing, untouched by the melancholy air. Io wished it might be the same for her; even the torch flame seemed to shrink from the surrounding gloom. They went down and down and down, until at last they reached level ground again—a wide, flat space very like a cellar, only larger and much more ominous. She saw tables with shackles, a rack strung with daggers and axes and wicked tools in nightmare shapes. More doors lined the walls here, none with windows, all heavily locked.

Amazingly, she smelled water too, and then caught sight of the well . . . surely a well, but so large and wide as to be a looming gap in the floor, the short barricade of stones around it giving way only to a device of wood and rope and pulleys, stretching out over the black maw. The wood was stained rust with a great deal of blood.

From far, far below came the ghostly sound of moving water.

Unfathomable, that men could devise and build such a place. Absurd, that she should be here, or aught that she loved.

The gatekeeper had strolled to one of the doors, identical to all the rest. He stood there, blank-faced, and let the torch spit sparks at him.

"Open it," Io ordered, and clenched her teeth together to stop their chatter.

He moved so slowly—she wanted to grab at him and shake him to speed his fumbling—but then the door was open, and Io hastened past the man and the torch, into the cell beyond.

Ah, such dark. Such fury. He slouched senseless, bleeding, against a wall, his wrists bound in manacles and a short chain pegged to the floor. Io crossed to him, cupped his face with her hands, and put her lips to his.

His flesh was ice and he tasted of coppery blood. She kissed him anyway, breathing what life she could into him. Nothing. Nothing.

She lifted his head and moved her lips more urgently to his closed eyes, to the smear of crimson down one cheekbone, his scar of before reopened.

He let out his breath, a sigh against her cheek.

"Awaken," she murmured. "Aedan, Aedan. Awaken."

The slumped weight of him tightened. Before she could move, he sprang to life, surging forward to take her by the throat, slamming her back with him against the wall, his legs between hers and his body a sheer force against her. The air was knocked from her chest; she could not breathe in again—he was squeezing too hard, his face a shadowed terror, violence and hushed death in every line.

Dots filled her vision; her fists bounced off his arms. He was stronger than she—so strong—he would kill her like this, he was going to kill her, and she could not say a word for her life, she could not even whimper. There was only hot pain in her throat and swift, ugly darkness rushing up to meet her.

When she could not see him any longer—when she could not move her arms or feel her body—his hands abruptly loosened.

Io took a shuddering breath.

There came blots of color; gradually his face fit together again like pieces of a puzzle that floated and teased. He held pressed against her, a tremor deep in his bones, his eyes clouded. Blood had smudged across them both; she tasted it on her lips. His fingers still encircled her neck.

She was afraid to move, afraid to look away.

"Ione?" Aedan said, in a tone of rasped uncertainty.

"Aye," she managed, her voice even coarser than his.

"Ione?" He stared at her as if he could not believe what he saw. He was scowling now too, a dawning outrage in his brows.

"Aye," she said again, clearer, and pushed at his hands.

He pulled away with a clatter of chains, checked fast on his knees, unable with the shackles to stand.

Io sat up, pushing her hair from her eyes. She was thrashed and sore and so happy to see him that for a moment all she could do was stare in return, her throat burning with pain and joy both.

He dropped his face into his hands. She heard his muffled groan and crept forward, touching his hair.

"All's well. Only see, love—I am not hurt."

"Begone," he said, still muffled. "You're not real."

"I am. As real as sunlight and soul. I am, my love."

His head lifted. She kept her hand in place, her fingers twined in black locks. He blinked at her from his haze, coming awake at last.

"You are a king," Io murmured.

"Indeed." He gave a broken laugh, sardonic in the dark. "I hope you are suitably impressed."

"A king enslaved is still a king."

They were running out of time. Io took up one of the manacles around his wrist; it was heavy and cumbersome, a thick clumsy band with a soldered loop for the chain and a slit for a key. Experimentally, she slipped her fingers between the iron and either side of his wrist, pulling, testing her strength.

Aedan's gaze traveled from their hands to her face.

"What are you doing here?"

"What does it appear?" she bit out, and gave up on the manacle with an irritated grunt. On Kell, this would be a trifle. On Kell, she could snap it with one hand—

"Go," Aedan said, jerking back. "Christ, Ione—are you really here? Go, now! It's not safe for you!"

"Nor for you," she muttered, surveying the heavy chain. It was a single length that ran through both manacles, bolted into the ground through its center by a spiked peg. She took up the links around the spike and pulled as hard as she could, her good foot propped against the wall. The metal creaked and stretched but did not give, and at last she fell away, breathing hard, her fingers numbed.

Aedan only watched, darksome, controlled. When she looked at him he smiled again, gentler now, no hint of mockery; she wanted to howl or weep or both.

One shackled hand lifted, a feather stroke down her arm, as if the irons were not there. "Beautiful siren. Go. You will not save me this time."

Io clambered to her feet. "Will I not?"

She had forgotten the guard, standing by the doorway with stupid patience.

"Enter," she directed, and he did. The sudden torchlight

made Aedan turn his head, sent rats squeaking into crevices and rotted straw.

"The key," Ione said, extending her palm. "The key to his bonds. Hurry!"

The guard frowned at her and began to shake his head. "No, no. No keys. He stays alone, no keys, they said, no name, keep him here—"

Her restraint shattered. She shoved him against the wall with both hands; the torch spun and fell, embers tumbling in a bright arc to the ground.

"The *key*," she demanded, but her magic was weakened, and the man only stared at her with rounded eyes, still shaking his head.

"No, no, no key, they said he had no name, I will not tell the secret, by my life, I would not tell—"

Io struck him across the jaw, crunching into bone. The gatekeeper collapsed with almost majestic leisure, folding in on himself until he hit the floor, arms and legs outflung. She kicked the torch away, knelt, and felt for the ring of keys at his waist. There, she had it. She ripped it from his belt—she had strength enough for *that*, by the gods—and ran to Aedan, searching for one that might be right.

He held out his wrists, wordless, as she tried the first one. The next one. The next.

A noise sounded beyond the door, a man's voice, echoing. She started, and the keys gave a musical jangle.

"That will be the second watch," Aedan said, very calm.

Io kept trying the keys. Her hands began to shake; she felt ready to jump from her skin, her heart hammering, bruising in her chest.

More noises from beyond. She heard footsteps approaching, the distant splash of the black well.

"He will summon another before coming all the way down," Aedan continued softly, watching her work. "They will be armed. You have to leave now."

"Be quiet," Io snapped, and jammed another key into the slit.

"Don't you understand?" Aggravation began to edge through his calm. "I can't protect you like this."

"You won't have to—"

"Leave me! There is another way out. A secret passageway beneath the stairs—"

"Quiet!" Another key. Another. They all looked alike—had she tried this one before? Which one *was* it? Curse it all, she could not stop quaking. . . .

Aedan's attention had focused past the doorway, his head cocked. She heard it too: new calls resounding, two men or perhaps more, coming closer.

He looked back at her, his voice a low hiss. "Ione, listen to me. You will go to the base of the stairs—"

"I won't."

"The seventh step from the bottom—"

"I've nearly got it—"

"For God's sake, *go*—"

"I didn't come all this way only to—"

"I won't let you sacrifice yourself for—"

"You must—"

"I *won't*—"

"Ione—"

"*Will* you be *quiet!*"

But her nerves were frayed and hands now beyond her control; she tried to stab another key into the lock and missed, dropping the ring.

"No, no, *no no!*" Io picked up the keys and hurled them against the wall, then, in wild desperation, grabbed the grounded spike and yanked with all her strength, nearly screaming with effort.

It gave.

She staggered back, then fell, landing on her rump with the spike held up before her.

Her gaze met Aedan's. Suddenly, foolishly, they both began to laugh..

The last of the torch extinguished; the cell swept to pitch. At the same instant there was movement from the doorway, a rushing figure holding a sword, blindly swinging.

She was scrambling to her feet, drawing air to warn Aedan, but he had already moved. Surely he was sightless too; he could not see what she did, the sword upraised, the man lunging—but Aedan spun and twisted, and the sword struck the stone wall. Aedan took the freed chain in his hands and swung it hard, crashing into the other man's torso. The guard bent and swore. Then Aedan was on him, the two of them rocking in furious, silent motion, Aedan with his chain and the man with his blade, slicing up toward Aedan's throat.

Io flung the spike. By stroke of pure luck it hit the guard and not Aedan, the blunt end striking his spine just as Aedan's fist hit his jaw. The man sagged to the ground with a sound like a moan, then lay still.

Aedan turned toward her, the chain a slithering prattle.

"Ione!"

"I'm here—"

His hands were cold and the chain colder still, slapping them both as he pulled her to him and kissed her, a delirious, hard crush of his mouth over hers.

"I thought you a dream." He pressed his lips to her cheek, her mouth again, fervent, as if to prove her truly real. "I thought I was dead again, to see you here."

"We both shall be if we don't leave soon." She leaned back. "More come. I hear them."

"The passageway—"

"This way."

But he did not need her to lead him. There was a gathering light beyond the doorway, brighter and brighter, and the voices were gathering with it, jabbering whispers and then sudden, suspicious silence.

Io and Aedan stepped past the cell door together and faced the column of men creeping down the tall stairs, blocking the exit above and Aedan's seventh stair. For a breathless moment only the shadows moved, flitting across walls and swords with the power of the three torches held high into the air.

Seven men—no, eight. Eight strangers staring, fit with armor and weapons. One among them seemed to gleam silver: the blond bossed man who had stood with the queen, and held her hand, and offered such steady comfort.

"Ease around them," instructed the man in a flat, dissonant tongue she had not heard in a long while. "Slowly, men, slowly."

"Stay," Io retorted, in the same language. From the hidden sheath beneath her belt she produced her dagger, wielding it before her. "Come closer at thy peril."

Everyone looked at her, surprised, even Aedan, coiled with tension at her side.

"Noble lady," said the silver-bossed man after a moment, with a tilt of his head. "I salute thee. But surrender this fight. Thou shalt not win it."

Io matched his cordial tone. "Ignoble man—by my life, neither shalt thou."

"*You*." Aedan started forward. "Filthy, murdering bastard, I know you—"

Io seized his arm, barely able to restrain him. He was wet there, but she could not look to see why.

The bossed man laughed a little, and his men laughed with him, their eyes sly and menacing.

"Good eve, my lord," he said, switching languages easily with a short mock of a bow. "Or good-bye, is it? I had not thought to end our time together so soon."

Something warm was sliding along her foot, something liquid.

"Oh, it is good-bye," Aedan was saying. "Most definitely good-bye, as soon as I find a worthy blade to put through your heart."

Io glanced down and then quickly up again, fighting to keep her face impassive. Bright blood dripped across the stones at their feet. Aedan was cut somewhere; he was badly wounded. Oh, they had to hurry.

The Saxon kept his ghastly smile. "Fine words, for a man more dead than alive."

Aedan took a step toward the stairs, lifting his palms. "Come to me then, cur, and I'll show you proof of life."

"Retreat," Ione said loudly, again in the Saxon's tongue. "Retreat now, and I will spare thy life."

The man paused, and turned his smile to her. "Most charming, gracious beauty. I think thy situation ill-suited for bargaining."

"Think again, trickster, thou baseborn thief."

"A trickster, aye," agreed the Saxon, still pleasant, and began to move once more down the stairs, slipping cautiously between his men. "Baseborn—rather not, little dove."

"But a thief." She took a sideways step into the chamber, pulling Aedan forcibly along. He followed, stiff-legged, never taking his gaze from the Saxon. "The boldest thief of all, to steal a crown."

The man matched their pace, coming closer. "Some say thief. I say explorer, seeking new lands."

"New riches," Io countered.

"New adventures."

"New conquests," she finished, and took another three steps.

The Saxon's grin grew as he stalked them. "But what is life, if not conquest? The strong rule, the weak yield. Let me show thee how I mean, my honeycomb."

"Nay," she began, but Aedan stumbled suddenly, righting himself with an ungainly pitch and turn. He had been following her lead until now, however reluctant. She risked a look up into his face—stark white, frowning. Blood had molded his tunic to his side, from his ribs to his hip; he shook his head, one hand reaching up to grip hard at her shoulder.

The Saxon noticed.

"Gentle princess, lady fair," he baited in that courteously insulting voice. "Why waste thy measure here? Come to me instead. I'll pleasure thee far better than ever this wretched cripple could. He'll not survive the hour, much less a night with thee. I would be grieved to have harm come to thee through him."

"I thank thee for thy concern, whoremonger's son." She ducked beneath Aedan's arm, slinging it over her shoulders to keep him upright. They lurched back again, one step at time, toward the center of the room. A trail of slippery red footprints followed. "But I prefer an honest heart to a curdled one, even in death."

The Saxon shrugged, still affable. "I'll have thee anyway, child. There is nowhere to flee, nowhere to hide."

His men had plodded behind him the whole while, listening, waiting for some silent signal. Io waited as well, trying not to take her gaze from the blond man's face, trying not to stare at the long, shining lines of the swords, splendid with firelight. Her dagger seemed woefully small against them.

Aedan was breathing hard now, his arm an awkward weight around her. She didn't know if he understood their words. She couldn't tell if he knew what she meant to do—she hoped he did; they were nearly there. . . .

"I shall make thee my favorite," goaded the Saxon, sweetly soft. " 'Haps we'll spare the cripple, to let him watch as I take thee. 'Haps he'll live to hear thy screams."

" 'Haps he'll live to hear *thy* screams as I slice out thy liver and feed it to sharks," Io snarled, abandoning her false goodwill. Her leg was afire, hindering them, and by the *gods* Aedan was heavy—how had he become so *heavy*—

Her heels knocked against the well wall. With a groan she couldn't conceal, she dragged them both atop it, balancing over empty space. The Saxons exclaimed and began to rush forward, caught only by their commander's outstretched arm.

"Wait," he said sharply, no longer smiling.

"My regrets to thy viper of a mistress," Ione panted, "but we've decided not to stay."

She wrapped her arms around Aedan's waist and stepped backward. The bossed man's infuriated bellow seemed to follow them all the way down the well.

She lost the dagger at once. It scraped the stones as they fell, was ripped from her hand and she let it go, concentrating on holding Aedan, on protecting them both as they tumbled against the damp walls—and then they hit water, cold, black water that swallowed them up and dragged them down deep.

They spun together amid silken bubbles; Io stayed stunned, disoriented from the fall as the currents moved them. Aedan's arms were still around her, hers around him—it was freshwater, she could breathe it—he could not—

She could not change in freshwater. She could swim, she could survive, but she could not change. She wrapped her fist in Aedan's tunic and kicked out, pulling him with her.

It was an underground river; she had recognized the scent of it right away. Even Kell had them, large, jagged fissures twisting through stone, countless feeder streams, water running swift, running strong. New jets pushed at them, joined the surging flow that swept them along. Io swam with it as well as she could. She had to find air for Aedan. She had to find the end of this tunnel or he would die, just as the Saxon predicted.

He was swimming with her. She felt his movements, caught a glimpse of his hands parting through water, the dark bands of iron around his wrists. He was struggling, blinded again, hitting rocks. The tunnel grew smaller, smaller . . .

She struck a curved aperture shaped like a snake, stone tearing at the gown, her chest and arms. Io turned, frantic, and tried to squeeze through while the river built and built around them, and Aedan fought to stay beside her . . . then began to drift away.

She made it! With both hands she tugged Aedan after her, helping him turn sideways, her hair in her eyes and her ridiculous clothing tangled around her legs, whipping with the current.

Somehow, somehow, she got him past the stone. They burst free together, spinning again so that his chain wrapped around them, and this time when they came out of it Ione knew exactly where to go.

She smelled the sea ahead. She felt the faint promise of the ocean, saltwater and an open sky.

Once more she pulled Aedan close, and then she swam as if for her own life: fleet, fierce strokes, using all of her human form to drive them forward, arms and legs and raging pain, her muscles aching, her entire body shot with anguish, screaming, *stop, stop, stop* . . .

She did not even have time to change. All at once, she found sand. She found the shore. Dizzy with relief, she fell to her knees upon it, drawing Aedan up with her, and the air was brittle and cool, the surf a whirling crush around them. He floated on his back, his face to the stars. She could not tell if he was breathing.

Io hooked her fingers into his tunic and hauled him farther up the beach, until the chain was covered in sand and the water seethed across only his feet. She sank down beside him, bending over his head.

*Sssssssst!*

The sand by her right hand exploded. She looked up, astonished, as the second arrow flew past her ear, landing in the surf.

*Sssst! Sssst!*

Io leapt to her feet and faced the woods as more arrows came, shielding Aedan with her body as best she could. They had not hit her yet—they were either very bad marks or very good ones, designed to pin her in place. She felt an awful, desperate panic—she had no weapon, she had no defense against unseen enemies. The ocean called from behind—she could do it, she could turn and swim to safety—but Aedan, Aedan—he needed help, he needed to breathe. . . .

From the darkness advanced a line of cloaked figures,

stealthy, arrows cocked, slinking through the trees. Starlight struck their leader first: a demon, horned and scowling, a face of glinting bronze and a bow tipped in silver, its arrow aimed straight at Io's heart.

She met the shadowed eyes of the beast. She had never seen a true demon before, but of course they would exist, because *she* existed. It seemed not all the ancient magic had yet fled the world—what a terrible, terrible way to discover it.

Very well. She sidled forward, crouching, ready to battle this thing, ready to die.

The demon seemed to catch sight of Aedan for the first time. It halted, appearing almost startled. Gradually the arrow lowered, the bowstring drawing flat. The bronze face turned away.

"*Ya-loh!*" it cried in a high, feminine voice, slightly smothered.

Not a demon—a human woman, masked and armed, who stepped warily through the sand toward Io and Aedan, her people trailing on either side.

Once more the woman paused, just within striking distance. With deliberate steadiness she released the clasp of her cloak, letting it fall away from her, catching the folds in one hand. She leaned forward, very slowly extending the draped cloth and fur. Io searched the eyes behind the mask, read the offer there, the caution.

She accepted the cloak.

The woman stood back, lifting her horned mask. Beneath the bronze scowl was a plainer face, round and flushed, brown eyes flashing and dark hair tied back.

Then she spoke again, her words now coming perfectly clear.

"I thank you, whoever you are. You have returned me my husband."

# CHAPTER THIRTEEN

H e is injured," Ione said, past the cold, cold space
that was her heart. "He needs to breathe."

The woman swept by her, the others followed,
and Ione stood back as they surrounded her sleeping
lover—*aye, only sleeping*—as they touched him and held
him and spoke his name, called him lord.

The cloakless woman was feeling his throat, his chest.
She glanced up and around, searching, and a new man
pushed through the crowd. The woodsmen closed in behind him; Io no longer saw Aedan at all.

"No," she heard someone say after a moment, a wizened voice. "I am sorry, my lady."

"Are you certain?" It was the leader, urgent. "Can you
not try, Urien?"

"My lady—"

"Try! Your herbs! Your potions—"

"He is dead," interrupted the man named Urien, louder
than before. "Herbs and potions will not alter that."

All the others began to speak at once.

*Dead*, thought Io, standing dazed and alone beside a stunted pine. *No. He is not dead. He is not.*

She was moving. She was stumbling toward the knot of them, shoving them out of her path. They shifted easily, divided like water before her, but Ione saw only Aedan in the pale ashen sand—oh, so handsome—his eyes closed, his lips parted and a puddle of blood yet seeping by his shoulder. One hand limp upon his chest, the other fallen into a graceful curve by his side, marred only by the shackles and that loathsome chain.

And her locket, Io saw at last. Her precious locket still about his throat, a bright band of silver against his skin.

She knelt beside him, removed his hand from his chest and brought down her fist over his heart, sending his body into a jerk.

Everyone shouted—everyone but the dark-haired woman, who raised her palm and watched as Io waited, then did it again.

"Stop," cried the wizened man, "stop at once, have you no respect—"

Aedan coughed, turning his head. Water poured from his mouth; he was gasping, choking, and at once the woman and two others pushed him onto his side, beating his back, supporting him.

Everyone else had turned to stare at Ione, who rose and took an uneven step away, feeling oddly light-headed.

"A Saracen," she said, disjointed, and found herself back on her knees in the sand. "I saw it once on a ship. A Saracen did it, and the drowned man lived. . . ."

The woodsmen's voices were distant now, their words made no sense to her. She closed her eyes and brought her hands to her face, bowing her head. She was so tired. She thought she might lay here and die, she was so tired.

THE LAST MERMAID · 157

*Her locket, bright about his throat. His lashes long and wet, his lips bleached blue—*

Something warm settled over her. A cloak.

His wife's cloak. His wife.

"A handy trick," whispered a voice by Io's ear. "Perhaps you might teach it to me someday."

Ione lifted her head. The dark-haired woman sat before her on her heels, examining Io's face as if it were of the greatest interest. Behind her moved her men, lifting Aedan, a mass of legs and arms, carrying him off into the woods.

"Now I must thank you again," said the wife. Her mouth lifted to almost a smile; tendrils of brown hair skimmed her cheeks with the wind. "Twice you have delivered him to me. I am in your debt."

Io looked out at the place where Aedan had lain, the scuffled sand. The wind seemed to sigh a little harder through the trees.

"You don't know me, do you?" The wife studied her so carefully. "You didn't know."

"I know that he lives," Io replied. "It is enough."

She got to her feet, shrugged off the cloak, and held it out. The wife shook her head.

"You need it more than I," she said, and only then did Io realize that the gown of gold was shredded, had fallen from her shoulders all the way to her hips, caught in place only by her linked belt. There were long scratches across her skin, red on white, some still bleeding. She touched one of the cuts, lifting damp fingers to inspect the blood.

"Our healer will aid you," said the woman, drawing the cloak back over Ione. "Come with me."

"No. I must go."

"No," countered the wife firmly, "you won't. I am Mòrag of Cairnmor. I control these woods. If you leave now you'll only fall under attack again. I've set men throughout the forest, and they won't know you from the enemy."

"I do not intend to be in the forest." Ione pulled back, wincing as the familiar pain tore up her leg.

"Don't go," said Mòrag, sounding genuinely concerned. "Not yet. Don't you want to see him again?"

Io hesitated, trying not to think of Aedan, trying not to imagine his face, waking to his wife, his people . . . embraced, adored.

*He is home and you are not; you will never be home here, siren. . . .*

A small something flicked to life within her, hot, like the high noon sun. Anger, she realized. Burning anger, overlapping the pain.

"Come." Mòrag gestured to the woods. "Come to our camp. You may eat and rest."

Io spared a glance to the trees. Aedan ahead, the ocean behind, and this mortal next to her, this woman, *his* woman—

"At the very least, come and tell me your tale, and his," said the wife, with her almost-smile. "Otherwise, I may ever wonder."

Ione pressed her lips together and stared back at her, silent, daring her to guess.

"No," Mòrag murmured finally. "I'd rather not wonder. Forgive me."

Perhaps it was her tone, so tranquil and kind. Perhaps it was her manner, open curiosity beneath modest calm. Perhaps it was only her hair, still flying dark with the breeze, long strands of deepest chestnut, unlikely elegant as they floated from her loosened braid.

Whatever the reason, Io felt the anger in her flame brighter, bitter jealousy, an intense, heated hatred of this woman, of herself and Aedan and all her careless, careless dreams.

"All right," Ione said curtly, turning on her heel. "Let us go find your husband."

Mòrag entered her tent just as the edge of night was fading blue into oystered gray. She had not slept or even rested in over a day, and the lack of respite was at last beginning to affect her. It took longer than usual to adjust to the light within; a horn lamp sent black smoke into the air, a timid glow, but still bright compared to the sky outside.

She crossed to the seated figure watching over Aedan, a woman who had to be as tired as she was but who glanced up at her in welcome with warm hazel eyes.

Mòrag nodded her greeting, her fingers grazing the other's arm.

"How is he?"

Sìne looked back at Aedan, breathing slowly beneath layers of furs.

"Still sleeping. And she?"

Mòrag sighed and found a space on the ground between the pallet and a jointed table, easing down, stretching out her back. "The same. Finally. I thought we'd have to drug her just to get her to sit down."

"She wanted to leave."

Mòrag gave a short laugh. "She wanted never to set foot here at all."

"Yet she came."

"Aye. For him. After she saw Aedan asleep she said she wanted only to be alone. She refused food, she refused water or ale. She refused treatment from Urien. Insisted upon seeing his herbs for herself and picked what she wanted from them."

"Oh," said Sìne faintly. "I imagine he was not pleased."

"No. He was not. Especially when she told him that his stores were old and his toadflax . . . *feeble*, I believe was her word."

"Dear me."

"Aye."

Sìne shook her head, her fingers threaded in her lap. "Interesting, isn't she?"

"Very."

Both women fell quiet. Outside, the morning birds began to rouse, song upon song within the trees. Sìne waited, watching Mòrag, then prompted, "Well?"

"Well . . . she wouldn't say much. If only Aedan could tell us—but her story affirmed what our sources reported. He was taken to Kelmere, imprisoned there. She went looking for him and somehow got him out—"

"How?"

"Ah . . ." Mòrag's face changed; she avoided Sìne's gaze, staring up at the ceiling of the tent. "Through the well, apparently."

"The *well?*"

"Aye."

There was a moment of heavy silence, broken only by Aedan's breathing and the warble of a finch, very close by.

"How many guards have you on her?" asked Sìne at last.

"None."

"None!" exclaimed Sìne, astounded. "Are you mad? She shows up here with him like this—*look* at him, Mòrag, he's been tortured, he's barely alive—"

"She *did* manage to resurrect him," Mòrag broke in, a distinct tightness around her lips.

"—chained up and half drowned and with a wound that would have *killed* a lesser man—and this woman says she *rescued* him through the fortress *well*? I suppose she *swam* with him all the way *here*, to the *other side* of the island—"

"Aye," said Mòrag again, and there was no mistaking the amusement in her voice now.

Sìne tossed up her hands. "I don't understand you! We are at war with these people—at any moment they might attack and destroy us and you play *games*, and you *jest*, and trust a *stranger* who might slit our throats as we sleep—"

Mòrag came to her feet with a sudden smoothness, approached Sìne and placed her hand over her mouth. Sìne's brows lowered ominously.

"I do trust her," Mòrag said. "Did you see the way she defended him on the beach, unarmed, against all of us? She didn't know who we are. She didn't know *me*. I still don't think she truly does," she continued, reflective. "But how else to explain any of it? Aedan was a prisoner in the fortress; now he is free. For all our grand plans, *we* didn't do it. She did."

Sìne stood, straightening her skirts with brisk, unhappy slaps, her auburn hair slipping loose down her back.

"Did you see her face?" Mòrag persisted. "Didn't you recognize the expression on her face?"

Sìne looked askance at the ground, the slant to her lips stubborn.

"Of course you did." Mòrag took her hands. "She loves him. She was prepared to die for him. I know that look well. I know that feeling. And so do you."

"You're naught but an extravagant dreamer," Sìne retorted, but her tone had lost its barb. "You look for love in everyone."

"There are worse things to look for."

"Aye, like adversaries, mayhap? Perfidy? Deception? It is only war, after all—oh, but seek out *love*. *That* will surely save us."

Mòrag tipped her head to Aedan. "It saved him."

Sìne made an impatient sound, trying to pull away, but Mòrag tightened her grip.

"Listen. We are of the woods, you and me. We understand enchantment. If the gods choose to favor us with such a gift . . ." One hand glided upward, past a fallen lock of hair, until her fingers curled beneath Sìne's chin. "Then who are we . . . to say nay?"

Mòrag's kiss was soft and light, almost a whispered touch. Sìne drew back, her eyes very bright, then turned and snuffed out the horn lamp.

"Her name is Ione, by the way," Mòrag added a long while later, as if in sleepy afterthought. "Uncommon, don't you think?"

His memory returned to him before consciousness did. He dreamt of his life, his death, of Ione and Kell and the elaborate, incredible events that all led to treachery, to capture in his own woods, imprisonment, rage, death again. Ione. Ione.

And then . . . nothing.

But when he awoke, Aedan remembered it all, every second, every thrill and miserable suffering. After days at sea he had found Kelmere only to lose it again—not to Picts, as he thought, but to Saxons. *Saxons* in the woods, disguised as Picts. *Saxons* who had ambushed him so long ago, *Saxons* who now crept and crawled through his kingdom like fat hungry worms, destroying his home, devouring his people and their lives.

Saxons. And Callese.

He listened as Mòrag explained it to him, watched her lips move and tried to comprehend the words. His father dead. His sister allying with the enemy. His sister betraying him, betraying them all.

Callese had set the trap. She had led the Saxons to their father's gate and then invited them inside. *Callese.*

He recalled her face at the twilight ambush, her look of amazement—a marvelous act. He felt the anguish for her fill him once more, how he had thought that she would die—but she hadn't died. Not at all. She had offered him to death instead.

Mòrag would not lie to him; they had too much at risk. She spoke bluntly, almost simply, as though to a lost child, and Aedan listened and nodded and silently raged.

Mòrag had mobilized her forces and was prepared to mount an offensive. She understood what would come; if Kelmere had gone to the Saxons, Cairnmor would be next to fall. She had planned to rescue him if she could. She had heard of his imprisonment, unraveled the devilish plans Callese had been so careful to twist and disguise.

He did not bother to doubt her. Mòrag always had resources where least expected.

"But what I do not know," she said at last, perched beside him on the mess of the pallet, "is what happened to you after that first battle. We thought you dead, all of us."

He closed his eyes and brought a hand to his forehead, smiling grimly.

"My scout half-feared you a ghost when he saw you seized in the wood," said Mòrag, after a pause. "Fortunately, he's a sensible man—at least when he's sober. He swore he hadn't had a drop that day. I believed him. He was poaching and needed his wits."

Aedan said nothing, the taut smile still pulling at him.

"And then, just days ago, I received another report, that of a lone woman, a princess, come to your sister's court. I thought, now, who could this be? It was said that she knew you. That she dined with the queen and wept salt tears at news of your death."

"She wept?" Aedan asked, lowering his hand.

"So I heard."

He glanced at her, skeptical.

"And I thought," went on Mòrag serenely, "who weeps for the lost prince at the feet of his slayer? What manner of woman arrives alone in the land of my enemy and speaks of my husband? I heard her beauty was enough to stun grown men, to render even the boldest soldier impotent."

He let out a huff of air, not quite a laugh. Mòrag nodded.

"Imagine my astonishment upon discovering her myself, here on my very shores. I have to agree, Aedan. She is stunning. Nearly . . . immortal."

He stared at the sloped walls of the tent, the soft play of leafy shadow across the cloth.

"No one found your body after the ambush," Mòrag said. "There were rumors that you had ascended straight to heaven, lifted atop the wings of angels. There were rumors that you were swallowed by the mountains, or stolen by the beasts of the forest, protected in their lairs. And there were rumors," she finished, slower now, "of a more human sort. That you were stolen by boat. Taken away to sea, to Kell itself, and buried there in the coldest waters, where none could ever find you."

The tent became very quiet.

Mòrag placed her hand over his. "I don't like rumors. I did my best to tease out facts, but there are some mysteries even I cannot solve. Yet I think perhaps this last one . . . might have been true."

"I was not—buried at sea," he said to the shadow leaves.

"No, love. Clearly not." She stood, brisk again. "It's been a long time, Aedan. Don't misunderstand, I'm delighted to find you alive. Surprised, but delighted. You've returned from the ocean, from death itself, with a woman who can swim so well and who is so—unthinkably—lovely. Truly the fates have blessed you."

"Truly," he muttered, and began to sit up.

"But you're not going to tell me who she is, or where you were," Mòrag concluded, unoffended. She watched him push back the blankets and moved out of his way. She would not order him to stay or rest. She knew him better than that.

"I could guess, of course." She gave him a sidelong look. "I'm very good at guessing."

"You could." He climbed out of the pallet, flexing the sore muscles of his legs, his arms, then met her eyes squarely. "But who would believe you?"

Mòrag smiled and turned away, reached for a tunic draped across a chair, and tossed it back at him.

"She's waiting for you, you know. She has been, all this while."

And his wife ducked out of the tent.

# CHAPTER FOURTEEN

❧

He was directed to the willow pond, and Aedan plucked the memory of it from a very distant childhood: a white-frothed stream emptying into an emerald pool, a ring of stout stones encircling the rim. Moss, minnows, black mud sparkling with mica.

It took time to get there. Once outside the tent he was set upon by a parcel of people, including the healer, who had not Mòrag's prosaic patience with him. Aedan greeted his comrades, ignored Urien's warnings, accepted the walking stick Mòrag had silently offered, and at last followed the path down to the pond, where air dipped cool and the sky became a blue cup laced with trees.

They told him that Ione had spent nearly all her time there, solitary, expecting nothing, demanding nothing, save that she see Aedan twice each of the three days he had lain in his stupor, fighting his fogged dreams.

Now he was awake. Still fogged, still fighting, but awake.

And Ione was here, alone as claimed, seated upon a

large white stone, gazing down into the waters below. She wore a gown—someone's gown—of softened wool, holly-green, long-sleeved and belted. Her head was bowed, her hair shining loose. She did not notice him.

With her chin tucked down he couldn't truly see her face, only a pale hint of brow, thick lashes, the straight line of her nose. She was resting on her hip, her legs crossed. One bare foot stroked lazily across the surface of the water, allowing it to caress her toes.

The contrast of the scene hit him with unexpected force. Ione, pearl and flame contained amid gray and green and black; lush, velvet hues, primal nature before him.

It was as if he were seeing a stranger. He thought he had known her so well on Kell, her bearing, her step, her scent. The glory of her, the mystery. She had seemed such a natural part of the island. Aye, there it had been easy. Kell was mystic and so was Ione. He had been the outsider then.

But now Aedan, leaning upon his borrowed stick, bandaged, fed, rested—a whole and rueful part of his own world again—saw plainly what had been so simple to accept just weeks ago:

Ione was a siren. Every bit of her, every lovely curve, spoke of Old magic, of myth and iconic beauty. She was out of place here, even in the borrowed gown. She sat so charmingly upon her rock, allowed the sun to gild her with amber rays, and she was, unquestionably, brilliant and wondrous and utterly foreign.

And these people who sheltered them—his mother's people—would surely recognize her for what she was, if they had not already. Mòrag could not be the only one with questions.

She looked up at him then, slowly, still pensive. There

were shadows beneath her eyes he had never noted before, a bow to her lips. She did not smile, she did not turn or rise. Only her head tilted as she took him in, standing beneath the willow leaves.

"You are awake," she said, in a voice of flat composure.

"You are dressed," he replied, the first thought that came to him.

She lifted a fold of the skirts, let it fall. "Your wife insisted."

"Ah." Aedan stepped into her vale, letting the willows close into a wall behind him.

It was tricky, managing the mossy stones, and he concentrated on that, and not the words that he had to say or the unfamiliar ache in his chest, as he made his way to her.

She waited for him, motionless upon her rock. When he was close enough to look into her eyes, it was almost as though he was wounded anew, a cold, slicing pain. Just the sight of her plunged his careful dignity into disarray—colors, gown, elemental beauty—and he had to glance away a moment, finding his purpose.

"How fare you?" He spoke to the pebbled ground, the tip of his walking stick.

"Well," came her reply, still even.

"Thank you." Aedan looked up. "For saving my life. Again. Thank you."

She shifted, drawing her knees to her chest, wrapping her arms around them with her heels against the stone. She watched him silently. Her eyes were very, very blue.

He took a deep breath. "I owe you an explanation."

"You owe me nothing."

"My life," he said, low. "My heart." He touched the collar of his tunic, where her locket lay. "My soul."

"I have returned you your soul, King Aedan."

"No. Don't."

"Don't?" she echoed, and that one eyebrow arched. "It is not your choice, Scot."

"I don't love her," he said abruptly. "She does not love me."

Both brows lifted now, exaggerated surprise. Her lips pursed, words held back perhaps, and he rushed on before she could speak.

"We were wed as children. I was eight. She was only five. We're cousins, our mothers both married to kings—it was for an alliance. My people, hers. She is my friend. She is not—my lover." The walking stick slipped a little in the mud. He repositioned it, seeking firmer ground. "She loves another."

"I know."

That startled him; the stick skidded again. He wavered a moment, unsteady, before Ione almost casually reached out and caught his arm.

"I am not witless, Scot. I've had ample time to observe these people. They talk, they come, they go. They shadow each other and game and plot and scheme until I wonder they don't drive themselves mad. Your wife has a companion, Sìne." She released his arm. "I like her."

"You do?"

"Aye. She's quiet. She does not babble like the rest."

He stared at her, torn between laughter and relief. "So—"

"You are hale again." She slid from the rock, moved so that it loomed between them. "I wish you well, King Aedan of Kelmere."

There was a note of finality to her tone that captured his full attention. "What does that mean?"

"It was all I awaited. Now you are hale. I must return to Kell."

"To Kell? No, Ione, I came to tell you—I came—"

All the fine phrases he had practiced fled his mind. She

held him in her blue-sober gaze and Aedan felt as if his mouth had turned to granite, gone as stubbornly silent as the great rocks surrounding them.

He was unfamiliar with wooing. He was never long enough at court to learn soft lover's ways, and God knew he had scant enough chance to practice, but right now he would have gladly traded all his years of battle for just the right words to hold her.

He had been wed so young. He had thought his fate well mapped for him, even after he came to realize that his wife would never be more than his friend. Even after he came to accept the fact that he would not live his father's life—he would not have the unspoken, burning passion that bound his parents; he would not have a steadfast companion in his bed, or children at his hearth. Long ago Aedan had surrendered these secret dreams, and gradually, painfully, he learned to embrace what he did have: a kingdom, loyal vassals. Obligation. Trust.

He had never sought love outside his marriage. It had seemed irresponsible somehow, although he knew Mòrag would not object. He had wrestled with it and finally reconciled it to the place he sent all forbidden things, the stuff of ordinary men, men who had not the destiny of a realm riding their shoulders. Men who might afford to forget who they were, even occasionally.

Aedan could never be such a man.

But now—here and now, in front of the one woman who had touched him, who had *saved* him—he thought perhaps love had found him after all.

He began to make his way toward her, the stick clacking against pebbles. Ione didn't back away; she didn't come to meet him either. She only stood there at the water's edge, just beyond reach.

"I told you Kell is my strength. I see now that Kelmere

is yours. I don't think . . . I don't think the curse can hold you. Perhaps you were right; perhaps it isn't even real." She shrugged, a slight move, almost weary. "Or perhaps you're simply too strong for it. This is your home. Understand that I must go back to mine."

Aedan freed his tongue. "But you came. I thought it meant you could stay. A while, even a short while."

She only looked at him, solemn, pale. Her answer was dark in her eyes.

"No," he said, rejecting her silence. There was a mounting anger in him, a deep and binding dismay he had never felt before. To have her once more, to lose her again—how could she leave? He felt on the verge of real life—of hope—for the first time ever; they stood facing each other in the mud, and the water rose to stain her hem, soak his boots, and if she took another step back it would mean she would go, she would vanish into emerald-green depths just like a dream, and how the hell would he ever reach her—

His hand was moving. While his thoughts raced and blurred, his fingers lifted, found the curve of her jaw, a faint warm caress. The familiar thrill of her rippled through him—smooth skin, delicate features, indigo eyes—and he saw the response wake in her, saw her blink, just once, before his hand slipped behind her neck and he leaned down to kiss her.

Aye, this was what he remembered, her taste, her touch, the slant of his mouth over hers, shared breath. Her hair was a glossy tangle between them, the color of coral, of clouds against the setting sun.

"Don't leave me," Aedan said, a rough demand.

"I—"

He stopped her with another kiss. "I need you." Against her lips the words became sensual, not a weakness as he had feared but something strong, something good. "Don't leave me, I need you," he said again, and dragged her to him, her body perfect, fitted to his just as it should be, everything right and just and fated.

Ione gave the smallest of sighs, relaxing into him.

He dropped the stick to the pond, plunging both hands into her hair, exploring her lips, their edges, their fullness, pink silky ripe. He heard a distant moan, realized it was his own. Her arms came around him, her eyes closed, and she tasted like strawberries, like violets. Each kiss seemed to free something in him, chip apart his buried doubts, his hidden worries. Her tongue met his and he brought her to him rougher yet, his hands roaming down her back to the swell of her bottom, tantalizing beneath soft wool.

She trailed kisses down his throat, her own hands traveling his body, knowing where to stroke, how to please him. When she found his arousal she pressed into him, her legs aligned to his, her fingers searching, rubbing. Hunger overwhelmed him, an urgent sharp crest though his blood. He began to pull her back with him toward the land, somewhere dry and firm—they didn't need the ground, even the damn rocks would do. They were both gasping, cool valley air, this green world, water at their feet and Ione in his arms, Ione in his heart, in every part of him, hot and coveted and so very welcome—

They made it to a rock. He pushed her to sit and shoved back her skirts; with a quick tug of cloth she had freed him. There was no fumbling, no awkward positioning. It was as if they had practiced this moment in this sunlit place, rehearsed it over and over, he compelling, she yielding, the rock, the water, the dark dance and panting desire. With one knee propped against the stone and her legs around his waist, he entered her; his hands under her thighs, her hips lifted, they moved together, they scorched and burned. She laid back against the stone, graced with sunlight, her arms thrown wide, her fingers curled. It was the most wanton and exquisite sight he had ever seen.

Pleasure rolled through her. He felt her come, saw her come, as she arched and twisted and cried out. In perfect beauty it flowed from her to him. He was drowned in bliss, he could not breathe with the sudden force of his release, emptying himself into her.

Their descent was much slower, a sweet, trembling conclusion. Aedan released her legs to lean over her, his body covering hers. Ione lifted her arms, her palms to his cheeks. Her eyes remained open as they kissed.

Someone—someone *else*—coughed.

"Sorry," said the someone, from over by the far willows. It was Mòrag. He could just see her feet, the backs of her boots. At least she was facing the other way.

Aedan raised his voice. "Go away."

"Sorry," she said again, obviously amused. "But I'm afraid we have need of you now, my lord. Your people are waiting."

He looked down at Ione. The soft acquiescence of her body had gone firm again, limber and controlled. With a final kiss he eased off her, rushing cold enclosing him once more.

Ione stood, pushed her hair out of her face and evened her skirts. She looked around, waded out into the pond, caught his walking stick, and handed it to him. Then, without a single glance back, she followed his wife out past the willow trees.


The meeting took place in the largest of the tents and still it was packed with mortals, men and women mixed, standing, sitting, practically hanging from the sparse furniture. The smell of them struck Ione like a fist: desire and fear and bravado, trouble and ambition and a curiosity so strong it was almost like wrath.

She thought of leaving—the affairs of these people barely brushed her own interests—but just then Aedan's wife caught her eye, beckoned her forward. Io began to thread her way through the crush, ignoring the mutters and stares, then gave up, stationing herself near the entrance, where at least there was air. Really, could they never gather outside, in fresh open spaces? What was it about humans that made them so afraid of the bare sky?

She picked out Mòrag again, her lover beside her. Io gave a little shrug; Mòrag nodded her understanding, while Sìne offered a smile. The old physician next to them turned his head away, sulking.

Even in this mass of bodies she could detect tokens of the brewing war: axes and maces propped against legs; swords and daggers; Mòrag's great bow outlined against the wall behind her, sinuous, lethal beauty primed.

The gossip rose and fell, racing words, narrowed eyes, a thousand useless stories and speculations.

A shadow stretched across the people. Someone new had entered the tent, held there against the autumn sun and the skin of the door, unmoving. Everything—all the whispers, the sweating, twitching, nervous prattle of the people—sank to sudden quiet. Io knew who had just come.

Aedan stood before them almost in battle stance, legs apart, a hand still pushed against the skin. In one swift and shining instant Ione saw him as the others surely did. Not mortal, not mere man.

A god.

A king, tall and lean and etched in light. Long black hair, a hard and watchful face, a silver shrewd gaze skimming the crowd. He did not wear a crown. He did not need one. No one seeing him now could doubt his power or command, even with the walking stick. The people practically wilted before him.

And Io . . . Io was held in his thrall as firmly as the rest. A singular pride filled her, seeing him there, a kind of wistful longing. He looked nothing at all like a man who had just made love on a pond stone.

Aedan searched the gathered faces, his shoulders stiff. She lifted one hand, a small crook of her fingers, drawing his eyes. The subtle stark edges of him seemed to gentle; he took the final step into the tent, letting the skin sweep closed behind him.

"Welcome, High King," called Mòrag from across the crowded space. "We are honored to greet you."

"I thank you," replied Aedan in a calm and carrying voice, just as formal.

Mòrag stood, facing the assembly. "As you all know, our situation has recently changed. By the grace of the gods our king is alive and returned to us. We may thank this woman for her invaluable aid." Mòrag gestured to Io. "And I know you will all show her the proper respect and gratitude due."

A few of the men dropped their eyes.

Mòrag continued. "The Saxons, however, remain as great a threat as ever. We've known for months—and now Ione confirms—that they have infiltrated every corner of the keep. They surround their false queen, they walk her court openly and armed. With Callese in their control, we may be certain they will not wait long to advance to Cairnmor. It is imperative that we strike first, and as far away from our homes and families as possible."

A chorus of "ayes" greeted this remark, and Mòrag paused to let the crowd grow hushed again.

"Yet we must remember one thing. The people of Kelmere are *not* our enemies. The Saxons are. When we march, we will need *them* to see that *we* are not their enemy. And the only way to do that is to show them the truth." Mòrag looked at Aedan. "We need you, my lord, to lead the line. We need you to open the battle, to show your people that you live and that your sister lies."

Aedan studied her, the waiting audience, then said, "You ask me to fight my own people."

"No, sire. Only the Saxons."

"Who are mixed with my own. Who, by your own account, control the armory and the court."

"But when they see you—"

"There will be no time to react. They will have no time to understand before the Saxons move in. It will be chaos. It will be slaughter."

"Aedan, this is our only opportunity—"

"It will be slaughter," he said again. "No."

Io watched Mòrag, expecting anger or, at the very least, resentment. Instead, the other woman only shook her head, her brow wrinkled with mild distress.

"What then, my lord, is your will? We cannot leave my people vulnerable."

"No, we cannot. But we shall not attack Kelmere just yet."

"There is scant time to wait."

"I have loyal men still, an army of them. All I need do is reach them."

"Your commanders are ensconced inside the barracks. Callese keeps them well apart from the Saxons. You'd never get near enough the fortress to send word."

"Your spy—"

"Dead. Just after we found you. They know now that we watch them."

Silence, thick and stifling. It seemed none of the people even breathed; everyone focused on the king, on Aedan, who stared at the ground with such a cool and impassive expression Io was sharply reminded of his sister. Finally he lifted his head.

"There's no other way. I'm going to the keep."

Mòrag stepped forward. "You'll be killed. My lord, we need our king."

"Once I reach the barracks, you will—"

"My lord," interrupted his wife, imploring. "I pray you, heed me. We *need* our *king*."

Ione said, "I will go."

A new silence gripped the tent. She felt the force of their attention, their astonishment, as if one of the tables had chosen to speak.

"No," said the king.

She faced him. "I will go and find your loyal men. I will tell them that you live, and not to fight."

His face remained stoic, frozen dignity. His eyes, however—his eyes were dangerous, bright piercing silver.

"No," he said again, so very controlled. "I think not."

"I know a safe way in, Scot. A way they will not think to guess."

His mouth thinned flat; slowly he shook his head. Io glanced back at Mòrag, who watched with her fingers pressed over her lips. There might have been the barest smile beneath her hand.

"Tell me how to find the barracks," Io said to her.

"No," said Aedan a third time, now with clear warning in his voice. Mòrag lowered her hand and then her head, and at once so did all the other people around them, one by one, a wave of motion. It was submission, complete and absolute. Io turned back to Aedan, galled.

"You know I know the way," she said, then added, rashly, "You can't prevent me."

A smile cracked his cold features, a very unpleasant smile. He moved toward her, past people who bobbled out of his path, until he had her by the arm, until he was propelling them both out of the reeking tent, back to air and light and sky.

They halted at the edge of the clearing, just where the woods began to knot tight. His hold on her arm remained pinching hard, surprisingly painful. She jerked free and he let her, inhaling deeply, a hiss past his teeth. When he spoke, his words came broken, though still deadly calm.

"You—will—not—"

"Saxons killed my mother," she said.

That gave him pause. His jaw clenched; the lines around his mouth chiseled deep.

"She had saved them from a storm, but their ship was damaged, and she was . . . hurt." Was that her voice, so faint and thin? "And afterward they hunted her. They chased her down and killed her for sport, or for vengeance. I know not."

He only gazed at her, sunlight dazzling behind him. She was blinded from it, her eyes stinging, and so Ione looked down, to the safety of deergrass and heather at their feet.

"I was younger then," she said. "I saw it. They had—spears. Nets. I could not stop them."

"You never told me this."

"I would have." She brushed the heather with her toe, watched the dry leaves tremble. "I would have, had you asked."

"Beloved." His pitch dropped, a graveled match to hers. "Sweetest heart . . ."

The frozen king was gone. Here was her lover again,

cherished and dear, and Io didn't know if she leaned toward him or he to her, but they were touching suddenly, their bodies close, and he was warm and solid, and his arms were strong. She pressed her cheek to his chest.

"But I can stop these Saxons. I have a plan. I will stop them."

"Ione—"

"I will."

"Not," vowed Aedan, "without me."

# CHAPTER FIFTEEN

❧

She was dying here. She could not stay.

In her heart Ione had known it all along, that she and Aedan were doomed to live apart. No force on earth would allow her to survive away from Kell; she was too much a part of the island, sand in her bones, salt in her blood. Away from her home she had narrowed to a shadow of herself, despicably weak, fearful.

Fearful, aye. Because she also knew that no force in heaven would settle peace upon Aedan were he at Kell. He would fret and burn and chafe until he left again, as they all did. She had not fully understood that until now. She had not understood the power of his world, a place of torches and princes and stone-built cities. He was rooted here, as surely as she was to her own realm, and to deny him his legacy would be unthinkable.

And such a legacy it was. Leader of men, commander of armies, of warrior women in demon masks, of crossbows and stealth. He would take back his kingdom, one way or another. Relentless as the tide he would fight to take it back, until he succeeded. Or until he was dead.

She had lied to him once again: She did not think the curse had truly let him go. She did not think the price of love would be so light; Io well knew her great-grandmother's song. It was not done with them yet.

She could hope—she could only hope for enough time.

It was nearing the moment to leave. Io waited at the fringe of camp as the men and women surrounded their king, embraced him, kissed his sword. She watched through her lashes, silent and apart, the early-day fog reaching up through the grass to enshroud her.

Aedan stood firm in the eddy of his people, checking his weapons, his supplies. He seemed stranded to her, a lone stroke of true life amid ghostly figures and trees. The fog had formed with the dawn and had not left; by dusk it would be cold, slick rain.

By dusk they would know one way or another if success was theirs, and rain would hardly matter.

He turned to her, his eyes searching, just as a web of mist slipped between them. For a heartbeat the image chilled her—he became a ghost himself, blank and hollow. Io looked away.

The fear for him enthralled her, snared tight around her heart and strangled her breath. She would risk anything to save him. Kell, her life. Time was short and her strength was dwindling, and she would risk anything.

She kept closing her hands to fists, reopening them. Her fingers were sore with it.

"There is a boat for you at the beach," said a voice behind her. Io nodded but did not turn.

"Will you reconsider?" asked Mòrag, at her shoulder. "Will you abandon this scheme?"

"No."

"The odds are against you. Most likely you will fail."

"So be it."

Mòrag came forward. "I had to ask."

"Aye."

Aedan was listening to someone speak, attentive, one hand on the hilt of his sword. He made some reply; the man before him shook his head, went to his knees, and took Aedan's hand, pressing it to his lips.

"I love him," said Mòrag, watching at her side. "I always have. He was my hero. As a boy he rescued me from pretend dragons. As a husband he has rescued me from—myself. From the opinions of others. From dishonesty, and the despair of a life choked with lies." She glanced at Io. "You love him too. I'm pleased. For you both."

The people began to break apart. Aedan moved toward Ione and Mòrag, his limp nearly disguised. A cloud of silver drifted in his wake.

Io bent down, reaching into the bag at her feet. "For you," she said to Mòrag, and placed the last of her jewelry upon Aedan's wife, the jeweled cuff, the loop of pearls. "For Sìne," she added, and handed over the linked sapphire belt as well.

Mòrag looked down at the gems, then up again. With one hand she unbuckled the sword belt at her waist, lifting it to Io, the scabbard swaying.

"And for you."

Ione caught the sword. She examined the blade—buffed and enscrolled—then fastened the belt across her hips. It was quite heavy.

"One last thing," Mòrag said. Draped with jewels, rich with gold, she took Ione by the shoulders and kissed her cheek. Soft lips, a delicate warmth, faint, fleeting. When she pulled back, Mòrag was smiling.

"It is a blessing among my people," she said, "to touch enchantment."

"Be blessed, then."

"And you."

Aedan was there. He scanned Ione, the gown she wore, her hair pinned back, his eyes lingering on the scabbard. "Until nightfall," he said curtly, turning to Mòrag. "Begin the siege then if we do not send word. You know the plan."

"Aye, my lord. All is prepared."

"We shall see you before sundown."

"So I pray."

Aedan took Io's arm. Together they walked out of the camp, into the phantom hush of the rising mist.

The boat was exactly where Mòrag said it would be, tucked beneath brush and leaves in a nook of trees by the shore. Aedan tore off the blankets concealing it, shaking out spare twigs. Ione stood back with her arms crossed, the sword at her hip absurdly large against her. She had already removed her boots, was curling her toes in the sand.

He threw the blankets aside. "I'll row you out."

"Unnecessary."

She began unfastening the sword belt. The wind had coaxed free strands of red around her face; they blew bright against the drab white day.

She seemed so small, almost girlish. He had never truly noted it before now, with his heart beating hard and dread for her acid in his throat. She seemed so fragile.

"I'll row you out," he said again, and began to haul the boat across the beach.

"No."

His temper snapped. "Damn it, Ione, for *once* will you listen to me?"

"No," she repeated, but the corners of her lips twitched.

"I am not jesting!"

The twitch vanished. "Neither am I. It would be pointless to waste your might on this boat, Scot, when I'll get there faster and easier without you. We don't know what lies ahead, but if any of this is to work, you must be able to fight."

"I'm damned well able to fight," he muttered.

"With someone other than *me*." She dropped the sword to the sand.

"You don't have to do this."

She made no reply, only reached behind her, untying the laces to the gown. It ruffled loose; she bent over and began to drag it over her head.

"You know I don't want you to do this." He was not pleading. He would not plead. Anyone could see this was an insufferable idea, disastrous. She would be killed, and it would be his fault. Why the hell didn't she understand that?

Ione emerged from the gown, glorious nude, supple curves and slender lines, her arms aloft. She wadded the cloth to a ball and tossed it at him. Aedan caught it, scowling.

"You said you would die if you left Kell. You said you had to return. Trust me, this would be a most excellent time to go."

She picked up the sword and scabbard, slung it over one shoulder.

"*Ione.*"

So then she turned to him, leaning near, lifting her fingers to his face. Her touch was cool as ever, unearthly cool and calm.

"Look what they have done," she murmured. "Scars

and bruises. Intrigue and woe." She spoke slowly, her voice tinged with an emotion he could not name, then shook her head. "It cannot continue."

He caught her hand and pressed it to his cheek.

"None of that matters," he said, very clearly. "None of that is as important to me as your safety."

"With the Saxons vanquished, you will have peace, will you not?"

She had managed to surprise him; he laughed in spite of himself, bitter. "Peace. No."

"You will have your throne," she persisted. "You will have your kingdom."

He couldn't deny it. He wouldn't admit it either, unwilling to hand her any excuse to continue with this lunacy. She read him anyway, nodding. Her lashes lowered.

"That is what I want, then."

She turned to go. His hand tightened around hers, pulling her back to him.

"You have two hours. If you don't appear by then, I am coming after you. Do you understand? I will come after you, alone if I must."

"I will be there. I will open the door."

"Two hours."

"I won't need that long." She looked pointedly at his hand. Aedan forced his fingers to relax, then remembered something.

"Wait." He worked at the clasp of her silver necklace, let the locket fall into his palm. "You should have this back."

"Should I?" she asked lightly.

"If it is my soul—if it is any part of me—then . . . I want you to have it."

She hesitated, then lifted it carefully, her fingers long

and pale, the silver a dull gleam between them. The locket gave a merry little spin against the clouds.

"I meant to ask you," he said, watching her fasten it back around her own neck, "how did you know to come for me, after I left Kell? How did you know I was imprisoned?"

"I did not."

"Then why did you come?"

She moved away from him, smiling. Without taking her eyes from his, Ione backed into the surf, letting it crash against her legs. Her waist.

"I came to tell you"—her voice was sweet over the ocean, melodic—"that we are going to have a child."

She slipped beneath the waves and was gone.

It didn't take long to find the opening in the island stone. Io was able to change now, for one thing, tail and fins returned, and that meant she could swim faster than the last time she was here. And the fissure was close to shore; she remembered that much. She came to it nearly at once, following the flow of freshwater until she reached the base rock, the black shaft beyond.

Io paused, one hand against the entrance. She looked up at the surface, a glassy heaven above. Twin otters swam by, playful, dark swift, speeding through the water like a pair of falling stars.

She turned back to the tunnel and pushed her way inside.

Now, this was more difficult. She was fighting the river, not accepting it, and the currents were strong. With the saltwater gone she reverted to her human form, resisting it, giving in, because she could not truly resist herself. At least she needn't worry about clothing to entrap her. At least she wasn't towing a man alongside her, frantic with worry for him. . . .

She was mindful of the basalt but it caught her still, scratching open new wounds. She could not let it plague her now. She could not slow. Aedan had marked the time and she fully believed his threat. He would come after her if she faltered. He would storm the fortress, her dauntless Scot.

Her hair worked free, a cloud of red-gold. Her legs began to ache, her arms. The sword dragged heavier than ever. She passed the fork for the keep well, caught herself, and doubled back. Aye, here it was. A smear of lead gray bloomed in black water, an opening to light. She approached it cautiously, finding the ring of stone that distinguished the well bottom, peering up to the top. No one looked back at her; there was only the blurred outline of that wooden device, far above.

Warily, soundlessly, she broke the surface, her hands pressed against stone. No voices cried out, no heads appeared in the circle of light above. Such perfect quiet. There might have been none but her in the whole mad world.

Io adjusted the scabbard, dug her fingers into mortar, and began the long ascent up the walls.

He waited by the cliffs where the secret exit to Kelmere was concealed, hunched and hidden, numb with cold, contemplating the fog and the strange fortune of his life.

A baby. With Ione.

Aedan rubbed his hands together, his breath hardened to frost.

After all this while, a child. A siren child.

For God's sake. Nothing was ever simple.

* * *

The climb took so much longer than she thought it would. She had rested during her time at the camp but was not truly healed; rest could not mend the loss of Kell's magic. Rest could not cease her slow death.

But she did it, one creeping handhold at a time, until finally she hung, panting, near the very top, her fingertips bleeding, her hands and feet throbbing.

She thought at first the chamber was empty. She still heard nothing beyond the river water, no conversation, no footsteps, no breathing. Io waited a while longer anyway, straining to listen, until at last she had to move or let go.

With a silent snarl she lifted herself up past the rim, one leg then the other swung over the side. She stood and glanced quickly around the room, directly into the startled eyes of the man who stood arrested, staring at her, not five strides away.

He wore the sword and plain leather of a guard—Aedan's or the Saxon's, she could not say.

"Greetings," Io tried, breathless, smiling. She shook back her wet hair to expose her breasts. "Thy master sent me to thee."

He gaped at her, his mouth slack. She approached in very slow steps, stroking her hand down the flex of her waist, the modest swell of her belly, red curls below.

"He thought thee in sore need of amusement, good sir." She kept her smile coy. "Of . . . recreation."

Still the fool did not speak. Io stopped just before him, wondering how best to proceed, as his face crimsoned and his gaze raked her body.

"How," he gasped, and cleared his throat. "How didst thou manage—"

It was all she needed to hear. In one quick and brutal blow she backhanded him, sending him falling, his head striking stone. Ione drew her sword, pressing it against his chest, but the guard did not move. She kicked him to be certain. Nothing.

"Saxon," she spat softly, and walked away.

Aedan had described the stone she needed to find in exhaustive detail: beneath the seventh stair, four rows up, two across. The left corner chipped, the suggestion of a grinning fox in the stain near the bottom . . .

There. She had it. The fox, the chip—she pressed the left corner, then the bottom right, and the foxstone swung free, just barely, enough to pluck farther to reveal the flat latch beneath.

And thus an entire door swung free, jagged and narrow, grinding stone against stone. She slipped through the slit of it and groped until she found the other latch inside, the one to close the door again.

Ione turned and sprinted down the unlit passageway.

# CHAPTER SIXTEEN

❧

The clouds had opened and rain was falling when she reached the false boulder that marked the end of the tunnel. She turned the lock and moved soundlessly past the new portal, searching until she found him, a shadow against trees and scrub, the outline of a horse drowsing, head down, behind him.

Aedan saw her, edged over. Water darkened his cloak, set his skin gleaming. He flashed a smile in the gloom; it filled her with unlikely warmth.

"Well done. I was just considering ways to charge the gate."

"I'm pleased to please you," she hissed, "but there is at least one Saxon behind me about to awaken, and I'd rather not listen to him scream for his companions."

His humor vanished. "You didn't kill him?"

"No."

Jet brows drew up in disbelief. Rain spiked his eye-lashes, rendered his silver stare potent. Io glared back at him.

"It is not my calling to kill humans." She waved him toward the tunnel. "We lull people, save them. We do not deliberately destroy them."

"The devil you—" He worked his way past the opening, squeezing into the slender space beside her, then stopped. "You're hurt. What happened?"

"Scratches. They will heal."

"You're *bleeding*, Ione. I knew I should not have allowed this. I knew, and let it happen anyway."

"You *allow* me naught, Scot. I choose my own path, and always have."

"Well I know it," he muttered.

The warmth of before had changed that quickly; he irritated her, her righteous lovely king, and she would have argued further but he cut her off.

"Do you mean that before—with the Saxons, and your dagger—you wouldn't have used it?"

"Couldn't."

"Why the hell not?"

"It is forbidden."

"By *whom*?"

"Shall we waste our precious day quarreling here?" Io reached past him, found the bolt that closed the door. "Or do you wish to salvage your kingdom?"

The tunnel plunged to night.

"Sweet Mary," Aedan swore, his voice a resonant echo. "You were damned convincing. I thought at any moment you'd gut them like fish."

"That," she took his hand, "was what I wanted *them* to think."

Ione led him back to the keep.

* * *

He followed her blindly, because that was all he could do, managing his sword, his stick, and the bundle of her clothing, her hand cool in his. She did not pause, she did not falter, although it seemed to him she was breathing harder than usual, a faint little hitch in every breath. He wanted to slow and knew they shouldn't; he stumbled over an uneven stone, and again over a root. His bad leg began to sting and eventually grow numb. Small mercy; at least he did not have to mind the hurt.

The King's Passage. Aedan had learned of it from his father, who had learned of it from his, and he from his, generations back, well into the mists of ancient memory. A cave transformed to tunnel; it had no entrance to Kelmere—no sleeping weakness for invaders to discover—only an exit, a last-hope escape for a leader and his people when the battle was done and flight the only answer left.

It had never been used in war. It existed only in the mountain and in the minds of the men who knew of it, fathers and sons, king to king to king.

Aedan had been planning to break that tradition. He was going to show it to his heir, his sister. Praise the fates he had never found the right moment to do so.

It occurred to him suddenly that Callese was no longer his heir. He felt an unseemly urge to laugh, and suppressed it.

On and on they went. He did not recall the Passage being so long. He could not imagine leading the masses of Kelmere through this ruthless dark. God shield it come to that.

At the end of the corridor they finally stopped. He put Ione behind him, one hand on the stone exit, listening, plotting, in case her stunned Saxon had indeed arisen. But there were no sounds coming past the wall—no sounds beyond the usual litany of misery he recognized from his own confinement here. He wondered, not for the first time, who those other wretched prisoners would prove to be.

No time to wonder now. Aedan released the latch and pushed open the door.

The Saxon, apparently, was alone in his duties, at least for now. He lay sprawled where she had left him, his mouth open in an expression much like the one he had when first he sighted her. Io bent over and snapped his jaw closed. When she straightened, Aedan was staring again.

"My lord?"

"Get dressed," he said roughly, and handed her the wadded gown. Their fingers brushed; a crackle of tension connected them, well apart from the danger of the moment. Ione smiled; she could not help it. He was so fierce, and so determined not to drop his gaze.

"She'll come late spring."

"Who?"

"Our daughter. But in the meantime, we need not worry about disturbing her. We are quite hardy, you know."

He blinked. A slow stain began to spread across his cheekbones.

"Perhaps you should bind him," Io suggested after a moment, gesturing to the Saxon.

Aedan sank down, found the rope they had packed. "Get dressed," he ordered again, not looking back at her. "For God's sake, be quick about it."

The clothing settled over her in almost familiar folds, the gown, the boots, the sword again. The hooded cloak, dullest black, a calculated match to the garb of the others who walked these halls.

Together they approached the stairs. Aedan threw her a speaking glance and went up; Io followed. The pain was still there, a growing rent inside her, but over it was her thumping heart, her hope, and her conviction.

A step at a time, lightly, quickly, hugging the walls. She could not see beyond the breadth of Aedan's shoulders, did not need to see. She knew what awaited them at the top. With her sword drawn she only stood back, let Aedan rush the guard.

He laid the body across the platform near the door, shielded from the grilled window. Io sheathed her sword again, adjusting her cloak as she watched him, swift hands, black hair that glanced gold from the torch above. He looked up at her, carved in light.

Without a word he straightened, drew the hood over her hair, tucked a stray lock behind her ear. They stood there a moment in silence, his hands on her shoulders, holding fast, as if he did not intend to let go. He inhaled, opened his mouth, closed it again. Frustration shone like heat from his eyes.

"If anyone should notice you—" His voice was a toneless whisper.

"None will. None but your own men."

"You must not be recognized."

"I won't be."

"Ione." He blew out his breath, took them both down a few more steps, away from the torch and the windowed door. "When I agreed to this I didn't realize you couldn't defend yourself. It's madness to go on. You stay here. I'm going instead."

"I can defend myself very well, as you know. I cannot kill. That's all."

" 'That's all,' " he grumbled. "A trifling detail you forgot to mention to me."

"I did not forget—"

"I know. I never asked. *I have a plan, I have a baby, I cannot kill.* Listen, damn it." His tone had pitched sharper; he dropped it again. "Is there anything else you haven't told me?"

She considered it, tilting her head. "Regarding the matter of Kelmere?"

"Aye," he bit out. "Regarding the matter of Kelmere."

"No."

"Good. Stay; better yet, get back down that well. I'll be out soon."

"No." She grabbed his arm. "It falls to me. Your sister's men won't recognize me. *You* will be noticed at once. You know I'm right."

He was incensed now, torn between protection and plain reason. She watched them war within him, waited for truth to settle in. His teeth were set and his eyes had that glitter she had seen but once, on Kell, when he told her he had nothing to offer her.

She understood. She knew his heart, and understood.

"You might make good use of your time," she offered. "Exchange clothing with our Saxon there. Just as a precaution."

As he gazed, affronted, at the much smaller man near their feet, Ione leaned closer, spoke to the hard pulse in his throat.

"I do recall something else, Scot. I believe I forgot to tell you that I love you. But you knew that already."

She moved to the exit. He watched her go, stone-faced, licked with changing shadows. The lock was simple, the handle easily broken. She eased out, shutting the door carefully between them.

Steps away she paused, gathered her breath and her composure. *Control the pain, control the pain, nearly finished now, control it. . . .*

She had reached only the second turn in the hallway when she felt the presence behind her, looming close. Io whirled, reaching for the sword. Her hand was caught immediately in a firm and inflexible grip.

"I have a new plan," came Aedan's voice in her ear. "We'll go together."

She jerked free, appalled. He took in her face, his lips lifting to a dry smile. "We go together," he reiterated softly, "or we don't go at all."

He was sincere. He stood there—*leaned* there, still with his cane—in clear view of any who might pass by, utterly indifferent to the peril. Torches were set more plentiful here. He was awash in light, completely exposed. He risked a kingdom and a people and his life, and for all the menace that lived and breathed around them he merely watched her, unwavering.

Somewhere down the hall a man called out, a name, a distant response.

Io glanced frantically around, found the alcove of a closed door nearby, and tugged him into it. "Are you senseless? You don't even have a hood! You'll be seen at once!"

"Change cloaks with me," he said.

"Aedan!"

"Hurry," he murmured, with that infuriating smile. "Nightfall won't wait, and your guard won't sleep forever."

More voices, a group of women walking much too near. They carried closer, faded off.

Aedan braced his shoulder against the wall in the manner of a man with boundless patience.

"You will be killed." Anger made her careless; she yanked at the clasp to her cloak, snagging it closed.

"So everyone keeps saying." He had freed his own already, brushed her fingers aside, and released the hook of hers. "And yet I find myself strongly compelled to live."

"Here." She flung the cloak at him. He caught it, shook it out to flare black around him, rippling. For some reason it sparked her temper all the more. Io squeezed her eyes shut, shaking her head.

"We'll *both* be killed."

She heard the small *click* of his cane propped against the door. He brought her to him with both hands, pushed his fingers through her hair and pressed his cheek to her temple, ignoring her wordless protest. "Not if *you* return to the—"

"Don't be an ass." But his touch was like silk, a sweet shimmer through her, and she leaned into him despite her displeasure. His hands moved across her back; he covered her with his still-damp cloak, drawing it closed around her, then lifted her hands to his lips.

She drew back, pulled the hood down over his head as far as it would go.

"Follow me, siren," Aedan said, and stepped out into the open hall.


The handmaid walked behind the royal party with her eyes fixed on the train of the queen's gown. It was a new gown, a gift from the people of the Northern Isles, and it distressed her to see the once pure ivory of the hem gone gray with dirt and dust.

Cold water, the maid thought. Lye. That might work. Or no, not lye, too harsh for such a fine fabric. Soapwort, then, aye. Soapwort and, perhaps, milk. Let it set overnight.

The queen's steps were constant and even down the hallway. She did not walk quickly; years at court had taught her, and her maid, the virtues of an unhurried stride. Yet Callese led this group of foreigners and courtiers, always just slightly ahead of the rest, nodding, listening, speaking in her soft settled voice, low enough that the men around her slanted close to hear.

The leader of the Saxons bent so near the queen that his arm lifted as if for balance, his palm grazing the flat of her back. It was the lightest touch, the swiftest stroke, intimate.

The handmaid dropped back another step. She did not like these rough men the queen held with her words. She did not understand why the queen suffered their touch. It was not her place to judge . . . but she was a child of Kelmere. She didn't trust Saxons, no matter how widely they smiled, or praised the fortress, or vowed to fight the Picts.

They smelled. They did not shave. She had heard, from the cousin of a cousin, that they preferred raw blood to mead.

But the maid cherished her position; she was the queen's hands and so held her peace, avoiding the eyes of the strangers, keeping her lips sealed tight.

Her pace matched the queen's precisely. It was a second rhythm to her now, a learned thing, routine. She no longer had to think about it.

Soapwort. She would fetch the cauldron herself, as soon as they reached the great hall and she was dismissed. She'd find lye too, just in case—

The queen came to a sudden halt, her voice abruptly silenced. The handmaid halted as well, still unthinking, and glanced up to see what had prompted this break in their march.

The ghost of the murdered prince stood before them in the hall, cloaked and hooded in devil black, burning eyes and a savage face, staring, staring at his sister, the queen.

Years of training did not desert her. The maid clapped her hand over her mouth to hold in the scream and fainted exactly in place.

# CHAPTER SEVENTEEN

❧

I o watched the queen's face drain of blood. There was a leisurely sort of suspension to the moment, a feeling of being caught in someone else's dream, where no one moved and no one breathed and no one even thought to speak. There were only these humans before her, their shock and surprise and rancor, flat as stick figures sketched in sand.

Up the wall beside them, as if by deliberate design, stretched a little square of daylight from a window, a spill of clouded gray into the hall.

A great despair washed over her, rooting her to the spot. After all they had dared, all they had planned, they were going to die here. The three of them, Io and her lover and their child. They were all going to die here in this simple stone hallway, far from help. The barracks, she was quite certain, were nowhere near this place.

*I'm sorry,* she thought, a drifting prayer to her daughter. *I am sorry.*

From behind the queen's retinue came a muffled thud;

Io saw skirts flare, a woman crumpled to the floor, but that was all. Not one of the queen's men turned.

"Callese," said Aedan at last, in a low and fearsome voice.

"No," she responded, almost conversationally, and turned to the Saxon at her side. "You told me he had died." She looked back at Aedan. "You are dead."

"I loved you." A deep, dragging pain scored his words. "By God, Callese, I always loved you. What have you done?"

She only shook her head. "Steffen," said the queen, with a little trill of laughter. "You told me he had fallen down the well. You told me he was dead."

Steffen, Io noted, was the bossed Saxon of before, the sickly smiling commander of men. He did not take his eyes from Aedan.

Beneath her cloak Ione found the grip of Mòrag's sword. It was a ready thing, primed for blood. She could feel the power of it singing cold against her hand.

"My lord," quavered one of the older men. "My prince! How can it be?"

"Aye," said the Saxon, with the beginnings of his smile. "How can it indeed?"

Io had the only answer to that. "Magic," she said, and stepped into the light beside Aedan.

A glimmer of unease crossed the Saxon's face. It gratified her to see his confidence shaken, even if only for an instant. He forced his smile again, thinner than before.

"And you," he said pleasantly, then switched languages. "Another rescue, little dove? I fear thou shalt find less success than before."

"It is not success I seek," Io replied, so that all the rest could understand. "Only justice. And I think you should fear that."

They were outnumbered. There were over a dozen men surrounding the queen—Saxons, certainly, but perhaps not all of them. The old man of before had called Aedan "prince." Three others stood beside him, dressed nearly the same. They might be loyal to Aedan. . . .

She could not rely on it. The bossed man would almost certainly strike at Aedan first; she would be his defense. Her fingers tightened around the grip.

"Fergus," snapped Aedan, jolting everyone. "Gannon! Niall! Do you ally yourself with this filth?"

One of the older men wobbled forward. "My lord— we—sweet lord, the Saxons came to fight the Picts, the Picts who attacked us. You—you remember that battle, my lord!"

"Aye. I do remember." He looked at the Saxon with shining menace. "That battle, and another. And I remember *you*."

The other man nodded, still smiling. His eyes flicked to Io, back to Aedan.

*Sorry*, Ione thought, cold and ready. *Oh, my love.*

"A sound defeat for you that day," said the Saxon loudly. "A pleasure for us, to prick the prince of the isles, to watch him bleed in the dirt."

"What?" gasped one of the old men.

*Come thee to me*, mouthed the Saxon to Ione. *Come, princess.*

"Aye, and did you weep for me, Callese?" demanded Aedan. "Did you cry on our father's shoulder and whisper honeyed lies? Did you tell him how you sold your soul to the enemy?"

The queen shook her head once more, her hands lax at her side. She looked as if she might join the woman upon the floor.

The square of daylight was fading, fading.

*Princess*, mouthed the Saxon. *Last offer. Come.*

His hand lifted, hovered. The hilt of his sword gleamed thick in the torchlight.

"Did you kill him?" Aedan began to move toward his sister. "Did you murder him as well?"

"No. I protected you." The queen was pale all over, her face and gown and hair, a girl-child robed in regal white. "You were alive. They swore to me. I sent you away, to safety."

"Your men," Aedan said. "The boat."

"To protect you!" Callese was trembling now, her skirts shivering. "I had no time to plan!"

"Oh, Callese," he said softly. "Protect me from whom? My truest enemy was you."

"No. No! I—"

"Betrayed me. Betrayed the kingdom. Why?"

"You don't understand—"

"Why?"

"He *loves* me," she burst out, defiant. "I will be queen!"

The Saxon threw a subtle downward glance to his right. The man beside him gave a scant nod. His fingers crept toward his waist.

"Queen," Aedan murmured. "Is that what you've become?"

Someone, a shadow from the back of the crowd, detached from the group, vanished down the corridor in fleet silent steps.

"I never meant you to come to harm," the girl said, almost pleading. "You must believe that."

"So you sent me to Kell." Aedan pushed back his hood, his face bleak. "Callese! To *Kell*."

"It was all I could think of! I had no time!"

Above the conversation, beyond it, the Saxon met Ione's eyes. There was laughter there, cunning. He winked at her.

*Too late, little dove.*

"My lord," stammered one of Aedan's men. "My lady—what are you saying?"

"Treason," said Aedan coolly. "Murder and treason. Here are your Picts, Niall, never Picts at all. It was Saxons at that ambush. *These* Saxons, led by my devoted sister."

Outrage, shifting forms, danger rising. The man named Niall was moaning his disbelief, his words tattered and choked. His hands wavered in the air, fluttering. He was frail and gaunt and aged. He was completely vulnerable.

Behind him, the little patch of light purpled gently into dusk.

Io began to lose her focus on the scene, distracted by the avid gaze of the Saxon and the hum of Mòrag's sword. Time became a crawl, heavy strokes, sluggish. The humans seemed to move and speak with exaggerated deliberation, set about her like figures in a Greek play: The girl queen, quaking like a snow-dipped leaf. The Saxon leering, about to spill blood. A mass of men filling the corridor beyond, a shaded tumble of feet and faces, coming closer, slow, slow. Aedan impassioned, his words lost, a harsh ripple of sound beneath her heartbeat and the single thought that now encircled her.

*Sorry, sorry, sorry . . .*

The Saxon's grin curled sharp; it pierced her very heart. He took his first step forward, and she did the same. There might have been no one else in the hall, so intent were they on each other.

*Sorry, sorry . . .*

Their movements matched. Their swords hissed free in awful harmony.

*Sorry—*

Without warning, Callese rounded on the man, pushing at him with both hands.

"You! This is your fault! You attacked too soon! You knew I was not ready, you knew the day was wrong, and you attacked!"

Everything changed so quickly, Io almost could not follow. The Saxon spun about, caught the queen by the waist and pulled her to him, his blade at her throat. She gave a strangled cry.

"Steffen! What are you doing? You're hurting me!"

"Am I, sweet?" He pressed the sword high against her jaw, then looked to Aedan, his hair a yellow spread across the girl's neck. "What do you do now? Are you a prince, or are you a brother?"

"I am a king," said Aedan flatly. "I have ten-score warriors in the woods. I have a hundred more within these walls. Do you dare test me?"

And Io saw then that Aedan was right; the new men approaching were his, surely his, warriors indeed, stealing forward with disbelieving eyes.

"Steffen—" A ribbon of blood trickled down the queen's pale skin. It stained the crest of her gown, a spreading flower of scarlet.

"I have warriors as well," growled the Saxon. "In every corner of your keep, I have men waiting, prepared to die. I have your queen—"

"My sister."

"—her heart in my hands. Back away, that she may live."

"No," said Callese quickly. "He is lying." The man jerked her again and she shouted the rest. "Aedan, he's lying, there are no more than four dozen of them—"

The Saxon howled and Aedan leapt and the entire scene erupted. All at once there was a great roar of voices, a flood of people, pushing, fighting. Io was shoved to the wall and held there; she could not see who had her, she could not see Aedan. Someone grabbed her hair, tearing her sideways, a flash of silver all the warning she had of a knife descending. She parried the blow, brought down Mòrag's fine blade and severed the caught locks, pulling free. Someone else pushed into her, an elbow into her stomach, and the agony of that left her sick and bent, groping at the wall so she would not fall and be trampled.

She heard Aedan call her name and labored to lift her head; still she could not find him. Wait, there—a glimpse of him past her tears, fighting, blood across his face—gone again, blocked by the mob. Io stood and twisted through a jumble of men, was yanked back by her cloak. She spun and struck out with the sword—a man screamed, hot blood down his arm, his fingers slipping loose from her.

Aedan ahead, more soldiers. A blow to her shoulder that sent her to her knees, but she recovered, stumbling, and pressed on. He was battling the bossed man. They were both spattered red, blades flying, striking sharp. They turned and she glimpsed his face: wolfen eyes, black hair streaming.

A new person swayed before her, familiar, blanched. It was the queen, shouting, but Io could not hear her over the noise. She ignored the girl, still trying to push forward, but someone hooked their arms around her and pulled her bodily back, crashing her into another and then to the floor, where her knees hit stone and the sword bounced from her fingers.

White-hot pain flared through her, stole her breath and her senses. Ione groaned, rolling, and pulled herself into a ball to avoid the scuffling feet.

There was a flash of ivory before her. Callese had fallen as well, just in front of her. They rose to their knees at the same time, face to face, eyes locked, and then to their feet. A man in green plowed into Io; her leg gave out. She caught herself with her palms, felt someone tread on her hand.

Mòrag's sword was kicked aside, lost to the throng of men.

The queen was reaching for her. Io scrambled back, knocking into others, but Callese followed, her hand outstretched. She was shouting still when the first spasm took her; her spine arched, her arms shot stiff. She looked down and Io followed: The very tip of a sword poked through her perfect bodice. The sword withdrew, and fresh blood bloomed across the queen's ribs.

She looked back at Io, her brows knit. For the shortest, strangest moment they were alone in the eye of the storm, close enough to embrace. Ione noted, remotely, how pretty she was—fair hair, sky-blue eyes—how very young. Then someone jostled her and Callese listed back, hitting the floor again.

The queen had been stabbed. The queen was dying.

Aedan's sister was dying.

Ione struggled to her side. On the hard stone floor, beneath the screams of war, beneath the blood frenzy and the confusion, Ione leaned over her and said, "You sent him to Kell. I thank you for it."

She placed her hands over the girl's wound, felt the heat of life ebbing. The pain was thin already but with the last of her strength she took what was left, held it in her hands and then in her heart. The queen's gaze grew slowly distant, a dreamy smile shaping her lips.

"Papa?" said the queen, and let out a long sigh.

\* \* \*

Aedan fought as he never had before. He could no longer feel his body, he could not feel pain, or rage, or fury. He felt only determination, a black lancing need to kill this man before him, to take his life and thus the battle, soon, soon. Now.

The Saxon was weakening. He was dense and strong but did not have Aedan's drive to win—Aedan knew that, exploited it. This was his home, this was his kingdom, his keep, his life, and the Saxon was only an ugly blot upon it all. Simple to wipe away. Simple to erase.

His hands were glossed with blood. He noticed this but did not let it distract him. He didn't think it was his own; it came from his enemy, and so became a beauteous thing.

Fallen men were everywhere. He leapt over and across them easily, and his leg held, and his sword shrieked, and the Saxon backed away, back, stumbling, slipping, the end in his eyes. He no longer smiled; that was something else Aedan had taken from him, his lips stretched tight with his own barbarous grin.

A part of him, the strategist, understood the battle was already turned. His men spilled into the hallway beside him, his loyal guard and more, outnumbering the Saxons. He thought perhaps Mòrag had found her way into the keep—in peace, he hoped, at least until this moment. Aye, Mòrag would be welcome here, but first—he would just—kill—this—bastard—

The Saxon stumbled anew and this time fell, blundering over the bodies on the floor. Aedan merely walked forward, confident in their finish, success soaring through him, raising his sword—

—and he saw that the bodies were Callese and Ione, and that the Saxon saw it too. Callese, a broken doll; Ione, dazed over her, lifting her head—the Saxon rose up behind her—Aedan was shouting now, running—Ione turned to him—

The Saxon grabbed her by the shoulder and plunged his blade into her back.

Aedan was screaming. He was flying, descending, and the Saxon's head was lopped from his shoulders, a fountain of blood showering them all.

Aedan dropped to his knees, gathered her into his arms. Her hair had tumbled across her face. He brushed it back, his hand shaking, and left scarlet across her cheek.

"No," he was saying, "no, no, no, Ione, no—"

She looked up at him with deep blue sorrow, her skin gone to chalk. Her hand reached out and found his arm.

"Kell," she whispered, and closed her eyes.

Aedan raised his head. "A ship," he said, and then bellowed it. "*I need the fastest ship!*"

But there was no ship fast enough. He knew that.

"My liege! We cannot come closer than this!"

Aedan nodded to the captain to let him know he understood, his eyes on the rain-sparkled water, the black misted mass that would be Kell in the distance. They were not close enough. They were not quick enough.

"Aedan." Mòrag stood beside him at the rail, facing the storm. "We can take the rowboat in."

"No." He turned, his eyes on the scene across the deck: Sìne with her head bowed over the limp figure in her lap, her arms raised to brace a sodden blanket over them both. "I'll do it alone."

"You can't possibly go by yourself—"

"*Alone, I said.*" He had alarmed her, not an easy feat with his wife. Another time, another day, he would be sorry for it. But not yet.

The rowboat was lowered in creaking jerks. Wind slammed them into the side of the galley, rattling his teeth, hulls scraping. They hit the water with a shallow splash; the boat was light, only two passengers instead of the eight it was built for, and after he released the ropes, the currents caught and carried them off like a leaf atop a whirlpool.

He found the oars, began to row. He did not take his eyes from Ione, curled in the bottom of the boat. Part of her hair had been shorn; shortened locks dripped wet across her face. Someone had removed her boots. He didn't remember who had thought of that. He supposed it might have been him.

The rain sheeted down in cold misery. Aedan rowed and rowed, and his blood was fire and his heart was frost.

She was so pale. He could not tell if she still breathed. He had placed her head to the side to be safe, but he could not tell.

*Kell, Kell, an island lost . . .*

He would get her there. He would.

He battled the currents at first, instinctive, then realized that they would take him at least partway to where he wanted to go. So Aedan stowed the oars, crept over to Ione, and took her in his arms as the rowboat swept toward the reef. The wind picked up and the waves grew rougher. Great ghastly ships pitched by, prows tilted out of the water, frames broken and torn.

The little boat smashed into one, lurched free. Kell inched closer.

At the dip of a massive wave he glimpsed the reef itself, higher than his head, black rock in blue-sable water. Then they were lifted up, away; they hit something he couldn't see and skipped off in circles. The galley spun out of sight, swallowed by the rain.

Aedan brought her hand to his chest, pressed hard over his heart.

"I love you," he said. "Damn you, Ione, don't you die. I love you."

And there was Kell, the shore taking shape. They were not there yet, there was such a ways still to go—

The boat struck into something new, snapped to a shuddering halt. Aedan righted them from the tumble and discovered the rowboat snared between a pair of skeleton ships, trapped at last. Water began to rush his feet.

He squinted out into the night. Kell was an eternity yet away.

Aedan stood up, lifted Ione, and jumped into the boiling sea.

They were sinking, sinking . . .

The water tore at him and he fought it, trying both to swim and to hold on to Ione, who floated beside him, listless. He found the surface, lost it again, saltwater in his mouth. A magnificent wave roared over them; he felt her rip away and reached out, desperate, only to have his head strike hard coral, or wood . . . reef or ship . . . it was all so dark. . . .

He could not find her. He could not see, or breathe. Darkness engulfed him, bitter salt darkness, and he tossed and reeled in the water. To come this close, to fail—he had almost done it, he had almost gotten her there.

Black and black and black—ah, it was a familiar death, perhaps even his destiny, to end here by her isle, to die where they had first met. They were together, at least; he would not regret that. . . .

He was moving. He was rising. It was an interesting sensation, because his head hurt—by heavens, truly hurt—

212 • Shana Abé

and he would have thought that in death the pain would be lifted away.

Aedan opened his eyes. The water had turned to flowing fire, long and curling. Tickling. He frowned at it, pushed at it. It was hair.

There was an arm around his shoulders. There was a woman before him, swimming swift beneath the waves, her face turned away. Tail and fins and silvered grace—not a woman, no. He reached for her, found her chin.

Ione glanced back at him and smiled.


It was a long while before she could move from the sand.

She kept her eyes closed, the fingers of one hand still clenched around Aedan's arm, and let the power of Kell slowly immerse her. The rain had been ferocious, but here the storm lightened to a shower, and then a drizzle, blown off to a thin, misty spray.

Yet it wasn't until the skies began to clear that Io opened her eyes and lifted her head. She tried a deep breath. The pain was tolerable again, not the terrible lethal ache of before, but slighter. She could move.

And so she did, turning over to see her lover at her side, spangled with raindrops and sand, breathing gently, perhaps sleeping.

She examined his peaceful face, then reached out and tapped her fingers against his cheek.

His eyes opened.

"You drown too easily, Scot," Io said.

He made a sound that was mostly groan and sat up, rimmed with clouds and stars. "I know it."

The storm had rolled out to sea, leaving Kell glinting in its wake. She pushed her fingers into the sand and felt the thrill of the island burn deep within her. Life to life, blood to blood, and she was home again—

"Ione!" Aedan had her by the shoulders. "Your wound—"

"Better now." She found her feet, hobbling a little, tore off the human gown and tossed it to the tide. "I'm so much better now."

He stood as well, steadier than she, and Io went to him, wrapped her arms around him, and pressed her lips to his. Oh, he was salt and sea and wonderful hope.

"Do you truly love me, Scot?"

"You heard that?" His voice was faint; he had buried his face in her hair.

"I did. Well—do you?"

"I leapt into the damned ocean for you in the middle of a tempest. I don't do that for women I don't love."

"A tempest," she teased softly. "Barely a spring rain."

"A squall. A goddamned gale."

"Say it again."

"I love you." He lifted his head. "I love you, siren of Kell."

She drew him down to her kiss and then to the beach, where they tangled together and it didn't matter if the wind or the rain or the sea swept over them; they made their own heat, their own place in the sand, nestled in the sweet safety of her isle.

Later, they gazed together at the lightening sky, dawn arising with a flourish of topaz and pink at the edge of the world.

"What will happen now?" Io asked, cradled in his arms.

"Now," Aedan said, turning, "we go up to your castle, where there is a room with a very fine bed, as I recall—"

She pushed him off. "No. I meant, what will happen now to *us*, oh king?"

"Ah." He relaxed back, crossing his arms beneath his head. "They'll return for me. Someday."

"Someday soon."

"Perhaps."

"Will you go?" she asked, very steady.

He watched the clouds above them, silent.

"I understand. I do. You are their king."

His hand found hers. "And you are my love."

The sun rose higher, warming the earth in spreading rays, kindling the surf to fiery froth. Io turned her face to his shoulder.

"Will you come back?" she asked, in a much smaller voice.

Aedan leaned up to skim his palm over her belly, sprinkling sand across her skin like powdered gold. "Every day, every week—every moment God grants, I pledge to you. You hold my heart, and so much more."

She looked up again, smiling. "I have your soul."

"Beloved siren." He gazed at her with wolf-lit eyes, his lips curved with sensual promise. "You have my everything."

# · EPILOGUE ·

She gave birth to their daughter in the calm blue sea, beneath the midnight sky and a bower of stars. Dolphins danced and sang their praises of her, and the moon smiled her sleepy smile and sent silver blessings down to the waves.

King Aedan in his boat took the baby in his arms, marveling, and lifted her up to the joyful sky.

# Book Two:

# The Hero

# · PROLOGUE ·

He was a man of the sea, not the land.

Kell spent his life on the marbled ocean, the wind in his smile, child of the sun, brother of the waves. He raced dolphins and whales, chased tales of giant sharks and fantastic squid. And fish, of course. Always the fish, which gleamed and glistened in the waters around him like living sand, like liquid stone, pulsing just beneath the glass face of the sea.

They came to him when he called, when he sang his mariner song, and he cast his nets and pulled them up to him, a thousand silvered tails beating in time in the hollow of his boat.

Some days he would simply drift, aside in the wake of a distant galley, careful to stay back, far back, watching the slave oars lift and drip and stab the water again.

How sad, Kell would think, to be so close to the sea and never truly touch her.

Back in port he always longed for the water, for the peace that filled him out there. If he could, he would have sailed away forever, to the very edge of the world.

But Kell was a fisherman. His work fed his village, and he took pride in that. Other men fished, aye, but none so well as he. So he did his job and came home when he should, spreading the bounty of the sea to his people, accepting their praise, feeling secret pity for those who never left the land. Pacing, planning, until it was time to sail again.

It was whispered, he knew, that he was not fully mortal, that his mother had known the sea god, that he was a favored son. Perhaps it was true. His mother never said.

Mortal or not, village girls threw smiles at him, lifted their skirts, beguiled him with flattery and long-lashed looks. Kell gave what he got, enjoying their pretty words, their pleasing ripe bodies and eager hands.

Yet the ocean always beckoned, and Kell always heeded her.

He did not love his life as much as he hungered for it. He lived for the sea and someday, he understood, he would die for it, just as all the men in his family did. Surely there could be no greater pleasure than to give his life to the one lover he cherished most.

He thought he understood his destiny, and was content with it.

But then . . . came the storm.

He knew storms. He survived them, shouted back at them, laughed at their purple rage and heaving fury. Storms could not hurt him.

This one was different. He felt it hours ahead, the bitter ache in the air, the roiling green center of the clouds. By then he was too far out to turn back to shore, so Kell did what he always had. He settled low and prepared to ride it out.

There was no laughing this time. He knew it in his bones: This time, the storm would win.

Hours later, days later—weeks or months, he could not say—it was over. He floated alone in his beautiful sea . . . placid now, sweet, flat sea . . . on what was left of his boat . . . three planks and half an oar . . . no water. No fish, no food.

No hope.

The sun gazed down at him, unblinking. The currents sucked gently at his legs. In time young Kell yielded to his death, sliding from his ravaged boat into the waiting arms of the sea . . .

. . . not the sea, no. The arms of a woman—the most comely woman he had ever seen, with salt bright on her cheeks, golden hair, a cold, cold smile. And her eyes, her eyes—deepest blue, the heart of the storm revived.

She spoke words he heard only faintly, dizzy with the spell of her and the fading cadence of his life.

*Fair youth. Shall I save thee? Shalt thou live?*

*Aye,* he croaked.

*A price,* she said. *Be mine, mine alone. Live thee with me, my hand, my heart. Thy soul. Always and for always.*

*Aye,* he managed again.

*Thy word.* She pressed his palm to the strange locket on her chest. *Give it to me.*

Her heart beat strong against him. Her skin felt like winter fire.

*My word, lady.*

*Then thou art home.*

And she took him to a place of dreams. It was an island like none other, brilliant colors, abundant life, lush flowers and vines and tame creatures, birds that would fly up and perch on his finger if he liked. It was land as he had never known land before, soft and giving, warm as a mother's womb, fertile, kind.

And she. His wife.

She was the extension of him: not half a god but a goddess entirely, magnificent, fearsome. A mermaid. Not woman, not fish, but wonderful both, her own silvered tail, rounded breasts, delicious voice.

Kell came to realize that while he had only skipped across the waves, she owned them, she *became* them. He admired her swimming, walking. On land she danced with him by music they made together, simple tunes hummed between closed lips, until they would fall into laughter and kisses.

She kept him close in every way possible. She held his promise in that locket of shining silver, on a necklace she never removed.

They built a home together, one stone at a time. A palace, a place for them and their children, safe and thick and laced with her magic.

Oh, he was blessed. Oh, he was content.

He held her at night, after she returned from the water. Wet or dry, he clasped her to him, her head above his heart, her hair a spill of gold against his dark skin. He listened to her breathe as she slept, one pale arm thrown across him, restless, as if she might still swim off.

He loved her so much he felt delirious with it,

both filled and empty, craving her, needing her, even as she slept in his arms.

He never knew it could be like this with another. He never knew he could love aught but the sea.

For a while—a long, long while—Kell didn't even miss the water. He was saturated in his wife. He was drowned in her, and the thought of leaving her, their children, and their refuge was beyond his ken.

But the sea was a constant whisper in his ear.

And finally one night, in the sly dark, Kell began to listen.

*Wherefore*, sighed the sea, *dost thou abandon me? Wherefore dost thou dwell on land, my own son?*

And he began to see those things he had not before. That he was on an island. That he was snared in sand, with no way back to the swift open water.

*Remember me*, murmured the sea. *Remember how I served thee, how I thrilled thee and made thee whole. . . .*

And he did remember, feelings he had not felt in a lifetime, the radiant solitude of the waves, the glory of the sky, master of his soul.

*Alas, thou art lost to me now.*

No. No, he was not lost. He was home. He had his wife here, he had his sons and daughters and the castle. He had birds and flowers and vines.

*Alas, my son . . .*

Kell began to dream. He dreamed of his youth, the village maidens, the writhing fish caught in his nets. He dreamed of sailing into port to the cheers of his people, a hero to all, admired and untamed.

His siren wife slept on, her perfect face ever

unchanged, her perfect body ever pressed next to his, and he felt—trapped.

She knew. She knew, and would not release him. When he spoke to her about it she turned away. She tossed her shining hair and left the isle, went back to her ocean with their children trailing behind her, leaving him alone on land, seething, helpless.

He missed her. He missed them all. And when she returned—she always returned—she would bring him news of his old home: famine, war, devastation. Plague and raiders and burning sod. But he never knew if any of it was real. He never knew if he should trust her, if it was truth or trick. It was driving him mad, the not knowing.

*My son*, mourned the sea.

One night he could abide it no longer. While his wife slept he reached down, nearly without thinking about it, and snapped the chain from her neck, the one that bound him to her.

In an instant he felt the power of what he had done, the danger, heady deliverance. He had broken more than a silver chain. He had broken his vow. His heart skipped and stopped and skipped again.

Her eyes opened. Her hand lifted.

Quickly, before she could touch him, before she could stop him, he opened the locket. She cried out, a terrible sob.

Kell felt the breath leave his body. He felt himself falling, falling, and he realized now—oh, too late—that he had broken too much. He had broken her wild, wild heart—

# CHAPTER ONE

❧

## London, 1721

I t was an extremely fine waistcoat, brocaded lemon silk that in the proper light flashed lilies, buttons of polished jet, and a lining of French satin. The don had managed to secure it from a desperate widow at a shockingly good price and was, naturally, quite pleased with it. When a half-washed barmaid leaned too close and dabbed him with the foam from a tankard, he backhanded her into the corner.

She sprawled there, red-faced, her ankles lolling white against the wood floor.

The don turned back to his companion and continued the transaction. Conversation in the tavern did not dim.

Slowly the maid stood up again, biting her lip, her hands trembling. He watched her from the corner of his eye, how her breasts strained against her dampened bodice as she leaned over, picked up the empty tankard. She shot him a quick glance—outrage, fear—then ducked her head and disappeared into the storeroom behind the bar.

Interesting.

He imagined following her into the storeroom. He imagined finding her there alone against the barrels and smoked meats and jugs of cheap gin. He imagined taking hold of that bodice, ripping loose the frayed laces, her breasts unbound—pale, of course, because the girl had been English, pale skin with pink English nipples—and she would cry out but he would stop her. He would put his hand over her mouth and press her back against the barrels, his fingers hard over her, her eyes very wide. . . .

What color had they been? Green, he thought, or perhaps gray.

Green, yes. Soft, frightened green.

He imagined holding her there while he pinched her, kneaded her, until she moaned beneath his palm. He would push back her skirts—he would be careful then, because her skirts were unclean, and he was also quite fond of his velvet breeches—and see those ankles again, worsted stockings up to her thighs, garters to be untied.

No, not untied. He would leave them, find the flesh around and above them, bare plump thighs that had never known the sun, never felt a noble hand—

She would hate him quite violently then, she would struggle, but really, she was only a girl, and he was a man. He was a lord, and she was merely a thing. For a moment, *his* thing.

The don smiled at the thought of her squirming. His handsome face fell into an expression of slack pleasure, enough so that his companion stopped speaking, leaning back in his chair, disgruntled.

"Did you 'ear me then, guv?"

"Of course," replied the don. "You have told me nothing new. Why have I wasted my money on you?"

"Mebe because you'd loike to live," suggested the companion, dry. "So I 'eard."

The don kept his lazy smile. "Tell me again, friend. *Why* do I pay you?"

"Because I knows what you don't," said the other bluntly. "Because I 'ave what you don't, guv, and that's me ears and eyes in the gutters. Because I can find out 'oo wants you dead, and quick-loike."

"And yet . . . you have not."

"I need more money. I know a bloke—"

"—*more* money? You English, so greedy. I am dismayed."

"—'oo says 'e knows the man 'ired for the job. A foreigner, 'e says, loike you, yer pardon, sir, and 'e'll talk for a bit more silver."

The don sighed. "Always more silver." He finished the last of his ale.

The barmaid reappeared. She worked alone tonight, he knew. The old witch who had served him his supper retired some while ago, and the man who apparently owned this miserable hovel was snoring by the fire.

The girl's cap had been retied, her lips set tight. Her hair was unpowdered, long and black; she had not been able to fully pin it up again. She walked nearly sideways to avoid them, dark locks floating behind.

He could sense the heat of her dislike for him, her anger, and felt himself grow hard.

"This man," said the don, still watching the girl—bend, stoop, serve, sweat gleaming across her skin—"you are certain he knows who the assassin is?"

"Aye. If 'e don't, no one do."

"And you are certain he will tell you?"

"With," said the companion, "the proper persuasion."

The barmaid straightened, swished back by, her skirts slipping over his leg. She vanished into the storeroom once more.

The don stood. "Do what you must, but hurry. I cannot bear this town much longer."

The other man pushed back his chair. "Aye, guv." He caught the leather pouch tossed to him, gave a wink and tipped his hat as the don made his way toward the bar.

It was more closet than storeroom, cramped, unlit. And she was not here, after all. He took a step deeper into the gloom, his eyes adjusting . . . and, ah, found the shadow of her by the far wall, slumped against a crate with a hand over her face.

There were no other exits.

He examined the narrow space, listened for voices, and heard only the drunken chaos behind him. The don entered the room. His heels scratched softly against the floor.

She looked up.

"A moment, guv."

The don whirled, his hand to his sword, then relaxed as he recognized the silhouette of his hired jackal.

"What is it now?" he asked calmly, beginning to unbutton his breeches.

"There was a matter of a damsel in La Seu d'Urgell."

Past the mangled pronunciation the don hesitated, found a glimmer of real surprise. Perhaps the man was better than he had believed. "Yes?"

He felt, strangely, a chill seeping over him, a dull curl of pain rising in his stomach. Cursed English food—he hated the stuff, could not wait to clear up this business and depart—

"A very young damsel," said the jackal, unmoving.

The don opened his mouth to reply but found that he could not. No words emerged from his lips—no sound— nothing. He brought a hand up to the lace of his jabot and heard a long, strangled gasp—it came from him.

Without warning his body snapped taut, his hands clenching. The last button of his breeches ripped free.

He was on his knees. He was on his back. Outrageous, to sully himself on this filthy floor—to touch the grit of rat droppings and dirt—his fine clothing—his wig—

His arm stretched high above him, ludicrous, as if it no longer connected to his body. The severed button was still in his fist. Blood began to dribble down his wrist and stain his cuff; the don's manicured nails dug deep into his palm.

The barmaid stepped over him, gathered her skirts, and leaned down very near. He blinked at her. The imprint of his hand was still sharp upon her cheek.

He had been right. Her eyes were green.

She held his gaze and said in the pure, graceful Spanish of his homeland, "Her father sends you his best regards."

Nyle watched the swell jerk and foam, saw his eyes roll and his face bleach to bone like a mask, like a monster. They both waited until the man stopped twitching, until the bubbles in his mouth stopped popping.

He looked back at the girl, repulsed in spite of himself. Her head was still bowed; with her hair falling down and the ruffled cap slipping sideways, she appeared even younger than she had before. The curve of her lips seemed sweetly docile to him, almost tender. Smoky light from the doorway bathed her from her jaw to her throat, revealing smooth skin beneath the grime of old powder.

Then she looked up and met his eyes.

Nyle felt something in him fall cold and very quiet. She was not young—not truly young. Not with those eyes, brittle fire, endless ice.

Without meaning to, he eased back a step.

"Right glad I didn't drink that ale," he said gruffly, to hide his nerves.

She angled past him. At the doorway she paused, offered a short glance from over her shoulder.

"It was not the ale. It was the meat."

And she walked out into the tavern.

When Nyle emerged a few minutes later, the girl was nowhere to be seen.

He watched her from the second-story window of the mercer's shop. Through the coal fog that clogged the alley, she moved smoothly, confidently, the stride of someone who knew where she was and why. She did not rush, she did not tarry. A mantle and hood hid all but a glimpse of her chin and the pointed tips of her shoes.

But Che Rogelio recognized her, of course. He knew her by night or by day, in his dreams or awake. He could predict her every step, every tilt of her head.

There was a woven basket tucked under one arm, the heel of a loaf of bread peeking out past the rim—a very pretty deception, he thought, that did not quite match the late London night.

She kept her head down, her eyes level. The hem of her mantle was whisked aside with a practical wrist over puddles of filth and the occasional stooped beggar.

Just beneath his window she stopped, turned, and retraced her steps. She bent over a pile of rags . . . no, another beggar. Che saw a hand dart out of the rags, pale and gaunt. He could not see what happened next; the mantle obscured his view. In a few seconds she walked on, and the hand was snatched back to darkness.

She looked around rather obviously until she found the blue door of the mercer's, although he had told her precisely where it would be. She did not need to look. He would speak to her later of that.

Che made his way down the stairs, a lone candle lighting his way.

He reached the door exactly as she knocked, three taps, two longer, their code.

"We are closed," he said anyway, because it would not hurt to remind her of the risks.

"*Soy yo*," came her voice, very low, and he opened the door.

She ducked in with a wash of cold air.

"Leila," he greeted her.

"*Padre*," she murmured.

"Speak English, if you please. It's safer."

"As you wish." She closed the door and turned to him, pushing back her hood.

Candlelight splashed gold across her face, warming her skin. He knew her beauty well enough not to be distracted by it: the elegance of her cheekbones, the wine of her lips. Exotic almond eyes, dark lashes framing a gaze of pale, absolute green.

Che Rogelio lifted the candle higher. She did not back away. It was permission to examine her, and so he did.

Her wig was loose, showing a wedge of fair hair beneath the black. The burned cork of one eyebrow had smudged to her temple; her rouge was uneven. He noted these flaws in silence, knowing that she knew already, that she allowed him this moment only to satisfy some inner notion of her own.

He paused, looking closer. He had been mistaken about the rouge—she was injured. The skin of her left cheek was pink and slightly swollen. She had been struck.

"Your cheek," Che said, dispassionate. "It presents a problem."

"Powder will cover it." Her lashes lowered. He knew this signal as well; he had been dismissed. Che stepped back and Leila swept around him, down the hallway to the front room.

The mercer's shop was stacked to the ceiling with bolts of cloth, velvet and silk piled thick upon themselves, spindles of lace draping the walls, a pair of shears hung up by a nail. Outside, past the shuttered windows, a hackney rolled by.

She began to remove her bodice. "How long have we?"

"Twelve minutes." He placed the candle on the cutter's shelf, next to where she had tossed the silly basket—now missing the bread, he noted—then turned and faced the window. "You are late."

"Don Camilo ate slowly."

"A pity."

She did not reply. He heard the rustle of her skirts. Her shoes were kicked against the counter.

"There is a looking glass on the wall," he said.

"I see it."

Ten minutes left. Eight. He kept his eyes on the light that seeped between the shutters, counted the seconds as they passed.

"How much did you give the beggar?" he asked.

"A pound."

"Good God," he said mildly.

"She had an infant."

Five minutes. Four.

At three minutes she was ready. She said his name, and he went to her.

The elderly couple that descended the stairs of the mercer's shop were clearly merchant gentry, on their way to a midnight game of whist, perhaps, judging by the lady's gloves. They were dressed well but not so well as to rouse the envy of the pickpocket slouched against the wall nearby. The cut of the old man's coat flared too wide for fashion, and the wigs of both were stiff with the fat, out-dated curls of their youth. Both walked with canes, his ebony, hers yellow pine.

The gent hailed a coach, helped in his dame, and off they went.

Less than two minutes later, the mercer returned to his shop, his cart loaded with goods, bleary-eyed from a long day at the docks. He never noticed the tiny scratch on the lock of his back-entrance door, and puzzled only briefly over the slight odor of tallow that lingered in his front room before he went to bed.

# CHAPTER TWO

L eila de Sant Severe sat curled alone by the window of her room in the modest inn Che had secured, looking out into the inky dark. A faint wind was rising with the night. It mixed with the London mist, blew the stars across the sky to twinkling, silvery dust.

The stars were different in Spain. Everything there was different. Spanish nights were sharper, the air more crisp. In Spain the stars shone with polished brilliance, the tears of a thousand angels, as her grandmother used to say, or a thousand wishes from little children, tossed up to God.

Leila preferred to believe the latter; she herself must have sprinkled half the sky with wishes by the time she reached ten.

A draft whistled in past the panes, cutting easily through the plum silk of her robe. She looked down at her hands, rubbed her palms together for warmth.

London was a cold place, as far from the arid heat of her home as anywhere she had yet seen. They had been in England for over two months now and still she hadn't adjusted to the change. She caught herself looking constantly up to the sky, toward a sun swallowed by clouds, or rendered small and distant in the brown winter haze that blanketed the city.

She liked the cold, Leila told herself. She would learn to like the cold.

As quickly as it had come to her, she pushed the thought aside. She did not dare even to think such things—not with Che so near.

A knock sounded on the door, which opened to reveal the chambermaid, hefting a platter of food to the table by the fire. Leila stood, wrapping her robe more securely around her, and walked over to inspect her meal.

Boiled beef and roasted apples. A square of gingerbread, her favorite, falling into crumbs. Simple fare but filling; Che knew she would be hungry.

Leila never ate on contract days. She moved forward through them on nerves alone.

The maid set out the plates and knives, her face downturned, limp hair, pallid cheeks, her apron worn and stained. She was the very picture of a city mouse scrambling at the edge of poverty.

Leila knew, better than most, how poverty bred desperation. How desperation could lead people to take any sort of risk to survive. Even bribery. Even murder.

Because she could, and because she knew she should, Leila lifted her hand to the girl.

"The ale," she instructed, and without a word the maid turned to pour it from the flagon. Leila reached for the mug she offered, opened her mind, and then, very deliberately, allowed their fingers to brush.

*Exhaustion, bone-weary sleep till six if she hurries I'll be done in an hour. Laundry tomorrow and baking I hope fresh eels but Jemmy needs milk. No eels then, next week, next week, treacle again. Dishes tonight Lud I hope he pays me, a fortnight behind Jemmy needs milk when will she finish? An hour and then home I hope, wee Jem needs me—*

The chambermaid let go of the mug and went back to the plates, arranging the beef and mustard. Leila stood there a moment, mastering her breath, resisting the inevitable, blinding white headache that began to wrap around her temples.

She moved back to the window, pretending to stare out with the ale clutched in numb fingers. Just the thought of drinking it made her throat close.

At least she knew the girl wasn't a spy. Surely that was worth the pain.

"If you please, mum, ring when you're done," said the maid behind her, and Leila waved a hand in response, not turning. The headache rendered her mute; she could not reply if she wanted to.

Silence settled across the little room, broken only by the rumble of the fire.

Slowly, slowly, the night came back into focus.

The wind past the glass began to lull. She concentrated on a whorl of leaves—*wee Jem, no eels*—following their dance—*needs milk, needs me*—until her vision blurred. When she could stare out no longer, when the leaves lost their shape to the spreading dark, she set the mug on the floor and brought her hands to her face, rubbing her eyes. The white pain began to let loose its claws in her head.

God knew she was tired. She needed to sleep.

Exactly on cue, Che tapped on the door. He did not wait for her to answer; he knew she would not be abed.

Unlike her, he had neither washed nor undressed, although he had removed the ridiculous wig. His hair was neatly brushed and tied back, yellow in this light, though that—like many things about him—was merely an illusion.

"You should sleep," he said, and she allowed herself a tight smile.

"I know."

He carried a cup with him, his usual offering on nights like these, setting it on the table with the food. He would not hand it to her. He was careful to never, ever touch her bare skin.

"Hot milk," he said, "and a trace of rum."

"Thank you."

He eased down into the chair closest to the fire, stretching out his bad leg with a sigh. Leila was granted his profile, a hooked nose and fierce gray brows, lips pursed in thought.

She crossed to the table, rested her hip against the edge, and broke off a corner of the gingerbread.

"We might not go," Che said finally, his voice sunk deep. "We might cancel the contract."

"No."

"A delay, then."

"No."

"My dear, forgive me, but you do not look well. A short rest—"

"No, *Padre*."

"Then for *me*," he said grumpily. "I am old. I cannot keep pace as I used to."

Leila lifted the cup of milk, examined it. "Oh? You appear much as you always have." She caught the scent of the steam, tipped the brim toward the light. He had poisoned her once, long ago. She did not enjoy repeating past mistakes.

No phosphorus, no telltale flecks or grit. She tried a sip and tasted only milk, the warm bite of the rum.

"We could return home," he murmured. "Think on it. Home."

"Then go," she invited smoothly, still gazing into her cup.

No answer. She did not need to see him to know his reaction: narrowed eyes, pinched lips. He would not leave without her. Just the thought of it was absurd.

He had been master to her apprentice, her guide and keeper for almost longer than she could recall. He had plucked her from obscurity and propped her up in a world of dazzling deceptions, fencing and riding and dueling wits, costumes and disguises, anatomy and potions and muskets and knives. . . .

She could not wait to escape him.

Eventually Che sighed again, an old man's sound, long and drawn out. "We have enough gold now. More than enough."

Leila slanted him a look. "Pardon?"

He turned his head away, hunching his shoulders.

"Is this some new character you're trying?" she asked. "You taught me there is never enough gold."

He lifted a hand sparkling with rings. "The Earl of Kell is a powerful man."

"We've dealt with others like him."

"A powerful man," he continued, louder, "with powerful connections. He reigns like a barbarian king up there in the north, surrounded by his people, walled up in his fortress. Getting near—"

"We've discussed this. We've made plans."

"Listen to me. I have a feeling about this one—"

"Feelings are *my* business," she countered.

A hit, and a good one; she watched him scowl into the flames.

"Very well," he said at last. "You are determined. Perhaps, then, this one time, we finish the assignment without going close. A simple thing—belladonna in his port, perhaps, or a bit of arsenic over his beefsteak, like the don."

"You seem to have forgotten that no one has ever actually seen him eat or drink in public."

"Then a gunshot—from afar. Your aim is infallible."

"You know I won't. I won't harm him—I won't harm *anyone*—without knowing the truth first."

"No." He steepled his fingers beneath his chin. "You won't. It's always been our dilemma, your little moral code."

"Your dilemma. Not mine."

The fire popped and flickered. The smell of the milk was making her slightly dizzy.

"It grows worse each time," Che said. "You don't speak of it, but I know."

Leila tapped her nails against the cup. "I can manage it."

"Indeed. Last time, for the don, you went to bed for two days."

She had no ready answer for that. It was true; a sennight past, in a carefully staged moment, she had grazed against Don Camilo in the street, and it had been like drinking Che's poison. It had sickened her, worse than ever, left her wretched and faint and gasping for air. Che had had to help her back to their carriage; she barely recalled it. Even tonight affected her—the instant his hand connected with her face she felt so ill she could hardly move.

But it was always like that with the evil ones. Poison.

One swift touch, one timeless moment. She had looked into his heart and what she had seen there would sicken anyone, she supposed.

*The little girl, weeping. Camilo laughing as he held her down, jeering—*

Leila rubbed her cheek, trying not to remember.

Che was watching the flames. "It was better when you were younger. You were stronger then, I think."

"I am strong now," she said quickly, offended, and he smiled.

"Well, then. Perhaps you were only younger. As were we all."

She stood. "We are expected tomorrow for the ball. The arrangements have been made. Should our situation change, certainly I will let you know."

"Ah, Leila . . ."

"You were correct, Che. I need to sleep."

"Had I realized when we met that you would prove to be so stubborn—"

"You would have done exactly as you did. You would have taken me anyway."

He glanced at her at last, gray eyes to match his hair. They were half-lidded and sharp; eyes that for five decades had gazed back into those of a host of dying men, princes and thieves alike.

*La Mano de Dios.* The Hand of God, Europe's most infamous assassin. Only the two of them knew that *La Mano* was no longer a man.

"You were almost dead in that dismal little village. Your father or his men would have found you. You would not have survived another week."

"Yes," she agreed evenly. "But you never offered me a choice, did you?"

Che clambered out of the chair, went to the door. "There was never a choice for either of us. I'd thought you understood that by now." The door opened on silent hinges; he did not look at her again. "Good night, my daughter. Pleasant dreams."

"Good night, *Padre*."

The village of Sant Severe had been hardly more than a few mud huts carved into the yellow hills with the good grace of a stream running near. That high up, the water cut clean and pure; in the lower plains it sullied down into a river, spreading out in wide, flat arms into fields until it vanished altogether.

But there, in the village of her birth, the stream washed fine and cool. Trees, so scarce in the constant sun, grew abundant at its banks, and Leila herself grew up in their shade. The trees and the water had been her joy, and she loved them only slightly less than she had loved her grandmother. Leila had learned to swim there, to play there, and—eventually—to hide there. To this very day the sparkle of daylight on water could arrest her, fling her back, without warning, to the vivid depths of her childhood.

The smell of burning grass could do the same thing.

In her new home, in the secret haven she would find, there would be many trees, and very little grass.

Leila finished the food, rang for the maid, and tipped her liberally, enough for both eels and milk. With her hair braided, the windows secured and the door bolted, she climbed into bed. She pushed down into the covers, turned away from the smoldering fire and closed her eyes, one hand, as always, firm on the hilt of the stiletto beneath her pillow.

She had drunk all of Che's milk and rum, because she did not want to dream.

* * *

The ceiling of the Duke of Covenford's ballroom was painted a rather spectacular pink, or so it seemed to Leila: pink clouds with pink blushing cherubs, a lilac-pink sky that bled down into pink marble columns. A great crystal chandelier swayed with the heat of the room, a geometry of gemstones and light. The faint, formal strains of a quadrille floated from the musicians fixed in the balcony; the notes bounced along the walls in odd repetition, over-lapping, nearly drowned in the din of conversation below.

It was a ball to celebrate the duke's recent marriage, a most exclusive event attended by only the bluest blood of English society. Che had complained a great deal about the cost of forging the invitations.

Privately, Leila was no better pleased than he to attend. She did not like crowds—too many hidden dangers—but there had been no choice. The mysterious and elusive Earl of Kell, the old laird of Clan Kell, was due to appear. He had come down from his Highland mountains on busi-ness, reportedly the first time in years he had left Scot-land. This was his only social engagement in London, as far as anyone knew, and Leila did not want to miss the op-portunity to observe him from a wide and safe distance before moving in.

She had learned, from experience, that it was far bet-ter to watch a tiger pace his cage before attempting to enter it.

But the Scottish earl was late. So was her contact, the man who would point him out to her.

Mr. Johnson. Not his true name, of course, but it hardly mattered. He paid in gold coin, half up front plus all ex-penses, and had sworn up and down on his father's grave that the earl was a fiend of a man, a vicious brute who had spent his life tormenting innocents, kidnapping children, ravaging women, and burning villages to the ground.

Burning villages . . .

She would find out soon enough for herself.

Leila stood by a potted palm, surveying the floor with simmering impatience. Her new pumps hurt her feet and one of her hairpins had managed to twist itself into her scalp. If Johnson did not come soon, she would have to forfeit the operation, Che would insist. She would have to concoct some new excuse not to return to Spain—

"Splendid, isn't it?"

Leila turned to the young man at her side, a gawky-thin nobleman with a nervous cough and a wilting cravat. He smiled gamely at her level look.

"I know it's hardly proper—we've not been introduced—but I saw ye standing here alone, and . . . er . . ."

Behind the leisurely sway of her feather fan Leila waited, watching the blood rise in his cheeks and his mouth open and shut again. He could not be more than eighteen, brown-eyed, and most unfortunately freckled. With a blush like that, his hair would be red beneath his frizzed wig.

Not her contact. She would have to get rid of him.

She lowered the fan. "I am Doña Adelina Montiago y Luz."

"You're not English! I knew it! That is—I mean to say . . ."

Once more he trailed off, gazing down at her.

"I am Spanish," she said. "I am in your country on tour."

"My country? Oh, it's not—on tour, did ye say? But that's splendid!"

The music changed, a minuet this time, and the couples on the floor broke apart, regrouped in a swirl of pastel colors and skirts. Her young suitor cleared his throat.

"I . . . er . . . would ye honor me—"

"It is very warm, is it not?" Leila waved her fan again slowly, smiling. "How I wish I had something to drink."

"Oh? Oh—of course. Please, madam, allow me—"

"Thank you so much. You are very kind."

As soon as he turned his back she moved, slipping off into the crush of guests. There were too many people here; the familiar cold panic begin to slide over her, and to distract herself Leila focused on the details of the chamber, taking in the configuration of the ballroom, the mob milling about.

Ten windows, double-sashed, tied curtains of maroon velvet. Wide enough to hide behind.

Nine potted palms, between the windows.

Six—pink—Doric columns.

Six doors, four of them leading to the courtyard, and from there to the garden. She had espied that earlier this evening, a prudish English thing with shaped trees and blunted bushes. Gravel underfoot, probably quite loud.

The musicians, flushed, earnest. At least . . . fifteen footmen, some bearing food, some drink, most stationed by the doors. Inconvenient.

Half as many maids, flustered, rushing.

Four long tables of food, punch, claret. An ice sculpture of what might have been a courting couple—or perhaps bears fighting. Melting very quickly. The tables were dressed, she noted. They would disguise anything beneath them.

A servant met her on her way to the courtyard doors. She accepted a flute of champagne, pretended to drink. A swarm of wide-skirted women hovered between Leila and the exit; she strolled idly around them, noting their calculated silence, the snap of their fans. Leila smiled and nodded as she passed.

Finally in place. She took another sip of the champagne—this one real; she was damnably thirsty—and waited. If Johnson was here, he would not be long. He knew that her time was expensive.

She turned away the next man who asked her to dance, and then the third. She fluttered her fan and pleaded the heat, and sent them both off for punch. It had the longest queue.

Over there, by the entrance, she took note of the be-wigged and ribboned dandy that was Che, flirting amicably with an infatuated matron. Poor woman. Che Rogelio could charm the devil if he wished; she had seen it time and again. The dashing adventurer, the exquisite lord, who appeared and disappeared at whim. The matron risked her reputation for naught; Che was examining her emeralds, not her décolletage.

Leila felt her lips curve, the driest smile. Che looked up, found her eyes. Without interrupting his tête-à-tête, he raised his eyebrows. *Has he come?*

Leila shook her head. *Not yet.*

He turned back to his matron and she to her drink. They did not mingle on assignment unless previously agreed. He was here as her watchdog, nothing more or less. Should the circumstances grow truly out of hand, she would signal, he would extract her, and they would depart.


He saw her long before she saw him.

She faced away from him, walking slowly across the crowded floor. Ronan couldn't say precisely what it was about her that drew his eye: From behind she appeared much as all the other ladies around her, fluffed and flounced, a tower of floured hair and too many ruffles. Perhaps it was only the color of her gown, exotic coral in a sea of marzipan peach and blue and white.

But . . . there was her back, trim and straight. Her neck, with a small, secret wisp of blond hair that escaped her wig, curled against her nape. Her skirts, barely swaying, as if she moved through water and not a mass of drunken Englishmen. Her skin . . . not the dull, flat white he was used to seeing here; beneath the powder her cast was warmer, more golden.

He'd never seen a gentlewoman kissed by the sun.

When she slipped behind a trio of lords, Ronan actually turned his head to keep her in view. A glimpse of color— he had found her again. She was sideways to him now, looking away toward the fountain of champagne. He let his inspection drift downward, following satin curves.

She kept her fan folded flat against her petticoat, her fingers flexed, her wrist quite straight—not the usual manner at all. Ronan recognized that hold. She held the fan as if it were a weapon.

Aye, she intrigued him, the coral-satin woman, and he hadn't even seen her face yet.

The orchestra began something new, a bright tinkling melody, and the lady turned. Against all odds—past the dancers and drinkers, past leering courtiers and countless red-cheeked debutantes, across the great room—their eyes met.

Ronan felt, inexplicably, as if he had just stepped off a very sharp cliff. He stared at her and she at him and he could only stand there, falling and yet still, held in a gaze of clear glass green that seemed to light down into his soul and catch there, illuminating.

He could not say if she was bonny or plain. He had only the impression of her features—dark lashes, winged brows, painted lips to match the gown—but he wasn't certain even of that. The rest of her blurred to colors and shape; only her eyes held steady, so keen and beautiful he felt as if he had been wounded somehow inside, bleeding hurt and rapture both.

*There,* said a voice that came awake inside him. *There she is.*

He was falling. He was still.

"Laird."

With great force of will, Ronan looked away. The world turned back into itself, a hot teeming room and auld Baird before him, sweating in his Sunday waistcoat.

"He's no' here, laird," said the man. "We've searched the place over. No doubt he'd heard ye'd come."

"No doubt."

Ronan took a deep breath to clear his head; he needed his focus tonight. Too much depended upon him now to lose his center. Too many hopes, too many plans.

"We await your word," said Baird quietly.

"Tell the others we're done. Lamont won't come now."

"Aye, laird."

In spite of himself, Ronan glanced back to where the lady had stood. There was a flash of sudden coral, brilliant with torchlight, as she walked out the French doors that led to the duke's garden. Alone.

*There she is.*

In the gilded heat of the ballroom, between the many ghosts of his yesterdays and the cold promise of his to-morrows, Anndra Ronan MacMhuirich made an instant decision.

"Baird."

"Aye?"

"On second thought, give the room another sweep. I'll join you soon."

And he shouldered his way through the crowd, follow-ing the woman in coral.

# CHAPTER THREE

Leila walked quickly out of the ballroom and into the violet dusk of the garden. She was moving because she had to move; she was walking because she could not stand still.

People were turning to look—slow down, slow down. She did not need attention now. Glancing figures in the shadows, phantom faces, the glitter of diamonds like fireflies in the dark. But she did not slow. Her heart was racing and her hands were trembling. She felt rather ill, as if her corset had been cinched too tight.

Of all the queer notions, of all the nights to come undone—

She could close her eyes and still see him. The man in the ballroom, the stranger watching her . . .

She'd never seen a man so truly, fiercely handsome. She'd never seen a face like his, clean carved lines and smoky shadows, the glint of his lashes and eyes of such devilish deep blue. He might have stepped to life from a Renaissance portrait, a painted prince of sapphire and gold, jeweled colors over jet. She had been turning, preparing to traverse the room yet again, and then . . .

Then she had seen him, by himself across the chamber, leaning against one of those ridiculous pillars with his arms crossed, unsmiling. A short wig and tailored elegance; he was done up in black, no velvet, no gaudy lace, watching her with utter concentration. As if he knew her. As if she knew him.

And the oddest chill had come over her, a most peculiar weakness in her limbs. For an instant—suspended there in sapphire—

The gravel was noisy, just as she had predicted. Leila rounded a corner, heard voices, and instinctively turned the other direction. She needed air, that was all. A few minutes in the November calm to find her composure, to breathe and think and remember who and what she was.

She found a gazebo of whitewashed lattice, a vine of barren ivy buried through it with lavish devotion. There was a bench inside, almost lost to the night, no one about but crickets and owls. She sat down gratefully, peeled off her shoes, and began to massage her sore feet.

Che would follow soon. She needed to consider what she'd say.

*I'm fine. It was too warm. Too many beaus. Too many eyes. I'm fine.*

Fine.

The cold air was like truth, a hard burn in her chest. She inhaled deeply, as much as she could hold, letting it out again in a silent hiss.

Silly chit, to lose her head over gold-tipped lashes and a square jaw.

The chant of the owl grew louder and then soft; lovers' whispers sidled by, not very near. And then, beneath the ghostly refrain of music still drifting from the ballroom, she heard footsteps. They paused and picked up again, coming ever closer, ending at the stairs to the gazebo.

Well. That hadn't taken long.

Leila didn't bother to look up from her foot.

"No," she said to her stockinged toes. "He did not come."

"I see," said a deep, sardonic voice. "Shall I offer commiseration or felicitation?"

Her hands stilled. She exhaled a single breath, very shallow, and looked up—and yes—oh, yes, curse it, it was he.

In the tame forest of the garden, the man seemed much larger than before, almost imposing. The fading light should have softened him but instead had the opposite effect: black coat, black breeches and stockings and shoes; against the frilled white gazebo he was completely austere. Formidable. His gaze held hers, and the same singular vertigo she had felt in the ballroom threatened.

With his long lashes and devil blue eyes, he seemed to see right through her, as if she were made of rice paper, or ice.

Leila forced her fingers to relax, tucking her feet beneath her. The air blew cool across her ankles. He seemed to notice; his lips kept the faintest smile.

"Neither, I should think," she said, with more assurance than she felt. "He will come soon."

The smile vanished. "Madam. Forgive me." The man looked down. "Perhaps you dropped this on the path?"

Her fan. She looked at it cradled in his hands. Her heart began to beat harder.

"Yes. Thank you," she said, and held out her open palm.

He hesitated, then unfurled it. "A most unusual design." The feathers nodded and waved. He turned and held them up to the light, ignoring her hand. One lean finger found the steel spine inserted in the center; he touched it cautiously, a bare prick.

It would draw blood. She had filed the point herself.

He glanced back at her, his brows lifted.

"It is the fashion in Spain," she said steadily.

"Spain," he murmured, and the smile returned.

"To guard against scoundrels."

"Of course." He closed it gently. "What is a lady without her fan?"

"Sadly defenseless," Leila said, and stood up to take it from his hand. "I thank you again, sir. Good evening."

But he was blocking the exit and showed no inclination to do otherwise, only stood there with his taut smile and a slanting, sideways look, watching her as if he expected her to say or do something more. The breeze settled just as the moon broke free of the clouds, rising ivory over the breadth of his shoulders. He was haloed in light, wild and plain and handsome at once, focused entirely on her. Leila felt, amazingly, a flush begin to creep up her throat.

*Don't look at him. Walk away. Leave before Che comes.*

But she did not.

"My name is MacMhuirich," said the man simply, when she did not speak or move or go. "Ronan MacMhuirich."

"Mr. Mac . . ."

"*MacMurray*," he repeated carefully, giving the word a sort of musical note. He waited, then prompted, "And you are?"

She knew what to do now, at least. Leila lifted her hand. "Doña Montiago y Luz."

He took her gloved fingers, bowing over them with full formality. She could see him more clearly now, with the moon through the trees; his coat stretched tight across his back, the black ribbon of his queue tied to a short, neat knot. His fingers pressed very lightly on hers, steady and firm, and she had the impression that this was his will more than his way; nothing about him spoke of the languor of an indoor gentleman.

"How do you do," he said in that marvelous low voice.

"How do you do," she echoed, soft.

The night seemed to grow very quiet. Clouds blew high above them in silent silver tumbles. Even the owl had ceased his plaintive song.

Leila wished, abruptly, that she was not wearing gloves. That she could feel the warmth of his skin against hers.

Wouldn't *that* make a mess of her evening?

The man straightened, releasing her hand. She took a step back, uneasy with herself, and him, and the sudden hush of the world. Where was Che?

"Are you a friend of the duke?" she heard herself ask.

"Not really."

"The duchess, then," she said, with a curious little twist to her heart.

"No."

He offered nothing further, nor did he move away. Leila felt her flush inch higher. To disguise it she concentrated on slipping her wrist through the loop of her fan, closing her fingers around the reassuring comfort of feathers and steel. With her head bowed, her eyes went to his hands, to the straight pale slash of his cuffs, distinct against his coat. His fingers laced together to form a loose cup; he appeared to be holding the starlight, letting it spill around them both.

When Leila looked up again, his expression was harder, darker; it seemed to steal her very breath. Their eyes held.

For a moment—a brief, dangerous moment—she let her imagination fly.

*Ojalá—oh, how I wish . . .*

"And you," he asked. "Do you know Honorine?"

She blinked, and spoke the lines she had rehearsed. "We have a mutual friend. The duke and duchess were kind enough to include me in their festivities. I do not know many people in England."

"How fortunate," said the man, cryptic. "And you traveled all the way from Spain to attend their delightful ball?"

"I am here on tour."

"With your husband?" he asked blandly.

"I fear I will be missed," Leila said. "Pray excuse me."

She wondered if he would let her pass; she walked boldly forward and she thought he might actually let her bounce into him. But he stood back in time, bowing again, not quite so deep as before. The scent of him rose with the breeze, fresh and unexpected, not perfume but something different, something pure and strong and bright.

The ocean, she realized. He smelled of the ocean.

"Madam," he called, as she reached the bottom step.

Leila looked back.

Ronan MacMhuirich said, with great gravity, "I believe you have forgotten your shoes," and held them up dangling by their heels.

He wanted to watch her put them on again, elaborate little pumps striped with pearls—he had never truly noticed a woman's shoes before, never really considered anything about them; he rather thought most of the women he knew wore boots, in any case—but she bent swiftly down. He had a glimpse of ankle, sweetly turned, the arch of her foot. Ronan looked away, up to the sky, up to the moon. Anywhere else.

She was awaiting someone. *He will come,* she had said, and he felt a strange loss tighten in his throat.

Enough, he chided himself. Go on. Find Baird and the others, figure the rest of the night, tomorrow and tomorrow and tomorrow. . . .

But he did not move. Doña Montiago y Luz—was it her wedded name?—had her head tipped down, her skirts spread in glossy folds in her hands as she worked her foot into the second pump.

It was rude of him to stare. But she wasn't looking at him anyway.

What manner of lady removed her shoes in a duke's garden—in the heart of November, in the middle of a ball?

He wanted her to look up. He wanted to see her eyes again.

She *was* bonny. He knew that now, at least. Fairer than that. With her eyes and her brows and her painted lips— with that secret, coy curl of hair at her nape—she was lovely. And she was as beyond him as the moon might be, or the tinseled stars.

The skirts were released; she smoothed them flat again over their hoops. Instead of looking at him, she shot a glance past him, down the empty path. Ronan felt the loss sharpen to irritation. He closed his eyes and considered that, the odd strength of his response, then pushed it aside.

Let it be. Wedded or no, she was waiting for another man.

"Good evening," he said as she walked past again, her heels clicking across the hollow floor.

She did look at him then, just once, those haunting

green eyes paled to gray with the night, and gave a small nod before gliding away.


Leila felt his gaze on her back and made certain to move normally, to keep her arms relaxed at her sides and her shoulders back. Thank God for the dark; her cheeks were burning. The cursed pumps were enormously loud on the gravel—she had seen them in a Paris window and succumbed to pretty buckles and fine color and the shopkeeper's smiling compliments—never again. She'd never wear them again.

She'd never wear them again without thinking of him.

Leila lifted her face to the wind. The cool felt merciful now; she resisted the temptation to fan herself too.

She passed a couple entwined by a statue and pretended not to see them. The woman made a small, startled sound, and the man chuckled and drew her deeper into the night. Gradually the trees and bushes grew tipped with yellow light. The ballroom should be just around the next turn.

"Doña," said a man falling in step beside her, and a hand took her elbow. "Allow me."

In a lower voice, Che added, "How are you? Do you need to sit? Can you make it to the courtyard?"

She glanced at him as they walked, uncertain. This wasn't anything they had planned.

"Leila," he growled, his grip very hard. "Are you going to faint?"

"No," she whispered back. "What's amiss?"

He stopped and so did she; they faced each other on the prim-straight path.

"Didn't you do it?" he asked.

"Do what?"

"You were with him all that time. You never had the opportunity?"

A group of young ladies approached, saw them, and shied back with smothered giggles. Che bowed extravagantly, eliciting more giggles, then took Leila's arm again and led her to a limestone satyr crouched beneath a tree. They waited until they could no longer hear the girls' lighthearted chatter.

Che looked at her squarely. "You never touched him, then."

"Who? Johnson isn't even here, and—"

"The man in the gazebo," he snapped. "I was watching from the arbor. I was certain you'd done it."

She kept her face very composed, though her heart seemed to freeze in her chest, guilt and fear and wonder: Che couldn't know her thoughts; he hadn't seen anything; he had no way to prove anything. . . .

Her voice, when she spoke, was tranquil.

"Whyever would I touch him?"

Che stared. "Leila, that was the Earl of Kell. You were with him all the while, child. Didn't you know?"

# CHAPTER FOUR

❧

She felt her mouth fall open. "*That* was the Earl of Kell?"

Che was shaking his head. "You'll have to go back, that's all. I thought the shoes a clever ruse—well, what else might you have forgotten? Do you have a handkerchief?"

"No," Leila said. "It can't be true. The earl is *old*, Che, older than you. We know that. This man was—younger."

"It was he. I confirmed it twice. I asked the duke himself, in fact."

"He said his name was *MacMurray*."

Che shrugged. "Family name. Or he lied."

She closed her eyes, imagining the man's face again, devil blue eyes and that slight, handsome smile.

No, he hadn't lied, she was sure of it. And he wasn't old enough either. Che was mistaken. Ronan MacMhuirich was no aging despot; he might be a rogue, or a sea wolf, or just a bored nobleman who enjoyed trifling with women.

But he was not the man she was hired to kill. Oh, surely not.

"Yes, your handkerchief," Che was muttering, pinching the bridge of his nose, as he always did when agitated. "You dropped it. You need it. Find a way to soil your gloves and take them off. That will do."

"Che," she began warningly.

"Can you manage it?" He looked up, frowning at her.

"I—" Leila thought suddenly of her dream, of the secret place in her heart that held her hopes, buried so deep sometimes she lost them completely. She thought of her future, and of Spain, and of the life she would have to live there.

"Yes," she said. "I'll be back when I can."

"I'll be near," he replied, but she knew that already.

And naturally, when she returned to the gazebo, the man who was not the Earl of Kell was well and truly gone.

Ronan accepted his hat and gloves from a footman. He unfolded the gloves and tucked the tricorn under his arm, walking out of the duke's mansion to inhale the scent of warm horses and chill night. It was early yet to leave the ball, but there was already a wait for the stables; there was a wait, it seemed, for every aspect of this monster city.

He did not mind waiting. He had, of course, a great deal of time. And there were some things that bore out his patience very well.

Ronan stared down at the cobblestones and considered the memory of a very fine ankle as his men fastened their cloaks and gathered around him in conference.

"An evening wasted," announced Baird in a grumbling undertone. "The devil take the man. Led us all the way to bloody London. And for what?"

"To attend *a ball*," answered Kirk, in disgust. "A fancy ball, for a fancy sir in powder and lace, who had more rouge on his lips than half the ladies there, I warrant. And Lamont never even shows his face."

"That 'fancy sir' is a duke, and our ally," said Ronan evenly. "We need him, especially now, if we are to get the king's permission to fire upon Kell's marauders. Do not forget it."

Kirk ducked his head, blowing frost to the ground. "Aye, laird."

"And not entirely wasted," said young Finlay, after a pause. "I met a lady—"

All the men groaned.

"No, no," said Baird, shaking his head. "Not again, lad. Ye fall in love with a pair of bonny new eyes every day— every hour. Clocks could toll by ye."

"I don't," said Finlay, with all the dignity of his seventeen years. "And her eyes *were* bonny."

Ronan looked up.

"Of course they were," said Kirk. "And, let me see, she had the comeliest face—"

"The finest smile," added Baird.

"The sweetest voice—"

"The lightest step—"

"The fairest bosoms—"

"I didna look at her bosoms," interrupted Finlay, stiff. "But as for the rest, aye. She had—all those things."

"Never fall in love with a Sassenach lass," advised Baird, scratching at his wig. "Summer on the eyes and winter in the bed."

"She was no Sassenach." Finlay was now clearly insulted.

"Oh, no?"

"No! She was from Spain."

"Ah," said Ronan, with more humor than resignation.

"What was her name, then, this Helen of Spain?" asked Kirk, slapping his hands together against the cold.

"Donya Adelina Montiago ee . . . eee . . ."

"Luz," finished Ronan softly. "Montiago y Luz."

Finlay's face fell, so quick and guileless Ronan almost pitied him. "Oh. Ye—ye met her too, laird?"

"Aye." He smiled at the boy absently and turned to meet the groom leading up his stallion. "But I was not honored with her given name."

"Oh," said Finlay, brighter. "Well, I'm sure if she had wanted to—that is, she would have if she had thought of . . . er . . ."

"Aye," said Ronan again. "If she had wanted to, no doubt."


Someone was attempting to kill him.

It was wasteful, tedious business, but it had been going on for some while, and the latest effort—a farce of a mugging in Edinburgh; the pair of men had let slip his name and theirs before he handled them—was so clumsy Ronan had decided it was time to deal with the situation himself.

It meant leaving Scotland, and Kell. He was not pleased with it; his lands held not merely his heart but his soul, if it could be said he possessed such a thing. Perhaps so, perhaps not. He had spun his life around his legacy, and his home reflected that: a glass web in the sun, near invisible but yet there, air and light formed mightier than the sky itself. He had made it as solid and safe as he could, but danger was fast encroaching.

He would not allow danger to come to Kelmere, or Kell.

He would not allow harm to befall aught that was his, not his holdings, not his clan.

There were rumors bubbling. Beneath the thin, slick veneer of society, Ronan knew he had enemies aplenty. His properties were fine, his wealth quite literally untold. He had farmland and islets and a wool trade that surely had the king chuckling with glee for the taxes he paid. But mostly, Ronan had Kell.

Kell, the deserted isle. Kell, with its ruin of a castle, and empty beaches, and deep, deadly waters.

Kell, with the relics of countless merchant ships beneath it, and all that sunken booty, only waiting to be harvested. Or so it was said.

The game had been set in motion centuries past, born of lost ships and legends and a very lethal reef. Greed was eternal, it seemed, and so the rumors of Kell had grown and abounded over the years. Not a month went by he didn't catch some luckless pack of outlaws in his waters, either in distress or about to be. Ronan had no patience with trespassers. He would let them all sink, if only it meant the trouble would stop. He knew, better than anyone, that it would not.

He had hoped to petition the king to fight back with an official force. He had hoped to be able to rely upon more than just legend and superstition to frighten away the endless thieves. But his petition was held up in the rigors of court: The king was *busy*, he was told; he had *concerns*, they said to him; you understand, old boy, the *duties* of the royal house, parliament and Jacobites and whatnot.

And Ronan—quite openly neither Jacobite nor ardent royalist—had needed no one to spell out to him the fact that the king had little inclination to indulge the request of a reclusive Scottish lord, no matter how prodigiously he contributed to the royal treasury.

Ordinarily, Ronan preferred to be left alone. Ordinarily, nothing would suit him better than to be ignored by the great pompous machine that was England. To take, as he always had, these matters into his own sure hands.

But now this. Some damned fool was out to rid his land of its laird, when all that would do was bring rise to another laird, and another.

None of them would be of Ronan's blood. None of them would be siren. Kell would become vulnerable; Kelmere and his people would be left without the ancient magic that encircled them still. His enemy couldn't know that, but it made Ronan's determination all the more unyielding. He was not yet ready to die. It annoyed him considerably that someone else had decided he was.

He even knew the name of his adversary: Lamont, the son of an old rival, a minor lord with lands not far from his own, a pretty new wife, and a great many debts. Lamont, who had, most inconveniently, vanished the very day Ronan obtained his name from those Edinburgh thugs.

All of which led him back to this bitter night, far from home, the steady clip of his horse's hooves over paving stones, the dim burn of the candle lanterns lining the London streets. His men surrounding him, as fierce a Highland guard as any could hope, garbed in old-fashioned capes and claymores and dirks.

Ronan himself carried a pistol beside his sword. He had lived long enough to place his faith judiciously in both the old and the new.

"A mistake," said Che Rogelio, in the tone of a tutor who could not quite overcome his disappointment in the failure of a favorite pupil. "You made a mistake."

Leila lifted her coffee, savoring the rich black scent of

it, the way the morning sun lit the steam to silver mist. "It's easily remedied."

"It's not like you." Che stirred his own with a clatter of spoon, adding another mound of sugar.

"I did not know who he was," she said, for perhaps the hundredth time. "How might I have known?"

Che opened his mouth to respond; the waiter arrived with more cream and he closed it again, glowering out the window of the stylish little coffeehouse.

They had argued this morning. They seldom argued, if for no other reason than Leila guarded her thoughts so closely against him. She had learned long ago that to give Che any sliver of herself was to further arm him against her. But he had come into her room this morning brooding and cross: She had failed him; the most rudimentary assignment, the most obvious facts before her; she had let the earl slide away; and he was old and weary and his arthritis was aggravated by the cold.

He wanted to end the job. He wanted to contact Johnson—whose fault all this truly was, in Leila's opinion—and return the monies given. Go home. To Spain.

Forever.

Leila had refused. They switched from English to Spanish to Catalan, exchanging barbs in the softest of tones. When the chambermaid scratched at the door, Leila had merely gathered her purse and left, leaving Che to huff after her or not.

And so they were here, seated together in the establishment of Messrs. Harvard & Gereau, Che glaring out the window at the rare winter sun and Leila glaring at him. A magnificent plate of tarts sat, untouched, on the table between them.

The waiter departed. Leila closed her eyes for patience and took another sip of her coffee. It was still very hot.

She did miss Spanish coffee. And olive oil. She missed that. *Tapas* and *sangría* and—

"By Jesus," Che swore, choking, and set down his china cup with an ominous *snap*. "I don't believe it."

"What?"

"There—across the street. Look there. It's him."

"Johnson?" She turned, searching.

"No. Lord Kell."

She lifted a hand to her eyes, blocking the light, and caught sight of him—tall and graceful, a heavy cape rippling, a long, easy stride—just as he turned his head their way.

"Oh," she whispered, as the sun slanted down and lit him to lucid fire. He wore no wig today, not even powder, showing hair that was lustrous deep gold, long and shining, mussed with the wind or his walk. He was surrounded by others, listening to someone speak, his eyes distant, distracted. They passed over hers without pause.

Someone new blocked him. Another man, with flaming red hair, talking with his hands in the air, quick, terse gestures. The angry shout of a coachman caused the new man to glance round—and stop short, seeing Leila past the bowfront window.

*Madre de Dios.* It was her beau of last night. The boy with the cravat.

Leila lowered her hand and turned back to the table. She gazed down at the granite top, tiny flecks of pink and cream and black dusted with sugar, then risked a peek back outside. The boy was talking still, actually pointing at her. All the other men turned to stare.

"Dearest Leila," said Che. "You have yet another admirer, I see."

"I thought myself rid of him last night."

"No longer." Che was smiling. "Here they come. Did you know he was with the earl?"

"Of course not. I don't even know his name."

She looked up again. They were all crossing the street in the middle of traffic, three—no, four men, old and young and Ronan MacMhuirich last of all, a purposeful stride and his cape open to the wind like the wings of a hawk.

She felt it the moment he saw her. She felt the power of that look, the attraction. Recognition. She felt it to her toes.

"Excellent," said Che, with resonant satisfaction. "We begin again. Remove your gloves."

"Che, I'm really not prepared—"

"Remove your gloves. You wanted to finish the job. This is our opportunity."

She watched the men come closer, the rattle of a carriage bouncing behind them.

"Leila," said Che in a new voice, his words a soft, slurred string of Spanish. "You need the truth, not me. I'll kill him either way, you know that. This is for you. Either seize this chance or don't, but I'm ready to go forward without you, if it will get us home the sooner."

She lowered her hands to her lap and very quickly pulled loose her gloves, stuffing them into her purse just as the glass doors opened.

They entered the coffeehouse to the scraping bows of the waiters, a mass of windblown men in unsettling dark cloaks, filing past the tables and hastily moved chairs. Several of the customers began a scandalized babble.

"Why, look," said the red-haired youth to his companions, as if he had only just noticed them. "It's Madam Montiago y Luz."

"Indeed," said a familiar voice, silky with boredom. "So it is."

Ronan MacMhuirich stood almost apart from the rest, larger, broader, golden hair and hooded sapphire eyes that seemed both heated and faintly mocking. He looked from Che to her. The expression on his face was very clear.

It wasn't the first time Che had been mistaken for her husband—even her cuckolded husband—but it was the first time it truly aggravated her. By God, who was *he* to toss her that condescending sneer? If she'd offered him the slightest encouragement last night, *he'd* be the one sharing breakfast coffee with her now, and they both knew it.

Leila lifted her chin and stared back at him, her own lips curling.

If the other two men noticed the tension, they gave no sign of it; they were ruddy and silent, standing in place with their hats in their hands. Perhaps they were shy; perhaps they were only admiring the tarts.

"I'm so pleased to find ye," said the young man, oblivious to all.

Leila sent him an artful smile. "Good sir. I had not thought to see you again so soon."

"I missed ye last night," he said earnestly. "I came back with the punch, but ye'd gone."

"I am sorry." She did not by so much as a fraction glance at Ronan. "I was unfortunately detained elsewhere."

"Oh," the boy said, shifting on his feet. "Well. I just wanted ye to know. About the punch. That I didn't forget."

Leila smiled again, this time warmer. "Thank you."

Che cleared his throat.

"I beg your pardon." She stood, forcing Che to rise and the others to step back, crowding further against the dainty tables and chairs. "How very discourteous of me. Please, allow me to introduce . . . but I don't know your names." Now she did look at Ronan, direct and clear. "Excepting yours, of course, Mr. MacMhuirich."

She lifted her hand to him, hoping she gave nothing away, that no one could guess at the fluttery knot in her stomach or the way her heart began to hammer in her chest.

He was arrogant and cold and presumptuous. His eyes were the purest blue she had ever seen. He had followed her and tempted her and discovered the spine in her fan.

She did not want it to be him.

Ronan MacMhuirich did not move; Leila didn't know if she should feel affront or relief. She stood there, waiting with the sun hot on her shoulders, and perhaps he wouldn't touch her after all—

"Madam," he said at last, and moved forward past his men to take her bare hand in his own.

# CHAPTER FIVE

❧

S he had a gift.

That was what her grandmother called it, and that was what the people of her village had believed as well.

Leila had been granted a gift from God. The night of her birth had been wreathed in lightning; it was said that her mother gave her life to the storm, that she had wandered out into the hills to draw the danger away from Sant Severe. Her child had been born in the white light of the Lord: A ring of scorched earth surrounded her body when they found it the next day. Her baby, tiny Leila, lay untouched beside her.

And ever since then, from those few hours after her birth until the day Sant Severe had ceased to be, Leila had been treated with a mixture of both awe and fear by her neighbors and kin.

She knew things. With the brush of her skin against another's, she knew *them*. Their hearts, small things and large, dark and bright—whether she wished it or not.

And each time after the touch, she paid a price. Minor pains at first, short headaches, a rare nosebleed. In the spirit of her youth she barely noted them. But they grew worse. And worse.

The little girl who was Leila began to dress in long sleeves in the heat, headscarves, abundant skirts. Grandmother stitched her a soft army of gloves. The few friends she had melted away, drawn to sunnier skies and freer days than her own.

And so wound her life. She was always shrouded. She was careful never to touch without permission. That was what she had been taught. That was what she had believed, until her father came, and then Che Rogelio after him.

It happened instantly. Ronan's fingers wrapped cool over hers and Leila had the immediate sensation of—

—*drowning. Black light, water above and below and inside her, warm and not warm, safe and not safe. A sea, an island, pebbles and sand and shore. A castle. Faces, gargoyles, carved into cliffs. Secrets and lies and drowning, drowning, foam and mist and endless water, a wilding way, the bottom of the sea, hushed and lonely, no hope no heart can't eat can't drink can't sleep—*

She jerked free and the room began a crazy spin back into itself, windows and candles and dark men around her, color and motion colliding to a strange blended whirl. The sound of her own heartbeat rushed like a river through her head.

Her skin burned where he had touched her. *Burned* like the sparks of a wildfire, a million feverish pinpricks racing up her arm.

Ronan MacMhuirich stood motionless before her, his hand still extended.

Very willfully, very consciously, Leila lowered her palm to her skirts. She had no idea how much time had passed. No one else seemed to move. No one else seemed real save him, watching her with sun-gilt lashes and a shrewd, penetrating look.

No headache. No anguish. Only that odd, brilliant burn, and the subtle tinge of salt on her tongue.

"Doña." Che was there, a hovering shadow. His voice seemed to travel a great distance to reach her. "You seem a bit pale. Are you well?"

She licked her dry lips. "Quite."

Everything righted at once, the clatter of cups on saucers, the hum of conversation, coffee and chocolate and the aroma of warm pastries filling the air.

"Perhaps you'd prefer to sit." Che was holding her chair.

"No." She forced a smile, and said it again. "No. Please. I haven't yet introduced you, have I? Mr. MacMhuirich, this is my father-in-law, Don Pio Rodriguez Montiago, of Barcelona."

Ronan's face did not change. He merely shifted his gaze from her to Che, impassive.

"Sir," he said, with a tilt of his golden head. "I am Kell."

Her heart sank, swiftly, utterly.

"Kell," Che repeated, carefully neutral. "A most unusual name."

"In some places," replied the earl, just as neutral. "And my companions. Baird Innes, Kirk Munro, Finlay MacMhuirich."

Each gentleman nodded in turn. Leila stood back with her hands pressed together and a smile frozen in place. For the first time in her adult life, she could not think of what to say or do next.

Kell. He *was* Lord Kell. He burned and he wore the ocean across his heart like a cloak, like a shield. And she had caught nothing of bloodshed or massacre in him. She had caught nothing but—the sea. An island. And something else something brutal strong but quenched in darkness . . . something feral and leashed.

He was to have been the key to her redemption. He had been her final hope.

She had to make a choice, very quickly. She had to decide.

For an awkward moment no one said anything further. Che sent her a brief, searching glance, then gestured to the table.

"Join us, my lord?"

"No," Leila said abruptly, and laughed to cover her rudeness. "Oh, dear. I meant, we are leaving, are we not, Don Pio? You mentioned how important it was not to be late to our appointment."

"Yes," said Che, making a show of checking his pocket watch. "Of course, my child. I had not realized the hour."

"Where d'ye go?" asked young Finlay. "Perhaps we might escort ye, at least part of the way."

"Far across town," Leila improvised. "Do not trouble yourselves, sirs."

But the Scotsmen accompanied them out to the curb, waited until Che found a hackney, a circle of men against the crowded walk and Leila held fast in their middle.

Lord Kell was more agile than Che; as the carriage rolled to a stop, he opened the door first and handed her in. She had her gloves on by then.

"Good-bye," Leila said coolly, with a fleet, hard spike of regret.

He matched her tone. "Perhaps we'll meet again."

"Perhaps."

His fingers tightened over hers, then released.

"Good day, doña."

Che climbed up. The Earl of Kell closed the door and rapped twice on the wood; the hackney snapped into motion, pulling away.

He was in a foul mood.

It had nothing to do with a lass with glass-green eyes, Ronan told himself. He gazed out the window of their private parlor at the inn, his men finishing the last of their supper behind him. The sun was sinking past the pointed peaks and riffs of the London horizon. He could nearly stare straight into it, fat and orange and ripe.

Nothing to do with her. Not her face, not her voice, with its tantalizing liquid accent. Not the swift, bright flash of anger he had glimpsed in her eyes as she had stared him down in the coffeehouse.

Not her lips, with their taunting, pretty curve.

Not even her hand, so slender and lithe in his own. The bare tremble of her fingers as he held her, quickly stilled.

The warmth of her palm. The sweet shock of her skin, a ripple of heat that had shone through him, so hot and pure as to be almost . . . erotic.

No.

He was disgusted with London, with England. With Lamont and wasted time and schemes and lies. That was all.

That was enough.

The parchment in his hand felt dry and weightless. Ronan unfolded it again, scanned the words in the fading light.

*We have discovered a Matter of Some Import,* read the missive from his steward at Kelmere. *It is a Foreign Appellation connected with a Certain Person of Interest. It appears a Figure of Some Professional Repute is now involved in this Concern, Zurich, Paris, London. Kindly send for Details.*

*Ys.*

*W.M.*

Ronan tore the letter in two and walked over to hold it above the fire until the edges caught. He watched the yellow flames—sulfur green at the ink—devour the writing, releasing it to the hearth only when his fingers began to hurt. The last wisp of parchment was ash before it settled to the stones.

The letter had come to the inn this afternoon, the wax seal apparently unbroken, the coded words unread. William was a prudent man; it was one of the reasons he made an excellent steward. But the message to Ronan came perfectly clear.

Lamont was not content with his petty crimes. He had hired a professional killer to do the job for him, a man who had traveled in to London from the continent.

Ronan smiled darkly at the fire. In Lamont's position, he might have done the same. Every other attempt on his life had been woefully bungled so far.

"News, laird?" asked Kirk, around a mouthful of food.

He turned to face his clansmen. "It seems our business in London is done. We are going home."

He could predict their reactions by their personalities alone: Baird, gruff and approving, who beneath his daunting scowl sore missed his wife. Kirk, disappointed; hotheaded and loyal, he wanted desperately a chance to confront Lamont himself. And Finlay, Ronan's distant cousin, his closest kin. Behind that diffident reserve was the mind of a scholar and a damned fine swordsman. Finlay alone nodded at Ronan's words, but the intellectual in him would miss the monster city.

Perhaps, when all this was done, Ronan would send him back down. Oxford, or Cambridge. The clan could use a man with a bit more way of the world. Especially from its future laird.

"When?" asked Kirk.

"Today. Now." He paused, then indicated the table. "When you're done."

All three immediately pushed back their chairs.

"When you are done," Ronan repeated quietly, and crossed again to the window.

The sun was nearly gone, a half-sliver left, then nothing but a sky of burning opal against the blackened buildings.

Aye, they'd be off tonight.

She was married. And he'd not find her again, anyway.


She had a dream.

It was not the stuff of grandness, Leila's dream. It was a simple thing, small and stubborn in her heart, soundless, timeless, like the truest dreams were.

It was a home.

And nothing grand there either, no mansion or sprawling country estate. Not the villa Che was building in Spain. Only a cottage, nestled back in the woods. She had wished for it so fervently and so often she could see it merely by closing her eyes.

There would be ivy upon it, thick and lush. There would be windows of glass *to see out*, and a cellar *to hide*, and a stone roof *no fires*.

There would be a garden for *not poison* cooking herbs.

There would be a little stream nearby, for fresh water *safe supply*. There would be locks and bolts *unbreakable* on every door, with keys only she held. She would keep a cat, and a pair of large messy dogs to follow her around *first warning*. There would be a special *secret* room for all her weapons.

And, Leila thought . . . perhaps a gazebo.

Just like the one at the duke's.

She would live there alone, and it would be fine. She wouldn't be lonely. She was used to being alone, in heart if not in company. She wouldn't miss—anyone. Certainly not a man she hardly knew, no matter how blue his eyes. Certainly not him.

Leila didn't know yet where she would find such a place, only that it would not be in Spain. No, not there. In fact, anywhere else but Spain, because that was where Che would be.

Che, wealthier than most landed lords. Che, with accounts in Madrid, and Zurich, and Paris and Brussels. Che, who held all the payments from the work of *La Mano de Dios* and thus all the power. Leila had no access to his banks. He had told her she need never worry about money; all she ever wanted would be provided her.

She did not worry. She planned.

One afternoon while he was away at the East End, she had taken the time to open her own modest account under a French surname, pleased to deposit the horde of paper and coins she had managed to scrape together and hide from him—tucked for years in clothing, shoes, hatboxes, and any other place she could find. It was a goodly sum but nothing near what she needed. Not yet.

Che Rogelio did not know about her account, or her dream. She hoped, she prayed he didn't know. Sometimes she caught him looking at her aslant; she imagined him

guessing at her thoughts, sifting through them one by
one like a miser searching for a gold nugget. He had raised
her, after all, and knew her well enough.

Yes, he had raised her. And so she knew how to lie, even
better than he did.

She had feigned illness all the way back to the inn. She
had drooped and sighed and made it to her chamber,
where she sent him off on an errand to find rose water for
her head. When he pressed her for details about Lord Kell,
she mumbled something about the sea and her head and
this terrible pain and *why* wouldn't he have the decency
to go get the rose water when he knew it was all that
would help?

And then, while he was gone, came the note from
Johnson.

She had decided to recover sufficiently to show it to
him when he returned.

*Meet tonight at Theatre Royal, Haymarket.*

They could demand the rest of the payment, Leila
pointed out. They could see how avid the man was.

Che had, in the end, agreed. She knew the promise of
more money would be too tempting to resist. She knew
him well enough too, *La Mano.*

"Late, late, late again," Che muttered. He was standing
beside her on the seething pit floor of the theatre, dressed
as a Cit with his eyes on the play taking place on the stage
above. He spoke nearly in her ear and still she barely heard
him; the raucous theatre was no place for whispering.

Leila was a kitchen maid on her night off, cheap gown
and apron and a battered straw hat, carefully slicing a pear
in her hand.

"If he cancels again, we are done," said the Cit, slightly
louder. An orange peel from a box above landed on his
shoulder, teetered there a moment, then slid off. She

watched it fall, silent. "I am sincere, Leila. This is the last time. He knew the terms when he first contracted us."

On the stage, a garish *comtesse* was screeching at her maid, who ran around in circles with her skirts held too high. The men in the pit let loose a lusty cheer.

"Yes," she said to her pear, beneath the noise. "I understand."

The maid collapsed with her legs in the air, increasing the hoots and whistles.

"You don't remember," Che said suddenly, glancing at her. "You really don't remember what you saw with Kell."

"It was confusing," she replied, honest in that at least. "Colors, shapes. Like no one else. A great deal of darkness."

"But not enough to satisfy you. Not enough to go forward."

"Not yet."

The *comtesse* was fanning herself, then the maid, scolding all the while.

Leila's pear was warm and bruised. She sucked at a slice, then spat a seed onto the floor. Che turned away, the edges of his lips tight.

She spat again for extra measure.

The dreadful play moved into the second act. She watched it without watching it, trifling with the blade in her hand, carving the pear into slow pieces. She yelled when the others did, laughed when they did, just a simple miss out to have a bit of fun. With her lank ginger hair and pockmarked skin, she was as invisible in the crowd as could be.

A thin, pale man began to edge his way toward her. She noted the movement from the corner of her eye, then leaned toward Che.

"He's here."

Like a sorcerer's trick, the Cit vanished from view, swallowed by the audience. She could just see the top of his wig, inching steadily toward the exit. Even before she knew him, he never met the clients directly; it added to *La Mano*'s mystique to remain unseen. Leila handled this part of the business—and, of late, most of the rest.

She turned back to her pear, now little more than a sticky core in her palm. The man stopped at her side, shoved back an exuberant young fop trying to squeeze between them, and ran a hand across his brow. He was, Leila observed, sweating quite profusely.

"You came," said Johnson, in such a loud and relieved voice she nearly winced.

"La, sir," she answered, in her best Cockney accents. "Lil' Sal always comes for you, don't I, luv?"

He dropped his voice. "I wasn't sure if I had reached you."

"Voilà. I am here. Where were you at the ball, Mr. Johnson?"

"There was a problem."

"Yes. The problem was that you were absent."

"No—" He wiped again at his face. "The earl was there."

"The earl was supposed to be there, I believe."

"He nearly *saw* me. He knows—" He choked off, made a strange grimace at the stage.

"Ah," Leila said, understanding. "He knows you. He knows what you do. Yes, I see. That *is* a problem."

Johnson took her by the arm. "I need him to finish the job now. As soon as possible. I cannot wait."

"I am afraid *La Mano de Dios* is most displeased with you." She spoke with the mildest of rue. "You have wasted his time and his talent. He talks now of leaving the country."

"No. No! I'll do what he asks. I'll pay more."

She admired her knife in the candlelight, saying nothing.

"Double," he said, desperate. "I'll pay double."

At least Che would be happy. Che would be—

It came to her then, a plan so clean and perfect it shone like a diamond in her mind. She had it, all at once, the solution to all her troubles—if she played it right, if she was clever and lucky and diligent—oh, it would work! It could work!

"Triple," she said to the man, rock calm.

"Triple," he gasped. "Are you mad?"

Leila smiled and ate another slice of pear.

"God, I can't—I don't . . ."

She waited. The mob around them roared at some dim joke.

"All right, yes, damn you. Triple, then, if that's what it takes."

She bowed her head in acknowledgment. "I am certain *La Mano* will be pleased."

"He damned well better finish the job soon, then. For that kind of money—"

"You pay for the best, Mr. Johnson. You will get what you want."

"God," he said again balefully, staring down at her.

Leila dropped the core and licked her fingers clean. "Your hand on it, sir."

Johnson hesitated, obviously revolted, then reached out and shook her hand.

*—damn her damn him sell the jewels Eva won't notice, she never wears the pearls anyway. It'll all be recovered. After Kell, after the isle, I'll have it back a hundredfold—*

He released her. It was swift and short but the headache

burst through her regardless, blistering white-hot pain, and she gritted her teeth and looked away, swallowing hard, fighting it, fighting. She could not succumb now.

Johnson began to move off. She caught him by the sleeve.

"A deposit," she managed, her fingers clenched in cloth. "Good faith."

"What? Oh." He fumbled with his waistcoat as she forced herself to let go. "Here."

Leila took the pouch, hiding it quickly in the pocket of her apron.

"When will it happen?" Johnson hissed.

She swallowed again. "He may well start tonight. We'll—be in contact."

He gave her another baleful look and turned to go.

Che was eating an orange near the door. As she approached, he tossed it aside, whisking a lace handkerchief from his cuff to wipe his hands. She kept walking. He walked with her.

"Yes, we go forward," said Leila under her breath. "Johnson has agreed to pay double."

"Your nose is bleeding."

"I had to be sure," she said, and accepted the handkerchief as soon as they left the theatre.

# CHAPTER SIX

❧

The road was sodden and rimed with frost; the horses' hooves cracked the muddy ice with each step. It was a gray, sullen day, with clouds that threatened sleet a few hours hence, by Ronan's reckon. November was ever a poor time to travel far north. But north they would go. North to Kelmere, and Kell.

Despite the weather, he felt his heart lift at the thought.

They had passed Hadrian's Wall yesterday morn; it felt good to be out of England, back to the open country with clean air and rolling fields and blue sky. Well—a sky that would be blue behind those clouds. From their faces he thought the others felt the same, even with the wind and cold. It was *Scottish* wind, and *Scottish* cold. It made all the difference.

The hills were growing steeper, long tracts shorn of barley or rye, followed with blocks of forest untouched. It had snowed not too long past, warmed and then cooled again, so that the trees and stubbled crops stood draped in icicles. Flocks of black-faced sheep waded stoically through, crunching on ice and straw alike.

In the distance Ronan fancied he saw the edge of the true mountains begin, jagged and sharp, a splendid harsh beauty awaiting them. And beyond them, the ocean.

It would be tossed now, frothed with winter storms. Black depths, white foam, cold and wild and inviting. At Kell it would hit the shore blue, green by the cove—pale green, like—

No.

He was doing it again, the thing he had privately vowed he would not. He was thinking of her. It wasn't like him to waste his time. And that's all it was: a waste.

The wind picked up, blowing wet on his face. He looked up to the sky, lifted his hand, and watched his glove speckle dark. Hell. Scottish sleet. He'd been wrong about it waiting. They'd have to find shelter for the night.

He turned in his saddle and found Baird adjusting his tartan to better cover his neck.

"New Cumnock, behind us," the man said. "Or Auchinleck, ahead. We'll no' make it to Ayr tonight."

"No," Ronan agreed. He studied the sky again, the sleet slanting down in narrow white darts. "Auchinleck. What say you, lads?"

They had come far, but not nearly far enough. Kelmere hung bright like a promise past the clouds. No one wanted to retrace their path. The horses puffed and sighed and shook their heads, and the four men of Clan Kell pressed onward through the growing storm.

Auchinleck was small, and there was only one inn— more of a tavern with a generous hearth. Ronan had stayed at the Quaichs before . . . long before, but he didn't think the innkeeper would remember him. It was at least a century past.

He was pleased to see the old building still standing, a fresh coat of paint beneath the ice and not one but two stableboys running out to greet them. He ordered an extra measure of oats for their mounts and grabbed his bags, stomped the mud from his boots, and led his men to the entrance, where a wall of warmed air pushed into them as he opened the door.

Aye, just as he recalled. The smell of woodsmoke and haggis, darkened stone and beams and a drowsing cat by the fire. The cat lifted its head and eyed them lazily, twitching just the tip of its tail at the draft.

They ordered food and whiskey from the stout owner, who welcomed them and pulled up chairs by the hearth. The tavern was near empty tonight; the weather had driven most his customers home, the man explained, and Ronan nodded and sympathized over the sleet. He thought he recognized the gleam of this fellow's eyes; the tavernkeep of the Quaichs those many years past had a gaze of just the same cheerful hazel gray. Perhaps a grandson. Or, more depressingly, a great-grandson.

He sat by the cat and stared down into his whiskey and tried not to allow that thought to take hold. Ronan never wished to be a man who outlived his time and place. He had a role; he was necessary to his clan; he was laird and leader and earl. He was myth and fearsome truth. His people—his many, many people—cherished him, who he was and what he was. As long as he lived, he would have that. It would be enough.

"Enough," he murmured to the cat, who watched him with yellow eyes, never blinking.

But so many friends and kin were gone. So many men and women precious to him, now dust in their graves. Only Ronan was left to live on. And on.

He was glad that he had never fallen in love. He was glad he'd never had the chance to outlive a wife.

An image of a face flashed before him, delicate fey and regal green eyes.

No, damn it all. He was glad.

His men ate bread and stew, exchanging comments with their host on the weather, the roads, and the likelihood of morning snow. Ronan didn't even pretend to eat; he tried a taste of the whiskey instead. It burned across his tongue, shaded of peat and Highland mist.

No doubt it was the sleet that dredged up this tiresome gloom. He was not usually given to melancholy.

He sipped more of the whiskey. Firelight danced bronze across the surface, a slide of colors between his palms. He hadn't indulged in liquor in a very long while. He was pleased suddenly that it came to this, this liquid smoke in his cup, a trace of home at last.

His men settled down by the fire, sinking into their capes and plaids. In a hundred years the Quaichs still had no private rooms to let. Ronan sat and listened as the inn fell deeper and deeper into the night, the silence broken only by Finlay's muffled snores.

The laird and the cat chose to stay awake together, guarding against the dark.


It was snowing in the morning. Ronan watched it from the tavern steps, a dull, frozen dawn and fat flakes that sifted from the sky. He knew this snow; it would cover everything in deceptive soft layers, disguising mud and black ice to pristine sameness. Still, he thought, all things considered, snow was better than sleet. They'd leave as soon as his men broke their fast. Baird was awake already, his morning grumbles coming clear past the door. It wouldn't be long before—

Ronan turned his head, looking sharply down the road. A horse was approaching at a gallop, no safe speed in this weather. He reached the front gate just as the rider came into view: frost and snow and spattering mud; the man and mount practically slid to a halt before him, both of them blowing white breath.

"Accident," called the man, before his feet hit the ground. "Bloody carriage snapped an axle—there's people 'urt—"

"How far?" Ronan asked.

The man was trying to catch his wind and keep control of his steed at the same time. He seemed relieved when Ronan reached for the reins. "Near four miles. It's a bloody mess, ladies screaming, one bloke's loikely dead—"

"Get inside," Ronan ordered. "Tell the men there. Tell them I'll meet them."

"Aye," wheezed the man, and lumbered away.

The horse was snuffling and wide-eyed, her muscles quivering beneath her lather. She'd still be swifter than taking the time to saddle his own stallion, though, and Ronan swung up on her back with a quick apology, a stroke down her neck before guiding her out to the road again. He didn't run her; the accident was done. It would do no one any good to break the mare's back or his own.

The snow grew thicker, a dense curtain between him and the sky. He followed the scattered prints of the other man's run until they were gone, filled to blank white. By then Ronan didn't need the prints to follow. He could hear the people ahead, a low, keening moan rising, jumbled voices. No ladies screaming, but faint broken cries and the nervous whinny of another horse. And someone—there was someone he could hear beneath all that, a soft feminine voice, calm and smooth, words he couldn't make out, but the moaning faltered and then stopped.

He topped a small crest and examined the scene spread out before him. A toppled carriage on its side in the middle of the road, erstwhile passengers loosely clustered next to it. One horse tethered to a tree, head hanging, two more on the ground. Twin angry slashes of dirt through the snow where the carriage had skidded and veered. And blood, oddly bright to his eyes, scarlet across pure virgin white.

Ronan urged the mare to a valiant trot.

No one seemed to notice as he rode up but the other horse, which twitched its ears and whinnied again. Ronan led the mare to it, dismounted with a final pat. The people were gathered against the exposed belly of the carriage, some slouched against it, some standing. A woman was weeping into her hands next to a figure laid out on the ground. A greatcoat had been draped across it.

"No, do not allow her to sleep," said a voice he knew, and, without the slightest sense of astonishment, Ronan saw that by the far side of the carriage was another woman, her skirts muddied, her pale blond hair unpinned and flying loose down her back with the wind.

The doña. Adelina.

She was holding the shoulders of a third lady propped against the coach, crouching down to peer into her eyes. Other people were talking around her, jostling. One of them, a man, was attempting to force her aside.

"Let her alone," the man was saying. "She's hurt, don't touch her—"

Someone grabbed his coat. "Babcock, stay back, she said she was a nurse, you saw what she did for Hamilton—"

"She's *hurt*," said the man, his voice rising. "Leave her—"

"I know she is hurt," Adelina replied, without looking round. "I am attempting to see—"

The man broke free and lunged forward, his arm raised. Ronan was there before he thought to move, catching the man's fist as it swung out, a solid *smack* of flesh on flesh, then shoving the fellow hard away.

"Back," he commanded, his voice revealing none of the outrage singing through him. "She's not harming your wife."

"Sister," the man muttered, rubbing his knuckles. "And who the devil are *you*?"

Ronan ignored him, finding the doña again through the falling snow. She looked up at him then, her face calm but her green eyes like an echo of the north wind.

"Lord Kell," she said. He didn't know if she was greeting him or announcing him to the group.

"My lady." He crouched beside her, taking in the smear of blood across her brow. "Are you injured?"

She shook her head, impatient, and turned back to the other woman.

"Open your eyes," said the doña loudly. "Madam— what is her name?"

"Glynis," said someone.

"Glynis, open your eyes. Do you hear me? Open them." The woman groaned; her lashes fluttered.

"You cannot sleep." The doña gave her a little shake, dislodging fresh snow from them both. "You must stay awake, Glynis, with your brother. Come here," she directed the young man Ronan had nearly crushed, and the boy dropped to his heels beside them, casting Ronan a suspicious eye. Ronan gazed back in flat warning. The cub was damned lucky to still have a hand.

Adelina poked the brother in the arm, gaining his

attention. "Listen to me. Hold her, talk to her. Do not allow her to swoon."

"How am I supposed—"

"Do you want her to die?" she snapped. "No? Then talk to her, drag her to her feet if you must. She needs to stay awake until a doctor comes." She pushed a lock of damp hair from her eyes and glanced at Ronan. "A doctor *is* coming?"

"Soon," he said, and she nodded and struggled to stand. Ronan took her hand without asking, intending to help her to her feet.

But it happened again: His fingers touched the skin of her wrist past her glove and he felt a tangible shock, real and warm and incredibly sensual. It pulsed through him, held him motionless, and did the same to her. Only her fingers moved, curling in his to sudden tightness, as if she felt it too. She was caught on the ground and he nearly standing; they stared at each other and the heat of her was like the sun to him, like spring thaw past the long winter chill, radiating into him through just this, her hand in his. He felt his entire body flush to life—as if he had been sleeping until now. As if he had been adrift in simple dreams.

Her hair was tangled starlight. Her lashes were brushed with snowflakes. Her lips—dusky rose, not coral—slowly parted. She looked at him with something akin to wonder.

And then softly, completely, there was no one else in the world. There was nothing else but snowfall, and hush, and her.

He wanted to kiss her. He pulled her up the rest of the way with the absolute intention of kissing her, because that was what would come next. That was what would happen, what was *meant* to happen. She rose and stepped toward him in a sweep of mantle and skirts, their fingers lacing between them, and she lifted her chin and he brought up his other hand—

"Doña," called a new voice, and the spell shattered. She pulled free and drew up her hood, color rising in her cheeks.

*No,* Ronan wanted to say, incredulous. *No, come back. Come back to me.*

The father-in-law was limping toward them, using a cane that punctured the muck of the road.

"My child," he said. "How is the lady?"

"Alive," replied Adelina, with a short, self-conscious tug of her skirts. "And you, *Padre?* Your—ah, your leg?"

"Not broken," he said cheerfully. "Unlike the coachman, I think." His gray eyes lit on Ronan. "And you, sir! A happy chance to find you here."

"He has summoned help," said the doña.

"Has he?" The man limped forward. "We are fortunate indeed."

Ronan stood there, silent, unable to rouse words through the haze of emotions that still filled him—passion and anger and rising remorse—as Adelina stared fixedly at the road and the don back and forth at them both.

The woman on the ground broke into fresh sobs. Two men stood awkwardly above her. One stooped to pat her on the back, offering stilted condolences. Ronan turned abruptly and crunched through the snow toward her. He surveyed the covered figure—a man, without doubt—and bent down.

"Madam," he said. "May I assist you?"

She didn't look up, didn't respond. Her eyes stayed fixed on the dead man, on the lumps and curves beneath the greatcoat. There was a large, ugly bruise swelling high on her forehead.

Ronan lifted his hand.

"She is afraid," said the doña behind him, quiet. "I tried to—to help her, but—she does not know where she is."

He nodded to show he heard, found the woman's chin, and, with great will, focused his scattered thoughts. She was older than he'd first perceived, lined and haggard; she stared at him blankly, red-eyed, weeping great, silent tears.

"It hurts," Ronan said to her gently, now touching her cheek. "Aye, it does. I know."

Her mouth trembled, another sob building, but he found it first, soothed it smooth and let it fall back. The pain in her was acute, not just in her head but in her heart, a wrenching sharp ache—he understood that this was her husband, that she had loved him, and his loss was so immense—so black and huge and paralyzing—that in this terrible moment she stood merely at the edge of it, peering down into a bleak and barren forevermore.

"I know," he whispered again. "I know it."

And because he was telling the truth, because he *did* know this pain, Ronan gathered it up into himself, pulled it from her and into him, and his heart was breaking now too, and his head was spinning, but he kept it close and sealed it up, just as he always had. Just as he always did. And the woman closed her eyes and relaxed her lips, and her breathing steadied.

Oh, God. It hurt. He remembered how this hurt.

The woman opened her eyes again. "Michael." She reached out, laid raw hands upon the coat. "My sweet Michael."

He heard the rising commotion only distantly, horses

and men shouting *hullooos*, but it took him a moment to find himself again, to shutter his heart and push the pain away for later, when he was alone.

When he could look up, it was into the face of the fair Adelina, standing above him, watching him carefully. Her hand stayed cupped on her elbow; she did not offer to help him rise.

"What did you do?" she asked.

"Nothing. Cold comfort." He found his feet and raked his fingers through his hair, clearing off the snow. She followed the movement with thoughtful interest. The green of her eyes shone very clear in the winter light.

"You touched her. She calmed."

"You've trained as a nurse?" he asked brusquely, cutting into the measured speculation of her voice.

Her lips curved, wry. "Something like that."

"What happened to your arm?"

She dropped her hand, flexed her fingers. "A sprain, I think."

"Let me see."

She took one swift step out of his reach. "Thank you, but no." They gazed at each other through the falling snow—*he would not think about kissing her, he would not think about tasting her, he would not think about pushing back her hood and pressing his lips to her cheeks and her mouth and the turn of her ear*—until she added softly, "Your friends are searching for you."

And they were. Baird and the others had come, the stableboys, even the tavernkeep. They had brought a wagon and were helping the other passengers aboard, but Baird and Finlay were clumping toward him, bundled and wrapped, only their eyes visible past their plaids.

The doña took note of this as well. She looked back at him, a fine furrow between her brows.

"You have no coat, Lord Kell, not even a cloak. You must be chilled through."

He said only, "I am accustomed to the cold." And walked away from her.

Che had gravely underestimated the roads, the climate, and the people. He had thought they could follow the Earl of Kell back to his little empire, slip them in unnoticed as gypsies or anonymous servants, and out again before anyone took serious notice. Johnson had made another partial payment—half neatly gone to Leila's secret account—and Che's hopes were high to finish the job and be done with it.

Leila had calculated she needed only one more payment. Less that, even; she could tell Johnson it was for expenses. And then she could vanish into the velvet hills of England—or Scotland, or Wales—without a trace.

But *La Mano* had not anticipated the storm, nor the fact that they were so close on the heels of their prey. Nor that the earl himself would ride out to their rescue—just imagining the expression on Che's face when he first saw Lord Kell made her want to laugh, but it wasn't really funny—when disaster struck and the carriage had snapped to pieces.

They were truly stuck now as the don and doña, ensconced in this tiny little tavern with the wind howling outside and the snow building and building, and the earl and his men talking in low voices over by the bar. She wished she knew if he was speaking of her.

Probably not. Certainly not. Why would he?

There were people swaddled throughout the tavern. The widow and the injured Glynis had both retreated to the landlord's quarters with the local physician, but the rest of them were not so pampered; there was food and shelter to be had, but little else.

Leila sat with Che and three others in a half-circle of chairs before the fire, trying discreetly to warm her toes. Her ruined skirts were steaming from the heat and her hair was still dripping down her back. Her wig and favorite hat had been left behind, hopelessly crushed from the accident.

Che kept throwing her curt, irritated glances; he wanted desperately to talk to her, she knew, but the confines of the chamber made privacy impossible. They had no good excuse to escape the room at the same time to the blizzard outside—not that she was eager to dawdle in the snow again, in any case. It irked him that they had to wait, and so perversely pleased her.

He had already taken up her hasty lie from the coffee-house and woven it into a crafty mix of fiction and half-truths, telling the others of a string of misfortunes: how their private carriage had become mired in mud past Dumfries—true—and of a sick maid left behind in Carlisle—untrue—and the don's own valet, her husband, remaining there with her for courtesy—untrue, untrue—and of how the little doña had so wished to keep traveling—*personal* reasons, the don had said, with a shake of his head—and so he had humored her, because you knew how the ladies could be, so impulsive, and now look where his patience had landed them. . . .

That was in the wagon on the way here, grousing to a cartful of sympathetic male ears. But the story would not hold without further details, she knew it as well as he.

Let him manage it. She had other matters to consider.

Leila leaned closer to the flames, holding out her hands. In this position she was able to keep the earl in the edge of her vision, a shadow of amber and dusk, colors that shifted and brightened with the mood of the fire.

She had seen the sea again when he touched her. More than seen it, she had felt it, buoyant and lifting, dark and mysterious and somehow essential to him. He was tied to the ocean, she understood that; his earldom was composed of a sprinkling of Scottish islands, and so naturally he would be of the sea.

But this time her impression of the ocean had been fleeting, swallowed by something deeper, wilder—a hunger in him. A hunger for *her*, shaped in devil blue and burnished gold and a dangerously subtle smile. The glint of morning beard on his jaw, the cool control of his hand over hers, holding her easily, bringing her to him as if it were the most natural thing in the world. He had gazed down at her through sleepy eyes, and she once again had the impression that he saw into her as well, as clearly and deeply as she could into him.

He was, altogether, like no other man she had ever met.

Leila thought now, in retrospect, that Lord Kell might actually have been about to kiss her. And she would have let him, right there in front of Che and everyone, destroying all her plans, all her careful ambitions.

Because, oh—she felt the hunger too.

She resisted the urge to turn her head now and look at him candidly. He was a threat to her, an incalculable risk. She had thought she could juggle them all, Che and Johnson and the earl, keep them tossed and busy with their own plans until she had what she needed and could fly. But the game was changing while only just begun; she was caught hard between her old dreams and this new desire, and *La Mano de Dios* standing guard over her as if she might bolt this very moment.

Leila stared at the fire. Her arm ached.

She could not abandon her dreams. She would not.

The pair of men to her right began to talk in heavy accents of the evening, and of rest, and the certain rescue to come tomorrow in the form of the weekly stage from Glasgow. They stood and crossed to the sole window, trying to peer out past the shades.

Rescue, she thought. She didn't think the stagecoach would do. There were too many of them in need of aid. A coach might hasten the news of their misfortune, but little more.

A look to Che confirmed it. He was scowling at the men.

She wasn't certain how much of her interaction with Lord Kell he had seen back there on the road, but she was prepared to deny anything. The touch had been too swift, she had been too shaken, she had no chance to *look*—anything to put him off the truth.

He would tolerate many things of her, she knew. But not this. Never this.

Che leaned closer. He drew breath to speak just as the red-haired boy—Finlay—broke away from the earl's group, approaching them.

"Doña," he greeted her, and then with a nod to Che, "Sir." He pulled up the chair next to hers, effectively blocking her view of Lord Kell. "If I may ask, how d'ye fare?"

"Well, thank you," she replied, lowering her hands.

"Hungry? Thirsty? I could fetch more cider, if ye like."

"No. All was fine."

"I promise I won't take as long as the punch at the duke's ball."

She tilted her head and smiled, and the boy blushed to his ears. Che Rogelio made a sound like a sigh.

"We're off soon," said Finlay. "And I just wanted to—er, ensure that you're comfortable. If ye need food—or, or aught."

"Where do you go?"

"Not very far. We're off to port. To Ayr."

"In this storm?" She did not have to exaggerate her surprise.

" 'Tis naught but a wee shower to us," he assured her. "There's far worse up north. This is only the beginning."

"Worse," she echoed faintly.

"Why, where were you headed, my lady?" asked the earl, just behind her. She hadn't heard him come up; not a footfall, not the smallest squeak of a floorboard. That was saying something, considering how hard she had trained over the years to absorb everything around her.

"Ayr," said Che, unexpected. "We go to Ayr as well."

"Oh?" Leila could hear the skepticism in the earl's voice, so deep and mellow above her head. "Forgive me, my lord, but have you been to Ayr before?"

"I have not had that pleasure."

The earl moved into the light, one hand resting lightly on the back of Leila's chair. She noticed for the first time that he was wearing a sword, not the ornamental bauble of most gentlemen, but one thick and plain and impressive.

"You might not call it a pleasure, sir. It's a port town, small and hardly worth . . . touring," he finished, with a look down to her.

"We do not go to tour," she said, after a moment. "We seek a ship north."

"There are better ports than Ayr."

"*You* are going there," she said pointedly.

"Aye. But *I* have a ship."

"Laird," began Finlay excitedly, and was silenced by the earl merely lifting his hand.

"What awaits you north, I wonder?" he asked, very mild.

Leila glanced at Che. She regretted now that they had

not conferred; Lord Kell was no fool, not by any account, and Leila was not deceived by the gentleness of his inquiry. Nothing was going as planned. She had no idea why Che had revealed their destination unless it was to force the earl to offer them escort. It made a sort of sense, from his point of view: Che would consider them closer to their target and thus to the completion of the contract—and Leila would have to work all the harder to keep him in check.

On the other hand, Lord Kell now knew that they were in Scotland, that they followed. If they separated now, and then by some calamity of fate he discovered them again on his trail, conjuring some new excuse for being near was going to be close to impossible.

Johnson had said the Earl of Kell knew what he was about, that he wanted to kill him. A man who knew he was marked would question everything, she supposed. Especially flimsy tales. Especially coincidences.

She had traveled Europe in shadow and stealth nearly all her life. She had conspired and schemed with the very specter of death at her side, and thought little of it, because that was simply her world. She had taken money for wicked lives as routinely as other women did for bread or clothing or sex, because that was who she was. It was who she had been raised to become.

But Leila knew suddenly, with every fiber of her being, that she did not want to cross this Scottish lord. That trying him, and failing, would be the end of everything.

She concentrated on her hands in her lap. There had to be a way out of this muddle—

"It is a personal matter," said Che Rogelio to the earl, sinking them deeper with every lie. "Concerning my son, the doña's husband."

She closed her eyes, helpless, waiting.

"I see," said Lord Kell casually. "He is up north?"

"No. He is in Spain. Ill, I'm afraid."

"How very regrettable," said the earl, still in that mild voice that sent a shiver down her spine.

God, she was going to have to intervene.

"We search for a place for him here, to recover," she said, lifting her head. "The cool, the ocean air. Do you see? His lungs are weak. He needs—" She hesitated, seeking the proper English word. "He needs *sanctuary* here, to recover."

The earl had been watching her, the very essence of untamed elegance with his disheveled hair and tawny gilt lashes and heavy boots. At her words, she thought she saw a flicker of blue something behind his gaze, she knew not what. Revelation, perhaps—or just wary interest.

She bit her tongue so she wouldn't say more to ensnare them.

"Can you ride, doña?" he asked.

"All children of Spain ride, sir."

Lord Kell gave a graceful bow to the dark. "Then may I offer you and your father-in-law the use of my ship? We are traveling north, to our home, and may land you at any port you choose. You'll find no finer galleon in Ayr."

She turned to look at Che, who suffered violently at sea. He was smiling and nodding.

"How generous you are," Leila said slowly. "We are most honored to accept."

# CHAPTER SEVEN

❧

It was well noted in Highland folklore the remarkable resemblance the lairds of Clan Kell all had to one another over the past two hundred odd years, each one golden-haired, blue-eyed, approximately the same weight and height—although accounts here sometimes varied; at times a laird was said to be a little taller than his father, or a little wider, but truly, beneath the plaid or cloak or cape or greatcoat, who could tell?

And some auld kin of the clan claimed that the lairds had always looked such, but others countered with tales of redheaded lairds, and raven-dark lairds, all the way back to the great King of the Isles himself, who was known to have hair as black as Solstice Eve.

So perhaps it was only a whim of nature that had all the recent lairds so golden blessed.

Perhaps not.

Only a very few knew the truth, even though most in the clan suspected it and some even boasted of it. But the real secret of Clan Kell stayed tight within the family, trusted to an inner council of men and women that had begun in those long-ago days of that black Solstice king, who had wooed and won a maiden of the sea and named their child his heir. From the beginning there needed to be a circle of protection around this noble secret, and so in the way of their people, the honor—and, Ronan suspected, burden—of guarding the blood of the king had begun. From the loins of those council members, new ones had been conceived, just as new queens and kings and then lairds had been, and they marched together hand in hand across time, across generations, partners in kinship and mystery.

And so had come Ronan, and then Baird and Kirk and finally Finlay, all of them born to their own rules and their own obligations. Family.

And it was family who knew that the man who had no children had become his own son, over and over again. Ronan had reached his fourth incarnation now. A false youth, a swift adolescence; then he could emerge once more as himself, as the old laird passed on and the new began his rule. Over the years he had taken care to always include his true name—Ronan—in every new leader he created. It was easier, certainly. But more importantly, it was his very first gift from his parents, the one piece of himself he found he was unable to surrender to time.

He *was* aging, but it was slow. So slow. He had wondered more and more of late how much longer he could hold on to his role before tiring of it completely.

All he had to do was stay away from Kell. He knew that. Just resist the lure of Kell and gradually slip full into mortal life. He would age as everyone else did. He would eat and drink and live and die, just like all the clan. Just like all the world.

From the deck of the *Lyre*, Ronan looked out at the

snowy wild sea, so painfully beautiful to him, green and gray and rocked. He thought he might as well pluck out his heart as to stay off Kell. He would have to stay away from the ocean itself to manage it.

And he could never do that.

Doña Adelina stood beside him, wrapped in her mantle, gazing out much as he was. Ronan studied her in stolen moments. She was windblown, her cheeks wet, her eyes tearing, her hair lashing about in silver-gold tendrils no matter how she tried to contain it.

There was a look of smothered horror on her face.

He smiled and steadied her with his hand on her back as the galleon slammed into a particularly high wave.

"You might wish to return below," he offered, leaning down to reach her ear.

She did not look at him. She only shook her head, her hands fisted on the railing, her lips set. She looked much like a cornered rabbit determined to face a wolf.

They had left port hours past and were well out to sea by now. The snow had lightened here but not stopped; it hung a cloud of white between the ocean and the sky, and the *Lyre* cut through it just as she did the waves: relentlessly, one purpose, one goal. To head home.

The doña had abandoned the inner warmth of the ship after they boarded. Ronan had watched her emerge from the hold, shaking her head at the bosun at her side, who was no doubt attempting to persuade her to turn around. Ronan hung far above them both in the foremast, his favorite place aboard any ship. He saw with interest that Adelina did not attempt to outreason his bosun; she merely ignored him, half-staggering to the railing of the forward deck, then standing there with the wind snatching at her and the snow parting around her like, he envisioned, Moses and the mighty sea. The bosun stood hunched at her side, no longer speaking, his cap tugged low over his ears.

Ronan spared the man the chill. He swung down the ropes and sent the bosun back to the captain, then turned to greet his guest.

"My lady."

She gave him a single glance. Her beauty, even wind-chafed, sent a barbed ache through his chest, surprising and unwelcome. He had to lower his eyes and retreat inward for an instant, shroud his heart and his mind to control this new hurt, and she looked away again, not replying.

Her skirts blew ruffled past her mantle, rose damask and satin braid, a swirl of blue flowers embroidered across her stomacher in improbable, feminine lines.

He could not help but notice she wore no wedding ring beneath her gloves. Not that he could tell.

In silence they watched the ocean lift and fall together.

The sky pressed low and gray and the waves leapt up to meet it; Ronan imagined it bitter and frigid and foreign to her . . . and yet she did not leave. She clung to the railing as if rooted to the spot. Her hood blew back and she didn't even bother to raise it again. She had hair like sunshine, he thought—like sunlight and stars. In the tavern he had taken unwilling note of it, long and waving, falling girlish to her waist. Damp from the snow, free of powder and hairpins and wigs, it had dried in reckless curls, showing no hint of proper ladylike restraint.

He had enjoyed seeing that, her hair loose. He wished, very much, to see it so again.

"Is it like this all the time?" Adelina finally asked above the wind. "Every winter?"

"The snow, you mean?"

She jerked her head yes. "And the cold. Is it always so cold here?"

"Aye. Almost always."

She closed her eyes and opened them again, glaring at the sea.

"Will your husband manage the cold?" he asked in spite of himself.

"Yes," she said, unhesitating. "He will like it."

Her nose was turning pink with the wind. He found it charming, although he didn't want to. It annoyed him now to find her charming. It annoyed him to find her so lovely and out of place, like a sunflower stranded in tundra.

"And you, my lady." His voice came harsher than he'd intended. "Will you manage it?"

"Yes," she bit out, her teeth clenched. "I like the cold."

Another giant wave; he kept his hand at her back and tried for a less personal tone. "Then you'll like Scotland. We have cold in abundance."

"Good," she said, and then again: "Good."

The snow felt like daggers on her face. Leila's lips and cheeks were raw, and she had to squint just to keep her vision clear. The smell of tar mixed with brine and wet wood burned in her nose, the deck heaved and sank beneath her feet in guttural animal groans—and the Earl of Kell seemed to notice none of it. He only stood at her side, an absolute calm about him, as though he had done and seen all this before, a hundred times before. And of course, she realized, he probably had. She didn't think he even blinked against the wind.

Beneath his heavy cloak he dressed much the same as his men, but *looser* somehow, entirely more nonchalant. There was the tartan—royal blue and emerald and soft crimson lines—but it draped across him in a way it did not the others, emphasizing the muscled width of his shoulders, a foil to the amber of his hair. He wore a plain shirt beneath it, but it wasn't even laced all the way; she had a glimpse of silver at his throat, a chain, polished and intricate. It seemed an unlikely adornment to a man who shunned even a ring.

Leila wanted to follow that chain where it disappeared beneath his shirt. She wondered if it lay warmed against his skin, and how her palm would feel against it.

Oh, heavens. She was mad; she was freezing. She wanted to escape her alarming attraction to this man and go below. But Che awaited her there with all his schemes . . . and this moment of freedom and possibilities seemed at once too precious to surrender. Not just yet.

She closed her eyes. She opened them. She took deep, guarded breaths.

The water leapt and churned. She had never seen waves like this. She had never seen the ocean this color before, the color of mass and weight and easy violence.

Wherever she ended up after all this, Leila decided, it would be far from here. It would be deep within a placid land, nothing heaving, nothing splashing. No savagely attractive men to disquiet her heart.

"Have you decided where you'll go?" asked Lord Kell.

"What?" She looked up at him, startled.

"Which port," he said patiently, with that keen, sidelong blue look she was coming to know. "Where shall we land you?"

"Oh. Don Pio will decide."

"Of course."

He let a while longer pass before saying, "I've heard the Mac Eanruig is considering a sale of land."

She stared out, frowning.

"He has islands, of course." Lord Kell spoke as if she had answered. "Your husband might like that."

"Islands."

"Aye. Like that one."

He lifted his hand and pointed past the snow to a shape she hadn't seen until this moment: dark and distant against the sea, passing swiftly off the bow.

An island. Out here. The very thought of it sent shudders through her.

"I don't believe we need an entire island," Leila said.

"Ah. Well, I've heard the Reverend Guinne has an estate to be had. A few hundred acres off Lochinver."

She held the rail more tightly. If she closed her eyes, the wind didn't hurt as much.

"Too large," she murmured.

"Let me think, then." She felt him at her side, felt the strength of him. They weren't even touching.

"Clan MacQueen might have something," he said. "Not an island. How about the tip of one?"

"A cottage," she said, her eyes still closed. "That's all."

"A cottage?" He shifted beside her, coming closer. "Surely with the three of you and your servants, you'll need a manor at least."

"No." She released the railing and hugged her arms to her chest. "A cottage. Discreet. In the woods."

He was quiet. "Your husband has simple tastes."

"Very."

"Yet Don Pio doesn't seem the sort of man to . . . celebrate the rustic life."

Leila opened her eyes. "Of course not. I was daydreaming." She made herself smile, though she still could not face him. "Please, don't mention this to my father-in-law. He—worries that I dream too much."

The ship gave a sudden lurch and the deck dropped out beneath her. She felt it drop, her stomach dropping with it, and Leila pitched and reeled and ended up firmly caught in the earl's arms. It happened so quickly, so breathlessly, that when it was over she merely clung to him, looking up at him with her feet misplaced and her heart in her throat.

"Dreaming is no sin," said Ronan MacMhuirich, and he leaned down and kissed her on the lips.

She had never been kissed before, not by any man. The most she knew of kisses were her grandmother's long-ago pecks of approval, brief and never lasting.

Lord Kell kissed nothing like that.

It seemed to Leila she hardly comprehended it at first; her lips were numb with cold, and all she really felt was the pressure of him, his body against hers between layers of clothing, his face and the fanned lashes of his closed eyes. The wind seemed to sing in her ears, a divine chorus rising, angels and cherubim and seraphim, and his breath warmed hers and his beard scraped her chin and then she felt him. *Felt* him, truly, exquisitely. Amazingly.

Not ocean or salt or dark, but all those things and him too, his tongue tracing her lips, teasing and sucking and stealing her senses, and his hands were sturdy against her back, and his hair blew like silk across her skin. She saw the ocean and the stars; she felt her spirit grow light and her body grow deliciously heavy, and her mouth opened under his.

He dragged her closer to him.

There was a sound between them, a low, sweet note of desire. It had come from him, or her, she didn't know which; it didn't matter, because it was both of them, a song they made together. His hands reached higher into her hair, then to her cheeks, and he cupped her face and held her still for him, an unhurried ravishment that beat in time with her blood and pressed hard and then soft and then hard again. She couldn't breathe and didn't care. She need never breathe again. She wanted only this, his touch and taste and form, the heat that sparked and burned between them like the angel chorus turned to wanton delight.

And the next moan that came was hers, small and wondrous. Expanding through her soul.

The ship heaved again. Ronan didn't even sway; he only set her gently apart from him and let the snow take the place of his lips, his hands slipping down to rest lightly on her shoulders.

Oh, no. Oh, no—no no no—

"*That*," he said unevenly, "might have been a sin."

Leila pressed both hands to her lips, speechless. Her face felt hot and stinging, as if she had rubbed her skin with rough wool.

"I wouldn't truly know, of course," Lord Kell continued after a moment, releasing her, turning to the rail. "I make it my business to avoid the specifics of what others call sin. I prefer to define my own. Can you forgive me, Adelina?"

She stared at him, his shuttered eyes and half a crooked smile angled down to the water. He glanced up at her again.

"Will you?"

"No." She said it without thinking. He cocked a brow at her.

"No," she said again, stronger. "You should not have done it. You should not."

"I know."

"Then why did you do it?" She was angry; she felt that and seized it for balance, the anger spreading through her, banishing the light and warmth and wonder.

He had kissed her. He had *kissed* her and turned her world upside down, and now she'd *never* stop wishing for him, damn his eyes. Everything was backward, everything was wrong. She needed to be ruthless but only felt powerless, full of longing and fire and restless dismay. The shards of the person she was—the person she had worked for and bled for and hoped one day to become—fell away from her and Leila could only watch it happen, all her hopes shattering at her feet. There was an awful pain in her heart she had never felt before.

She was incomplete now, and she knew it.

Both of the earl's brows raised; his smile drew thin.

"I cannot apologize," he said. "But . . . I regret . . . if I hurt you."

"Yes, fine, very well." Her voice was shaking with emotion; she pulled the mantle around her tight. "We won't speak of it. We won't think of it."

"Perhaps *you* won't," he countered, very soft.

Leila spun around and left him brooding at the sea.

# CHAPTER EIGHT

~

S upper aboard the earl's ship was a stilted affair. Leila was barely able to pay it any mind at first; her thoughts were jumbled and her lips felt swollen and she was certain—absolutely, unquestionably certain—that everyone in the main cabin could tell exactly what had just happened to her.

She had been kissed. She had been kissed by the man she had agreed to kill.

She had kissed him back.

He had followed her in a minute later. She'd barely had time to smooth her hair and her thoughts before the door opened and he filled the empty space, golden glittering and a shower of snowflakes. Nothing on *his* face revealed his thoughts; the Earl of Kell shook off the snow and entered the opulent cabin with the complete composure of a man who knew he was in his element, who appreciated his power and station. Near the corner of the chamber he stopped to confer with a dark-hatted man, the captain, she thought, and then glanced round to find her in the shadows, standing beside Finlay—who was speaking enthusiastically about salmon, or sturgeon, she didn't know what—with her mantle sopping over her arms.

Ronan walked over, took the mantle from her and handed it off again to Finlay, then offered his arm to the table.

"Supper is prepared," he said, as impersonal as could be.

Che was already seated, along with the earl's two other men. Ronan placed her to his right, holding the chair out for her just so, pushing it in again as easily as if she were a child. He greeted the others cordially, nodded to Che, and took his place at the head of the table. It was all very civilized. Perhaps only Leila had seen the look he sent her under his lashes as he settled into his seat, a deliberate, smoldering examination. She could not help but meet that look and then, worse, drop her gaze to his lips. They lifted into that faint, slight smile, a bare acknowledgment of her, of what she was doing. Leila tore her gaze away and placed her napkin on her lap, fighting to keep her color and her pulse under strict control.

The main cabin was not a small space, a monument to both organization and unabashed luxury: a polished mahogany table bolted to the floor, pressed linens and shining flatware, pillowed chairs, oil lamps hanging with etched-glass globes and blue-yellow flames. There was even a crystal vase serving as the centerpiece, a spray of holly and something else, delicate silvered leafy stems, like branches from an enchanted forest.

The earl was close enough to nearly touch arms. If she moved her foot too freely, she would surely encounter his own. From the corner of her eye she studied his right hand—so tantalizingly near—the elegant union of muscle and bone, his fingers relaxed and lean, dark skin against pale linen. He had touched her with those fingers. He had stroked her cheeks with them, and sent her world spinning.

A manservant in a tartan and green jacket bent to pour her wine. It rocked in her glass, glowing ruby, the sultry dark color of . . . blood.

Only then did she look over to Che. And what she saw on his face snapped her back to her senses.

Ten years ago Leila had been successfully poisoned by *La Mano de Dios* for the first and last time.

It was part of her lessons, he had explained afterward. He had been instructing her for months in the subtleties of poison, the textures, the tastes, the invisible smells of hemlock or nightshade or monkshood. At least he had waited until she turned fourteen; by then Leila had already been through the rigors of fencing and shooting and the basics of combat. That he had waited, she supposed, was meant to be a kindness on his part.

It happened during supper one night at their house in Madrid. She had accepted the milk he poured for her without question, as she had a hundred other nights. They had spent the day in his laboratory, dividing chemicals and burning oils for their essence. Her hand was cramped from scribbling notes, and she had a headache already from the lingering odors of their work. When it increased over the course of the meal she made no connection. Not at first.

But it grew. And the food on her plate began to lose its color, blurring together into strange shapes. She had looked up across the table and seen Che's eyes, whetted and brilliant, fixed on her. Waiting.

Leila had stood and knocked over the milk. It splashed across the table in a long ribbon of grayish white, and Che did not move.

She recognized it then: a scant metallic aftertaste, like touching her tongue to copper.

"Orrisroot," said her mentor, still seated in his chair. "What are the properties, Leila?"

Nausea. Dizziness. Loss of sight.

She groped at the edge of the table, sank down to her knees, fourteen years old and feeling her heart slow in her chest like a stone settling to the bottom of a deep, dark lake.

"A small dose," Che had told her, kneeling down with her, pressing a foul-smelling antidote to her lips. "But remember it, child. Trust nothing. Trust no food, no drink. No matter who hands it to you."

And Leila had remembered.

*La Mano* had that same look on his face tonight, an avid, scarcely veiled sharpness to his gaze as he pretended not to watch the earl. She felt a cold sweat break out on her brow.

She had been gone above deck too long. Che had pockets and rings of deadly little powders about him at all times; he might have poisoned any of the dishes, he might have done anything. How foolish she had been, to leave him to his own devices for so long. She had lingered and dreamed and been kissed amid the rough Scottish seas, and now, unless she acted, Ronan would die for it.

The ship swayed and the wine in her glass swayed with it, rising just to the rim, falling back again. The flames in the lamps seemed to burn thin in the dark.

The servants began to serve soup. Leila's stomach was tied in knots; she could not look at the meaty brown broth, could not guess what Che had done. She tried to catch his eye, desperate, but when she managed it, all he did was wink at her between sips. Her stomach twisted tighter.

The earl ate no soup. Was not even offered soup, in fact. He sat there and conversed lightly with his men, no food, no plates before him. There was only an elaborate silver goblet nearby. She tried to remember if she had seen wine poured for him, and could not. Without rising from the table it was impossible to tell if there was anything in it at all, and Ronan had yet to drink. He lounged in his chair with his tartan and open shirt and the light falling dim into his hair, and when he felt her nervous stare he turned to her, too late for her to glance away.

"Does the meal not please you, my lady?" he asked, impersonal again.

"It is excellent."

"You've not tasted much."

"Nor have you," she tried, bold.

He gave her a look she couldn't interpret, half lost to shadow. "No. I dined earlier."

Leila's gaze flew to Che. He met her eyes guilelessly.

"But I see you are drinking." She nodded at the silver goblet. "It is superb wine, my lord."

"Thank you."

"Indeed," commented Che, "I've not tasted anything so fine since Paris. French?"

"Portuguese."

"Ah," said Che, with a pleased little smile. "How unusual."

Leila brightened her voice. "What an interesting—¿cómo se dice? El cáliz—"

"Grail," said Che.

"Chalice," said the earl, and lifted it with effortless grace.

"Yes, thank you, chalice. It appears quite old."

And valuable. It would have drawn Che's attention like nectar to a fly. The silver was hammered thick, with opals spreading a ring of fire around the lip and large purple stones studded beneath.

"It is ancient," Ronan said. "A family heirloom, you might say."

Without looking at Che, without looking at anyone, Leila extended her hand, an unspoken request. She was counting on his manners, on a well-bred gentleman's inability to refuse a lady, and the earl did not hesitate. He leaned over to offer her the goblet, and just as the weight of the silver came down heavy on her palm, she let her fingers slip loose. The vessel bobbled and fell. Wine sprayed a red crescent across the tablecloth.

"Oh!" Leila exclaimed, and quickly retrieved the goblet, ensuring at the same time that all the wine had spilled. "How clumsy of me! Please forgive me, my lord."

He had stood as she had; his fingers closed over her wrist. A sharp, wicked jolt of pure carnal desire rushed through her.

—*her skin like honey, her lips, heat and rose and cherry dusk, to touch them again, to feel her*—

"You've done nothing to forgive," Ronan murmured just in her ear. "Adelina."

He took the goblet from her. When Leila moved back to her seat, Che was watching them both.

He spoke quickly as they said their good nights at her door, hissing at her in Spanish.

"Explain yourself."

"You know what I thought. It's too dangerous here to risk—"

"What's become of your sense, girl? I'd never be so witless. We're on a ship. There's no way out. I always have an escape route."

One of the sailors walked by them, doffed his cap.

"I am sorry, Father," Leila replied in English. "You taught me better, of course."

"Did I? I begin to wonder."

"Good evening," she said, and closed the door on him.


Cloudlight poured in from the window of her cabin, too blurred for true moonlight, too sullen to spread far. Leila undressed carefully in the pearly gloom, wincing as she eased her sore arm out of her sleeve. She had shuttered the lamp left for her use, preferring to know the night, allowing her eyes to adapt to the shadows. After years of training she was used to hiding, more comfortable unseen than seen. Some days she couldn't even remember what it was like to enjoy the open sun.

Her trunks, rescued from the carriage, had been thoughtfully stowed at the foot of the iron bed. Thank goodness for Spanish steel; had the locks broken open, the earl and his men might well have wondered at a noblewoman who carried little fine clothing but an arsenal of weaponry and costumes and herbs.

The ship rose and sank. Past the paneled walls the hull kept up its steady groaning.

In her chemise and stays, Leila crossed to the cabin window. The snow had ended and the sea appeared calmer than before. No hideous whitecaps scraped the sky, no sputtering spray. It wasn't entirely tranquil, but . . .

She touched her fingers to the glass, forming instant foggy halos, then oddly, impulsively, pressed her lips to the pane, imagining that the smooth coldness was him. That Ronan kissed her again.

When she drew back and opened her eyes, she saw him in the water.

He wasn't far out, a head, a torso, strong arms moving and gleaming with rhythmic certainty. He turned to the ship and the tarnished light reflected back up at him from the waves.

Ronan. The Earl of Kell, with his hair streaked dark and his face like marble, swimming unclad and alone in the icy ocean.

Leila stood motionless, staring, her breath coming in small, incredulous puffs. She was imagining it. She was asleep, she was dreaming.

But it was he. She wiped her palm down the glass, clearing the mist, and yes—he was still there, a man adrift in endless black, growing more distant as the galleon sailed on.

Great God in heaven!

The ship had neither slowed nor stopped—hadn't anyone seen him fall overboard? Leila ran to the bed, grabbed her robe and threw it over her shoulders, yanking at the door handle—she had bolted it, damn it, she forgot—slammed open the door and stumbled out into the hallway, leaping the stairs two at a time.

The night wind struck her with a slap, forcing her back a step, but Leila clutched the robe to her chest and scanned the open deck, searching wildly for anyone nearby. There—wan light and shadows over there, by the main mast—

"Stop, stop," she called out, running still, and realized that she was shouting in Spanish.

The hulking figure of one of the earl's men—burly, hirsute: Baird Innes, clicked her mind—turned in surprise, hurried forward to take her by the arms.

"Why, now, what's this, lass? What's amiss?"

"The earl," she panted, "your lord—overboard—"

Another man appeared behind him with a horn lantern, younger and slimmer, dark hair flying.

"What's happened?" he demanded. "Who's overboard?"

"The *earl*." She tried to shake Baird to get him to move. "Lord Kell! You must turn the ship around!"

"The earl," repeated the young man blankly, and looked to his companion.

"Did ye see him go over?" asked Baird, intent.

"No—no, I saw him from my window—he is trying to swim, to stay afloat—"

"Now, lass." Baird's expression had relaxed; he adopted a soothing tone. "I dinna ken what ye saw, but it was no' the earl. We've seals aplenty here in the isles, they follow the ships for scraps. By night ye might well think—"

Leila wrenched from his hold. "It was no seal. I know what I saw. He's out there right now, and you *must* turn back for him—hurry!"

Again the two men exchanged looks.

"Don't you understand?" Her robe flapped behind her with the wind, a silk bird ready to tear off into the sky. "It is *cold*. He is *lost*. He will *die*. You must return for him!"

"Kirk," said Baird. "Go on to the laird's quarters. See if he's there."

"Aye," said the other, and ducked around them both.

"I can show you where he was," she said, moving toward the rail. "Where I saw him last—"

"No, no." The man had her by the elbow. "Wait here a bit, lass. The deck's rare slick tonight."

"But—"

"Just wait."

She stared at Baird and he at her; he seemed utterly rooted in place, as if he would never budge, as if the slick deck had sprouted a man. Leila began to glance around them.

"Where is the captain?"

"Around," said Baird comfortably. "No need to fuss at him yet."

"Every moment you wait, every second—"

"No need," insisted the old man. "Kirk's a swift lad. He'll be back soon. The laird's safe as houses. Ye'll see."

"Listen to me! The water is freezing. At that temperature he won't last more than a few minutes—his limbs will deaden and his heart will fail—"

"Ach, I expect we've a few minutes more." And then, infuriatingly: "The laird's a strong swimmer, anyhow."

Leila made a sound of disbelief, trying to back away. Baird finally broke from his position.

"I wouldna do that, lass. Stay here with me, keep an auld man company."

"Release my arm," she said icily, but he only tightened his grasp.

"Or better, why no' wait in your cabin? It's warmer there, to be sure, and bonny as ye look, you're no' dressed for the weather."

"Not dressed for—*Dios mío*, did you misunderstand? Your *laird* is out *there*, in the *sea*!"

He smiled at her. "So ye say."

Outrage whipped through her; the man had no idea what danger he was in. She knew a thousand ways to hurt him, to bring him to his knees—he was wasting her time and Ronan's—she would not stand for it—

Leila turned and twisted and freed herself, spinning with the robe twisting around her in a neat, quick move that left Baird Innes holding nothing but air. Before he could blink, before he could close his mouth, she whirled around and ran—

—straight into a solid, masculine chest. A very *damp*, solid, masculine chest.

"Hullo," said an intimate voice. "What's this, doña?"

Ronan steadied her, a light touch that grazed the thin silk of her robe and was gone.

"I—you—" Leila stared up at him, words trapped in her throat.

She had *seen* him. She *had*. But here he was anyway, smiling down at her with that warm crooked smile—most definitely *not* drowned—his eyes lashed with shadows, his hair lifting in strands. He had dressed hastily, his shirt untucked—moist, clinging—breeches and bare feet, no stockings, no sword. He was not even wearing his plaid.

A drop of water slipped and clung to a thread of golden hair, splashed down with tiny emphasis on the back of her hand.

"I beg your pardon," said the earl. "I was just washing up. Kirk came and said you needed to see me."

"I—no. No, I thought . . . I thought something else."

For the first time he glanced down at the rest of her, taking in the robe and stays, the chemise that plastered to her with the wind.

"It's not wise to be out here at night," Ronan said easily. "We leave few lamps burning, and there are many hazards to the unwary. Come below with me, my lady, and get warm again."

She turned away at once, not waiting when he paused to say something to Baird, barely catching the man's muttered reply. Kirk was there too, holding up his lantern for Leila to see, and she moved past him with her spine straight, feeling slow and flushed and ridiculous.

Lord Kell caught up. She couldn't bear to look at him, couldn't bear to have him see her. But in the narrow corridor of the hallway he stopped her in place with just the stroke of his hand down her back. A lone lantern on a hook flickered two doors down; it lit blue into his eyes, the shade of absolute midnight.

"Adelina."

She stared down at the planking of the floor. Her bare toes, pressed white with cold.

"Lina." His voice was velvet. "Baird told me what happened."

She crossed her arms, found her sore elbow, and gripped hard.

"I'm sure it was a seal," he said, so close his breath ruffled her hair.

"Yes."

"Were you worried?"

She shook her head. She would not cry. Never, never—

"I'm sorry," Ronan said quietly, and she felt his lips against her hair, a brief, forbidden contact.

"Sorry," he breathed again, his face very nearly touching hers.

Leila shut her eyes. There was a terrible melting going on inside her, her bones, her heart and blood; it was hot and miserable and lonely. Every inch of her wanted to lean into him, to take one little step and be in his arms and feel him again. Be warm again.

He was not drowned. He was not.

"Lina, Lina." He spoke the word like song, making it long and lyric and dear. It nearly undid her, hearing that tender note in a name she had made up.

She fixed her gaze on the chain around his neck and kept it there, linked silver blurred with yellow light.

Ronan bent toward her. His pulse beat hard in his throat, a living desire, a consuming ache. She should leave, she should turn away—God help her, she wanted him too much to move at all. But all she had to do was lift her head.

His lips hovered over hers. His breathing came as broken as her own.

She was a statue, she was stone. She was dying inside.

"Go to bed," Ronan whispered at last. "Please.—Lina. Go to sleep."

He didn't even open her door for her, only walked away down the corridor without looking back.


Leila made it to her bed and sat down, ignoring the shivers racking through her. She tucked her feet beneath the blankets and gazed around the unlit cabin, seeing the black ocean instead. Seeing him in it.

She lifted her hand to her mouth, touched her tongue to the place where that drop from his hair had landed.

*Salt.*

# CHAPTER NINE

~

They came upon Kell in the morning, just as the early fog began to dissolve, suddenly— although Ronan, of course, had known it was there—magically, an island revealed from misted nothing, *terra firma* fixed in a vast cosmos of water.

He watched it appear with Finlay and Adelina and the don, the four of them convened by accident on their way to breakfast, halted by just the supple bending of the light. Without a word, Ronan had pointed to the break in the mist and Kell had done its trick, appearing full and lush and glorious in just the space of a heartbeat.

He heard the doña gasp. Even the old don seemed impressed.

For a while Ronan said nothing. He watched Adelina instead, the expression on her face. The way her eyes picked up the color of the sea, deeply luminous. They were beautiful eyes, by any light. Last night with the lanterns they had appeared more opaque, jade . . . or . . .

Last night. She had worn next to nothing; he'd noticed

THE LAST MERMAID • 323

that just after her eyes. It had taken a restraint greater
than he knew he possessed not to gawk at her, not to pull
her to him, all lace and ribbons and sheer, sheer linen.
Thank God she had the robe, that false-pious little wrap of
purple, more not there than there. It wasn't near enough
to conceal her. He remembered the instant she had run
into him, the startling soft feel of her body against his, almost free from fashion and corsets and stiff resistance. Almost, almost.

Ronan had spent the rest of the night burning in his
bed, trying not to see her again in his mind, trying not to
feel her, that one swift moment blossoming in his imagination to endless possibilities. He grew so painfully
aroused he considered returning to the cold sea and
couldn't risk even that—he had to suffer it, suffer her, the
thought of her sleeping alone on his ship just cabins
away. In her gauzy chemise. Or naked. Wrapped in his
sheets, her arms around his pillow, her hair spread, her
legs bare, long and bare—

Above them a sail snapped against the sky, abruptly
ending his fantasy. Ronan realized he'd been staring at
her. She was done up proper this morning at least, a modest gown of turquoise and her hair pulled tight into a
coronet. Beneath the folds of her mantle he could glimpse
the swell of her chest where the bodice ended, silken skin
exposed, her breasts bound and the faint sparkle of powder, a most *im*modest temptation.

He was growing weary of that mantle. He would like
nothing better, in fact, than to take it off her, to untie the
laces and brush his knuckles against her skin, let the material slip from her shoulders, revealing full that décolletage, the line of her throat, perfume and heat and the
sweet, dark edge of her nipples. . . .

Delicate pink began to stain her cheeks. Adelina kept her face angled studiously away.

"A charming sight," said the don, breaking the silence. "What is it called?"

"Kell," answered Finlay, with obvious pride. "It belongs to us—to the laird."

"To the clan," Ronan corrected and turned, not without regret, to observe it again.

The southern forest was coming into view, pine and birch and oak, some still resplendent with autumn leaves beneath their sugaring of snow. There would be red deer in those trees, foxes and stoats. There would be squirrels hoarding pinecones, and blackbirds singing from the boughs.

There would be starlings in the castle. Tapestries, treasure. His bedchamber. His home.

He had an immediate vision of Lina there. In his bed there, in his arms, surrounded by satin and furs and him. It was so real—he could taste her.

Ronan set his jaw, banished the image. *Goddamn it. She's wed. She is wed.*

The ship sailed on and the forest gave way to moors and scrub, rising cliffs with the surf a white flourish below. The doña stepped closer to the railing, her eyes narrowed; without looking, Ronan knew what she saw carved into the stone, what they all did.

Monsters.

"Gracious," she said. "What is that?"

Finlay spoke again. He had, Ronan knew, told this story many times before.

"Spirits of the isle, my lady. So 'tis said. They guard Kell against interlopers. 'Tis a sacred island, y'see, home to our ancient sea gods. Legend tells they come to life whenever the isle's in peril."

Against the ashen sky, the cliffs were bathed in light and shadow, the carvings upon them vivid as black and white: crude gargoyles and harpies, double dragons and a fierce spitting cockatrice. They writhed in silent warning, shining near as sharp as the day Ronan had hewed them from his island, all those years ago.

*Beasties,* the clan called them. *Our own wilding kin.*

"Legend, eh?" chuckled the don. "Was it legend that carved those creatures? Who lives there?"

"No one. No one human."

The don laughed outright but Adelina did not. She was standing very still against the wind, her lips parted. She looked shaken.

"A pretty place," said the don. "What do you think, doña? Would my son like it there?" He addressed Ronan before she could respond. "How much for such an isle, my lord?"

Ronan smiled, mirthless. "Kell is not for sale."

"Oh, come! All things are for sale. Is it not so, Adelina?"

"Perhaps not all things," she murmured.

"Nonsense. If I've learned anything over the years, it is that enough coin will buy a man whatever he desires."

There was a fine edge to his tone that garnered Ronan's full attention. "Sir, I assure you. You cannot afford this island."

The don looked back at him, smiling, his eyes cold.

Finlay was busy whispering the legend to Adelina. ". . . and she went mad without him, went weeping into the sea, and all her children since have sought love everlasting. . . ."

"No one can afford Kell," Ronan said with deliberate force. "Not for any price."

The *Lyre* slashed by a broken caravel, still trapped and rotting upon the reef after forty long years.

". . . thus the siren's heir haunts these waters yet, chasing off pirates and innocents alike, brewing storms from calm waters . . ."

"Ah, well," said the don at last. "A passing thought, my lord."

The sun was breaking through the clouds, blue sky teasing and disappearing in patches. The cliffs and caravel were growing distant; the course of the *Lyre* made it seem they spun away like a child's toy globe, revealing new woods, the sheltered cove . . . the castle.

Finlay's voice dropped even further. "D'ye see it, my lady? The siren's ruins, there amongst the trees?"

"Yes," she said, thin. "I see it."

"On dark nights 'tis said the siren's heir comes down from his auld home, offering death and woe to any who trespass in his waters. He waits at the bottom of the sea, ne'er eating or drinking or sleeping. Only watching. Only waiting for those who dare risk his wrath."

Lina seemed to wake from a spell, a slight shake of her head. "He waits . . . ?"

"Aye. To defend Kell."

"The *siren*?"

"Not the first one, my lady. Her heir. There's always been a siren heir. There's always been siren's blood here."

She flattened a hand to her chest, as if to affirm her own heartbeat. "But, you said—the siren now—he is a man?"

"Aye. So they say."

Adelina went very white all at once; Ronan reached for her but the don had her first.

"Lina—"

"What is it? My child, are you ill?"

She pressed her lips together and turned her head and looked straight at Ronan, blanched skin and pale green eyes, beauty and clarity and a soul like bright burning truth.

He thought, shocked: *She knows.*

"Come inside." The don began to hustle her away. "Come along, my dear. It's been too long since you've eaten, I fear. I'm sure the earl has a fine meal at hand. . . ."

Ronan watched them go together, feeling his feet turned to lead, unable to move, unable to walk after her and touch her and see those eyes again.

Finlay stood beside him with his red hair blowing. "She didna take the story well," he observed.

No. She did not.


She would not look at him again.

Leila kept her eyes on her plate, on the smoked salmon and capers and runny eggs—on the hot tea with bits of leaves swirling at the bottom of the cup. At the tablecloth. At her own hands.

She would not lift her eyes to him.

He was staring at her, however; she felt it, the prickle on the back of her neck, an excruciating awareness that did not subside. She watched her hands move, pouring milk from the sterling pitcher into her tea. Lifting, a sip. Down again.

There was no food or drink before the earl. She knew that without looking.

It could not be. It could not. She was crazed to even think it—

"How do you feel, child?" asked Che, seated next to her.

"Much better."

"Eat," urged Che. "Try the kippers, Adelina. They are excellent."

"Don Pio," said the earl in an unhurried voice, "we're only hours from Kelmere. Perhaps it would be best if you and the doña came with us to our own port."

Leila looked up, snared instantly in the earl's dark gaze.

"Until you decide where else to go," he continued smoothly. "You'll be most welcome in my home. Take a day . . . or two. And the *Lyre* will remain at your disposal, of course."

"An admirable suggestion." Che was slicing into his fish. Not a sliver of excitement betrayed him at this offer; it was a plum landing square in his lap. "We thank you, sir."

"Not at all," replied the earl, and gave her a smile that could only be described as disturbing, a hard curve of his mouth.

She saw it and remembered the black ocean. She saw it and thought, *How can it be?*

It was laughable. It was absurd. It was as ridiculous as a girl who could read hearts through her touch.

And her gift did not lie.

She had found the island of his visions. She had witnessed the gargoyles, the castle, and the cove. In his mind she had seen the seabed and the glimmering sky of water above.

*—can't eat can't drink can't sleep—*

He was handsome and apt, uncannily so. He was supposed to be old and was not; he was supposed to be brutal but had kissed her with languid sorcery. He had always smelled of the sea, tasted of the sea, been of the sea. And last night—out here, by his mysterious haunted isle—he swam in it. She would stake her life on it.

Siren.

The earl never loosed her from his gaze. He said in his soft, lazy drawl, "I'm certain my lady will find Kelmere quite as interesting as Kell. In the meantime, perhaps we may persuade Finlay to tell you a few . . . less worrisome family tales."

She knew then that he had deciphered her thoughts. That he knew what she knew.

Leila tossed her napkin aside and stood. "Excuse me. I think I must rest awhile."

She was out the door of the cabin while the men were still finding their feet.


She threw everything she owned into her open trunk. There wasn't much to pack, a few cosmetics, her brushes and undergarments and the spare stiletto left under the pillow. The banded glass jar of powder landed against something with a sharp *clink*, and before she could move, a cloud of scented white lifted and spread, settling like ash across everything nearby. Leila coughed and waved her hands about, kneeling to shut the trunk anyway.

"Now I know why you always smell of violets."

She inhaled too quickly and coughed again, looking up to find him past the dust: Lord Kell, appearing much as he had that first time she had seen him at the duke's ball, shadowed and intent, leaning against her closed door with his arms crossed. A gold-painted prince wished to life.

"I have a key," he explained gently, when her eyes flew to the door handle. "It's my ship, Lina. I have all the keys."

"Don't call me that."

"What? Lina?" He said the name like it was music, an incantation, something to bind her in place amid her belongings and the sifting sheen of her expensive French powder. And it worked; she could not move. She could not run or hide or force him to leave. She only knelt there with her hands flat on the unbuckled straps of her trunk, a haze of white fading between them.

He studied her with just a slight tilt of his head. His eyes had that sleepy look, both soft and hard, sapphire blue beneath gilded lashes.

Her heart thudded in her chest. She tasted flowers on her tongue.

"Walk with me," he said, and again it was as if he had woven a charm around her. She thought *no* but found herself nodding, rising to her feet. She shook her hands free of powder and he opened the door.

The corridor was dim. They did not go in the direction she knew but the other way, toward darkness and unlit passages. The hallway was too narrow to walk side by side; she followed him silently, watching his back, the leather tie of his queue with a sort of helpless dread. Why didn't she leave? Why didn't she turn around?

He opened a door—a storeroom, barrels and fat bags of grain, kernels of wheat scattered at their feet—and then another one, with daylight streaming down at them and a ladder to climb. He went first, turning back to take her hand—

—*cold, cold, hungry sea*—

—and she gathered her mantle and skirts, climbing the rungs carefully in her stacked heels.

They emerged on a small lower deck she had not seen before. They were at the back of the ship. The water cut in wide waves behind them, a blue-green wake she could follow for miles.

They were alone. No one could possibly see them here.

"Tell me," said the earl. "What did you think of Kell?"

Leila found her voice, slender as it was. "Your gods are terrifying."

He gave an odd smile. "Not all of them," he said, and lifted her hand to his lips, brushing a kiss across her fingertips. She felt pressure and breath and perhaps it was that she was so very afraid—she could not read his thoughts at all.

"We are an ancient family," he said, lowering her hand, staring down at it. His thumb stroked her skin. "And all families have secrets. Don't you agree?"

Leila nodded, swallowing.

"Have you any secrets, Adelina?"

*No.*

She couldn't say it. She tried, and only her lips moved.

He raised his other hand to spread his fingers against her cheek, giving her a look that made her throat close. She felt calluses, cool skin. Burn.

"Aye, everyone has secrets," he murmured, and with just that simple touch brought her face to his, a fleeting kiss. "Perhaps we might keep each other's."

*No.*

But if he could read her thoughts now he didn't care; after a moment's hesitation the kiss abruptly deepened and the burn became a starburst, a pinwheel of light behind her eyes. His arms came around her and his tongue found hers, an advance, retreat, his body hard as iron, nearly as cold. She was trapped and bent with the strength of his will, his hand cradled behind her head and the other firm at her waist. There was nothing languid about this kiss; it was power and force and painful pleasure. He showed no mercy, held her and scorched her with his mouth over and over, drawing the air from her lungs, her life, into him.

Leila put her palms on his shoulders and pressed her

fingers into his plaid. She didn't want to kiss him. Oh, she didn't want him to stop.

When she was weak and dizzy and her knees no longer held her, when she thought she might die of bliss and fear—he finished it. He drew back carefully, still supporting her, a spark of something lost and unsettled in his eyes. They stayed like that a long minute, panting together, the wind teasing gold from his queue and billowing her hooped skirts out toward the sea.

"Tell me of your husband," he said roughly.

Leila shook her head.

His hand tightened in her hair. "*Lina.*"

"Kind," she managed in a broken voice. She felt tears gather hot, threatening disgrace. "A good heart."

"Does he love you?"

"Yes." But it sounded false, even to her.

"He let you go," said the earl, harsh. "He let you leave Spain, and him."

"Only to find—"

"Aye, a home. A cottage. Christ." He released her without warning, turning to scowl out across the water. "You might have gone anywhere else in Europe, but you went to London. To dance at balls and . . . meet . . ."

He did not so much end his sentence as slowly abandon it. She watched the transformation come over his face, a gradual comprehension, his expression lifting, whetting, to become one of sharp arrest.

She had thought she was in danger before. He looked back at her again, and she saw a demon awakened.

"That first night we met, in Covenford's garden. Of whom were you speaking?"

"What?" She tried to put innocence in the word, bewilderment, but it was only a stifled whisper.

"I found you and you said, 'He did not come.' Even if

you thought I was Don Pio, your husband is in Spain. So who was it—who did not come?"

She couldn't breathe, she couldn't speak. A single tear fell from the corner of her eye.

He understood her silence. Heaven save her, she saw that he did.

"The ball," he said, low and awful. "And you were in the coffeehouse. And on the road to Ayr. You've—*always* been where I've been."

She was trembling. She judged the distance from him to the ladder and knew she'd never succeed. The ocean was far closer.

"Lamont," he said fiercely. "You work for Lamont."

"I don't know who that is," she cried.

*"Don't lie to me."*

She tried to bite back the truth, and could not: "He said his name was Johnson."

He held savage and stark and still. His eyes were arctic blue.

Then he moved. Without looking away, without saying anything more, his hand went to her throat, to the ties of her mantle. His fingers jerked against her; the knot ripped free with the small popping of severed threads. Satin and wool slid down to a heap on the deck.

And then, his gaze still frozen on hers, Lord Kell began to remove his clothing.

# CHAPTER TEN

❦

She had her dagger out before he finished unlacing his shirt.

"Away," she said to him, and the sun gleamed along her blade like a slim silver snake. Leila knew how to wield it and knew that it showed; her hand did not shake, although it seemed every other part of her did.

Lord Kell paused, his hands lowering. His eyes went from the dagger to her face. His lips lifted in that dangerous smile.

"Do you mean to kill me now, Lina?"

"No. All I want is—just stay there. Don't move."

"Where would you go? You're on my ship. You're miles at sea."

The wind blew her hair into her eyes. Leila blinked it away, her mind racing. The ladder, the door. Had there been a bolt on it on the other side? Surely so. Surely there had to be something to secure it against storms and thieves—

"Walk to your left," she instructed. "Slowly—don't think I can't hurt you."

Tawny lashes lowered. "No. I wouldn't think that."

"Excellent. Then listen to me, my lord. I do not wish to harm you. I want only to go free. To your left, if you please."

He did not stir.

"Lord Kell!" Her voice cracked on his name. "Left! Now!"

His eyes raised to hers. He did not smile again.

"How much did he pay you?"

He wasn't going to move. He wasn't afraid of her, or the dagger. Her heart was thumping and she felt sick inside and nothing in the world was going to move him.

"Lina. How much for my life?"

"I *said*," she began to inch sideways herself, toward the ladder, "do *not* call me that."

"Stop."

He said it quietly, but the word rang in her ears like a bell that tolled and tolled on one long, repeated note. It numbed her feet, her legs. She tried to pick up her foot and could not.

No! No, she would not succumb to this, not again. Leila clenched her jaw and thought, *Focus!* The wind gusted and pushed her back; she was able to save her balance and then step back yet again. The dagger wavered but the earl still only watched, his face hard and calm and beautiful.

She thought of a hawk floating noiseless on an updraft of air, a savage death held high aloft, waiting patiently for his prey. For a single, inevitable mistake.

"What shall I call you?" Ronan asked softly. "You have another name, I know that. What does Lamont call you?"

She shook her head and got her hair tossed back into her eyes.

Another step. Another. She dared a glance to the ladder; it was getting nearer. She could do it—she was going to do it—

When she looked back, Lord Kell stood directly in front of her. His eyes kept that steady flat look.

"Give me the knife."

Her fingers uncurled. A sound like a sob rose from her chest.

"Give it to me."

He held out his hand and the dagger dropped to his palm. He lifted it, examined it—noting the worn leather of the hilt, the small scratch on the blade from the time she had missed her hay target and nicked the baling wire instead—then he turned and threw it into the sea.

While she stood dumb and staring, he ran his hands down her front and back and sides, a brisk, dispassionate search that revealed the hidden slit in her skirts and chemise, the garter at her thigh that had held the dagger. With their faces close and his gaze locked on hers, his hand opened against her bare skin; he followed the garter all the way around and then did the same to her other leg—but the spare stiletto was stashed far away in her trunk.

He stepped back, his eyes dark.

He took off his shirt.

He removed his belt and scabbard.

He set his boots and the sword carefully aside so that they lay against the pitched wall of the hull.

He began to undo his breeches and Leila closed her eyes, thinking *run, run, run,* but never moving at all, not even when she felt his arms encircle her and his breath in her ear.

They tilted together and fell; the cold water hit her like oblivion.

\* \* \*

It would be too cold for her. Ronan knew that. He held her and waited for the change, for the feeling of foam and light to peak through him, for his heritage to consume him as it always did in saltwater, and then he was his whole self again.

She tried to twist away but he didn't let go, her gown spinning and opening like a lotus flower in the waves. It was cold and she couldn't breathe it; he wanted to hurt her and found he could not: Ronan crushed her to him and followed the currents home. To Kell.

He kept her head above water. He made certain of that, his fingers hard against her throat. He could feel her pulse beneath his palm, how it beat warm and swift and then cool and swift, and then slower, slower.

He pushed her up onto the sandy cove, and her eyes were closed and her lips were pale. Her hands fell limply to her sides, lax fingers and drenched lace. He leaned over her and pressed a grinding kiss to those lips, unable to help that much, and then forced the change to come again, stronger and easier on Kell than anywhere else in the world.

Ronan lifted his assassin in his arms and stood, nude and shining with water, carrying her up the crumbling old stairs into the siren's ruins.

Sunlight slanted across them. She turned her face into his chest, made a small moan.

Alive at least, he thought grimly.

She weighed almost nothing. Most of the weight of her, in fact, seemed to be the turquoise gown, now sodden and trailing droplets and sand.

He remembered the fan with the silent needle inside it, the concealed dagger. God knew what else she had hidden about her person.

He intended, very soon, to find out.

* * *

Leila awoke chilled and with a throat that felt scratchy and sore. It was dark, and she sat up to find the cup of water she always kept beside her bed, her hand sweeping only empty space.

There was no cup. There was no nightstand. She had a queasy lurch of disorientation, of confusion and panic. She scrambled to her knees and then to her feet, discovering the shock of a hard stone floor instead of the warm rugs of her room.

"Awake?" said a voice from the dark, and Leila started and turned, her reason rushing back in a flood—the earl and the ship and the sea—

She reached instinctively for her dagger but it was gone. She felt only her bare leg—she wore nothing, not even her chemise. No wonder she was freezing.

"Don't bother," he said, as she whirled back to the bed. "You've nothing left to hide from me, love."

She groped until she found a blanket and whipped it around her. He had even unpinned her hair; it snarled in the folds as she tucked the corners in. Leila climbed atop the bed and stood ready there, trying to see past the utter black, trying to listen for any clue of him over the muted boom of the surf and the narrow whistle of the breeze through stone.

She felt the tingle of his gaze. He could see her. He could see her in this pitch night, and she could not see him.

"I'm not frightened," she said, but her voice was hoarse and thin.

"Aren't you?"

He was to her right, she guessed about twenty paces away. Leila turned in that direction.

"If you had meant to kill me, you would have done so by now."

"Perhaps not. Perhaps I mean to . . . torture you a bit first."

"You may try," she said with deadly menace.

He made a sound that might have been laughter. "There are different methods of torture, Adelina."

She was quiet, listening. He seemed to be moving closer. She was skilled enough to know how to fight blinded; if he came within striking distance, she thought she could manage his throat or his groin. One hit would have to suffice. Leila knew she wouldn't get a second chance.

"You're thinking of physical torture, of course," Lord Kell was saying in his melodious voice. "But I know of other ways. Tell me, Lina, do you know what it's like to lose everyone you love?"

"Yes," she said.

"Oh?" He had paused no more than fifteen paces away. She thought she could almost see him, large, a shadow among shadows. "I don't believe you."

"I don't care if you do."

"Prove it to me, Adelina. Perhaps I'll show mercy. You never know."

"When I was ten my father butchered my grandmother and burned my entire village to ash." She bounced lightly on the bed, testing the spring of it, judging her kick. "And that was all that I loved."

"A sad tale indeed."

"Not entirely. He died an unpleasant death himself, I heard. Madness. From the pox."

The room—chamber?—fell silent. She took shallow breaths and lifted her fists.

"Who is Don Pio?"

"My lover. My husband. The man who will kill you."

"Something in your tone lacks sincerity, Lina."

"Oh," she said, "I am most sincere. If he finds you, he *will* kill you."

"No doubt." The earl sounded amused. "But he's not your lover, is he?"

He had moved again, switching sides, to her left now. She countered his maneuver, stepping back on the bed, clearing a blanket at her feet.

"No," said the earl, decisive. "He's not your lover. You don't kiss like a woman well loved."

It stung, as she knew it was meant to.

"Why don't we discuss you, Lord Kell? How many women have you seduced and kidnapped and tormented in the dark?"

"There have been so many," he murmured. "I'm afraid I've lost count."

The wind brought the scent of him—or was it the ocean again? She shifted on the uneasy mattress, trying to keep him in front of her.

"You haven't even asked where you are, Adelina. I'm surprised. Usually it's the first thing my victims want to know."

*Not frightened,* she thought, curling her toes into the soft bed. *I am not.*

"Perhaps you've already guessed, then. You seemed so drawn to it on the ship, I thought I'd show you Kell first-hand. What do you think, love? Does it please you?"

"Give me a light," she said steadily, "and I shall tell you."

"Hmm. I'd rather not. I enjoy watching you search for me. I can see you, Lina. Perhaps you've guessed that as well. And so I must suppose you know what I am. I wonder—I really do wonder—how you might have put that together. It is a secret very well kept."

The wind and the fright and the dark—she was growing too cold, involuntary shivers that rattled her senses. The blanket began to slip loose, but she would not lower her guard to tie it up again.

Lord Kell seemed to sigh. "Why don't you sit down? I'm not quite ready to ravish you yet."

"Go to hell."

But the next shiver sent the blanket to her feet.

"Lina." His voice was definitely warmer. "How will you fight me if you catch a fever first? Go on, pick it up. I promise I won't move."

She hesitated, then snatched up the blanket, yanking it around her again with vicious tightness.

"What's your real name?" Ronan asked, softer now, gentler.

"Come," he said when she didn't answer, "does it truly matter to you if I know?"

"Does it to you?"

"I could make you tell me." He was closer than she thought. "You realize that. I'd prefer you choose to tell me yourself."

His voice was so calming; it made her think about the breeze blowing across her uncovered shoulders, and the knot in her stomach, and how her arm still hurt.

"Leila."

"Ah. *Lay-la*." Oh, God, he made it lovely. Her heart ached, to hear him say it like that.

"Do you miss her, Leila? Your grandmother?"

And because he was so calm, and because she was telling the truth anyway, she replied, "Every day."

She sat down on the bed and dropped her head into her hands.

He came silently before her; she felt him without looking up.

"I found a vial of liquid in your dress. What is it?"

"Laudanum," she mumbled. "For headaches."

"A potent drug."

"They are," she said, "potent headaches."

The mattress tilted as he sat down beside her. He touched her, very lightly, his hand on her hair. "Why did you run to Baird last night when you saw me in the ocean? Why did you try to save me, when you've been hired to kill me?"

She didn't answer. She couldn't think of an answer clear enough to say aloud.

He waited, stroking her hair. She blew a breath between her palms.

"Does your head pain you now?" Ronan asked.

"No."

His hand slipped down her back, slowly pulling free the hair trapped in her blanket, smoothing it again.

"Something does," he whispered. "I feel it. Aye"—his hand glided lower, found her elbow—"here. I feel it here." He made a cup with his fingers over the joint. There came a surprising heat, as if he warmed her arm and then her whole body, and it made her raise her head.

"Are you merely being nice to me before you kill me, Lord Kell?"

"No," he said, husky. "I'm never nice to ladies I mean to kill, Leila."

His kiss was soft. Like kissing a cloud, or feeling butterflies against her face. He put his hands to her shoulders and laid her back onto the bed, coming over her, beside her, large and lean, and the feather mattress sank beneath their weight, his forearms beside her head, pinning her hair to the pillows.

His thoughts came to her like a shimmer of distant light: *sleep now she should sleep, let it settle think and come back, she'll sleep safe now. . . .*

There was a pendant on the chain he wore. It lay trapped between them, hard and round and cool. His hair brushed her cheeks; in the dark of dark she fancied she could see the outline of his face above her.

Every touch was tender warmth. Every kiss was gentle peace.

Perhaps he told her to sleep. Perhaps she only dreamed he did.

Leila closed her eyes and, with his lips still on hers, drifted off.

# CHAPTER ELEVEN

᚛

The beach was deserted. Leila stood alone at its edge and stared out in dismay at the endless expanse of sand and pebbles and water. She glanced back up at the remains of the castle behind her, columns of stone and tumbled walls and ice-licked vines buried throughout. The flash of a raven's wing by the lone standing tower caught her eye; the bird dipped and swerved and vanished between arches, swallowed by the utter stillness of the snow-dappled woods past the ruins.

She wore a gown of supple wool that, judging by its cut, was at least two centuries old, yet looked and felt as if it had been sewn only yesterday. It lay slender and sumptuous upon her, pale minty green trimmed with brown sable, long-sleeved and hooded.

It had no pockets at all.

She had found it draped over a chair this morning, along with slippers and a comb. There was no trace of her own dress—or her stays or chemise or stockings or petticoats—or the vial of laudanum. There was no trace of the earl.

He had truly done it. He had brought her to Kell. And *left* her here.

The day was clear and the angle of the sun told her it was still early noon. She was hungry and thirsty but alive—alive!—stranded on an island with no company but birds and seals and the hushed omniscience of the white and dark forest behind her.

She turned and a new flash of something sparkled in the sand by a rock. Leila lifted the heavy skirts and walked over to pick it up; it was a coin. A gold coin, stamped with a laureled king's head and a scroll of Latin on the back. She had seen its like only once before—Mr. Johnson paid his primary fee in such coin.

*La Mano* had wanted to know the source—nothing was worse than marked currency—and Johnson had claimed it came from a small fortune he had legitimately inherited from his uncle, a privateer. When she told Che he had laughed, saying that *privateer* was simply another word for one English society could not properly pronounce: *pirate*. Either way, of course, he was satisfied.

As if the mere thought had invoked it, a ship appeared on the blue line of the horizon, not a galleon but a sloop, sleek and fast and riding the wind toward Kell. She clutched the coin in her palm and watched it come in— could it be Che? Could he have understood already what had happened to her? Was it a rescue, or—

She didn't care. Leila ran to the surf, waving her arms, hopping in the sand, shouting. The sloop nosed close and then slowed, turning her starboard side to the isle. A flurry of activity centered around the mast; Leila saw a skiff on ropes, starting to lower to the sea.

But it stopped. Across the water came a quick crest of sound, men yelling and dashing about. The sloop seemed to give a sudden shudder—but that was her imagination, surely. A ship that size wouldn't . . .

It was listing. Definitely listing, and the men were bellowing still. There was a bright flash of light followed by a noise like a report, one smart blast, and the waves in front of Leila erupted to the sky.

She cried out and staggered back, nearly tripping on her skirts. They were *firing* at her, they had fired a *cannon*, and just as she realized it they did it again, this shot hitting wider, farther out by a cove of trees.

Despite its list, the sloop was edging away, the bow swinging toward the open sea, the single sail ballooning to hasty life.

She sank to her knees in the sand and watched it go, oddly tilted, sailing off to clouds and sky.

Well. Hell.

She sat there and let the breeze lift her hair, her stomach empty and the gold coin still tight in her hand. Damp sand began to stain the green gown dark; the sable at her shoulders fluffed and swept with the will of the wind. She watched the roll of the breakers as they came in, one line after another of slow spooling cream, and, at last, saw Ronan in the waves.

Not a seal. Ronan.

Burnished blond hair and that flawless tanned face, his arms opening and closing across the water in easy cadence. He saw her, seated on the beach. She knew that he did.

He came to the very brink of the surf and surveyed her without speaking, the ocean dividing around him as if he were not flesh but solid stone.

She felt herself rise, drawn forward on legs that did not want to move yet were. Leila halted with the sea hissing at her feet, surging and falling to drag at her gown. She kept her gaze on his face, refusing to look lower than that, to the gleam of his chest and arms and the tapering lines of his belly, or below, God, to that part of him that was like nothing she had ever seen, indigo scales and fins the color of the sky.

"Afraid now, doña?" asked the earl, softly mocking.

She was strong; she was resilient. A shower of fire could rain down from the sky and she would no longer be surprised. She would not retreat now.

"What did you do to the ship?"

His lips curved to a feral smile. "Nothing fatal. A hole in the stern—a somewhat large hole."

"Nothing fatal," she repeated carefully. "They'll limp out to sea until they're stranded and the ship slowly fills. I suppose you are correct. It isn't fatal. Not immediately. Tell me, why do they deserve such a fate?"

"They came to Kell," he said, blunt.

"As did I." Leila opened her fingers, dropped the coin into the clear water. "I remember last night, Lord Kell, and my arm. In addition to this"—her hand lifted, a gesture both short and baffled; she had no words to describe him now—"to—how you are—you are able to feel the pain of others?"

He didn't answer immediately. She watched the sea rise at her feet, suck back, forming an eddy of sand at the hem of her gown.

"Aye," he said at last.

"Is that why you brought me here? To feel my suffering?"

He was silent again.

She nodded, still following the slip of the water. "I see." She turned away, dragging her wet skirts and slippers back up the beach.

"Leila."

She kept going, headed for the line of stairs that led to

the inner keep of the ruins. It seemed she heard him coming after her in no time, brisk footsteps in the sand.

"Wait, damn it."

There was no spell to this demand; she lifted her chin and marched on, tackling the first of the uneven steps, the next, and the next, until he had her by the arm and spun her about.

He looked human once more, a tall comely man wearing nothing but that pendant and chain. In the cool sunlight he shone like a god, all gilt and fair, so truly stunning she was amazed she had never realized it before. That he was unlike her, unlike anyone else. That he could only be magic, gold dust and gemstones and hard, gleaming muscles.

"You blush rather a lot," he said, "for a woman of your trade."

She shrugged her arm free. "I want to be very clear, Lord Kell. I will fight you. I'll do whatever I can to fight you, and I don't care how I die. If you mean to enjoy my pain, you won't have an easy time of it. I won't merely limp off like that ship of doomed sailors."

"They were pirates," he said evenly. "They came to steal what is mine, and in case you didn't quite regard it, they also fired upon you. I believe you gave them a fright," he added, with a hint of that wicked smile. "But they won't die, Leila. At least, not by me. One of my patrol ships will come across them soon enough."

He reached for her hand, and she pulled away. His expression changed, his mouth growing tight, and he took hold of her forcibly, his fingers threading through hers.

It bothered him that she shied from his touch; even as Ronan understood why, it bothered him. He had come to her open and honest with who he was, literally exposed before sun and earth. It was too late to hide himself from her, even if he had been inclined to do so, which he wasn't. She had enmeshed herself in his life, and if she suffered a little the consequences—he could not pity her. He would not.

But he didn't want her to shy away. He didn't want her to lean from him as she was doing now, her almond eyes wide and her chest rising and falling just a little too fast. It touched him in some deeper place, and he didn't want that either.

He asked, "Are you really wed?"

He could see her consider it, weighing truth and lies and consequences, and then a mask slipped over her: Her green gaze shifted, watching something over his shoulder, her lips flattened to a line.

"No."

"I told you last night I didn't mean to kill you," Ronan said. "It's certainly more than you've offered me, and I don't lie, Leila."

She looked back at him, her brows raised. Her eyes flashed, very quickly, over his bare body.

"I don't often lie," he amended, and was pleased to see that blush return.

"Am I to thank you for it?" she asked in a suffocated voice. "You refrain from killing me, but I am to be stranded here instead? You said also last night that you would show mercy. Is this your idea of it, my lord?"

"I believe I said only 'perhaps.' "

She tugged again at her hand and he only held tighter.

"Come eat," Ronan said, curt. "I've gone to some trouble for your pleasure, doña."

He tucked her hand into the crook of his arm and towed her up the stairs with him.

As a child he had liked to imagine what the castle was like once upon a time, when it was new and whole. He could nearly see it today, with the sun shining in pale spears through the roof, and each long window still framed perfectly in stone. There was cloth rippling over some of those windows—medieval pennants or ship's flags, he thought, in faded ghost colors. They had hung all his life and he had never taken them down; he didn't know why. He supposed they had always seemed silent and graceful to him, visible wind to follow on long, dreamless nights.

But Leila glanced at them dubiously, and now Ronan saw them anew: tattered and frayed and a weightless, eerie lifting. She walked slower than ever, inching closer to him. The furred sleeve of the gown he had chosen for her skimmed softly across his skin. Like a wish. Like an invitation.

He could just see the curve of her shoulder where the gown ended. He could just see the fall of her hair against the hood. She had made a braid of it, a thick rope of light, and its contrast to the chocolate sable made him think darker thoughts. Of undoing the braid. Of spreading his fingers through it, and seeing her body—her lovely, willowy body—entirely naked upon his bed. In daylight. Encompassed, beset in sable—

Leila pulled, quite forcefully, at her hand.

He did not release her.

Ronan took her to the kitchen, to where the south wall had long ago fallen away and formed a sort of stepped terrace to the sea, gray stone and clean air and the whisper of pines above them. She paused and stared at the meal he had set out upon the stones, at the blanket and candles and covered plates. The wine, and his chalice.

"What is this?" she asked, suspicious.

"Luncheon," he answered, and drew her forward. "Your luncheon, in any event."

At the blanket's fringed edge she turned to him, her brows puckered. He loosened their fingers and she quickly hid both hands in her skirts. Nervous, he thought, and offered her a heartless smile.

"I thought we might . . . talk, Leila of Spain."

She looked around them at the snowy ferns and shrubs and glistening pine needles that swayed overhead. Her bottom lip jutted out, dubious again; she expected a trap and couldn't yet see it.

"Please," said Ronan, making the request a command. "Sit."

She did so, gingerly, taking care with her sanded skirts, perching upon the blanket as if she meant to spring to her feet at any moment. Her chin lowered and she glanced up at him through her lashes; once more that pretty burn came to her cheeks.

"Does it trouble you, my lady?" he asked lightly.

"Not in the least."

"What a fetching liar you are." He turned and found the tartan he had left by the chalice, made a quick wrap around his shoulder and waist. "But then I suppose you've had a great deal of practice."

She only sat with her facade of distant calm, her hands in her lap.

Ronan eased down beside her, removed the dome from the plate of spiced venison. "I thought you'd be interested to know that your—associate, Don Pio, managed a most effective escape."

Her lashes lifted.

"Aye," he said. "I've been to Kelmere and back. The *Lyre* docked and your don vanished with the rats. Not a very loyal consort, I would think. Baird made a good guess about where we had gone. He told the don you were locked in your cabin with a dreadful case of sea illness, but apparently Pio saw through the tale. He must have jumped ship just as she reached port. I am sorry," he continued, his hand tightening over the silver knob of the dome, "*very* sorry, that I did not get to the *Lyre* sooner to save my people the trouble of hunting him down."

"Safeguard your people," she said soberly. "*La Mano de Dios* won't be caught, and if cornered he will kill without hesitation or regret."

Ronan drew upon his rusty Latin. "God's Hand. How very biblical."

Her lips curled, and she turned her head away.

"Who is he really, Leila?" He moved the plate of venison before her, unfolded her napkin. She accepted it woodenly, not meeting his eyes.

"Leila," he prompted, silky.

"He is the man who raised me. After my father came, *La Mano* found me hiding in what was left of my village. He . . . he took me in."

"Generous. And exceedingly unbelievable."

"It is the truth. He came across the remains of Sant Severe and rescued me. He meant to ransom me, you see." She gave him a level look. "My father was a rich man."

"Who kept his daughter in a village?"

"His bastard daughter, yes."

She wasn't eating. He began to cut the meat for her. "Then why did your father burn it?"

"Because he was drunk. Because he could." One shoulder lifted, revealing a deeper glimpse of honeyed skin as the gown slipped down her arm. She pulled it up again briskly. "I don't think he needed a reason. Don Federico was our lord, and whatever he wanted, he did. Whomever he wanted, he had."

"Whomever," Ronan echoed, his hands falling still.

"My mother. My cousins. Any pretty face would suffice."

He set the knife down and reached out, caught her by the chin. "Any?" he asked, very soft.

"Oh, fear not, Lord Kell. I ran away." Leila stared hard into his eyes, refusing to show weakness, refusing the warm rush of sensation that came with his touch. "I went to the woods. I left her there alone."

"Your grandmother."

"Yes."

She pulled free. The memories were crowding back and she didn't want them: Abuelita and her weathered face, her bright silver hair like moonlight against the cottage door; the horses and the screaming, children scattering to the hills; Federico and the first torch, tossed laughingly upon the blacksmith's thatched roof.

Abuelita pushing her out the back window, panting, *Run, run, my heart, run and hide*—

"But you were only a lass," said Ronan. Leila blinked and came back, startled to find herself seated here beside him on this snowy little island, far from Spain and that bloody night.

She looked down at the plate of cold meat. She picked up the fork—Lord Kell kept the knife—and set it down again.

"Leila," he said. "Don't you think she'd prefer that you lived?"

The fork had sharp tines. It was silver, heavy, layered in roses and vines. Another Leila, in another life, knew how to make it into something awful. Into a weapon, a quick and brutal force.

That was the Leila her father had forged. That was the Leila born on the night of her grandmother's death.

She lifted her gaze to the earl's. He was studying her

with every appearance of casual interest, one knee propped up and his arm relaxed across it; elegant fingers toyed with the knife, turning it round and round in thoughtful circles. She forced herself to watch him, to meet his eyes without flinching, to ignore the flash of the knife and the sly temptation of the fork.

She was not that person. She did not have to be that person.

"It is done now," she said. "It is of no consequence what she wanted. All that matters to me is what happens next. Will you let me free?"

The knife stopped twirling. "No. I will not."

She accepted that with a nod, looking out to the ocean. "Then what *is* next, Lord Kell?"

"Lunch," he answered drily. "As I believe I've mentioned before. And you needn't worry. I haven't poisoned it."

"Of course not."

"I'm gratified, doña."

"Don't be." She speared the meat, held it up to the light. "You wouldn't drag me to this rock of an island only to poison me. You might have done that anywhere."

"True." There was laughter in his voice; when she looked up at him, his face was closed and his blue eyes glittered. "I confess I have a much more diabolical plan in mind."

She shrugged again, pure bravado, tugged the gown back up, and began to eat.

Venison, potatoes, grilled asparagus. Stilton and cheddar. Wine. It was a lovely meal, worthy of the finest house, laid out with dreamlike delicacy upon china and silver on a thick blanket by a ruin overlooking the sea.

But this was no dream. None of this came from the wreck of the kitchen behind her; he must have brought it all back from the ship somehow. And he must have planned it well—the food was cold but dry, not anything hauled through the ocean as she had been. Perhaps he had brought it in a rowboat.

Perhaps there was a boat on Kell. Somewhere.

As if she could discover it. As if it would do her the slightest ounce of good to find a rowboat out here in the middle of the northern sea. She might as well ask him nicely for the direction to Hades, for all the help it would be.

Lord Kell was a mystery beneath the changesome shade, watching her with hooded interest, every bite, every motion of her hand. In time he leaned forward, lifting the gemmed chalice to her lips. "To your health," he bid her, low.

She took the chalice from him rather than drink that way. Self-preservation wouldn't allow her to ignore the obvious; she paused to stare down into burgundy depths, then inhaled carefully. Essence of vanilla and black cherries filled her senses.

"It is safe, I assure you," he said. "Unlike the last time this chalice held wine."

"It was safe then as well. *La Mano* hadn't touched it."

"You spilled it intentionally, my love."

She tried a taste. "I was wrong."

"Dear me," he murmured, with a lift of his brows. "Imagine that. It would be twice, then, that you've attempted to spare me a certain death. You're a strange assassin indeed—else a very ineffectual one."

"If I had wanted you dead, Lord Kell, you would be dead."

"Do you think so?"

She bit her lip and set the chalice down on the blanket. A circle of sky flashed and caught in liquid red.

"What stopped you, Leila?"

She ran a finger around the rim, rubbing warm opals. There seemed to be no better answer than the truth. "I never planned to actually kill you."

"You've done a damned fine job of pretending."

"Yes." She looked up at him. "But that's all it was. I—before we ever met I had decided not to complete the contract. I needed money, so I agreed to accept the assignment, to take the payment—but that was all. Before you could be harmed I would vanish."

"Leaving Don Pio to tie things up, I suppose."

"No. He would have followed me. He would drop everything to follow me."

"How reassuring." Ronan's eyes held hers, ruthless and sapphire dark. "He loves you that much."

She flicked sand from her skirts. "It isn't love."

"No?"

"It's never been love. With him, it's simply—possession. For as long as I can recall, I've wanted to be free of him." Leila gave the skirt an extra swipe. "And now I suppose I am."

The earl was silent. Far down on the beach below, a seal began to bark. The noise bounced up the hill, rolling sharp across the stones. Out in the ocean another seal answered, a lonely sound, mournful and deep.

"I saw a boy once," she said suddenly. "A shepherd boy, in a straw hat and no shoes, and lambs all around him. I was sixteen, and we were in France, stopped at a country château for dinner. He played . . . the pipe. I think it was the pipe. He was walking through the village, playing a song with the little sheep following behind, and the sun was coming past the clouds, and he stopped and looked back at me, and he smiled. . . ." She trailed off, remembering.

Ronan only gazed at her, with his hair drying straight and the plaid a slash of color across his chest.

"He was all I ever wanted." She laughed. "You'll think it so foolish. But I knew it then; if he had crooked his finger at me, I would have followed him with his flock, followed him into the hills and beyond, just to hear him play, or see that smile. Just—to be free, as he was."

" 'Tis a hard life, a shepherdess," said the earl after a while.

"Yes." She touched a finger to the wine, watched the drop that fell back into its circle. "But there are compensations. Trees and grass and clouds. The bare blue sky."

Ronan stood. "Come with me," he said seriously. "And I will show you the sky."

He held out his open palm. Daylight streamed behind him and blinded her with gold; he was man and not and beast and not—an angel or a devil touched to plain earth—either way, his offer was the same.

Leila moved the chalice aside and accepted his hand.

# CHAPTER TWELVE

⁓

The wind at the top of the tower rushed fiercer than down below. She could not understand how it could gust so hard and still leave the caps of snow on the trees undisturbed.

She paced the squared turret with her arms hugged to her chest, biting her teeth closed against their chatter, struggling with the slap of the gown against her legs.

"Leila." Ronan beckoned her to where he stood in the center of the square. When she reached his side, he lifted his arms and said only, "Look."

Up and out and around: She hung like a bubble in infinite blue. There weren't even any clouds so high up, only the sky, pure deep azure straight above that flowed and faded to the edges of the world. No sea. No forest. Only this, the untouchable exile of birds and spirits and the burning sun.

"It's even better if you lie down," he said.

And so she did, flat on her back with her arms still

crossed, the tickle of fur from the hood at her cheek. Ronan sat beside her, not too near, leaning back on his hands.

Nothing loomed above, nothing kept her bound to land. She imagined that the slightest push would spill her up into the sky to blow thin and gossamer like a single lost feather. Feeling reckless, she flung her arms out, embracing open space. It was dizzying; it was exhilarating. Even the wind tasted like freedom.

"Now you needn't bother with the sheep," said Ronan. "Or the shepherd boy."

She laughed in spite of herself.

"Tedious business, sheep," he continued, very solemn. "Believe me, I know. I've got a few thousand or so. They eat anything."

She angled her eyes to him, watching him with blue all around.

"Brush, grass, clover. Dresses, buttons, bottles. Once I had one that ate an entire cake of perfumed soap."

"Truly?"

"Aye. She belched bubbles for a sennight. We named her Lavender," he added, watching the corners of her lips lift, "in honor of her discerning tastes."

She was so beautiful when she smiled. She looked just as he dreamed—dark, dark dreams—she would, the opposite of him, the opposite of what lived inside him, a savage churning boil beneath his surface calm. Ronan made himself return her smile, feeling his mouth draw tight with it, and it was false, because he did not want to smile at her.

He wanted to take her. Cover her, overpower her. Push up the skirts, feel the sable and her skin together. Kiss her and breathe her and join with her here at the march of heaven. Make her his.

Her smile faltered. He heard his own breathing, how it rasped in his chest, betraying him even as he kept his

expression easy. She lay so bright and open against the
dove-gray stones, revealed to him in ways he was certain
she didn't even realize. In the medieval gown, all her
modern padding—starched linen and ruffles and petticoats—was gone. He saw every sweet stroke of her figure,
the contour of her legs, her waist. Her breasts. The pale
blond of her braid, slung carelessly over her shoulder. It
was coming loose at the end, unwinding in curls he
wanted to tangle in his fist.

It had been like this for him from the beginning. From
the moment he first saw her at the ball—in the moonlit
garden, a silver nymph dressed in coral, full lips and deft
grace, the fan and the shoes and the flutter of her fingers
in his—and then later, and later, a willing flame that
seemed always to return to him, a temptation ever present. He had held on to himself because that was what he
had to do. Or so he had thought.

But things were different now. They were on Kell, and
everything was different.

Scrubbed free of civilization, she was fairer than even
before with her ribbons and powdered wigs. She was
wilder here, honey peach skin and glass-green eyes and
the scent of the sea still caught in her hair. Aye, up here, in
the siren tower on the island he loved, she became a creature less tamed, more of salt and sunlight than of the
earth.

More like him.

She was his enemy and his champion. He had her
trapped and smiling and could not imagine not touching
her any longer.

His hand moved, taking up the braid, letting the curls
slip across his knuckles. The texture, the color; it was sleek
and glossy and fine—he was utterly fascinated. She lay
quiescent as he drew his fingers through the strands,

three separate locks neatly twined into one, starlight in the fullness of day. He could count every breath she took, could see the peaked tip of each breast pushing past the gown, how her lashes lowered and sent her eyes to bottle green. She said nothing as he undid her hair, thinking about undoing the gown. It had laces up the side. He took good note of that last night. He had chosen it for color and softness and that short stitch of lacing, because even then he knew. Even then he had dreamed himself here, with her, had made it a mirror to the future he wanted so much.

"You don't speak as the others do," she said abruptly— and so, so slightly breathless. "Your accent."

"No." He combed his fingers through ashen gold. "I suppose it's that I've . . . traveled more."

"Where?" Definitely breathless.

"All the seven seas," Ronan said absently, and with great care spread the fall of her hair across her bodice, stroking it into the shape of a fan, discovering the warmth of her body through the pads of his fingers. His thumb grazed her nipple and he felt the quiver run through her, so he did it again, slower this time, circling and rubbing. Leaning over, he brushed his lips across the firm nub, and he had never felt anything so erotic in his life.

Leila pushed up, very quickly, and then stood. She backed away from him with her arms crossed again and her hair streaming behind her, all the way to the edge of the turret. Ronan remained where he was, unmoving.

"I'm cold," she said in a tremulous voice.

"We'll go below," he offered, calm. "Out of the wind."

"No. You don't understand."

He came to his feet, watching her, the visible shivers that took her.

"Leila—"

"I'm *cold*," she said urgently, almost pleading. "I'm always so cold."

"I can help you. If you let me."

She didn't say yes but she didn't say no either, and so he untied the knot that held the tartan to his waist, let it soar with the breeze as he walked to her and drew it around her shoulders. Ronan held it in place with his arms a loose shelter; she gazed up at him with her lips downturned and that pucker returned to her brow. They stood there together, she bundled and he nude and the wind a hollow ballad between them.

"There," he said, striving for composure but hearing only strain. "Better now?"

Her hand lifted to curl over his. By the look in her eyes he wasn't certain who was more surprised, she or he. He held frozen under this lightest of restraints, steady and still as if they weren't half a breath away from the tower's precipice, so close he need only tilt his head to press his cheek to hers.

"Leila," he whispered, and turned his hand over, bringing both the tartan and her fingers to his lips. "Come with me. Come be warm with me."

Leila closed her eyes. There was panic in her throat, caution and apprehension, and deep, deep inside her a brash demand that matched the ache beneath his words. She should let go. She should pull away. He was a being of song and misted fantasies, but right now he felt like only a man, one with a need so sharp and fervent she felt it as her own.

She was cupped and cradled in his embrace. He stood unclothed, unashamed, the stiff arousal of his body full evident, and instead of turning from him in dismay, she felt more alive and thrilled and welcome than ever she had in her life.

He was saying her name. He was stroking his fingers down her face, tracing her eyebrows, her cheekbones and chin. His thoughts sparked and blended to glimmering confusion, not words but feelings, images, of her and him and the grand bed down below them, and the fire in his blood that fed into hers and joined them in a great flame of light.

"No," Leila said, and pushed forward, away from the edge. He stepped back with her, taking her weight. "Here," she said. "Not below. Here, with the sky."

She brought her arms up around his and pulled his mouth to hers. His fingers lifted, then gripped her shoulders tight—but his kiss stayed faintly tender, like last night.

Leila pressed harder against him. She didn't want tenderness. She wanted burn.

He responded with a groan, finding the curve of her hip, the nape of her neck; he pulled her to him with a rough murmur, a sound she couldn't make out, but in his heart she read it, a hammering chant, plain and stark:

*Yes, mine, now.*

She ran her hand down the satin gleam of his shoulder, warm from the sun or from this fire they made between them. His muscles flexed to steel and he turned them as one, brought them both back to the center of the tower, to that place of infinite suspension where there was only him, and her, and the vault of blue ether.

The tartan drifted to the stones and they followed it, the wind now not so chilled, the stones cushioned with the colors of his clan. He moved above her and it seemed so natural to be here with him, eager for his hands on her body, his lips at her throat.

She felt light-headed. He shoved at the skirts and skimmed his hands up her calves—no stockings—to the soft inner curves of her thighs, then higher, a delicate stroke to the wet heat of her that left her gasping. Her hips lifted with each long slide; she had no will over it, she could not control it, and he smiled at her as he petted her there, that fleet wicked smile that transformed him from light to dark.

"Ronan," she panted, and grabbed his arm. She didn't know if she wanted him to go on or to stop, but he kissed her then anyway, a hot, bruising delight.

"My name," he said, harsh against her lips. "Say it again."

She shook her head, mindless. He eased a finger inside her and she whimpered in pleasure, and then he lowered his head and drew her nipple into his mouth, teeth and wool scoring her as his hand still worked, stroking high and low and in and out.

"Leila," he grated. "*Again.*"

"Ronan—"

She couldn't resist, couldn't think. She clutched his shoulders and tried to pull him to her, to hold her down because she was turning to light and energy and would fly off soon into that endless blue. He shifted and came between her legs, rigid and smooth, stronger, heavier than she'd ever realized. His face was taut and his eyes were rapt; he closed them as he pressed into her, a little push, and then another, longer, and another, until the pain blended with the thrill, Ronan above her and around her, his lips on hers, his tongue tasting her as he moved and sent ripples of that sensuous pleasure all through her. She felt the rising crest again and reached for it, wanting. She fisted her hands in his hair and opened her legs wider, taking in more of him, lifting to every thrust.

The sky loomed closer and closer, held back only by the bright golden beauty that was him. He dragged his lips across hers and pressed deep into her and she fell—sweet, long spinning waves of bliss, right up into heaven while held in his arms.

He pressed deep again, her name in his throat, another heavy thrust—a gasp, a shudder. His body clenched tight . . . and then slowly relaxed. One hand spread across her breast; he buried his face in her hair.

*Mine*, he thought, but never said it.

*Mine*, claimed every inch of his body, still warm and thick inside her.

"Are you cold now?" he breathed, ragged in her ear.

Leila, half clothed and pinned to stone by a large, brawny man, brought up a hand to shield her eyes from the day. "No," she said, marveling, because for the first time in a very long while, it was true.

He couldn't keep her here.

Ronan wanted to. He actually did. On Kell she would be safe and secure and alone. There would be nothing to tempt her, or him, beyond themselves, no plots or schemes or Spanish madmen to cloud his time with her. He thought he'd like nothing better than to laze with her here in these pale winter days, to wrap her in his plaid and kiss her and keep her until the shadows vanished from her eyes.

But she couldn't stay. Kell was a place both charmed and cruel; mortals never did well here. He had brought her here in anger, a rash and reckless gesture, and although he was not sorry for it, he needed a remedy. Soon.

It was difficult to think of remedies with her nestled in his bed. It was difficult to think at all when he had her beneath him, and her head tipped back and her lips parted and he filled her with himself. He had followed his own dream and draped the pillows and sheets in furs. She was a jewel in lush smoky colors, a star in the night that teased and tempted and ultimately drowned him in ecstasy.

She couldn't stay. As morning broke and he watched her sleeping, he laid his hand over her heart, feeling the fragile beat of it, smelling the sweet woman scent of her. Kell would turn on her, one way or another. She didn't hate him now, even after all he had done. But if he kept her here, trapped in his castle—she would.

He didn't think he'd be able to brook that.

There was the curse, of course. Deep down, Ronan didn't really believe in it, which was ridiculous, considering what he was. Yet he had always considered his body a tangible thing, a gift both real and painful, while the story of his family was so thin and distant it had faded in his heart to simple legend, with no lasting meaning. Was there still the living curse placed by that first siren? Certainly there was the reef, and the castle, and all the accumulation of treasure he had buried beneath the isle. Certainly there was hidden death for any who dared come uninvited. But would there be death for those who left too?

Something else came to him then, a corner of a verse of a very old song:

*Child of the sea unveiled . . .*

He gazed down at Leila, lit all to rose with the dawn sliding in past the windows. Was he beloved of his enemy?

No. Not likely . . . not yet.

Ronan touched his hand to her temple to brush back an unruly lock. Her eyes opened instantly, as if she had never slept.

"I have a business proposition for you," he said.

She waited, creamy curves and that luscious scent, one arm curled above her head.

"It appears I am in need of a bodyguard. I propose to hire you."

She blinked at him once, just one slow blink, and took a longer breath than before.

"I consider you the ideal candidate," Ronan continued. "You seem familiar enough with weapons and pretense. I presume you understand the man who will try to kill me better than anyone. And you told me you needed money. I'll pay thrice whatever Lamont offered."

Her brows raised. "You don't know what he offered."

"Thrice," he said firmly.

"He paid in gold," she yawned, stretching like a cat in the sun.

"As can I."

"He wants your little island."

"As do I," said Ronan grimly.

She sat up, holding a king's ermine to her chest, watching him with veiled speculation.

"What if I won't?"

"Then you may learn to enjoy Kell."

Dark lashes swept low, hiding her gaze. "What if I fail?"

"Then I suppose I'll no longer need a bodyguard."

She pushed her hand through the thick pelt across her legs. "*La Mano* is relentless, but he will leave you be if I go to him."

"Is that what you want?" he asked, gruff.

"What I want is irrelevant. I am telling you that your true problem is this man Lamont. He hired us. He will only hire more after us."

"No," vowed Ronan softly, "he won't. Of that I assure you."

"He paid in gold," she repeated, looking up again with green eyes fringed in light. "He paid in the same coin I found on your beach here. Do you understand?"

"Aye."

"More gold from Kell. That is what he actually desires. I believe your death to him is—incidental."

"Nevertheless, I have put an offer to you. A simple business deal."

"With only your life at stake," she finished tartly.

"What say you, doña?"

"If you let me go, I swear *La Mano* will follow me."

"No. Come with me, else stay here. Those are your only choices."

For a moment her steely poise wavered; he saw doubt in her, distress. Her fingers twisted to a knot on her lap.

He covered her hands with his. "I have surprising faith in you, Leila of Sant Severe. But if you think to trick me, know this—I'll find you wherever you go. You know what I am. I have powers you've never imagined. You'll be very, very sorry you lied to me again."

"I am already sorry," she muttered. "Very well, Lord Kell. I accept your offer."

"Ronan," he insisted, pulling her to him.

"Ronan," she whispered, and raised her chin for his kiss.

# CHAPTER THIRTEEN

❦

They would wait for the black of the new moon to travel to Kelmere.

That was Leila's first directive. Voyage in darkness, as smugglers did, without lanterns or moonlight to reveal them. The Hand of God—*Shay*, she called him now—would be monitoring the shores, prowling the streets of the main island for any hint of either of them. She thought time enough had passed for him to find his feet again; Ronan had the image of a sly and grizzled fox, leering from dank alleyways.

Pistols, poisons, sabers—even the faint scratch of a fingernail from an innocent-looking hand—she ticked off the possibilities of his demise in a matter-of-fact tone, seated cross-legged on the bed as he stared out the castle window and watched the snow melt in rivulets from the eaves.

"And I'd like payment in advance, if you please," she said, cool as ice.

He slanted her a look from over his shoulder. "Don't think I'll live long enough to draw a draft at Kelmere?"

She gave him that small, graceful shrug. "In my profession, one does not take unnecessary risks."

"Very wise."

"I am four and twenty, Lord Kell. I did not reach this age by luck alone."

"No," he agreed gravely. "No indeed. Quarter payment, then."

"Half."

"Done."

So he took her down into the depths of the island the only way anyone still could: by the sea.

She wasn't pleased with that idea, it was clear. A day and a night of lovemaking hadn't truly melted her reserve. She stood on the beach with him and held her hair with both hands, her back stiff and straight and her jaw tight with resistance.

"It's quick," he assured her, which was almost true. "You'll hardly notice it."

She narrowed her eyes. "I'll wait here for you."

"You're going to enjoy this, Leila. I promise."

She didn't believe him, but it didn't matter. He drew her to him, one step at a time into the surf, knee-high, thigh-high, waist-high, the dress she insisted upon wearing trailing out behind her. When the water reached as high as his heart, he slipped under all the way, still holding her hands, a tug to bring her to him. She resisted a moment; he granted her time to take a breath and then pulled again. This time she came.

He waited for the change until she could see it. He wanted her to see it happen, to know him in this way. He wanted no more secrets between them.

It was swift. He took them deeper out and let the ocean

fill him. It hurt—it always hurt—and his hands might have tightened around hers. He arched back and let it wash through him, and when it was done she was wide-eyed, her arms stretched out, not even kicking her feet to stay in place.

He brought her up to the surface again, turning her in his arms, pulling her back to rest against his chest so that they floated together facing the clouds. Ronan pressed his lips to her wet hair.

"And . . . there's the sky again, doña."

"So it is," she said faintly.

"Breathe," he advised. "It's not so terrible. Breathe, my love."

He wrapped his arms beneath hers and began a slow backward glide. She found his wrists and gripped hard.

"Cold?" he asked, though he knew she wouldn't be.

She shook her head. She did not release his wrists.

"Nearly there. Very good. Are you ready? Hold your breath."

Her chest expanded; he sank with her into cobalt depths.

The water was warm to him, velvety; because he felt it so, she would as well. The truth for her was, however, quite different. He had only a short while to keep her here in his primal home before her body would begin to die. He had chanced more than that just to get her here, and wasn't about to court further harm now. But he wanted her to see the grotto.

The currents pushed strong but he moved surely, easily though them. Sea light dimmed and flowed; the mouth of the cavern was deep off the isle, a great oval mystery no man or ship had yet discovered.

Nor would they, he thought. Never, ever.

He brought her up quickly to air again, held her lightly

as she coughed and bobbed and wiped the hair from her eyes.

"Come." The platform wasn't far, still sound after all this time, a wide wedge of marble braced against the sea. But Leila wasn't looking at that. She was looking at what was upon it: all the riches of Kell.

Stacks of coins, mounds of jewelry, majestic statues and ingots and Roman armament freckled with rust. The light seemed to shift with each lap of the water, refracted sunshine sparkling over centuries of silver and gold and gems of every color of the rainbow.

He took Leila to the platform edge, lifted her up, and set her down with her feet still dangling in the water.

"Choose whatever you wish," Ronan said, his breath frosting. "Half payment."

She cupped a hand over her mouth and began to laugh.

She was blinded; she was dazzled. Leila crept between mountains of treasure, held the hands of alabaster gods, admired briefly a long curving scimitar engraved with pear blossoms. She stepped over helmets and torques, and once nearly lost her footing between a cache of muskets and a brass coffer of pearls.

In the end she could not choose. She only sat, dripping, on a closed chest by the cavern wall, resting her chin on her fists. She had never seen anything like this—never dreamed of it but perhaps as a child in the flowery extravagance of Moorish fables. All the pashas and princes of the desert could not have such hoards as this. She wasn't even certain she had seen it all yet. There had been stairs farther back, leading up to who knew where, but they lay buried beneath a hill of ossified debris.

"This," said Ronan from the water, his words echoing, "is what Lamont really wants."

"He knows of this place?"

"He suspects. He has an island not far from here. Coins have washed up on his shores for decades. Every scrap of flotsam and jetsam in Scotland is rumored to come from Kell. His father suspected it, his grandfather. They were greedy men but not stupid. I never really thought Lamont would be the one to attempt anything so asinine as murder. I suppose he thinks that with my death the clan will be thrown into chaos. He'd be right, for a time."

"Long enough to come here and steal the gold."

"Aye."

"How old are you?" she asked suddenly.

He smiled, enigmatic. "Old."

She threw a guarded look to the statue of Poseidon posed beside her, trident in hand, and he chuckled. "Not that old."

Ronan climbed onto the platform. He had human legs again, thick and handsomely muscled. He bent over and shucked the water off his body with flat palms, his hair corded amber across his shoulders. The chain and pendant he wore clung tight to the base of his throat.

"We won't linger here long, my lady. Have you decided upon your payment?"

She stared at him, at that silver pendant, a lone and modest ornament amid all this luxury. It had struck her strange before, on the ship, that first time she had noticed it. But thinking back she realized she had never seen him without it. Not once.

He walked to her, elegant and masterful, stood before her as imposing as the stone gods all around.

"Shall I decide for you?" he asked quietly.

Leila rose and touched the pendant with one finger. It

was a locket, she saw now, bright and shining with a pattern across it that reminded her of a flowing river.

"It's so warm," she said, surprised.

"No. It's only that you're cold."

"I'm not." Her eyes flashed up to his. "Not now."

He pulled gently away. "You are, you know. You don't realize it, but you are." His face changed, his eyes shuttering, his mouth growing hard. He took another step away. "Your payment, Leila. And then we must go."

She lifted her hand once more, and once more he pulled back, sharper than before.

"No," he said. "Don't ask. You can have anything else." He turned, vanishing behind a florid baroque screen. She heard rustling and a tinkling clatter; a single silver coin rolled out past the screen to bump against a strongbox. Ronan reappeared to thrust something into her hand, saying, "That should secure you something a bit better than a cottage." And he pulled her to the edge of the platform.

She looked down. He had given her a cut stone nearly the size of a hen's egg, blazing white set in plaited gold. A diamond.

Her jaw dropped; she was about to speak but he dragged her into the sea with him.


The ocean was very, very black.

Leila had not quite envisioned it being so dark at sea without the moon, though she had, on many occasions, made use of such nights on land. It was a darkness that consumed all else, and she sat in the rowboat with her hands clenched fast to the sides, not to steady herself—the little boat moved like silk over glass—but to assure herself that it was still there.

The wind had finally died, leaving only the breath of their voyage to push past her. There was no fog. There were no stars. There had to be clouds overhead, but she couldn't see even those. She missed them so much her throat ached with it.

Ronan towed the boat by a single rope tied to the bow. She did not want to think about it breaking, what she would do out here if he decided to abandon her sightless and so alone.

His voice floated out of the emptiness, a low welcome sound over the whisper plashing of the waves.

"Tell me, did Finlay manage to finish the tale of the first siren and her fisherman?"

"Lost love. Sad ending." She spoke to blank nothingness and was glad he swam ahead of her, where he could not see her face. "Your family history appears full of woe, my lord."

"Aye, some of it. But there's been happiness as well. There was a king, in fact, who once loved a siren here, many years past. She had saved him from the sea and decided to keep him for herself."

"Rather like a puppy," she said sourly.

He laughed; the boat gave a little bobble. "As a lover, my lady. And though the king was already wed, it was a happy alliance indeed."

"Perhaps not so much for the queen."

"The queen was a wise woman. She loved her king well enough to understand his fate. They had a child, the king and the siren, and the queen took her into her home and raised her as her own daughter."

Leila said nothing, thinking of that long-ago woman, of how it must have felt to be presented with her husband's enchanted child. How lonely she must have been behind her royal trappings and her crown. How generous.

"That daughter became my great-great-grandmother," Ronan said.

"What happened to the siren and the king?"

"Ah. The king was only mortal, you see. At first he didn't understand the siren, or Kell. He wanted only to return home, for he was an important man and had many lives depending upon him. But the siren was very patient, and, in time, he grew to love her."

"Did she love him?"

"With her whole heart."

He fell silent. Leila let go of the boat, tucked her fingers under her cloak.

"But she released him," Ronan said at last. "Because he had the spirit of a wolf, and like all wild things he could not survive entrapped, not even entrapped on an island. One day there came a war to the king's land. He was in danger. The siren decided to forsake her life on Kell to stand with him, and she nearly died because of it. Yet the wolf king was brave and clever. He managed to save her the only way he could—he took her back to Kell. He had to leave her there."

"Without him?"

"Aye. As the years passed he would visit her, one man in a boat, ever alone. When he would draw near Kell, she would lower the mist and calm the seas, saying, 'Come over, true love, come over.' And he would."

"Can you do that?" she asked, skeptical. "Lower the mist, calm the sea?"

"Well . . . she could. And that was the way of it, until one day the old king never returned from Kell. It was said that he and his love had lived their lives to completion, vanishing together into the sea, arm in arm. Never alone again."

The air brushed by, liquid black as everything else, no color or light left in the world.

"It seems to me a sad tale yet, my lord," she said softly.

There was a small purl of sound ahead, as if he turned to see her. "I only tell you it because of the boat. I think it must have been very like this one."

She frowned at the darkness, uneasy with his tone. There was a secret behind his words, an unspoken message. Before she could think of a reply he murmured, "We're here," and the rowboat scraped into sand.

They had agreed to land away from the main port, which, Ronan informed her, would be full of people at almost any hour, a very easy cover for a man of stealth. The earl had chosen a remote beach instead, no cottages or roads. She stood up in the wobbling boat with the bundle of his clothing in her arms and was consoled by the fact that he at least could see; he found her waist in the dark and then scooped her up to his chest, splashing them both to shore.

He set her down and helped straighten her skirts. She had dressed the part before they left, an ordinary Scotswoman now, no hoops but petticoats aplenty, her own corset and a plain gown tied with the plaid.

The diamond Ronan had given her was pushed firmly down into her right boot.

His hands paused, lifted. He cupped her cheeks and kissed her, a deep, sliding kiss that made the mushed sand at her feet and the nearby odor of cattle far less important than they had been a second before. Leila found his shoulders and returned it, the two of them breathing warmth into the wintry night. She wouldn't admit it aloud, but it was a heartfelt relief to have him touch her now, to feel the strength of him before her when all else was mystery and frosted darkness.

He spoke against her cheek, his lips shaping hushed words. "It's a long walk, little doña. Shall we begin?"

But she knew he wasn't thinking of what awaited them ahead. He was thinking of that solitary king in his boat, a shrouded figure in mist, alone, alone, but who had finally found his love, and who had one day faded into legend beside her.

# CHAPTER FOURTEEN

inlay would be waiting for them at the hang-
man's tree. It was the prearranged meeting spot
Ronan had used time and again, and tonight was
no exception. The clan would send someone down from
Kelmere every day, every night to wait for him, until the
laird returned or until a full year passed—and it was time
to designate a new laird. Finlay had the job of late; Ronan
hoped he was wrapped well against the frigid air.

The great barren oak stretched its limbs into the black
sky. It was older than he was, massive and gnarled, a local
landmark that had never, to his knowledge, actually been
used to hang anyone. A shadow beneath the branches
stirred as they drew nearer.

Young Finlay had eyes like a cat. Ronan had long suspected a hint of siren blood still lingered in this cousin
of his.

"Ye've brought *her*?" he asked first off, his voice a hiss
of disbelief.

"I have," Ronan responded, so coldly the lad's mouth

snapped shut. "She's with us now. May I present Señorita Leila de Sant Severe."

Leila inclined her head, silent. Finlay gave a stiff bow, his expression mulish.

"The señorita has agreed to act as my personal protection," Ronan added, just to gauge the boy's reaction. He was not disappointed. Finlay's eyebrows pulled down into a scowl worthy of Baird Innes. But at least he had sense enough to hold his tongue.

Ronan placed his hand on Leila's elbow. "Kindly lead the way home, lad. I fear my lady grows chilled."

Without another word Finlay turned and almost stomped away, his cape swelling to ebony fullness, flipping out and down again.

"He is displeased," said Leila under her breath.

"He is disillusioned." They began to follow the lanky figure up the dirt road. "I think he was more than a little in love with Doña Adelina."

She sighed, a weary sound, small and pensive. "Well. I am sorry for it."

"No matter. 'Tis a valuable lesson. The next time he won't fall so easily for a splendid face. Not even one as splendid as yours."

She threw him a glance in the dark, but he didn't know if she could actually see him yet.

"Mind your feet," he said mildly. "It's a stony path ahead."

And it was. Past heather and streams filigreed with ice, along beds of peat and glens that would green and flower come August's full bloom, all the way up the winding lane that led to the great house that stood on the hill—half fortress, half something else, the haphazard culmination of generations of dreams and practical hopes. Kelmere.

Finlay made certain they were still behind him, then

hailed the sentries at the front gate. A short conversation ensued; a lantern lit, three men now marginally revealed in dull muted color. Ronan slowed and Leila slowed with him. One of the sentries vanished behind the gatehouse and came back, lifting something to his mouth.

The conch sounded, that unmusical blast of notes that shattered the night to herald his arrival.

Ronan felt Leila's start. "It's a greeting to the laird." He tried to think of a better way to explain it, but in the end said only, "It is our way."

Almost at once, lights began to appear in the darkness above. The auld mansion began to wink to life, one candle, one window at a time. Ronan moved forward again.

She could nearly see. With the gathering pinpricks of light, Leila could nearly make out the shape of the building before her, towers and parapets and long rambling wings. Yes, she *could* see it now, and even past the windows, to the ragged line of trees and vegetation—and then beyond even that, to the slopes of a colossal mountain, snow-streaked and stark, that seemed poised to swallow them whole.

The lights were dancing. They met bright near one spot in particular, an open doorway on the bottom floor, far-off people standing in miniature against the heavy edifice like dolls set up to play. Leila saw the lancet arch of the entrance, the glow of a hundred candles flung over stone, shifting shadows that slurred across every pit and crag.

"Come up, Leila," said the earl. Tempered gold hollowed his cheeks, enmeshed in the gilt of his hair. Without looking at her he held out his hand. "Come up and meet my clan."

She placed her palm in his. He felt cool again, the warmth

he had on Kell drained away. It was like touching the hand of Poseidon but that he breathed and spoke.

"Wait," she said.

His glance back was hidden blue. "Yes?"

She moved ahead of him, scanning the people. "There are too many. They should disperse before you approach."

His face cleared. "Not here, doña. There are no enemies secluded here. This is Kelmere."

"Yes, Kelmere, the ancestral seat of the Earls of Kell. I'm well aware of it. You may be sure that *La Mano* is too."

He shook his head at her. "Come."

She tugged free her hand, irritation rising through her. "You've hired me to guard you. I cannot do so in such a crowd."

"Then consider this a recess," he said casually, and walked on.

"If it is a recess, then I can leave," she called to his back.

"No, you can't." He kept walking.

Damn him. She should turn around right now, to hell with what he said. She should take her fat diamond and just go. She could make her way back to London, sell the jewel. He had been right, it was far more than she required. She could live off the profit for years to come. She did not need him.

The earl climbed the steps of slate that lined the manicured path to the manor. No cape, no cloak. Only a man, or the fashion of one, in a sweep of plaid and damp boots, taking each stair alone.

The thought came to her from nowhere, from everywhere, clear and keen: He needed her.

She let out her breath in a white cloud of exasperation.

The three huddled men were looking at her, the two sentries shifting uneasily but Finlay standing fixed, indignation radiating from every line of him. Leila lifted her skirts and walked after Ronan. Let the *niño* think what he would.

She caught up with him only because he let her, and because there were a great many of the slate steps embedded in the grassy slope. By the time she reached him, the mountain air felt a good deal thinner than before. He made room for her without speaking; together they ascended to the top of the knoll.

She looked around them at the united faces and thought again that there were too many—far too many to read and judge at once.

At the sight of their laird, the people hummed and surged. There were grins and blank stares and plain astonishment at the subsequent sight of her. Ronan linked his arm with hers, and the astonishment turned to shock.

The earl smiled and greeted the people by name as they walked past, unchallenged, unquestioned, strolling down the open center of their mass while Leila scrutinized their faces, searching for any twitch of Che among them.

"Welcome home, laird," said a man, and more salutations followed. Everyone pressed close and Leila had a moment of panic—she tried to draw in front of Ronan but he held her at his side with his arm gone to iron over hers, turning his lips to her ear.

"Not here. We're safe here."

She freed her other arm from the cloak and let her hand glance against the bodies surrounding them.

*Whist! look at the lass, bold as ye please—*

*—home safe—*

*—looks fit, why a fell bonny lad—*

*—in the larder? he'll like raspberries now—nay, the tayberries and—*

*—brought her here? it's no' right—*

*—so green, like a cat—*
*—in our colors—*
*—who is she—*
*—home praise be—*
*—so pretty—*
*—who can—*
*—came back—*
*—he walks—*
*—she—*
*—laird—*
*—our laird—*
*—that lass—*
*—who is she who is SHE SHE SHE SHE SHE—*

She shouldn't have done it; the voices were growing too loud in her head; she tried to pull away from them and found she could not. The pain was born as a little pea in her mind, it grew and grew to white dragon ferocity, devouring everything—she couldn't see, she couldn't reason. There was the impression of shadows and flickering light, of a hallway and the hard echo of footsteps over stone. There were voices outside and in, a strange babble of sound she didn't understand, and Ronan's response, equally incomprehensible. She thought she had stopped walking. She didn't know.

Leila closed her eyes, almost panting. She was sick. God help her, here, in front of all these strangers, she was going to be sick.

Ronan said her name. She came to feel, gradually, his palms on her cheeks, rubbing, heat. His face came into focus, holding grim before hers.

"You did not exaggerate," he said, "about the headaches."

She swallowed. "No." Logic began to seep past the nausea. "The people—where—"

"Peace," he whispered, distant. "Be still. They're gone now, doña, we're alone. Sit calm. I'll be finished soon."

She didn't have to ask what he was doing. She felt it, the warmth spreading through her, smothering the dragon, turning it meek and meager and then gone. She watched him as he did it, the faraway aspect that slipped over him, the hardening of his features that in the wavering light turned him to carved effigy and then flesh again.

His eyes were so dark. They never left hers.

"Thank you," she said.

His lashes lowered; he let his hands fall and leaned away from her, blowing air past his teeth. She noticed then they were in a chamber that had to be a bedroom— his bedroom, of course, and she was seated on the bed, four posts and knotted rosewood, sunk deep into blankets and down.

The light came from a fireplace, from silver sconces fixed to walls covered in Chinese silk. By the fire there were chairs and a table for backgammon, a scattering of porcelain figurines watching from the marble hearth. There was a painting of a horse framed between black-glassed windows; a cabinet; a mirror; and a clock whose hands informed her it was well past three.

Ronan squatted on his heels on a tasseled rug. She slipped to her knees before him, found his hands, and held them in hers.

"It pains you, doesn't it?" she asked, knowing the answer already.

"No," he lied, blunt.

She contemplated him, spreading her fingers to lace with his. He appeared more tired than she had yet seen, comely even with shadows beneath his eyes and that hard line to his mouth.

"Don't do it if it pains you. Not for me."

"If not for you," he said with quiet tension, "then I cannot fathom for who." He looked askance at their hands, then pulled them slowly together until they met behind his back, bringing her to him, her chest grazing his. He pressed a hot kiss to her throat.

"Better," he murmured, his mouth drifting, exploring. "That's so much better."

He released her hands and she slid them up his back, beneath the tartan, holding herself steady as he trailed kisses across her cheeks.

"The door," she protested faintly.

"The devil with the door."

"It must be bolted."

He eased her down to the rug. "It is."

"The windows—"

"Aye, them as well."

She turned her face to take a clear breath while he grappled with the bulk of her skirts.

"Is there water set out? A basin?"

His reply was muffled. He was inhaling deeply, as if he could drown in her scent. "No."

"I can see it, my lord, from here. Don't drink—"

"Yes." His fingers found her center; his voice went harsh as he touched her there. "Yes to whatever you say. Only let me . . ."

She was losing the thread of her reason, and tried, with hazy urgency, to find it again. "Ronan, you must listen—"

"Layla." His hand worked at his breeches. She felt him come free, hard and ready between her thighs.

"Everything," he said with a groan, pushing into her, "is just as it ought to be."

* * *

By morning there was no longer any doubt in anyone's mind regarding the identity of the lass who spent the night in the laird's bed. Ronan made certain of that.

Guardian, he said to the clusters of his people. Protector. As we shall protect her.

He didn't tell them much more than that; a few hints in the right ears about her history, her heroism, her daring twice to save him despite the villainous bastard who crushed her in his grip. *Damsel in distress*, he might as well have said, and saw the gleam catch and spark from eye to eye.

There was nothing a Scotsman, or woman, enjoyed more than dire intrigue spiced with romance—topped with a dollop of grief. The laird was happy to provide the fodder for their gossip. He wanted it clear that the señorita was welcome here.

He did not tell them of the sweeter things, about how he lay awake at night to watch her, to follow the gentle passage of her breath. Of how when she turned in her sleep she always rubbed her nose and gave a little sigh, almost wistful, before relaxing back into her dreams.

Of how she had forbidden him to take her into the bed until she stripped it to the wood base, shaking out each sheet, each blanket and pillow, searching for serpents or scorpions or some other slight evil thing. He stood aside and watched her skim the finest sheet across the bare mattress, hunting for any sort of snag to catch the flow, and wondered at the life she had led, at the depths of a mind that would think to plant a deadly needle in the heart of a man's bed.

When she was satisfied, he helped her put it to rights again and then tumbled her into it, where she had turned to his chest and fallen instantly asleep.

Hence, his staying awake.

She was not going to be pleased to wake up alone, he knew. She had seized the role he had offered her with a steadfast vehemence; he didn't know whether to be more flattered or alarmed.

Ronan wondered how she would react if she had any real idea of how hard he was to kill. He wouldn't tell her. The truth was, he wasn't even sure himself.

But the laird went and had a talk with his steward and then with the chatelaine and the guards. He had told Leila there were no enemies at Kelmere, and it was true—for now. But word would soon spread down the mountain that the señorita was here. He had a legion of men entrenched in the hills, a horde of strapping souls and shrewd Highland cunning. Lamont himself had gone to earth, but when his assassin stole into Ronan's kingdom, Ronan fully intended to be ready.

For Leila. For his heart.

# CHAPTER FIFTEEN

❧

S he awoke alone.

It was a normal thing at first, all by herself in a
soft bed, yellow sun warming her face. She pulled
a pillow over her head and smelled roses, which was
enough to make her open her eyes and have a look
around.

Ronan was gone. She sat up too quickly, had to wait a
moment while the dizziness passed. When it cleared, she
saw the chamber door creeping open. She was on her feet
before the first woman stepped foot past the frame.

"Ah!" said the woman in a glad and open voice. "The
laird thought ye might sleep the morn away." She carried
hot water, and the one behind her carried towels, and the
next clothing, and perfume, and the last one of all a tray
of food.

It was a ritual, Leila could see that, and an alien one to
her. She was unused to being waited upon; she did not
know what to do while they bustled around her and set
up her breakfast and bath. To depend upon others was a

weakness—Che had taught her that in her first days with him. Not merely a weakness but folly, for danger could readily hide behind a servile smile, and death was always easier to inflict upon the careless.

Leila was never careless.

She took the hand of the woman who helped her into the bath *why thin as a post poor lass talk to Cook summat fine to fix her*, glanced fingers with the one who gave her the towels *right bonny child I suppose he could do worse*, let the other pair help her into the fresh gown *shy barely a word mayhap she don't know proper English* of ruby silk, and finally kept her hands to herself as they fixed their plaid around her.

She thanked them, but they were not done. Her aching head was hardly helped by the final brushing and tugging of her hair, but she submitted to it quietly, letting them think her shy, keeping her eyes on some lower point in the looking glass, watching not their faces as they worked but their hands, their skirts, as they produced brushes and combs and pearled pins from pockets unseen.

The pins were a difficulty. It took all her will to remain still for that part of the ceremony, to trust these strangers with needle-pointed objects against her head. She had to concentrate very hard on the brooch the eldest woman wore, committing to memory every detail of the silver, every facet of the squared garnets arranged in a circle.

"There now," that lady said. "Don't ye look fine. What, lass—afeard of your own face? Lift your chin there, that's the way. What a bonny sight to greet the laird! We'll have some color in those cheeks soon, I warrant."

She did look. If *bonny* was the word they wanted, she would not argue with it, but in her reflection Leila saw something more severe than that: a woman with softly tamed hair and dark winged brows, and eyes of light restless searching.

"Where is the laird?" she asked.

"Oh, about," was the comprehensive reply, followed by assurances that he would find her soon, now that he knew her to be up and dressed.

"No," she said, standing. "I will go to him."

And for some reason this pleased them enormously. Leila followed them out of the laird's sun-stroked room, seeing for the first time—the first time, truly—the halls of Ronan's more conventional home.

The ruby silk swished and floated like a bright zephyr at her feet, the color so warm it reflected back off the polished floors. The Scotswomen walked ahead, deliberating over where the laird might be, and Leila took silent note of walls, portraits, marble busts, memorizing her way back. They passed doors open and closed, and then an open door with voices within.

The tone of those voices caught Leila's attention at once—cracked and worried, the sharp shades of crisis.

She slowed and then turned around, moving soundlessly back to the door.

". . . what else to do? He willna eat, I canna force him to drink. He wakes and wheezes and the pain won't stop." A woman, standing by a canopied bed.

"He's sleeping now. Let him rest. Give him this when he wakes."

"Unless ye mean me to tie him down, doctor," said the woman bitingly, "I dinna see how I'm to manage it."

"Let him sleep," repeated the man in a firm whisper. "Fetch me when he wakes."

"Aye." It was an aggravated sigh.

"Poor Baird," murmured one of Leila's women in her ear. The physician came to the door, saw the clump of them, and pushed past with a nod. Leila followed his form down the hall, then looked back to the darkened room.

"Baird," she said. "Baird Innes?"

"Aye. Came home not a fortnight ago—well, ye know that, of course—but within days caught the fever summat terrible. Won't let Allie there do aught but wring her hands and fuss."

The woman—Mistress Innes, Leila assumed—stalked across the hardwood floor, tall in a white cap and frilled apron.

Leila drifted into the room.

He could not wait for her any longer. In the midst of his ledgers and sheets of accounting and the endless stack of numbers recited by his placid steward, Ronan kept glancing out the paned window to the sun. Watching it rise. And rise. Past the woods, across the saffron grass. Over the arbor and up the side of Kelmere's eastern flank, flooding his study with unmistakable daylight.

She had been exhausted. She needed to sleep. That was all it was.

No use. He couldn't focus, couldn't stop thinking of her, some tiny, tiny detail from last night scratching at the back of his thoughts, elusive. Ronan apologized to William, told him to reschedule their appointment at the man's later convenience, and reached the door just as the chatelaine arrived with news of "the foreign lass" tending to Baird.

That was where he found her, standing over the prone figure of his friend, his hand clutched in both of hers and her head bowed, while Allie and a gathering of women stood in an anxious cluster by the foot of the bed.

For a moment he felt his heart drop. He knew of Baird's

illness; he had consulted the physician early this morning, as soon as he'd heard. It was only a fever, the man had
said, most like caught from the storm in Ayr . . . but Allie
was red-eyed, and the slender shape that was Leila had a
droop to her shoulders he had not seen before. He stepped
into the room and the women turned as one to see him.
All but Leila, with her chin to her chest and her eyes
closed.

"What are you feeding him?" she asked, and opened
her eyes when no one answered. She lifted her head but
did not move otherwise; Baird let out a snort that choked
into a cough.

"Mistress," she said, sharper. "What does he eat?"

"Naught," said Allie, with a quick, anguished glance to
Ronan. "He'll eat naught, not even by the doctor's command."

"What medicine?"

"What the doctor gave—"

"Show me."

Allie presented a brown glass bottle; Leila gently released Baird's hand to the quilts. When she moved, Ronan
had a clearer glimpse of her face. She was pale, her skin
drawn. She looked nearly as ill as Baird. She looked—as
she had last night. The headache.

The tickle in the back of his mind grew stronger.

Leila uncorked the bottle, took a short whiff, and
winced.

"*Dios mío, es hisopo.*" She turned a fierce eye to Allie.
"Hyssop. You'll kill him with this."

"But—the doctor—"

"It is not fever," Leila snapped. "It is his heart."

"But he said—"

"His nails are blue, his hands are ice. Your husband has

pain here"—she touched his chest—"and here"—then his left arm. "It is his heart."

"Well, I . . ." For the first time since Ronan had known her, Allie seemed at a loss for words.

"What medicine should he have?" asked Ronan softly.

Leila pressed her palm to her forehead and shook her head, mute.

He came closer, looking from her to the man in the bed. "What should he have?" he persisted, still soft.

"Foxglove," she said at last, in a burst. "His heart. For God's sake, I'll mix it myself. The wrong dosage will end him for certain."

"Leila."

"I need my trunks. From the ship."

"Leila, stop." He reached up, dabbed his fingers to her upper lip. "You're bleeding."

She turned from him with a small little sound, bringing both hands to her face. One of the women hurried forward with a handkerchief. She accepted it, keeping her back to them all.

"Ladies," said Ronan, "pray excuse us."

They left in a trickle, Allie last of all, throwing Ronan a final heavy glance. He closed the door after them, then approached the bed.

Baird slept on beneath the covers, nearly serene, his companion and adviser for many a year. Ronan remembered, quite vividly, the day Baird had been born. It had been cold then too. The core of winter.

Ronan adjusted the quilts carefully around his old friend's shoulders.

"When I touch him," he said, "I see only a good man. What do you see?"

She lowered the handkerchief with a sniff but did not

turn. He had an excellent view of her nape and that one persistent curl.

"What do you see, Leila? Or is it more of an awareness?"

"His heart troubles him," she said at last.

"Well." Ronan felt himself smile. "I understand that, at least."

She walked to the window and pushed a hand between the closed curtains. Sunlight split past her into the room, falling in an arrow across the floor. The red of her gown was lit to flame.

He asked, "Does it happen always, or only when you wish it?"

"¿Qué?"

"The sight. When you touch."

The kerchief was crumpled in her fist. "Only eyes can see," she said shortly.

"Sweet doña, I'm really too old to dance tactfully around uncomfortable subjects. This is Scotland, the very end of the civilized world. We have faeries here, and goblins and moondust and even mermaids. You knew what I was long before I showed you. You never touch anyone without gloves—except me. But you touched Baird today, and the clan last night—I saw your hand go out—" Ronan stopped, arrested, as another mystery began to dissolve in his mind. "That's why *La Mano* took you from your village," he said slowly. "Isn't it? Because you could see."

"No." She hesitated, then turned around to face him. "That's why he did not ransom me."

He nodded, encouraging. *Magic happens every day,* said his expression, even though he knew very well it wasn't true.

Real magic was rare. As rare as true love.

Her eyes dropped again. She smoothed a hand down the fan of her skirts, the ruby light softening and shifting with her movements. He could see very clearly the outline of each velvet lash, the fine arch of her eyebrows. There were pearls in her hair, delicate silvery beads caught in woven starlight.

"Che understood how it could work for him, my gift. Because I could tell him things about people, and no one guessed what—no one knew." Her fingers fretted the handkerchief, turning it round and round. "If he asked the right questions and I was touching someone, I saw answers. Where money was kept. Who might be trusted. Who not."

"But it hurts you," Ronan said.

"Yes. It always has."

"And he forced you to continue."

She looked up at him, a wisp of gold and green and flame. "I wanted to live," she said simply. "He offered me the way."

"Leila," he said roughly. "When . . . I touch you—"

"No. It's not like that with you. It's different. It's . . . very nice."

*Nice.* Not the word he would have chosen. *Incredible. Glorious. Soul-stirring, life-altering—*

Baird let out another sleepy snort, followed by a loud and extremely lucid string of oaths.

Leila brought the kerchief to her lips. Color began to flag her cheeks; her shoulders shook.

Ronan felt something hard and jagged inside his chest start to ease. "I suggest we take our talk elsewhere, my lady."

"Not outside," she said quickly, around the kerchief.

"No, love. We'll stay in."

\* \* \*

Three days passed.

Three days of pretending that his world was normal, that nothing miraculous had come to stand beside him in the form of a gravely beautiful woman. She took her duties to heart; Ronan was given a list of rules to obey for his safety and he did so, Leila nearly always by his side. So he watched her and consulted with her and beheld the charming of his clan. She was exotic and reticent and unknown; by her very silence she intrigued them, brought them circling to her one by one until they hung in her orbit like comets to the sun—much as he did.

He had her trunks brought to his room. The keys were lost. Kirk of the nimble fingers worked to finesse the locks until Leila requested his metal files; she had the tumblers turned in under a minute. Even Finlay asked how she managed it.

The kitchens were given over to her for her potion. She held command over boiling pots and copper coils, filling the room with the distinct smell of an apothecary. She mixed and stirred and muttered measurements to herself, and when Allie showed up, Leila made a second batch, just so Baird's wife could see how it had been done.

No magic there, she had said. But she was wrong. There was magic in every breath of her.

In the great dining hall on the third night, Baird was up again, white-lipped but present. The clan was so heartened to see him, the hall rang with conversation, wine and whiskey lifted in a flurry of toasts that lasted the meal.

Kirk, seated across the table, had lured some green lad into a wager and acquired a fine new dirk as the result. He was boasting of it, showing off the blade and sending Finlay into black-eyed envy, when Ronan held out his hand.

Leila, he later recalled, was to his right, speaking to

Baird. Not just her head but her entire torso was angled away from him, as she was gently harassing Baird to eat.

Kirk tossed him the dirk across the haddock.

Before Ronan could make the catch, Leila had shoved him hard with both hands. If he hadn't been so surprised she couldn't have moved him, but she threw the full force of her weight behind it. Ronan and the fine-legged Gibbons chair both tipped and fell, Leila and her chair toppling after.

Above them hung a significant silence.

Between carved satinwood legs and needlepoint cushions, he brought his hands to her hair and kissed her, making a mess of her coiffure and not caring.

"Are you injured?" he asked, just as the worried face of Baird appeared over her shoulder.

"No. Are you?"

Ronan smiled. "No." And he kissed her again.

Baird helped her to rise while Ronan handled the chairs. When he turned back to her, Leila sank into a formal curtsy, then found the dirk and presented it by the hilt.

All at once laughter broke out, whistles and applause and stomping feet. She stood there a moment with her hair falling down, then gave a second—more bashful—curtsy to the table.

He took her hand and thought, *I love you.*

Her eyes lifted to his. The glow of her smile spread warmth like a summer day though his heart.

She had forgotten. She had forgotten what it was like to be the girl who once knew only trees and hills and hugs, and nothing of morbid death for hire. She had forgotten how it felt to be surrounded by innocence; no codes or subtle suggestions tucked between words. She had forgotten how it felt to walk in confidence, to release that dull, constant ache between her shoulder blades, mark of a lifetime of dread. She had forgotten warmth, and comfort, and love.

But then, early on her fourth morning at Kelmere, came the message from Che.

In the arched granite glory of the formal vestibule, a pair of maids found the supine body of Mr. Johnson arranged with tender care, his eyes pressed closed and his hands folded piously over his chest.

Leila stood alone in the ensuing commotion. She stared down at the corpse and realized—she had forgotten herself.

# CHAPTER SIXTEEN

❧

After that, it was only a matter of waiting. Waiting, and attempting to convince Ronan to let her go.

"No," was his answer, unwavering. And sometimes, "God, no." And finally, "For Christ's sake, Leila. Never."

He met with men and women of his clan, summoned the physician and the magistrate and sent the body off to the old empty granary until it could be transported back to Lamont's holding. With a full accompaniment of men she went there to examine it, searching for any extra clues.

Mr. Johnson—Lamont—had had a steel wire through his heart. That was all she could tell. It was one of Che's favorite methods from his youth.

Swift, he had taught her. Nearly bloodless.

She felt a terror so tight and controlling that for a moment she feared she would splinter from it. She knelt in front of the dead man and focused on keeping her face blank and her eyes empty, tricks she had mastered as a child. Hard and bitter lessons; they served her well now, here in the cold stone loft that still held the dusty chaff of grain in its corners.

*He is here.* The thought circled round her, strangling, inexorable. *He is here, he is here.*

How was she going to save Ronan now? He would not hide; he would not run. He would not even return with her to Kell. He could not leave his people vulnerable, and how could she fault him that, even as her mind and heart screamed in warning?

She moved through the day as if the night would be her last. She changed her gown, from fawn to ivory, the better to be seen. She refused food, wine, anything but water, because she did not wish her senses dulled. Her body had the same light smoothness that came to her on contract days—another reason not to eat.

She became his shadow. It was her talent, and she used it well. She followed Ronan down the long halls of Kelmere, paused when he did. Often he took her hand as he spoke to the others, dallying with her fingers, sliding their palms together. She caught echoes of his thoughts and had to work hard to push them from her mind, because they were sweet and sensual and distracting, and she could not afford to be distracted now.

In the bronze and green decor of his study, she stared out the window and listened with half an ear as he made arrangements and plans that would do no good at all. She didn't bother to tell him that a dozen men—five dozen—could not stop *La Mano de Dios* in a rage.

She wished she had never crossed the channel into England. She wished she had never met Che, had died in Federico's fire. She looked once back at Ronan—mythic and precious and a true beloved heart—and wished she had not been born, because then he would be safe.

She would not endure his death. She would not survive it.

Leila realized the study had fallen silent. When she looked back again all but the earl had gone. Ronan was seated alone behind his polished desk, watching her with a blue cryptic gaze.

"Come away from the window," he said.

She moved, shifting from light to shadow.

"Come to me," he said, and she did, standing before him in her ivory and lace like a penitent child. He rubbed a finger over his lips, thoughtful, but made no move to touch her.

"I've been informed you're not eating."

"I have no appetite."

"None?"

"No."

"Nevertheless, you're going to eat," he said. "I've ordered tea for you."

Despite her fears, she felt her lips curl. "And how will you get me to eat, Lord Kell?"

"I'll sing you a song," he said steadily. "I'm damned well tempted to do it anyway, just to get you to sit down."

She fluffed her skirts and sat, without ceremony, at his feet.

"Well," he said, with an arch of his brow. "That was simple. Kiss me."

Sunlight turned golden red against her closed lids. His lips were cool but the burning came anyway, fiery sparks across her skin. It gathered and raced through her with sudden reckoning: She read him as clearly as that first time they had touched.

*My soul. My heart. My hope.*

Leila pulled away and put her forehead to his knees.

She watched a tear fall and spatter into a star on the gauze of her petticoat.

He drew his hand down her neck, rested it there.

"He won't kill me," Ronan said quietly. "Stop thinking it. It won't happen."

"You don't know him."

"I know *you*. I know what I have to live for. God grants such scarce favors, beautiful Leila. But when they come, I know to hold tight."

His hand lifted, then came back. She felt him loop a chain around her neck, his fingers brushing her skin as he worked the catch. The silver locket slid heavily down her chest.

He cupped his hand beneath her chin and lifted her face.

"There. It looks far better on you than ever it did on me, I think."

She covered the locket with her palm.

"Half payment?" she asked, attempting to smile, but he did not return it.

"No. No payment. A gift. Only . . ." He searched her face, a gaze like the dark mountain mists that haunted his home. "Only me. My promise to you, Leila. All will be well between us."

"I'd rather you promise me you'll return to Kell awhile."

"Hmm. I suppose we could"—he bent his head to hers—"merely outlive him there."

She arched her neck, relishing the scrape of his cheek against hers, his teeth on her earlobe.

"Stay on Kell," he murmured, tasting her. "You'll play mermaid for the pirates. And I"—his voice grew deeper—"I'll play with you. A thousand years, just you and I. That should do it."

"A thousand years, and no water closet. I think not."

He laughed into her hair. A knock came on the door; high tea had arrived.

Leila sat back as Ronan accepted the tray, stroking the silver locket. It had gone from cool to warm, very warm, in just the space of his kiss.

He invited her politely to the table. Because he wanted her to—because he asked—she ate.

It would be soon now. He knew that.

The surest way to catch a thief was to set a gem in plain sight. So Ronan did naught to alter the appearance of his life, moving freely through his home, talking to those who sought him out, striding through the course of his day as if the morning had not revealed a slain enemy.

At Kelmere, meals were done in the old way of his people, which meant that any who came to the great mansion were welcome. The clan took their cue from their laird and carried out supper as if all were well. Conversation was more subdued, perhaps, but the hall was packed with faces. Clan Kell had full faith in him to see this matter through.

Which was more faith, he acknowledged ruefully, than had Leila.

The servants accommodated the extra people with aplomb; there was food and drink for all—except Ronan, of course.

Leila sat beside him with her hands resting lightly on the arms of her chair, slightly pushed back from the table. In her pale gown she glowed with the candlelight, her gaze unsettled, scanning his people. She was a sylph with ice green eyes, too taut and austere for his pleasing. The siren locket nestled just in the curve of her breasts. He had not been flattering her before—it looked as if it had been poured and molded exactly for her.

He would tell her the tale of it tonight. After he had loved her, and melted that ice from her eyes.

The meal ended, and no one had died. Leila's plate was still full.

He leaned over to her ear. "Tonight," he murmured, "I'll make you poached pears and claret. I have a fine idea of how to use the sauce."

She turned her head and kissed him, heedless of their audience. She felt too warm, almost feverish, and when she broke off her eyes glinted bright.

"Leila," he said with sudden aching, and closed his fingers against her cheek. He drew the back of his hand down her smooth skin. "Later, love. Later."

She nodded and looked away again, unsmiling, a shining lethal shield dressed like a bride in lace and white.


He was a footman. He traveled as they did, served what they did. He wore a brown wig and the same livery as all the others, and Leila did not want to think of how he had procured it.

Che met her gaze as he bent to pour someone ale. He was a ghost who moved in cordial silence; she could not believe no one but she had read the death in his eyes.

Ronan turned to her, whispered sugared words in her ear. With Che watching, she shifted in her seat and kissed him, kissed him very well—heat and heart and burning—then pulled back and made herself look up into sapphire eyes.

He was a fell bonny man. She understood the meaning of the words now.

When Ronan turned to answer a question from the

steward, she slipped the bone-handled knife from her plate and kept it flat in her palm.

The laird rose; the meal ended. Leila stood beside him, her gaze on Che, who stood by the door watching her with a fold of linen over his wrist.

In the confusion of the exiting, Leila found Finlay, caught his plaid. He looked back at her in wary expectation; she came close and spoke in a soft, even tone.

"Do you love your laird?"

His lips thinned; he shook her off. "He is my family."

"You would defend him?"

"Of course!"

She gripped his hand and held hard. "You would die for him."

"Aye," he said tersely. "I would."

And she saw that it was true.

"Then listen to me, Finlay MacMhuirich. Keep him here." Before he could answer she pushed by him, going quickly to the door. People spilled behind her in couples or groups; she heard no one calling out her name.

In the dim-lit corridor, Che paced ahead of her. Without his cane he had a marked limp, yet his feet made almost no sound over the checked marble tiles.

He did not look back to see if she followed. He knew that she would. He knew she could not walk away.

A turn, another. The smell of beeswax became overwhelming to her, the cloying perfume of church and guttering candles. He led her to a room with garden doors already cracked open. She stepped outside into the blood-chilling night.

It was a garden, a small one leading to a black wall of woods. Beside a hedge he stopped, waiting. There was a moon tonight, a sickle shaving, but it was enough to make out his face. He looked older than his years, older than she ever remembered.

Che said, "If it was compliments you were after, I could have provided them."

She only shook her head in response. She kept the knife in her hand hidden in her skirts.

"I have a ship ready, Leila. I have a way home for us."

"Why did you kill Mr. Johnson?"

"He displeased me." Che lifted his arms, a broad move that encompassed her, the mansion, the garden. "Someone had to pay for this debacle."

"Did you kill the man who owns those clothes?"

"No." He smiled. "I considered it, I admit. But I knew you wouldn't like it. He sleeps sound in the dairy."

"You must go," she said seriously. "Go, and never come back."

"Without you? How could I?"

"I am going to reach into my pocket, *Padre*. I am going to move very slowly. I want to show you something. It is not a weapon."

She found the diamond, held it out to him. Even under the sickle moon it flashed and flared blazing white. There could be no mistaking what it was.

"My quittance," she said, and tossed it to his feet.

Che made no move to pick up the stone. "Quittance. Is that what you think of me?"

"Please go. Take your ship, go home to Spain. Live a long life in your villa."

"It's your villa," he said. "The villa and my life. All of it yours. Didn't you realize?"

She gripped the knife tighter. "Will you go?"

"No, child. Not alone."

He spoke with utmost assurance. It was the voice of reason, the voice of her childhood and her nightmares.

"I've closed your account in London," he said. "Oh, yes, I knew of it. I always knew. I'm afraid dear Mademoiselle's father caught up with her and her rash, spendthrift ways. The bankers were quite easy to dupe. I had them apologizing all the way out to the street."

Leila felt a clear, cold sanity fall upon her, seeing him before her, the hedge, the starry night, tearing up the last of her illusions with just an indulgent smile.

"I cannot pretend I wasn't surprised, Leila, and a bit hurt. All that money. How could you have come by it but for cheating me? And now this." He scuffed at the diamond with the toe of his boot. "What else have you been hiding?"

"Go," she said, but it was too soft.

"I've a better notion. Take my hand." He lifted his palm up, to show it empty. She did not move.

"Did you truly think you could stay?" he asked. "Did you think this was how it was to end? You're not made for this place. You're not made for him."

"Nor you."

"Take my hand."

"No." This time the word came strong.

Che began to walk toward her, brittle grass crunching like glass with every step. His smile turned tristful. "Would it be so disagreeable? Would it be worth risking your life—or his?"

She bared her teeth. "Kill me, if you think you can. Because I won't let you near him."

"Such devotion. What could he have done to inspire it?"

He kept creeping toward her in that small, stealthy way. She had seen it too many times before. The bone knife was cold and narrow in her palm. She kept her arms relaxed, no hint of what she had hidden, her eyes on his. If he sensed weakness he'd strike like a snake.

But his hand was still outstretched.

"Think of how it would be," he said in his comforting voice, "if you stay now and I go. You'll never sleep again, will you, *niña*? I know you. You'll always wonder when I'll be back, what I'll do. And I *would* be back, Leila. I will always come for you."

He was right. If she allowed him to walk away now, it would never be over. He would never let her—or Ronan—alone.

She allowed her lips to tremble. She allowed her eyes to tear. Her feet were so cold she could no longer feel them at all.

His fingers curled gently upward, a plight, an invitation. His eyes were the color of the moon.

She lifted her empty hand, reluctantly, and let the winter night shiver down through her fingers.

Leila thought of Ronan. Of his heartbeat when he held her to his chest. Of his warm crooked smile. Of how he had fed her scones and jam today, a bite, a kiss at a time.

"Good girl," Che approved, and just as his hand reached hers she moved, slashing her other arm up, turning sideways and thrusting forward with the tip of the blade aimed at his jugular as if she held a rapier and not a paltry supper knife. He pivoted nearly as she did, twisting back, and the serrated edge only grazed his skin. Too late to stop: Her momentum carried her into him—his arms closed around her, the short blade of the *baslard* he had strapped to his wrist slicing into her forearm. They staggered back together and landed against the hedge, toppled and rolled.

From somewhere, a man shouted.

Leila kicked out, felt her foot connect with flesh, although she couldn't tell what she had hit. Che snarled above her and brought his hand down as they fought; his blade flashed before her eyes and there was bright pain across her chest. She cried out and drove the bone knife toward his heart.

"No—no—" Che caught her by the wrist and held her there, far stronger than she had ever realized. She swung her other hand to his face and he caught that one too, his fingers pressing into her.

"Read me," he gasped above her. "Read me, Leila—reeeeeaaaad . . ."

His voice faded out on an awful, scratching note, the single word turning and distorting in her mind, filling her head like the whine of a scythe slicing air.

Oh, God.

The poison welled up, black and viscous. It clogged through her lungs and she couldn't breathe with it, and still it didn't stop, filling her, filling her. Che in her mind seeing her, yanking her from her hiding place in the river trees, a small quaking waif with a nobleman's eyes, stealing her, keeping her locked away with a key and then with her own fears. Teaching her *this will burn holes in iron* her little face like a flower *this will freeze blood*, growing older, a rare deadly blossom his own creation *this is how we live and shall always live. . . .*

Leila was moaning. She thought it was her. A light struck past the night and glared ferociously over her face; she tried to hide from it and could not. The poison gagged in her throat. Her lungs had a death rattle she could not stop.

*Leila. Leila. Open your eyes Leila look at me love oh look—*

Not Che. Ronan.

*Leila!*

He was so loud in her head. His voice shook through

her and she squinted up at him. His face blazed with gold, a tiger caught in the light with a wild and barbarous fury behind his eyes.

She reached up. His palms were pressed flat to her face, his lips drawn back. A thin trickle of blood began to seep from his nose.

"No, no," she said, and tried to push him from her. He was the mountain, he was the sea. Nothing moved him.

The flow of blood increased. Her hand fumbled against it; scarlet slipped between her fingers.

"Stop." Her voice came ragged. She pushed and pushed. "Stop, you must stop."

He took his hands from her cheeks, wiped the blood from his mouth with his sleeve. "Don't move," he said. "You've been stabbed." And then: "God. God*damn*, you frightened me."

She felt it now, the sting across her chest. It didn't seem so awful, a sparse razored ache. He had torn off his plaid, was pressing it hard over the wound.

"Don't move," he said again, glaring at her. But she did anyway, turning her head to see blades of grass blurred up close, the booted feet of men, more distant—and then a hand, slack on the ground. Che, flat on the grass with leaves in his hair, watching her with glazed eyes.

The feet moved. She had a good view of the blood staining his stolen livery, the hilt of the bone knife barely visible past the neat green waistcoat.

"Oh," she said, suddenly winded. "Did you do that?"

"No." Ronan leaned down and kissed her with a violence that cut her lips, his blood and hers mingling between them. "You did. Thank God. And if you ever try anything so stupid as running off like that again, I swear to God I will kill you myself."

He lifted his head. *"Finlay,"* he roared, "where the *hell* is that doctor?"

As it was wont to do, the Scottish winter descended with full force, locking up the mountains and the roads in slick glittering ice, painting snow in generous layers across the purple-green woods and glens. From the very top of Kelmere's old stone donjon, Ronan could see the fresco of the sea, a push of sunlight breaking through clouds, soon swept away with the wind.

Up here, alone, he could believe the fortress was its own kingdom again. That nothing could touch them but nature and time.

"You are a difficult man to find," said a feminine voice behind him.

He smiled at the leaden sky. "Not so very difficult. You found me."

"Yes." He heard her walk up behind him, soft feet padding over stone. "But I have a gift, you know."

"I do."

He'd been avoiding her and she knew it, as Leila seemed to know all things about him.

"Do you miss the ocean?" she asked, standing at his side.

"Aye." He shrugged. "But the thaw will come soon."

He thought of telling her of the Celtic well far below them, and the underground springs. But he didn't. Perhaps she wouldn't want to know.

Ronan angled a look down at her. She was dressed in woolens and a cloak and still had the Kell tartan pulled over her like a blanket. The tips of her fingers where she pinched it closed at her throat were red and white, to match her cheeks. He remembered something he had thought of her once—a sunflower. A being of heat and light caught in his icicled, prismed world.

"What sort of cottage will you have?" he asked. She glanced up at him from beneath her lashes. "I mean," he said awkwardly, "where will it be?"

She turned back to the rolling view.

"By water?" he persisted.

"Perhaps."

The wind circled past them. Ronan clasped his hands tightly behind his back.

"With the diamond you'll have enough money to buy an entire village by the sea. I'll give you more, if you don't." He kept talking, because she was so quiet. "I was told it once belonged to Hadrian's empress. It could be nonsense. Who knows."

"I don't want a village," Leila said. A corner of the tartan lifted playfully in the wind; he had a glimpse of the long pink scar down her chest, the locket—and the fresh scratch across it that had probably saved her life when deflecting *La Mano*'s blade.

He had been nearly too late. For all his strength and magic, he had nearly lost her that night. Finlay pulling him aside in the hall, telling him she'd gone. The deep, spiraling panic of realizing that she had melted into shadows, that she faced his nemesis alone.

In those minutes without her, he'd tasted madness. He'd imagined a different ghastly death for her with each running step. And then, when he'd found her—

Two months had followed and Leila was mending well. He knew it for himself. He had kissed and stroked and loved every part of her, telling her without words how cherished she was to him, how dear. He had lain at her side and lost himself in her, in the pale wave of her hair and glow of her cheek, in the promise of the future in her glass-green eyes.

But this morning Ronan had awakened before dawn. He had stolen softly from the bed to leave her sleeping, crossed to the window to find black ice on the sills and the sky swollen dark. And he had stood there, perversely reminded of spring, of the day that would come when the ice would flow to water and new life would begin.

She never spoke of leaving. She never spoke of staying, either.

He would not be the new master who held her. He would not be her keeper. She was free to leave Kelmere whenever the elements allowed.

Ronan thought of her going and felt like he'd never find the sun again.

"Won't you be lonely?" he asked.

Her lips pressed up to a smile. "No."

"Are you certain?" He closed his eyes, addressed the raw clouds. "I've been alone all my life. I can tell you it's much overrated."

Her answer was peaceful. "Well. It all depends on how often you'll be going to Kell."

Ronan gave her a sidelong look.

"And, I suppose, if you can—lower the mists and calm the seas." Her fingers rolled the ends of the tartan into twists; she did not meet his gaze. "I'm skilled at many things, Lord Kell, but sailing is not among them."

"Leila," he began, but lost his breath. He did not want to hope. He did not want to feel these things and have the world pulled out from him—he remembered her on the grass, all the blood spilling over her, and her slow, drowsy smile at him—

She stood so straight, a hint of uncertainty in her eyes as her hair and skirts were tossed wild with the wind.

"I am cold," Leila said to him, very dignified. "I do not wish to be cold any longer."

The edges of the tartan parted; her arms opened to him.

"And I love you," she added, when he couldn't move. "Will it matter? I love you with my whole heart."

He came to life, suddenly, splendidly. He took her in his arms and folded her to him, tartan and all. He pressed his lips to the tender warmth behind her ear, her arms around his waist and his hand tangled in her hair.

"I love you," he whispered. "Little doña. I love you so much."

"You're cold too." It was a faint muffled complaint to his chest.

"Not for long, Layla." Ronan rocked her close, his head bowed to hers. "Not for long."

# Book Three:
# The Siren

# · PROLOGUE ·

Once I swam the seas alone. It was well for me, all I thought I wanted or needed. The ocean was my mother and my heart; my island, my father and my peace. I was *siren*—sovereign and wild and thoroughly delighted with everything about myself.

But I was alone. I had no sisters, no brothers. My siren mother died young, and there was none such as me left in the world. I was the last.

For many years it suited me. What being could compare to me, to my raw power and splendid elegance? What need had I for men, who were weak mortal things, unblessed by the sea?

But I was alone. Ever alone.

And slowly, strangely, men became . . . intriguing.

I began to spy on them. I began to hunt them, to follow their ships closer than ever I dared before. I began to listen to them, to take their measure by their eyes, by their voices and hands. One would

have a comely smile, but at rest his lips turned small
and mean. Or one might have the gift of song, but
his legs were bandied and frail. Strong hands but a
bent back. Copper hair but a cruel laugh. None was
altogether perfect like me.

My loneliness began to weigh heavy upon me. I
spent more and more time at the bottom of the sea,
too weary to rise up to the sky.

And then came the storm. Oh, it was a transcen-
dent storm, a boon from the gods, danger and fury
and barbarous swells. It pushed me hither and yon
until I had no choice but to wake from my stupor, to
swim and fight for my life.

And when it was done, like a pearl in a nacre
shell, I found him waiting for me.

Kell.

Fairest youth ever I had seen, a creature of such
dark beauty and warmth I knew instantly that he
was mine. He knew it as well. We were bound from
the moment I touched his hand. With the sea surrounding us, we exchanged our vows. Then I pressed
my lips to his and took him home with me.

Hallowed days. Breathtaking nights.

Our young were as beautiful as I—and as he, a
school of sea children laughing and racing about our
isle, swimming and diving with me in the water.
Never before had I known such completion.

Kell and the little ones and me: We were, quite
naturally, the perfect family.

But he changed. Small things at first . . . how he
began to glance away from me when I arose from
the waves. How his lips drew tight with disdain before our kisses. He grew rougher with me, more
careless with his words and hands.

He became cold at night. No amount of heat from me would warm him.

I tried to win him again; I tried to woo him and please him as I had of old. He spoke of certain foods and spices and I brought them to him. He spoke of kin and I ventured out to find them—long dead, of course. He spoke of his homeland, and I delivered him news of it, telling him of the wars that had come while we played on our isle, of the savages that had swarmed and burned and ripped all they touched to tatters. Yet Kell, my beloved Kell, did not open to me.

He no longer met my eyes. He no longer touched my body.

I would flee to the sea to weep, so that he would not see the breadth of my pain.

One night I slept deep, dreaming of a curious land, of glass palaces so tall they pierced a brown heaven, of hard rivers of stone with countless people trapped upon them, all leading to a bitter ocean that I did not know.

A hard tug at my throat. I awoke—and Kell was above me, his face a dreadful mask, my precious locket in his hands.

I moved as quickly as I could. I was young and he was old and I was swift and he was slow and still he beat me, still he won: He opened the locket. I saw it happen. I saw our dreams dissolve before my eyes, and my one true love—the man I had lived with for so long, who had embraced me and cherished me and known me as none other, the man who still held my wounded heart in his hands—fell dead to my feet.

Who would survive such a thing? Who would not go mad?

Who would not cast a wish for one more chance?

424 · Sh

margarita mix red...
glass to her lips a...
She... Call now...

# CHAPTER

❧

# Storm Lake, Iowa, 4:41 A.M.

Jessie sat slumped on the davenport, the remains of her fourth—fifth?—margarita melting to sludge in its glass. The television squatted brightly straight ahead of her, a blinding succession of infomercials and fake psychics chattering on, inviting her to call them *right now* to discover her *true* destiny.

Right. Like she needed a psychic for that.

The wind picked up and sent the leaves of the old cottonwood outside the window trembling with moonlight. Another night, another time, the effect might have been lovely. Tonight the tree—standing so gaunt and alone— only reminded her of her loss. Jessie turned her face away from the window. God, she was tired. Why didn't she just go to bed?

"Call now," tempted a gorgeous redhead on the screen, voluptuous and practically dipped in gold jewelry. "Call now, and have all the mysteries of your fate revealed. Our psychics are waiting . . . just for you."

Jessie glanced down to the pitcher by her feet, ice and

...ed to sticky dregs, then lifted her ... and drained that too.

... Why not?

... straightened, setting the glass on the floor next to ...e pitcher with a dull *clink*.

Yeah. Why the hell not?

Quickly, before she could change her mind, she grabbed the phone and punched in the number to the psychic line. There was a wait, and then a hum, and then a weird crackle of static as the line began to ring. Jessie worried her lower lip nervously. This was stupid. This was a new low. She should just hang up right—

Another click, more static. Then:

"Hello," greeted a woman's voice, darker and even more sultry than the one from the television. "This is Natalya. Please tell me just your first name."

"Um, Jessica." She began to twist the phone cord around her finger until it hurt.

"Hi, Jessica. Have you ever had a Tarot card reading before?"

"No."

"There's nothing to worry about." The psychic's voice was melodic and very feminine, somehow both soothing and smiling, like your best girlfriend about to tell you a delicious secret. *Contralto*, that was the word.

Jessie pictured the redhead from the commercial reclining luxuriously on pillows in a room filled with incense and beads and crystal balls.

"You have a question you'd like answered, don't you?"

"I—maybe. I think so."

"That's fine," said Natalya in her throaty, disarming way. "You don't have to tell me the question. Just keep it in your thoughts while I do your reading."

"Okay."

"I'm going to pull the first card of the spread, Jessica. We call it the Significator. It represents you in your current situation. Are you ready?"

"Yes." She felt, abruptly, much more confident. She looked down at the phone cord caught between her rings and began to free her hand.

"Here we go. Ah. THE CHARIOT. Interesting . . ."

Jessie relaxed back again, the phone cradled to her ear, letting the other woman's words lull her deep into the davenport cushions.

*Goodness*, she thought, with a kind of distant admiration, *I could listen to her talk all day.*

"TEMPERANCE," Natalya was saying smoothly. "Crossing you. You don't find forgiveness easy."

"No. No, I suppose not."

"You should let go of old hurts, Jessica. They harm only you."

Past the double-paned window, past the lonely cottonwood, the morning stars were beginning to fade. The eastern edge of the sky took on a paler hue.

"Do you understand me, Jessica?"

"Yes."

The sky was turning lavender. At the lip of the world, it was the exact color of the lavender chiffon dress she had worn to her senior formal, so long ago. Dan had looked so handsome that night, like a bright golden god in his tux. No wonder she had let him—

"Jessie," said Natalya with sudden sharpness.

Jessica snapped upright, blinking. "Yes. I'm here."

"Do you . . ." For the first time, there was hesitancy in the psychic's tone. Natalya paused, then finished softly. "Do you have a cat?"

Jessie's throat cramped; her eyes burned. She couldn't speak.

"I'm getting a strong image of a cat . . . is it a cat?"

*No*, Jessie mouthed, her vocal cords still frozen.

"No," said Natalya at nearly the same time. "Not a cat. A person. A girl."

"Yes," Jessie said, a rush of sound. *"Yes."*

"She's close to you."

"My daughter. Catrina. I call—I called her Cat." Her voice broke. There was more she wanted to say, that she was dying to say, but the words were stuck in her throat, clogged with hot tears, *she's been gone six months now, only thirteen years old, my little girl, my runaway, god oh god I'm so sorry and I miss her so much—*

Natalya spoke again, her voice pure as spring water. "No, Jessica. I mean, she's close to you physically. She's not far away."

Beyond the cottonwood, the lavender sky began to lift to perfect rose. The psychic said, "It's the answer to your question. Your daughter is coming home."

And at that very moment, in the clean stillness of the new day, there came a soft knock on the kitchen door.

# Pasadena, California, 3:13 A.M.

Ruri Kell ended the call, unclipped the phone from the waist of her jeans, and tore off the pinch of the headset, tossing both to the coffee table with a little more force than necessary. She felt restless, achy in a deep sort of way that had nothing to do with the fact that she'd just spent the last half hour or so cross-legged on the floor for a reading.

It came over her sometimes, this itchy annoyance of her own skin, as if her bones and joints wanted to keep growing past their twenty-five-year-old frame.

*Crazy-bones*, Dad used to call it. *Family trait, Rurigirl. Guess you're not the milkman's daughter, after all.*

Ruri knew, from experience, there was nothing to do for it. Nothing banished the ache but time—not exercise, not food or alcohol, not sleeping.

Not sleeping. Definitely not that.

She slipped her hands through her dark hair and stretched hard anyway, yawning and testing her limits, then wandered over to her front door, opening it to moonlight and charcoal shadows.

It was the sort of April night that seldom blessed L.A., cloudless, soft and warm but with a sweet-scented breeze that settled like flower petals over dry dusty streets and curbs. Ruri stood there awhile in silence, appreciating that faint, pretty scent, then turned back to the deliberate gloom of her apartment.

She kept it dim because it was easier for her to read that way. No lamplight but plenty of candles layered across the furniture: a fat white one on top of the CD player, slow burning; a trio of slender pink tapers flickering on the windowsill, doubled flames bright against the glass; and last of all a creamy brick of light on the coffee table, a gift from Jody the witch.

The brick candle, heady with lily, was Ruri's favorite. Lily for calm, and for hope. It was why she kept it by her Tarot cards.

She was barefoot, enjoying the polish of her old maple floor as she walked to the table and sat again before it. She had a sofa—a fat, overstuffed hand-me-down from Aunt Setsu—but seldom used it. The floor was almost always more comfortable.

*Nature-girl*, the family teased her. *Little pagan.*

Ruri tucked her hair behind her ears and surveyed the black sweep of cards curved out before her. Her hand lifted, the pads of her fingers drifting lightly over the spread. She knew their worn edges, the thick cardboard slap of them as she shuffled and plucked and rearranged them. This was her very first set of Tarot cards and still her favorite, designed in rich jewel colors and bold, simple illustrations. Back in junior high, she had squandered eight months' worth of babysitting money to afford them.

*Guess they've paid for themselves by now,* she thought, and didn't know whether to laugh or sigh over that.

*Ruriko,* Aunt Setsu had scolded last week, *are you still working that terrible job? A girl like you! Why are you playing games with silly cards?*

And Ruri had smiled and murmured something vaguely apologetic, because it was an old, familiar argument, and Ruri never won. It would be impolite to win, to say the only things she could say to defend herself:

*Because Mom and Dad died, and I need the money.*

*Because the night is never-ending.*

*Because I can't sleep.*

And because sometimes, sometimes . . . it wasn't a game at all.

The phone rang, two short peals. Business line.

She lifted the headset, adjusted the mike, and put on her *you-can-tell-me-anything* voice.

"Hello, this is Natalya. Please—"

A wince-inducing blast of static screeched in her ear. She swore and tore off the headset, scowling at it as it practically vibrated in her hands. The static burbled and chattered and then finally dropped to a mutter.

Damned phone. It was her third one this year. She had the worst luck with phones.

Gingerly, she held the headphone out by her ear.

"Hello?"

The static chirped and broke into a staccato series of snaps—but there was a voice coming through. A man's voice.

". . . mackinnez. Are you . . ."

"Hello? Can you hear me?"

". . . is ee-un mac . . ."

Definitely a man's voice, clipped and impatient beneath the noise.

"Just a moment, please." She unplugged the headset, shook out the cord, and plugged it back in. The static settled down to a sullen hiss.

"I'm so sorry," Ruri began, "would you mind—"

As soon as she slipped the headset on, the static flared back, a hum that dipped and rose and rose, and beneath it she caught one final, irritated word before the line died:

*"Kell—"*

With a soft *pop*, the little red light on the phone burned out, sending up a wisp of smoke as if in spiraling farewell. Ruri stared at the smoke, then at the useless headset cupped in her hands.

Slowly, intentionally, she lowered her forehead to the coffee table and banged it once. Sleepless, alone, flat broke . . . and now she didn't even have a phone.

Iain MacInnes was annoyed. He stood with his hands clasped loosely behind his back and contemplated the view from the tall, spotless windows of his library, the green roll of the island hills, the dense forests that fingered the sky. The ocean, a coy sparkle of silver that flashed between the treetops.

Aye, annoyed. His life had been a series of shrewd calculations, one step to another to another. It took a great deal of will and energy to maintain the tight control he required in this dance, and that he had managed it so well for so long was not so much a point of pride for him but one of stark necessity. He had done what he must to lift himself from poverty and shame to climb up to here, to Kelmere, and he was so close now—so damned *close*. . . .

Months of hunting had finally located the last Kell heir, not a Scot at all but an American. It was a complication so unexpected, so ludicrous that his annoyance wavered, threatened to turn to grim humor before he quashed it.

His eyes narrowed against the sea light. Telephoning had been singularly unsuccessful; there was a storm boiling to the south, and in any case, international calls from the island were notoriously unreliable. He'd try again later.

Deliberately he released the tension from his fingers. There was no doubt he would achieve what he wished. He always had. The annoyance came from waiting.

The dark humor rode up anyway, became a wry smile. Very well, he'd wait. It'd been forever already. What was another day?

# CHAPTER TWO

❧

*T*he ocean was roiling, surly and thick and hideous, and the sky was an evil welt above her, bruised clouds swelling and splitting open to drown her in rain. She was going to die here, it was time to die, because she couldn't breathe and she couldn't fight and the sea was going to gobble her whole, suck her down to inky cold depths until her lungs were crushed paper and the fish would come and eat her in pieces—

Ruri woke, sobbing, twisted in her sheets with her hands pushing at the wall above her head. It took a long while to come back to the sun-washed room that was her studio apartment, to swallow and wipe her tears and accept the fact that she was not dying, not drowning, but only tangled in bedclothes and light. She sat up, breathing deeply, shoving her hair from her face. ·

God. It had happened again. She had meant to rest just a while, a few hours at most. Usually the Nightmare crept only into her longer sleeps, waiting until she sank to the deeps of her dreams. It began always the same, a dragging, gathering sense of pressure, growing heavier, more potent, until it welled into pain—blistering, searing—into panic. And then the storm would come.

Ruri glanced at the clock by her futon. Ten fifteen. She'd slept three hours, then. And the Nightmare had come anyway, stronger than it'd been in months.

She dropped her head into her palms, rubbed her eyes. What was she going to do? Nothing helped.

Karma, Jody would say. This is what you have brought with you into this life. This is what you must understand, and embrace, in order to overcome.

She did not understand it; she would not embrace it. How would she ever overcome it? Until her parents had passed away, Ruri had never suffered a nightmare in her life. It was as if they had all been saved up, pressed together, massed into one ugly black horror that she relived over and over. . . .

Ten fifteen. Her head lifted. She'd be late for Sunday brunch if she didn't get moving.

Setsu's home was the unofficial center of family business, a small Craftsman filled with *shoji* screens and clever corners. There was always green tea and welcome, and sometimes a great deal more; in those first blurry, dreadful days after the accident, Ruri had spent untold time nestled in the easy chair by the fireplace, covered in blankets yet icy cold, clutching endless cups of tea just to warm her fingers.

And although the 210 unspooled more easily than usual, Ruri was still late. There were cousins already spilling out the patio door, milling beneath the purple jacaranda just beginning to come into bloom. She tried to duck in but Toshio saw her first, shouting out her name so that everyone turned, and she grinned as he did, sliding up to pull her into a hug.

"What'd you bring to eat? More rabbit food, little bunny?"

"Hummus. And pita bread."

Toshio, at thirty-two the oldest of the cousins, rolled his eyes in exaggerated exasperation. "Thank God Mallory brought the sushi. I'd starve around you."

"Wouldn't hurt you much." Ruri poked him in the ribs.

"Ouch! The bunny bites!"

"Shut up."

And Toshio, who had once infamously said, *God gave Ruri a voice that could melt glaciers. She could tell me to strip naked and dye my hair blue, and I'd ask, navy or baby?*, only replied, "Okay," and ambled away.

They were a rainbowed family, a disparate collection of colors and sizes and temperaments, from geisha-lovely Amanda to green-eyed Hanako. Ruri paused by the fireplace mantel to glance at the family portrait taken two Christmases ago: smiles and near-smiles, beloved faces ranging from coffee to cream to china-white. Ruriko stood quite literally somewhere in that middle, neither tall nor short, neither pale nor tanned, deep-brown hair that in full sun threw glints of copper, her mother's dark tilted brows and rosebud lips. Her father's eyes—blue, like lapis. Like midnight.

Setsu found her. There were more hugs to be shared; the hummus and bread were carried to the crowded kitchen table, settled meekly between an elaborate platter of confetti-hued *sashimi* and a box of pale, powdery balls of *mochi*.

"I'm making you a salad," Setsu said, squeezing Ruri's hands. "Vinaigrette and candied pecans, just the way you like it."

"Aunt Setsu, you don't have to go to all that trouble."

"What trouble? I enjoy it. Sit down. Sit."

Ruri took her favorite chair, the one with the lopsided arm and the back leg a hair too short that gave everyone else fits but always managed to lean back just right for her. She sat a moment with her hands in her lap, watching her aunt move—brisk, trim, economical grace—then kicked off her sling-backs and drew up her knees for a chinrest.

People came and went through the kitchen, and the platter of *sashimi* began to resemble a jigsaw puzzle missing most of its pieces. Eight-year-old Molly darted in and tried the hummus, pronounced it delicious, and then began to chase Toshio across the room, brandishing a piece of dipped bread like a sword. Family scattered, began to laugh and scold, but Ruri was watching Setsu. She was standing motionless at the sink, her hands cupped around the glass bowl filled with green lettuce, her gaze dropped. There was a pull to her lips Ruri hadn't seen before.

She came to her feet, put her hand on her aunt's shoulder.

"Auntie? What is it?"

Setsu looked up quickly, too quickly, and gave Ruri a vacant smile. "Are you hungry? What an old woman I am today, standing here daydreaming. Where's your plate?"

It was the smile more than anything that alarmed her. Aunt Setsu, Ruri's rock and her faith, never, ever shirked from the truth, no matter how unpleasant. "Setsu, please. Tell me what's wrong."

Her aunt's eyes lowered again, her fine skin wrinkled to a frown. She turned the bowl slowly in her hands, then set it down on the counter.

"Something came in the mail yesterday."

"Something bad?"

Setsu opened a drawer, rummaged inside, and pulled out a padded brown envelope.

"Something for your father."

There would come a day, Ruri hoped, when her heart wouldn't freeze up and turn to stone in her chest, when her blood wouldn't just stop and fall and leave her so barren and dry. She saw her hands reach out, accept the package, crisp brown paper and thickly taped edges. Her father's name, *Dr. Samuel Kell*, typed neatly on a white sticky label.

She didn't recognize the return address. It was foreign, a string of surnames and ampersands. Scotland.

"Why did it come here?" How normal she sounded.

"It went to the law firm first." Setsu tapped the address beneath her father's name. "See? They forwarded it here. Probably just got our addresses mixed up."

"Probably."

The envelope was larger than anything needed for a letter but not big enough for much else. Ruri felt a curious reluctance to unwrap it, this final, mysterious business of her father's; whom could he have known in Scotland? He had never been there, had never even been in touch with his very distant family there, she knew. Maybe it had something to do with the university, or . . .

She stared down at that plain sensible label and felt an unlikely chill begin to snake up the tendons of her hands.

Don't ignore your instincts, Jody had taught her. Your inner self is smarter than you think.

Molly ran up from behind and threw her arms around Ruri's waist, hard enough to rock them both.

"Hey, Ruri. What is it? What's in the package?"

"I don't know, baby. It just came."

The arms tightened; a head of shining black hair poked

through the crook of Ruri's elbow. "Aren't you going to open it?"

"Molly-*chan*, leave her alone," Setsu chided, but Ruri shook her head.

"No, she's right. I should open it."

*I should, I should. But I don't want to.*

"Maybe it's money," offered Molly hopefully.

"Or just some more paperwork." Ruri began to peel back the tape.

It wasn't money, or papers. It was a box, a long one, heavy cardboard, like the kind used to hold jewelry. Molly was jittering up and down now on the balls of her feet, so Ruri's hands shook—*that was the only reason*—as she lifted off the lid.

"Oh," said Molly in a surprised voice, and stopped bouncing.

"My," said Setsu, with a swift, small gasp.

Ruri said nothing at all. All her breath had left her; she was hollow and light and lost in the burning glow of silver trapped in the box she held.

It was a necklace. A necklace with a locket, nothing very delicate, but bright polished metal that was both heavy and fine. The links looked distinctly handmade, each one with slight variations in shape or size, but the locket itself was what drew her eyes. Clearly an antique, it gleamed with a subtle waving pattern chased across the metal, like moonlight rippling over water. There was a long, shallow scratch along one side, rubbed soft with time.

Ruri lifted it from the box. It lay so warm, cupped in her palm.

*I know this,* she realized. *I've seen this before.*

And with that knowledge came something else, sharp and prickling, like winter breath blown across her skin.

*It's dangerous.*

"Wow," said Molly. "It's so beautiful. Is it yours, Ruri?"

"I . . . I don't know. There's no note, no explanation."

"Open it," Molly demanded, wiggling free of Ruri's arm. "Maybe there's something inside the locket."

Ruri hesitated, then pressed her thumb against the rimmed silver edge. Nothing happened.

"It's frozen shut. I might be able to force it open, but I don't want to damage it."

Molly stretched out her hand. "Let me try. I'm strong."

"Not as strong as Ruriko," said Setsu firmly. "Go wash your hands, child, you've got—what is that?"

"Hummus!"

"—hummus all over them. And you've gotten Ruri's blouse dirty."

"Sorry." Molly skipped off.

Setsu came close, stroked one careful finger across the surface of the locket, her eyes shadowed. "Molly's right. It *is* beautiful. Luminous, really."

Ruri spoke quietly. "Yes. It is."

"Are you going to keep it?"

"I don't think it's mine, Auntie."

"Don't you?" Setsu looked up at Ruri, that odd pull back to her lips, her gaze level. "Whatever was your mother's and father's is now yours. If this belonged to Samuel, he'd want you to have it. You know that."

*Danger,* sang Ruri's intuition, her fingers rubbing the warm linked chain, learning its curves. *Sweet, silvery danger.*

"I don't think this was ever Dad's. There must be some sort of a mix-up. Whoever owns this will want it back. Besides, I don't wear jewelry, especially not heavy things."

"Yes. But if you were to start . . ."

Ruri forced a smile. "Frankly, I'm far more likely to pawn it for cash than ever wear it."

And she dropped the necklace back into the box and closed the lid.

She had spent her life well loved, protected. Ruri had never fully realized it until her parents were gone: that she had been so protected that money was never openly discussed; that debt was something that happened to others—unfortunate others. That when she asked for help with tuition, they gave her what they didn't have. That they had borrowed, and borrowed, and borrowed.

That it was her fault.

*Not your fault,* said Setsu, the attorneys, everyone else. *You didn't know, no one knew, how could we have known?*

The car accident stole them so swiftly. They were alive one morning and dead that afternoon, and Ruri was left with nothing but the memory of her mother's laugh and her father's tired voice on the phone, assuring her that they were leaving the house in five minutes and would see her soon for lunch. But she'd never seen them again.

Toshio had to identify the bodies. Ruriko, in her daze, couldn't rise from Setsu's chair.

Her phone was fried. There was no possible way to receive a message on her answering machine, but when Ruri walked into her apartment she discovered the message display flashing a bright red *1*.

Puzzled, she dropped her purse and the Scottish envelope—the strange necklace quite, quite tucked away—on the pine table by the door, then stood before the answering machine, her hands on her hips. Could it pick up a call even without the phone working?

*1, 1, 1*, winked the display.

Well, okay. Ruri pushed the Play button.

Static again, shrill and crisp. For God's sake, she paid a small fortune to the phone company every month and this just kept happening—

"—Kell. It is extremely important that I—"

That man—it was the same man as last night; she'd recognize his voice in a heartbeat, even through the static. Deep and almost musical, he spoke with an accent she couldn't quite place—

"—at once. If you might kindly meet—"

Irritated. A deep, musical, irritated voice, fading thin against the buzzing background and then surging back, loud and clear as if he were standing right next to her.

"—by Wednesday in Los Angeles. Good day."

She tapped her nails against the plastic cover of the machine, frowning as the recording ended and the *1* turned to *0*. Whoever he was, he certainly was persistent. Ruri turned away with a mental shrug. If he wanted to speak to her badly enough, he'd call back. By Wednesday she'd have a new phone.


Despite all precedent and quite a few weathermen's firm predications of eternal spring sunshine, in the small dark hours of Tuesday morning it began to rain. Ruri pushed her futon close to her window and watched, her elbows propped on the sill, as the clouds began to stack and plump, shifting from misty blue to violet, swirling darker to plum. Lightning sparked and lit the world to sudden brilliance; the trees and sidewalks blinded her in black and white. For an instant it wasn't Los Angeles at all but some eerie, magical place, with elves and fairies revealed—and then gone.

The heavens opened up, and the rain shattered down.

She trailed a finger down the window, following drops of water as they splashed and wept down the pane. A gleam caught the corner of her eye; her gaze went to the heavy charm of silver by her legs, nearly hidden in covers. The necklace.

Against her better judgment she had left her bed to pull it out of the box again, let it slip across her hands with a soft, inviting whisper of chain. The locket felt cold now, far colder than the room, but still it drew her in a way she'd never felt before; it tempted her and warned her and bothered her until the urge to try it on had become nearly overwhelming. And then Ruri had set it aside.

It wasn't hers. She didn't want it to be hers.

Another trident of lightning splintered the sky. This time there was thunder too, a rolling deep rumble that shivered through her with baritone delight. Ruri kicked off the sheets and came to her feet.

In her tank top and pajama bottoms she walked outside, lifting her face to the wet. Rainfall bit her skin; she opened her palms to the sky and felt the water slide between her fingers, a joyous sensation. It hadn't rained in forever. She had forgotten how wonderful it was just to do something simple and childish and fun like getting soaked in a cloudburst.

No elves, no fairies. Only a lone woman, standing on the flagstone path to her door with her arms outstretched and her head tipped back, grinning like a fool, somehow madly, ridiculously grateful for the downpour.

She didn't see the stranger approach until he loomed right in front of her, phantom-fixed, silent and still as the night was not.

# CHAPTER THREE

❧

He had left Scotland in a pelter of storms, by sea, by air, and then by land, thrashed and buffeted the entire journey. It seemed the rain gods had followed him even here, to a place he had thought would be as parched as desert grass.

Was it a sign, or merely a spate of bad weather?

A sign, Iain decided, pushing aside his cynicism. A gift from Kelmere flung with him across the wide ocean, the gods blowing hard at his back.

*Come home soon.*

Aye. He would. At long last, he would.

From the shelter of his rented limousine he watched the woman step out of the dark, her delighted little skip across the stones of the path, the rain sheeting off her lean body to leave her sleek and gleaming as a seal. Her rapture was so manifest, so absolute. She couldn't possibly realize she was being observed.

"Wait here," Iain instructed the chauffeur, who was no doubt half asleep, since they had parked over an hour ago.

But the man turned his head and nodded, and Iain climbed out of the automobile into the cool tumult of the night.

He had been somewhat taken aback when the driver had brought him to this rambling, unkempt neighborhood and pointed out the unassuming row of flats that matched the address Iain provided. They didn't seem the proper sort of quarters for a respected university professor and his wife, but there was no denying facts. This was the place.

He'd been waiting for a decent hour to knock on the door, for sunrise at least. But then the woman had emerged from Dr. Kell's flat, unhurried, uncovered, as if it were the most natural thing in the world to spin beneath the pouring clouds without a slicker or even, he saw as he came closer, shoes.

She looked too young to be a professor's wife.

Interesting, and unforeseen. Yet it might offer him an edge to the game he was about to effect. And Iain had long ago made it a custom to seize whatever edge he could, deserved or no.

Raindrops slanted iridescent through the night, glanced off him like a shower of diamonds. He moved with the muscled stealth and eloquence of over two decades of hard-core *shaolin* training: instinct, survival, the hunt merged as one. But it occurred to him to make some noise to warn the young woman, footsteps at least; he let his heels clip the flagstones.

She didn't seem to hear.

So he walked up to a view of the lady's throat, bared and lovely as she faced the heavens, her hair a dusky tangle down her back. What there was of her nightshirt had turned translucent with the rain, molded to her in pale willowed lines. He couldn't help the fleet, appreciative glance at her breasts, their pleasing curves and the hint of taut nipples—he wasn't a monk, by God—but it was only a brief slip of control.

Then her chin lowered, and her gaze fell to his. Iain found himself looking straight into the deep blue, almond-tipped eyes of a siren.

*The* siren.

His heart stopped in his chest.

Ruri yelped and danced back, raising her fists in a gesture both protective and enraged. "One more step, mister, and I guarantee you'll end up missing some vital body parts."

The man didn't move. Through the bruising rain Ruri held her stance, her nerves screaming, ready to strike. She wasn't a trained fighter but knew she could hit hard— very hard. If he twitched, if he *blinked*, she'd let loose— the door was just behind her—*why* had she walked outside alone, for God's sake, she was smarter than that, she'd lived in the city for years—

"Yuriko Kell?"

It took a moment to register that, the deep, familiar voice, the fluent accent. Her mother's name, with the emphasis on the wrong syllable.

He spoke again, hoarsely, water splashing between them in a thousand sizzling beads. "Are you—Yuriko Kell?"

She didn't drop her fists, not really. But she did stand up a little straighter. "Who the hell are you?"

"Iain MacInnes." He lifted a hand, lowered it again when she hopped back. "I called. I said I was coming."

"Did you? Guess I missed your message."

If he caught her sarcasm he gave no sign of it, but answered only, "I see," in that rough, attractive tone. And then, when she didn't move: "I mean you no harm."

In the raindark Ruri examined him: taller than she, with

thick black hair that curled in licks down his forehead and dripped water down his neck; a long gray coat that concealed most of his body. No hat. He was staring down at her, dark-lashed, heavy-browed, twin lines etched around an undeniably sexy mouth. Despite the lines, his face held something close to beauty—hard-edged, masculine, but more than that. There was a severity to him, a sternness, that cast the handsome lips and lashes an ascetic depth.

He had eyes the color of lit amber. They studied her with unshielded intensity, a panther sizing up its prey.

Ruri remembered, all at once, what she was wearing. How it would look wet.

"Please." The man nodded toward the open door behind her. "Might we go inside?"

"Absolutely not." She began to back up, never looking away from his face. But the man didn't follow, only watched her go with that light, burning gaze.

"I've come a long way."

"Cry me a river."

"I beg your pardon?"

She had reached the door, took shelter behind the hard, heavy wood. "Do you know what time it is?"

"I've come to—to talk to Dr. Kell. I know it's late—or early—I've just flown in from Scotland. It is urgent that I speak with him."

"You're too late."

He took a step forward. "What?"

She was tired suddenly, the adrenaline that had whipped through her before collapsing in her veins, leaving her small and weary. "You're too late," Ruri said again, and felt, awfully, her chest tighten with that dull, angry pain that meant she was about to weep. "Samuel Kell is dead. Come back tomorrow."

She closed the door before he could say anything else.

* * *

Far and away, on a small, perfect island, every living creature, from the nimble rabbits in the woods to the mam-
moth gray seals on the rocks, paused in its day to catch the
new scent riding the sky. Waves of turquoise leapt and
rinsed the shore in white sprays, tossed reflections of the
clouds above. And in the ruins of an ancient palace, where
the breezes swirled and turned, the starlings in their sheltered nests began to sing.

She did not sleep.

She tried to, because even the Nightmare was better
than remembering, and hurting, and shedding tears into
her already-damp pillow. But Ruri didn't sleep, and she
cried only a bit before wiping her face and getting up to
take a shower. Hot water usually helped.

Dawn crept through the paper honeycomb shades,
tinting the ivory to orangy pink and lighting the whole of
her little home like the inside of a seashell. Ruri brewed a
pot of coffee and drank it slowly, concentrating on each
sip, each small movement of her hand so that she
wouldn't have to think or feel yet. Soon she would. Soon
she'd face the day.

Outside began the sounds of the city awakening, cars
grumbling down the street, neighbors stirring, dogs with
fast-clicking nails being walked across cement and puddles.

The coffee was gone; the rain had stopped. Ruri opened
her door and looked out at the fresh-washed sky—cloudless now, pristine—and the water-jeweled trees and darkened buildings—

And at the limousine parked across the street, exactly
where it had been the night before.

A man exited the limo. A tall, good-looking man in an expensive gray coat.

"Great," she muttered, and watched him cross the street to her.

At least she was dressed.

"You're still here," she said, when he was close enough.

"It *is* tomorrow," he countered, smooth.

She didn't shift from the doorway, only crossed her arms and gave him a very meticulous, very obvious inspection from his tousled head to his Italian leather-shod toes.

"Did you sleep in the car?"

"No. I have a hotel room."

"Don't they provide razors at the hotel?" she asked sweetly.

He smiled at that, but there was no humor in the sharp curving of his lips. "I found myself in rather a hurry."

"Mr. MacGuinnes—"

"Mac*Innes*," he corrected, soft.

"I'm sorry you've come from Scotland. I'm sorry you couldn't bother to shave. But I told you last night about Samuel. Any business you had with him, you'll have to take up with the law firm that's handling the probate. I'm not dealing with the creditors—"

"You're not Yuriko."

In daylight his eyes took on the glint of polished topaz, an extraordinary color, both pale and splendid bright. They gazed into hers and Ruri felt some of her antagonism falter, caught in that gilded stare.

"No. I'm not."

"You're . . . their daughter."

"You seem to know a great deal about me and my family. And since I know nothing at all about you, I think you'd better either produce some solid evidence of your identity or else get out of here before I call the cops."

"Of course."

Nothing seemed to rattle him; he took her defensive tone with the cordial poise of a man used to dealing with uncivilized creatures, only reaching into his coat to pull out a wallet, and then a card, offering it to her between two long, tanned fingers.

Ruri took it delicately, careful not to touch his hand.

*Iain MacInnes, Ph.D.*
*Dept. of Marine Archaeology*
*University of St. Andrews*

"My apologies for the confusion," he was saying calmly. "No one informed me of Dr. Kell's passing, or that he had a daughter. Please accept my deepest sympathies for your loss."

Ruri looked up. "Did you know him?"

The golden gaze shifted, studied the lacework of English ivy embedded in the wall behind her. "I'm afraid that I did not."

Damn. Iain still found it difficult to hold her eyes, but when she spoke like that—sugar and smoke and that slight, poignant catch in the back of her throat—it became impossible. It simply hurt too much.

She didn't remember him. He couldn't believe it, but it was thoroughly, obviously true.

How could it be he had recognized her with a jolt that had slammed through his entire being, that had left him mute and staggered—and she didn't remember? Thirty-three years of hard mastery and discipline and hell-bent sacrifice had abandoned him in just the blink of blue eyes; shock and dismay had numbed his mind and his body to useless nothing.

She didn't know him.

And if she didn't know him . . . she might not know anything. Not of Kell. Not of herself.

He focused on the ivy, followed the elaborate tracery of vine over stucco as he exhaled in a silent five-count. Peace, stillness. Push away distractions, concentrate on what must be done.

Iain allowed himself another glimpse of her. She was examining his card again, holding it by the corners as if it might contain some hidden message in the unprinted space. Her hair was glossy and richly dark, a bittersweet-chocolate fall past her shoulders, shorter strands around her face curving softly to brush flawless cheeks. Pink lips were pursed, sooty lashes lowered. Her nails, unpolished, had the hard crystal gleam of quartz. Even clad in the sort of worn T-shirt and jeans so many women today seemed to favor, she shone with the pure, elemental radiance that marked all her kind.

Aye, she was siren.

It was clear he would have to tread very carefully with her. Strong as her body no doubt was, he could see that her spirit was wounded—although she probably didn't realize that either. He read suffering, reservation, behind her every glance. It rocked him to his bones.

No good. He would have to get past emotion, past this rather unpleasant sense of betrayal, to reach the heart of his plan.

"Driver's license," the siren said.

Iain looked back at her. "Pardon?"

"I want to see your driver's license," she explained slowly, as if he were especially dim-witted. "Anyone with a computer and a printer can make up a business card."

"It's *embossed*."

She shrugged, exquisitely nonchalant. "Still."

Offense warred with admiration warred with amusement; amusement won. Silently he reopened his wallet, withdrew the license, and handed it over.

"Would you like a thumbprint as well?" he asked, ruthlessly polite. "A blood sample?"

"Not at all." She matched his tone precisely. "This should do."

"Splendid. If I have passed your test, Ms. Kell, I wonder if we might continue our conversation inside? Unless you'd prefer the limousine . . . ?"

Her look to him was endless blue, measuring. At length she nodded, stepped back, and invited him to pass with a supple sweep of her hand. Iain walked into her flat.

Small. Very small. Yet appealing in a modest way, the plain furnishings, the simple, brilliant accents of color scattered about: a duo of Moorish lamps suspended from a corner, their pressed glass flaring emerald and white against the sun; a line of stones winking on a windowsill, agates and amethysts and the half cup of a tiny black geode; a rumpled futon on the floor with a cover of shot crimson silk; the gold and rust grandeur of an Imari plate fixed to the wall.

A large spider conch on an end table.

He moved to the conch, raised it to the light. Instinctively his hands knew the way of it, the spines pressing hard into his skin, his fingers finding the rose-flushed lip. The apex was still uncut.

Not a clan shell, then. But, ah . . . it could be.

Ruri watched him turn to the window by her futon, his head bowed, a spill of sunlight sending rainbows through pirate-black hair. There was a brooding, distracted air about him, a lift to the corners of his lips that she found, for no reason, faintly unsettling. Yet he held her father's conch as if it were precious, as if it were spun glass. It was oddly fascinating, to watch his fingers slip so gently over the stony coral tips and curves.

A word began to tease the back of her thoughts—the tanned skin and unruly hair, the hint of morning beard sharpening his cheeks—an old-fashioned sort of word never used anymore . . .

*Rogue.* Of course. It suited him.

Ruri cleared her throat.

"Dr. MacInnes—"

He spoke without looking up. "Call me Iain."

"Dr. MacInnes," she repeated firmly, "have you come about the necklace?"

He lowered the shell, gently again, and met her eyes.

"No," he said with peaceful disinterest. "What necklace?"

Without warning, goose bumps pricked her skin; that wisp of winter slid over her once more, leaving her cold and wary. It happened sometimes, a chilled, drifting awareness that would settle into her like silent falling snow—Saturday night, with Jessica and Cat, and now. . . .

Ruri knew, with all her heart, that it was not peace this man felt. The mild look, the tranquil voice, the gracious manner—all a lie.

There was hunger beneath the calm. There was ferocity.

And he knew about the necklace.

She stuck her hands in her back pockets, didn't miss the way he followed that, a quick, keen flicker of a glance. "You know what? Never mind. It's not important."

"It's not?"

"No." She hoped he wouldn't turn around and notice the glimmer of silver in her blankets. As casually as she could, Ruri took a step back toward the door. "Why *are* you here, then?"

He crossed to the coffee table, ran a careful hand over her Tarot cards, still laid out. "I've come to ask your plans for the island."

Her silence was unmistakable; at last he looked up.

"The Isle of Kell. You've not heard of it? Ah. I see." Almost leisurely he turned back to the cards, chose one, glanced at it, and set it down again. "Will you have dinner with me tonight?"

"No," she said, startled.

"Why not?" He straightened, faced her squarely. "I've never been to your city before. I could use a proper guide. I thought we might go to someplace . . . by the ocean."

"I'm busy."

"Jealous husband?"

"No—"

"Possessive boyfriend?"

"No—"

"Then what?"

"Look," she said, irritated. "I don't even *know* you."

"Aye," he murmured. "I do realize that."

And then he did something truly unnerving: He smiled at her. It was a slow smile, one of heat and charm and clear ambition that seemed to send the warmth of the sun all the way through her. She saw, with shock, that Dr. Iain MacInnes was more than handsome. He was gorgeous.

"My interest is purely professional, Ms. Kell. You're about to come into possession of an island. A very special island. And I would like to purchase it from you."

"I think you should leave now."

"As you wish. You have my card. My cell phone number is on the back. Perhaps you'll reconsider dinner."

He approached the door, waited stoically until she

gathered her wits and moved out of his way. In the cool bloom of daylight he turned, offering his hand.

"I hope you'll call."

"Good-bye, Dr. MacInnes."

She reached out, preparing for a brisk handshake, but in a courtly, surprising move his fingers slid under hers, warm and strong, lifting; he bent to skim his lips lightly over her skin.

"I assure you, Ms. Kell, it's only good morning."

As she stood there, staring, he offered a shadow of that smile again, then turned and strode away.

She was actually afraid he had pulled THE LOVERS. But when Ruri picked up the Tarot card Iain had chosen, she saw the bright, bold lettering of JUSTICE instead.

It wasn't until he was back in the hotel, on the phone with his harried solicitor, effectively roused from his supper, that Iain realized he didn't even know her first name.

# CHAPTER FOUR

❧

R uri dug her nails, very lightly, into the leather arms of her parents' attorney's—*her* attorney's— chair. It was burgundy leather, the polished surface very clear to her in the circle of lamplight that fell gracefully over her shoulder to land in her lap; when she relaxed her hands, faint crescent moons were left behind.

It had been three days since Iain MacInnes had found her. Three days, and now, here in this artfully lit, excruciatingly tasteful law office, everything he had said was, astonishingly, coming true.

The office had called yesterday. Mr. Saito himself had told her she needed to come in, that new business regarding her parents had surfaced.

Not creditors, he assured her. An inheritance.

And Ruri had thought instantly of her enigmatic Scottish visitor.

He had not contacted her since that morning. She had thrown away his card, then, chagrined, fished it out of the trash again, brushed it off, and buried it away in the mess of her address book. She'd puzzled and pondered his visit, reviewed every aspect of it—especially that smile—and, in the end, dismissed him as a provocative but misguided academic who had stepped, oh so briefly, into her life.

But he had been right. She had an island.

Mr. Saito was speaking. Ruri heard his words, but the meaning was rapidly becoming lost to her, overwhelming news buried in the flat, even monotone of business.

She stared at the little leather moons, began to rub them out with her fingers.

". . . that in Scotland there was some confusion regarding the location of the true Kell heir, which is why we've only just now learned of it. It appears your father was considered the last of the direct descendants of a very strict, if somewhat obscure, family line. As he was named heir just prior to his death three months ago, the entire inheritance now falls solely to his progeny—to you, of course. . . ."

The crescent moons were fading, fading.

". . . and it is an entire island. A small one, uninhabited, in the Outer Hebrides. There appears to be a significant early ruin upon it, which would explain the interest of the National Trust for Scotland, but no one outside the family has been allowed on the isle for decades, and so this information remains unconfirmed. . . ."

A ruin. An island. Scotland.

Hers. Her father's, and so . . . hers.

A terrible, helpless pressure began to build in her temples, expanding darkly. Cold began to sink through her— quiet snowfall—

No. Not now.

"The island—" Mr. Saito said, but the rest of his sentence was lost because his voice caught in Ruri's head, rolled over and over her, *the island the island* and somehow became the Nightmare, living here in full daylight, complete and absolute *the ocean* in its consumption, filling her until she could not breathe *roiling, surly and thick and hideous*—

"—quite isolated, even for Scotland. The currents around it are considered extremely dangerous—"

—*the sea was going*—

"—with numerous shipwrecks thought to be concealed beneath the waters—"

—*to gobble her whole, suck her down*—

"—of minimal value to you, as the currents render any attempts at excavation infeasible—"

—*to inky cold depths until her lungs were crushed paper and the fish would come*—

Stop!

Ruri forced her fingers to uncurl, sucking air past her teeth. She lowered her eyes, staring fiercely at the new marks left in the chair. This time, the crescent moons bit deep.

A discreet rock fountain hummed by the door. She focused on that, the water whizzing through the hidden pump with the dullest purr, splashing up again over river stones in easy, distracting notes.

". . . these first three letters of query. We will, naturally, review them very thoroughly before submitting to you any recommendations. Not having seen the island, it is difficult, if not impossible, to ascertain if any of these offers are at fair market value. Or, indeed, if you even wish to consider a sale—"

Ruri looked up. "Sell it."

Mr. Saito sat back in his own leather chair, removed his reading glasses to rub his nose. He was far too diplomatic to frown at her, but there was the smallest hint of disapproval in the line of his brow.

"Ruriko, I understand that your financial circumstances are . . . less than ideal. But as I mentioned before, the island has been in the family—your father's family—for generations. Perhaps you might wish to consider the matter a while longer."

"I don't."

There was a heavy pause. The fountain splashed on.

"Very well," said Mr. Saito, putting his glasses on again. "We will begin review of these current offers at once. I presume you wish to place the property on the open market, which will, perhaps, increase the price. A reputable realtor will be of paramount importance. . . ."

His voice receded into that distant drone. Ruri found her fingers once more gripping hard into the leather of the chair. From the black corners of her mind, the Nightmare still threatened, lurking.

What the hell was happening to her? She felt winded, dizzy, as if someone had lobbed a softball at her stomach.

". . . and there is the matter of the missing necklace."

Her attention dragged back. "What?"

Mr. Saito browsed the papers in his hands. "An heirloom, I'm afraid. It was meant to be passed along with the isle, but thus far no one has been able to locate it. As at least one of the purchase offers for the Isle of Kell is contingent upon receiving this necklace, it is a matter of some concern, but I'm sure we'll be able to—"

"Sorry." Ruri held up a hand. "Can you describe it?"

"Well, no. From what I understand it's merely a very old family item. A locket, I was told. The solicitor from the estate mistakenly handed it over to a new apprentice in a box of general goods. He was quite distraught—"

"I have it," Ruri said. "It's not missing."

"Oh?"

"Yes. And—it's not for sale."

Mr. Saito accepted that in his unblinking way. "I will inform the Scottish firm."

"Thank you."

"Of course. And, Ruriko?"

"Yes?"

"Think about what I said, about waiting to sell. As your attorney, I am your advocate, no matter what you decide. But as your father's friend, I would be remiss if I did not put forth all the options." He smiled at her then, his round, smooth face crinkling with kindness. "And after all, it's not every day you're given your own island."


She didn't know why she had said that, why, when the necklace was mentioned, she had leapt to protect it. To keep it. Alluring as it was, she didn't even like it.

But the words had just come, and then, after she had said them, they had seemed right. They felt right.

Her apartment welcomed her with the familiar, steady and sane after everything that had happened this morning. Her own uncomplicated space, bits of her life and her loved ones' captured in one cheerful room, a view of the little Zen garden just outside and the wide, tree-lined street beyond.

She found herself looking at the conch, walking to it. The spiraled top, the fan of spines had always seemed so playfully exotic to her, a drop of the tropical in her everyday world. But as Ruri touched it now, she wondered how it had felt to him. To Iain MacInnes, cupping it so carefully in his sun-darkened hands.

She had left the door open. In daylight the manic energy of the city was better contained, held apart from her home by the massive oak in the front and the sheer crooked caprice of her flagstone path; a breeze passed through the room in an underbreath, not even stirring the blinds.

Ruri replaced the conch on its little table, pulled open the shallow drawer recessed beneath it.

The locket lay there in its box, lid off, a dull ashen sheen. She stood there a moment staring down at it, then, almost unwillingly, lifted it to the light.

It seemed heavier than before: The chain slid between her fingers, slithering fast before her fist closed and she captured it again. The locket snapped into a twirl above her open palm, caught the sun and tossed it back again in a salvo of silver sparks. She had to shut her eyes against it.

"You didn't want dinner," said a voice behind her. "How do you feel about lunch?"

She turned without the slightest sense of surprise, as if she had been expecting him. As if she had been waiting.

"Because I've found a place," Iain continued, matter-of-fact, paused in her doorway. "And I thought of you."

His eyes went to the locket—he could hardly miss it, a shooting star trapped in her hand—and his brows lifted. "Ah. There it is. I wondered . . ."

Ruri lowered the pendant, discomfited. "What?"

"Where it went. It's quite valuable, you know. I'm pleased you have it."

"You know about it." There was accusation in her tone; it brought forth a slight tip of his head.

"The Soul of Kell. Of course I do."

"It has a *name*?"

"It's famous—among certain circles. Don't you know the story?"

"No."

"Shall I tell you?" he asked, very soft. "Wear it to lunch. I'll regale you with history."

"No, thank you." She placed the necklace back into its box, shut the drawer firmly. "And I don't want lunch."

"Don't you?" He hadn't moved yet, only stood there in her doorway, narrowing the light. The breeze stirred again; this time she thought it carried a subtle, inviting scent, man and intangible earth.

She gazed down at the conch, chewing her bottom lip as his voice turned coaxing.

"Come with me. You'll enjoy it. Open space. Wind chimes. Fresh air."

"Fresh air," she echoed, rubbing a finger across a fragile spine. "In L.A.? I don't think so."

"Come and find out. You know who I am now," he said, when she still didn't move. "You know why I'm here. I've told you. What have you to fear?"

"Are you stalking me?" she demanded, and regretted instantly how childish it sounded.

But the chiseled lips only lifted in smile; he plucked a word from her thoughts. "No, lass. Merely waiting."

Ruri sent him a sidelong glance, considering. Combed today, shaven, he still had that air of disreputable charm laid over brawn. Faded jeans and a biscuit-colored sweater—it had to be cashmere—emphasized a well-toned frame; one shoulder was propped casually against her door. He stood there, relaxed, with his hands in his pockets and the breeze in his hair, a man of light and shade edged with the dapple of oak leaves.

She knew, without doubt, that he wasn't entirely what he seemed. And yet . . .

Ruri picked up her purse. "I'm a vegetarian."

"Aye," he replied evenly. "I had a feeling you were."

\* \* \*

He took her to Malibu, that fabled stretch of fashionable beaches and movie-star mansions that rubbed wall-to-wall. She was silent on the ride over, accepting the new red convertible he'd procured with just one slanted, satiric look, but he handed her in and she only unfolded her sunglasses, facing ahead.

Iain hadn't wanted the limousine for her. He hadn't wanted to trap them both in such a private, enclosed space. Not yet.

The wind tore at them on the freeways but she managed it, holding her hair with one hand, watching the buildings and then the mountains flash by. The linen skirt of her sundress blew up to her knees; he was distracted by a pair of long, pretty legs, crossed at the ankle, little sandals that made her look barefoot.

In Malibu Canyon she leaned out the window, following the faint, twisting line of the creek they shadowed, until the hills opened up and the Pacific spread before them in a wedge of hazed indigo.

After that, he noticed, she watched the ocean.

The restaurant was small, secluded, perched high on a cliff atop a narrow, winding drive. He allowed the valet to open her door, made certain to take her arm to lead her inside.

It was, as he had said, a place that spoke of her: cool limestone floors and gracious Spanish archways, slender ficus trees with braided trunks and fairy lights strung in their leaves. The wind chimes, a soft serenade from the garden patio, and a series of Tibetan copper bells, no larger than roses, hung from the eaves.

He could not stop looking at her. He could not seem to turn away from her face, the lovely lines of her profile, her wind-combed hair, as she lifted her head and took it all in. She wore very little makeup. She didn't need it, of course; she had the mythic, unconscious splendor of siren that nearly shimmered with her every step. The light caressed her, the air sighed. As she walked through the restaurant, men in tailored suits and silk ties swiveled in their seats to stare.

He wondered how it was that she wasn't married.

But she wasn't. He'd done his research by now, knew all there was to know of her through public record—and a few things not so public. Full name, date of birth, social security number, bank-account balances, college transcripts, previous addresses . . . all the parts and pieces that made up the official Ruriko Catherine Kell and rubbed away some of the mystery of her life.

He knew already, of course, the mystery of her private life.

Creditors, she'd said that morning at her door, and he'd found the stack of bills that had haunted her parents, and now her, a growing debt and nothing left to pay it. That she worked at night, as a fortune-teller—part of him still had to smile at that—and kept afloat a paycheck at a time.

That she was an only child.

That she had a degree in English, and wanted to teach.

That she'd been in graduate school until her parents had died.

That she was alone, and vulnerable. Exactly as he wished.

"Have you been here before?" Iain asked, as the maître d'hôtel bowed deep and pulled out her chair.

She threw him a glance that might have held irony. "No."

"I've heard it's excellent."

"I'm sure it is." Irony, without doubt.

The copper bells outside released a perfect *fioritura* of notes.

"And," Iain said neutrally, "the view is outstanding."

She shifted, gazing out the wide window at her side, but he caught the disquiet that had shuttered her face, took note of the way she searched the ocean and then the cliffs, and then the ocean again. Reflected sunshine gave her skin a peach-blossom glow, tipped ebony lashes in honey gold. The top of her dress was overlaid in lace; it reached up to her collarbone, angel white next to the sweet hollow of her throat.

Iain said, "I thought perhaps afterward we might walk on the beach."

"Is this a date?"

His smile was bland, cover to the abrupt reaction of his body to the full blue force of her gaze: a scorching hurt, a nearly violent desire that arced to life within him and kindled there, burning.

*Not yet, not yet.*

Waiters came, water, fresh rolls. He ordered appetizers and wine, waited until they left before forming his answer.

"This is only business. But there's no reason business can't be conducted in a bit of sand and sun. Especially with the weather so fine. It's much cooler this time of year in Scotland."

She contemplated the bread plate, brown hair spilling forward to mask her cheeks. There was a faint, unhappy curve to her lips.

"Was it something I said?" he asked, and her lashes lifted.

"I almost drowned once."

He couldn't hide his surprise. "You did?"

"Yes." She took a sip of water, her fingers pressed pale against the glass. "I was very young, but I remember it—

scenes from it—like pictures. Like it happened to someone else. There was this pressure—in my lungs. Like they
were being pulled inside out."

He managed to keep his voice placid. "Was it the ocean?"

"No." She gave a brittle laugh, brushed the hair from
her face. "God, no. Not the ocean. I'd never go near it. It
was just a swimming pool."

"You mean, you've never been in the sea?"

"Never. Ever." She spoke with complete conviction.
One hand lifted, dismissed the view. "I don't even come to
the coast."

He was silent a moment, mulling that, then had a new
thought. "Who saved you? In the pool?"

"Oh, my mother. My father couldn't swim a stroke.
She wanted me to have swimming lessons after that, but
I—" She shrugged, a flush rising in her cheeks. "I didn't
want to. I stayed away from pools. And that was the end
of it."

Iain leaned back, torn between the sudden, irrational
urge to tell her everything and the wisdom to keep his
mouth shut. It seemed so improbable that the secret of the
family had died in this American branch, but her kin had
left Scotland so long ago; he supposed anything was possible. God knew heritages had been buried before. So,
Samuel Kell did not swim, his daughter did not swim—

It was as Iain had suspected. She knew nothing of
herself.

He was going to have to show her.

Ruriko laughed again, lighter now, abashed. "I can't
imagine why I told you any of that."

"Because . . . you don't want to walk on the beach."

She fiddled with the butter knife. "No. I really don't."

How mortifying; she was babbling, telling him stories,

*personal* stories, things she normally wouldn't tell any-one. Her face actually hurt with the rush of blood; the contrast of her heated skin against the crisp briny air was sharply unpleasant. Composure, composure! There was something about this man that made her too nervous, that twisted her stomach into pretzels and disconnected her brain from her mouth.

She could feel his stare, the bright topaz intensity that did not relent. In time Ruri managed to look up again, met his gaze with what she hoped was an expression of supreme aplomb.

"Business," she said. "I've had several offers for the island."

His smile returned, dry. "My. How things change in just a few days."

"Well. I've been to my attorney now."

"Oh, attorneys," he said knowingly, and the smile grew even drier. "Patron saints of the business world. Very well, Ms. Kell, let us proceed forthwith. I'll give you twelve million for it."

"I . . . you—what?" The butter knife fell from her fingers.

"Twelve million dollars, U.S."

She could not think of a single thing to say.

Another waiter approached, presented a bottle of wine with the reverence of a sacrificial tribute. Iain glanced at the label, nodded, then turned back to her. "It's a very generous proposal."

"Generous?" Her heart began to beat again. "No one else has offered nearly—"

"Nearly that much?" His eyes lit with humor, sensual, sympathetic. "In business, Ruriko, it's never good form to tip your hand. Who knows? I might have gone higher."

She gaped at him. "You are crazy."

"No. Just very, very rich."

Should she leave? Was he playing a game? Good God, how could he possibly be serious—

More waiters came and hovered, pouring the wine, setting down plates with a showy snap of bleached napkins, but he ignored them, clearly used to such treatment, waiting only until they faded back into the pale walls of the room.

"Ruriko," he said. "What do you think?"

Suspicion held her to her chair, made her scan his face with new insight. "Why would you pay so much?"

"Perhaps I'm eccentric."

In spite of herself she felt laughter come, pressed her lips together hard to stop it. "I believe that falls under 'crazy.'"

And he laughed for her, a deep, wonderful sound that sent an unexpected lick of pleasure through her, warm and intimate.

"Have you seen it? Even a picture?"

She took a breath, shook her head.

"I think you should," he said gently. "In fact, I think you should see it in person. Then you'll understand."

"Oh—no. I won't. An island . . . that would involve water, the ocean."

"Aye. It would."

"A picture will do fine."

His fingers dallied with the stem of his wineglass, sending the merlot into a slow maroon swirl. "No," he said.

"Sorry?"

He did not look up from the glass. "You need to visit the isle. In fact," he went on, reflective, "I believe I'm going to have to insist."

All signs of humor were gone. He spoke with an assurance that sent a crawl down her spine and tight warning into her throat.

"What are you saying?"

At last his eyes raised. "You should come back to Scotland with me."

She let out a sound that was more gasp than laughter; he did not smile again.

"Would you sell the home of your ancestors without even a look?"

"Yes!"

"Really? How interesting." He tried the wine, impassive now, utterly cool. "Yet I fear I could not, in clear conscience, take Kell from you without knowing you had been there first."

It had been a trick, Ruri realized, dismayed. All of it— the smile, the pleasant repartee, the engaging veneer—a device to get her here, to listen and believe—and despite her doubts of him, she had followed along as willing as a lamb.

*Here* was the true man. Here was the man she had glimpsed back in her apartment three days ago, the steely ruthlessness that belied his amiable facade. And here was his real agenda, or at least a portion of it.

He wanted her to cross the *ocean*—

Twelve million dollars. Oh, God.

"Only think of what you might do with such a sum," Iain said, his gaze going past her, to the wide-open sea. "Pay off debts, finish school. Open your own school, if you wish."

"You . . . you've had me investigated."

"I am a thorough man."

"You had no right—"

"It's not about rights, lass. I told you, this is business. Large or small, I never walk into a deal blind, and *this* deal is . . . significant. Aye, I know who you are, I know what you want. And I know that I can give it to you." He looked back at her again, golden-eyed, black-haired, smiling a faint shrewd smile. "Money," he added quietly, "can change everything. I wonder if you're bold enough to let me prove it to you?"

The soft-hued room seemed at once too light, too exposed. Ruri lifted a hand to cover her eyes, closing them, craving the dark.

"My parents were not . . . good with money."

"No," he answered, in a tone that might have meant anything.

"They died so suddenly. They didn't intend . . ."

He waited, silent, as the smooth buzz and hum of the restaurant washed around them.

"I don't have to sell it to you," she muttered finally.

"But you're going to, aren't you, Ruriko Kell?"

She lowered her hand. "I'll think about it."

Iain lifted his glass to her, charm and grace once more, the merlot a cupped berry between his fingers. "That's all I ask."

Ruri hesitated, then lifted hers in response.

He added, "For now," as the crystal goblets touched rims.

They waited for his car beneath the deco fronds of a Queen palm, a stately giant swaying above them. Ruri's gaze traveled up the column of the trunk to the neon bowl of the sky, jagged blue behind green leaves.

"You were right about the air here," she admitted. "It's nice."

Iain leaned close to her ear, his words a silken whisper. "Wait until you taste the air of Kell. You'll feel like a new woman. I promise."

# CHAPTER FIVE

ور first years together on the island passed in a
maze of happiness. The moment he reached
the golden sands of his new home, Kell paused
and turned to me with great solemnity. With the tide
washing over our feet, he bestowed both a promise and a
kiss: This was our domain. This island, this instant, belonged to us alone.

"And to the beasts and the trees and the sea," I added,
smiling through the kiss.

"Aye, and them," he agreed. "For we are all thy servants."

I linked my fingers with his, looked up at him through
my lashes. "Not a servant." I tugged him closer, sank to
my knees to the welcome sanctum of the beach. "Not
thee."

His hands loosened from mine. I felt the faint stroke of
his caress over my hair, my brow, and then he knelt before me, his face lovely and taut.

"No, lady, not a servant," he said, his voice low, and his
palms cupped my cheeks.

"Husband," I said softly, watching the sun warm his eyes.

"Lover," he replied, and bent his head to my neck, his lips glancing my skin, light and spare as air brushed by a sparrow's wings.

I stretched my body against his and reveled in it; his slightest touch sent liquid pleasure through my limbs and I was curiously, delightfully, helpless to it. I knew it would always be so between us. At last I had found my worthy love.

Time sailed by. We danced and played and let mankind abide without us.

It was Kell who, one day as we lazed in a glen, thought of the palace. This was not perhaps unexpected, for it was Kell who had come from the world of men, and what was a palace but a worldly thing, a hollow haven for mortals? We didn't need it, I pointed out. We had the blessings of the woods and the island creatures. Of what use would be a palace, an onus of heavy walls and stone?

And he smiled his tender smile and laid his hand upon my belly, where our first child was growing.

"A home for her," he said. "That we might give her—a cradle, and a hearth. A window from which to watch the waves. And . . . a place where she may keep all the flowers I will bring her."

"And me," I said quickly, and his smile deepened into laughter. He pulled me into his arms, the finest shelter yet; as his mouth covered mine, his mirth shook us both.

"Aye, and thee. Naturally, thee."

Was ever a man so intoxicating?

I raised Kell his palace, stone by stone, spell by spell. Inevitably it became a splendid place, for everything I did became splendid, whether I willed it or no. That was my nature.

We walked the halls together, hand in hand, and even I had to admit it was a wondrous home.

He filled it with flowers, our chamber first—our bed—and then later our daughter's little room.

We named her Eos, for the great joy she brought. Never a day passed that Kell did not offer her some small gift, a shell, an opalescent scale, a pretty piece of quartz. A perfect stem of orange blossoms, honey-sweet.

For me there were deeper tributes, poems and songs, fragrant blankets of petals for lovemaking. Once he found a golden chain washed ashore amid the pebbles, a noble-woman's vanity capped with ruby beads; he wrapped the chain around my waist with hot lickerish kisses, let the rubies ride between my legs until I moaned in ecstasy.

The island celebrated his adoration, and fields of wild-flowers seemed to bloom wherever he roamed. He'd bring armfuls back for us: poppies in summer, pale roses in spring. Gentians in autumn and crisp holly in winter. In our palace, nature's perfume washed and mixed with the ocean wind, unique and ever inviting. Sometimes at sea I would turn my face toward the isle, however far away I might be, and imagine I could still breathe in the scent of his devotion.

When I'd swim back to shore he'd greet me with our daughter in his arms, her flaxen curls crowned with lavender and primrose, her tiny fists clutching another garland for me.

I would wear his flowers and steal his kisses, while Eos chortled at us both.

# CHAPTER SIX

⟡

The airplane seat was sinfully comfortable, plush leather that reclined into a bed, her own video screen, padded headset, warm hand towels. Ruri had a window seat; outside, mounds of French vanilla clouds lofted by, a soft cottony blanket that covered the earth.

She found herself watching more and more of those clouds, and not the ingenious little video screen. They rolled and tumbled, spread and folded. She never caught a hint of the planet beneath them.

A week had passed since she had seen Iain. He had not called or come by since. She had finally reached the point where she stopped peering out her windows, searching nervously for a gleaming new car, a handsome man with unruly black hair, when Mr. Saito phoned. Dr. MacInnes had gone back to Scotland. Along with his official purchase offer for the Isle of Kell, he had left a sealed envelope for her at the law office.

Inside the envelope was a plane ticket to Edinburgh, and a short, folded note.

*I await your pleasure.*

Disturbing words, layered with meaning. Or not. She nearly drove herself to distraction, trying to decide.

*Postscript: Bring the locket.*

A flight attendant walked by, offered to top off Ruri's champagne. She declined, turning instead to contemplate those fat creamy clouds past her window.

First class. If she didn't end up accepting Iain's bid for Kell, she might have to sell a kidney to pay him back.

"Go," Setsu had urged. "For heaven's sake, Ruriko. Go. You don't have to promise him anything. But he was right, you should see the isle."

"Go," agreed Jody, casting her runes. "Your path awaits you, and it's never any use to avoid fate. I have a strong feeling about this."

"Go," finished Toshio, at last Sunday's brunch. "And if he messes with you, I'll fly over there and kick his ass."

She would have to deal with the ocean. Fine. It was only water, after all. Yes, a great deal of water—but she wasn't going swimming in it. She didn't even have to get her feet wet; if it was an island, there had to be a boat to it, for God's sake. Or even better, a helicopter. All she had to do was look at the Isle of Kell, admire it—yes, delightful, how very cozy—sign Iain's contract, and leave. There was no reason to panic.

But what ultimately convinced her was not her private rationalizations, not even the wishes of her family or friends, heartfelt as they were. It was something else, something much darker and simpler: the challenge of that note. A careless scrawl on a sheet of hotel stationery, an unstated provocation. Come to me if you dare. She could almost see his face as he penned it, the arched brows, the slight, mocking lift to his lips.

So she dared.

But for all her nerve she hadn't quite managed to read her own fortune before she left. Her Tarot cards remained safely back at the apartment, waiting for her return.

The champagne was dry in her mouth, the bubbles smarting over her tongue. She tried to drink it slowly but it seemed the alcohol went straight to her veins anyway, golden and heady, like the clouds. Like Iain MacInnes's eyes.

Below her, the world turned and turned.

Ruri wished, suddenly, desperately, that she had brought her cards after all.

Too late for regrets, she knew. She was already stranded above the sea, far, far from home.

She was coming.

In the solitude of his study Iain felt it, a low electric hum in the air, a sizzle of energy that surrounded him, the land. The sea.

Anticipation of Ruriko.

He felt awake and alive, both ravenous and filled, rudiments of feelings that had haunted him all his life but were deeper now, achingly raw. Even as a child, the knowledge that there was *something* waiting for him—something stranger and wilder and more profound than the plain ordinary life that contented others—had teased at him, beckoned him around every blind curve and bend.

With the whisper of the wind he had felt it; with the changing of the seasons he had felt it, stronger every year. And now Iain knew the source. Not Kelmere, this place he had fought for and earned through blood, sweat, and whetted plans. Not even Kell, the isle of dreams he had yet to conquer.

It was Ruriko, all of it, all along. How astonishing that he'd never realized she lived until now.

He had received her confirmation by fax, had acknowledged and affirmed all her plans. She'd be here today, this morning, stepping foot on the soil that had not welcomed her in so long.

He wondered if she'd remember it. What he'd have to do, if she didn't.

When he closed his eyes, her face all but eluded him. He could summon only the most general of features, chocolate-brown hair, straight nose, winsome lips. But what he always recalled—what always stayed crystal clear—were her eyes: dark and fragile and the color of storm, gazing into his own with just the slow, shy suggestion of budding heat.

A knock on the study door interrupted his musing. Rupert entered the room, hunched and dour, deep-set green eyes that saw, Iain knew, far more than most.

"The car's ready," he said, standing stiffly before Iain's desk. "I'm off for the ferry."

"Good. I'll meet you at the quay on your way back."

It had caused no small scandal when auld Rupert Munro, pure-blood descendant of one of the last clan families, had defected to the side of the brash young man Iain had been a decade ago and decided to work for the upstart who had purchased Kelmere. Iain had been born to a branch of far-distant kin—too distant, it seemed, to matter much to the tight-knit community that safeguarded Kelmere, and Kell. Despite his wealth, it had been rough going then; he was the invader who had dared to buy what many believed should never have been sold.

He used to speculate, not without just cause, if one

night some bloody irate clansman would decide to burn the mansion down about his head rather than let him keep it.

Only Rupert had stood firm beside him—though not without a biting remark or two when he felt the need. It was clear from the beginning that Rupert Munro served because he wanted to, not because he needed to. His loyalty had been grudging but absolute, and the key to Iain's eventual acceptance by the people of the land.

Iain had never revealed the full truth to him. He had the strong feeling that Rupert, with his canny old eyes, knew it all anyway.

"Is there something else?" he asked mildly, when the man remained standing, glaring out the window behind Iain.

"Nay, what else could there be?" Rupert asked, too light and brisk to be anything but scathing. "I'll fetch the lass, just as ye wish. I'll bring her to ye right as rain, so she'll be signing yer wee bit of paper."

"You don't like her." He made a statement.

"Like her? What right have I to like or dislike her, I'd like to know?"

Iain stood. "You tell me."

"Just because the lass wants to sell the isle sight unseen—the isle that belonged to us, all of us, for lo these many years—what's to grieve over?"

"Rupert—"

" 'Tis only the Isle of Kell. Why should it mean aught to her? Only the land of her father, her father's father, that she shucks off like an auld coat—"

"She won't sell it."

Rupert fixed him with a beady eye. "Oh, won't she, then?"

"No."

"You're a cocksure lad, aren't ye?"

Iain smiled. "I am. As you know." He came around the desk, put his hand on the other man's shoulder. "Don't worry. She'll change her mind as soon as she sees the island."

Rupert huffed a sigh, only slightly mollified. "I suppose I'm to take yer word for it."

"Aye."

"Tell me this. What be the purpose of bringing her out here, if she willna sell?"

"I think you'll know the answer to that—when you see her."

They stared at each other a long moment.

Rupert scratched his chin, glowering, and turned to the door. "Well enough. I'll fetch the lass. And I'll *see*."

It was as close to a concession as Iain was going to get, and he knew it.

But he was right. With all his heart, with all his being, Iain knew that he was right. She would come, and she would remember.

And if she did not remember . . . it was going to be his most gratifying obligation to remind her.


Iain MacInnes had sent a driver for her. In the crush and swarm of the Edinburgh airport, a man in a sober dark suit held up a sign with her name written on it. Before she could even approach, he came to her, an olive-green gaze and a weathered face, iron-gray hair that grew long over his collar.

"Come along, then," he had said to her brusquely, and Ruri, bewildered in the mob of chattering people, had clutched at her purse and followed.

Without asking, the man had assumed control of her

roll-away. There was only the one bag, just enough for the basic necessities; she had no plans to linger long.

He led her to yet another limousine, black and polished as obsidian.

"Where is Dr. MacInnes?" Ruri asked.

"Waitin' for ye." He hefted her luggage into the trunk of the limo, far more spry than the hair and suit would suggest.

She walked to the door he pulled open for her. "How did you know it was me, in the airport?"

His eyes flitted over her face. "Lucky guess, I reckon."

Ruri sank into charcoal cushions, stretched her legs, and refused the drink the man—curtly—offered. He did not glance back at her again as the car slid into the snarl of morning traffic.

Gradually the impressive dun mass of the city melted into countryside, into velvet farmland and long lines of trees whiskered with new leaves. The sky was overcast but in a lovely, smudged way, watercolors that spilled across the heavens, wolf-gray clouds lapping low against the rich colors of the fields. In the distance she could just make out the suggestion of hills, purple-backed, slumbering beasts . . . dreaming of an enchanted call to rise. . . .

Ruri smiled to herself, rubbing a hand over her face. She was tired. The flight had been long but she hadn't slept—as usual. As always. She was used to going days without rest, but here in the cradled, rocking indulgence of Iain's limousine—how many did he have? she wondered drowsily—her eyelids grew gritty, too heavy to lift any longer.

She shot a glance to the driver, who was still ignoring her, then tugged her peacoat over her shoulders and settled lower into her seat. She'd only close her eyes for a little bit. She just needed a few minutes, that's all . . .

*. . . at sea, the unbounded sea, with the dead flat tang
of a storm in the air, a pressure rising above and around,
and the waves throwing tantrums in swelling peaks of
blue glass and foam. The clouds gathering, the light si-
phoned away, and the dull, distant moan of the wind rising into a roar—*

She sat up too quickly, panting, her heart a frightened
tattoo in her chest.

"Nightmare?"

Like a fantasy, like a willful new dream, Iain now sat
beside her in the car, one arm draped across the seat behind her in a curve that brought the tips of his fingers to
her shoulder. His eyes were hooded as he took her in, the
pale, transparent topaz shadowed with lashes, his mouth
unsmiling.

"Awake yet, lass?" he asked, more softly, and his gaze
dropped to her lips.

She twisted to push his hand away, then, unthinking,
pressed her palms to her chest, feeling the tremors that
still shook her. Her coat had fallen open and down one
arm, urchin-loose.

He pulled back without offense, no change in either his
manner or that shadowed look. She stared back at him,
wide-eyed.

"You were sleeping so deeply, it seemed a shame to
rouse you. But we're at the quay, ready to go. We cannot
wait much longer."

Ruri realized that the car was no longer moving, that
the door behind him was open to the wind. Even as she
thought it, a chilled draft snaked in, sifting through her
hair, sending goose bumps along her unprotected skin.

"Sorry," she said. "I didn't know—I didn't mean . . ."

She looked around again, disoriented, then back up at
him as he inclined his head.

"Welcome to Scotland, Ruriko Kell. I'm very pleased you're here."

He climbed out of the limousine and after a moment she followed, accepting his hand, stepping onto gravel that crunched like marbles beneath her feet. The wind picked up, gusting, left the taste of salt on her lips.

They were at the end of a town—more of a village, she thought, with picturesque stone houses and a single dirt lane that led from the buildings to the dock. A scattering of vessels bobbed in the water, a few trawlers, fewer still sailboats, but most were runabouts or skiffs, sun-bleached with rust-stained motors clamped astern. Men moved like careful crabs around a few of them, hauling nets, oiling parts, throwing frequent, furtive glances at the car and the man beside her.

The entire town was ringed with mountains, green and gold slopes dotted with heather, rough granite bluffs crumbling boulders into the meadows below.

Ruri turned her face to the sea. Not just the mountains had changed while she slept. The clouds had waxed darker too; at the smear of the horizon they dulled and bled into a fuzzy leaden line.

Squall's coming, she thought, but couldn't say how she knew that.

"Ready?" Iain touched her lightly at the elbow, indicated a craft straight ahead.

Ruri dug her heels into the dirt. "You want me to go on *that*?"

His look was conspicuous innocence. "Aye. Why not?"

Why not? She hardly knew where to begin. It was a powerboat, for one thing, long and skinny and obviously built for speed, already bucking against the waves. Two seats and a half-moon windshield were all that stood between the sky and the purgatory of the North Atlantic. In the chopped gray of the water, the entire thing looked as sturdy as a toothpick.

She would have thought that a man who could offer twelve million dollars for a little island could surely afford a yacht.

"No," said Ruri, as firmly as possible. She saw with alarm that the surly driver of the limo was already slinging her suitcase aboard.

"Ach, she's faster than she looks," said Iain calmly, still urging her forward. "No worries there."

"I'm not worried about how fast she is. I want to go in a bigger boat. A more *enclosed* boat."

"Good heavens. I had no idea you were such a snob."

"I'm not a *snob*," she said, enraged. "I told you about— I told you of that time—and I *can't* . . ." Her voice rasped to silence; she had to pause to breathe, to control the fear ricocheting through her.

The Scotsmen of the quay were now openly watching, nets and oily rags forgotten. Iain took in the fact of their attention, then glanced back at her, inscrutable. The wind ruffled up through his hair.

"I can't go on that," she said helplessly. "Please."

His hand dropped from her elbow; his fingers found hers, warm over the coolness of her skin. He lowered his eyes and spoke to her quietly, the lilt of his brogue turned solemn, more pronounced.

"I would never let anything hurt you," he said, and looked up at her again.

She was breathing too fast. She was light-headed, woozy, and couldn't tell if his golden-bright scrutiny was making it better or worse.

"Ruriko," he murmured, his fingers tightening, "I promise you. No harm will befall you. Just . . . come with me."

He was moving her, one foot, one step at a time, their

gazes locked. She was afraid to look away, afraid not to. The sound of the gravel was like drumfire in her ears.

At the edge of the dock he had her by the waist, lowered her carefully to the cockpit of the boat, where the chauffeur caught and steadied her. She swallowed and sank into the nearest seat, her hands frozen against the leather cushions.

Iain followed at once, leaping to her side with the careless finesse of a pirate.

"That's my girl," he said, and brought the boat to life.

# CHAPTER SEVEN

❧

It was easy to believe she'd never been on the water before. Easy, and at the same time madly absurd, because even as she clutched fast to her seat and kept her chin at a defiant tilt against the wind, she was clearly, dazzlingly in her element, a muse of magic and storm against the black-pearled sea. True, Iain thought, she did seem a tad paler than she had on land, but he had no doubts she'd soon relax into the dips and vaults of the charging boat like a native—which, of course, she was.

"What happened to that man? The driver?" she shouted over the yowl of the engines.

"He'll be taking the ferry back."

She faced him fully. "There's a ferry?"

"Aye."

"Why didn't you tell me that before?"

"It won't be leaving today, Ruriko. Look there, to the north. See those clouds? The calm will break soon. He'll have to wait it out on the mainland, mayhap for days. It's why I've come to get you myself. Everyone will be heading into harbor by now."

"Everyone but us!"

He grinned. "Aye. But we'll be fine. Don't worry."

She grumbled something he didn't quite catch, looking ahead once more. Some of the tilt was gone from her chin.

Iain gestured to the whitecaps, bright and perfect as snowflakes over the dark waters. "Beautiful, isn't it?"

She didn't answer.

"Truth of the matter is, lass, no boat but this could reach Kelmere in time, anyway."

"Kelmere?" He'd caught her attention again. "I thought we were going to Kell."

"Not today. Not unless you'd fancy being stranded on a deserted isle with no proper shelter in the middle of a tempest."

The wind slammed hard to port; he compensated, feeling the surge of horsepower ramming through state-of-the-art fiberglass and burled wood. Ruriko felt it too—she was back to gripping the seat. The din of the engines over the cloud-cold wind soon made talking impractical; for a good while Iain let her retreat into her silence, giving her time to grow accustomed to the sea.

The light began to dim, the air to thicken. The bank of thunderheads to the north cascaded ever closer, a greedy black curtain devouring the firmament. Roaring and planing over the waves, the speedboat headed straight for them.

He became adept at stealing seconds of her, taking wordless note of how hard her fingers squeezed the seat, her knees; of when she finally began to investigate the waters around them, instead of holding fixed with that glassy, trapped-deer stare.

"Oh," he heard her say, and she was pointing off the

starboard bow, rising from the seat. He stood to see what she did.

"Dolphins," he said, and killed the engines. The sudden quiet was breathtaking.

A pod flipped by nearly close enough to touch, their dorsal fins slicing the water, their silvered bodies weaving in and out of the combs in a tapestry of grace. The lead female rose high and skipped across air, landing again with a mighty splash. Ruriko tossed him a swift, delighted smile from over her shoulder.

It tore him up. God, he should have anticipated it. Iain realized he had never seen her true smile before, but of course he recognized it, passed down through the ages: bashful and bold and sweet at once, an unspoken invitation, a comely refusal. It suited her well—too well. Just looking at her made him uneasy.

"They follow the boats sometimes," he said, glancing away, trying to distract himself. "They like to race."

"But you're not racing them now."

"No. I've something else to show you now."

His gaze slid back to hers. She was regarding him quizzically, her cheeks abloom, her eyes sparkling. Right now, in this slender moment, she had forgotten her doubts and fears. She trusted him.

Just above her, the clouds were about to unleash.

Iain moved to stand behind her, turned her so that her back was to him and her hair slipped soft against his chest. Her scent drifted up to eclipse his reason, ocean and jasmine and sky.

He wanted, with painful intensity, to bury his face in the curve of her neck. To hold her body against his. To feel that perfumed hair against his bare skin, his lips. But none of those things would bring him his true desire, not here, so Iain kept his hands to his sides and his voice well controlled, saying only, "Look." He did not need to point where.

Kell had been waiting for them. A shadow, a far-off mirage stroked with mist, it lay still and calm ahead, emerald and violet and gold, forest and mountains and shore. After all this while there were no more visible wrecks to encircle it; instead, a ring of buoys marked the boundary of the reef, bright red warning to any ships passing by. The Isle of Kell was protected now by both magic and men's laws, and the only shipwrecks that survived this day lay deep, deep down in the ocean bed.

Still it shone, still it enchanted, as pure and lovely as the day he first stepped foot on it. The clan's final home. His final home.

Ruriko stood transfixed before him. Iain angled his head to see her better: a sleepwalker alone in her reverie, lips apart, pulse slowed. All the color had drained from her face. She was an alabaster girl, too bonny to be real. Only her hair seemed mortal; it danced and blew into her lashes and she didn't even blink, only stood there, staring, letting the breeze play.

If he touched her skin now, he knew she'd be cold. Cold and rigid, truly like stone. Aye, he remembered that.

"Kell," she said, but it was a distant whisper.

The dolphins called to each other, descended to become water wraiths that swam lazy circles around the boat.

He didn't mean to, he didn't want to, but Iain saw his hand lifting, reaching for her. Her hair stirred again; he opened his palm to it and let the strands slide between his fingers, splendid dark brown . . . the color of seals, of the ancient woods. He was crumbling, crumbling. . . .

The first raindrop landed on his wrist. The next hit the top of his head, and then it was a deluge.

She didn't move. He took her by the shoulders and

pushed her back into her seat, a quick examination of her face, her rain-lashed eyes, her ashen cheeks. He found the helm and revived the engines, soaring away from Kell, toward the heart of that storm. Kelmere lay just beyond.

Her blood was ice. Ruri felt frozen, broken, drenched in rain. But as the boat battled ahead, she didn't see the ocean before her, or the terrible clouds. She saw the island. She saw Kell, and felt—she hardly knew what she felt. Incredulous. Amazed. Terrified—that a mere jot of land in the middle of the sea could pull these emotions from the dregs of her heart, so deep and bitter sure—it was like her soul had been struck by a sword of lightning, cleaved in two: Old Ruri. New Ruri.

She'd seen the Isle of Kell . . . and it looked like—home.

Rainwater was pooling in the soaked lap of her coat. She looked down at it, brought her hands together to form a cup and watched that fill too. It occurred to her that she should be worried, caught out here in the middle of a Scottish squall—if ever there was a moment for the Nightmare to dip down into reality, it would be this—but instead she felt only the numb safety of the discovery of this new and glacial self.

A glance to Iain showed her the hard slant of his jaw, lowered brows. He wasn't even wearing a coat, only a taupe wool sweater and heavy jeans, but he didn't look chilled, only . . . fierce. Alive.

His head turned and his gaze met hers, amber eyes rimmed in black, the starkly handsome angles of his face lucent with rain.

*Pirate.*

His lips moved. She heard his words, distal, edged with thunder.

"How are you?"

She made some response; she didn't know what. It

must have been the right one, though, because he nodded and turned back to the sea, long fingers firm on the wheel. The racer tore through the mounting waves.

Ruri looked up. A spear of real lightning flashed overhead, seemed to dissolve into forks exactly at the tip of the prow.

She felt, weirdly, the urge to laugh. Iain shot her another look. As if their thoughts connected, his mouth lifted; in an instant the fierce charisma of him transformed to something else, something both warmer and more enigmatic, breathtakingly seductive. Even the cropped raven curls of his hair were sexy, whipped with water and wind.

A fissure slid through her wintry calm, and then a break. Her entire body awoke to the lash of the rain and the heat of his look.

His smile widened. She felt her own lips curve in response, and in that moment—with the gust and the storm and the ocean chasing them in thick savage swells—Ruri realized that despite his promise to her, she was in danger. Deep danger.

It'd be far too easy to fall in love with a man who granted her smiles like that.


The port was called Lir Haven, and Iain obviously kept a slip there, because despite the rough sea he glided into the largest open space with skilled familiarity, mooring the powerboat next to a particularly sleek and stylish yacht.

"Yours?" she asked, as he helped her up to the pier. He swiped the water from his eyes and nodded, ignoring her disgruntled look, only grasping her hand to lead her away.

"My suitcase," she protested.

"It'll be brought up."

Ruri was a child of the city; the thought of leaving anything of her own in the unprotected wide open was as alien as handing her purse to a stranger. "Somebody will steal it!"

His glance held banked humor. "No, they won't." And he kept pulling her along.

The pier was slick and the ocean rushed over it like her pulse, a pounding, rhythmic surging, gray foam and shiny dark wood. She wanted to hurry but Iain's hold on her hand was too tight; even as the water lapped over their shoes, they walked. At least she wouldn't fall in.

The rain seemed heavier here ashore. She wouldn't have thought that possible. Their steps shook the pier and then they were on land, blessed land, sand that squished underfoot and gave way to long stems of sea lavender, and then grass.

Lir Haven was not much larger than the village they had left on the mainland, with the same quaint stone cottages and old-fashioned, romantic air. But the streets here were cobblestone, and as they darted along the sidewalks she saw that most of the buildings had been painted into merry rows of Easter egg colors, yellows and mauves and powder blues.

Beyond the buildings, beyond the pitched roofs of the homes, stretched a mountain that seemed to belie the town's deliberate cheer, powerfully austere, vapored slopes masking vivid green, the rain a sapphired mist across its peak. Behind it rose another, and then another, and another. She could not see the end of them.

"In here." They had stopped in front of one of the paler-pink buildings, this one with wide-spaced windows speckled with rain. The panes closest to her bore tarnished gilt letters that spelled, in a rather grand arc, *The Syren*.

Iain opened the door, vanished into smoke and darkness. Ruri took another look at that mountain, then followed.

It was a pub. Of course it was a pub, stuffed with people, men mostly, gathered at tables with pipes and glasses, standing at the bar. Here were the folk who had sense enough to stay ashore, Ruri realized; there would be no fishing today, not with this weather. Essence of tobacco and the distinct, sour tinge of ale knocked into her, actually stopping her in place by the door.

Conversation in the room ceased. Completely. Utterly. Everyone was staring at either Iain or at her, dripping rain all over the entry mat.

Iain, undaunted, sloughed the water from his hair and made his way to the bar.

"If I might borrow the phone, Mab," he said to the woman there, who looked from him to Ruri with wide, then narrowed eyes. She was small and plump, with a crown of braids as bright as new pennies.

"Why . . ." she breathed, watching Ruri, but the word only faded into the hush of the chamber.

"The phone, Mab," said Iain, gently.

"Aye. Here 'tis."

Without taking her eyes from Ruri, she pulled it up from behind the bar, plunked it down on the wood.

"Reliable wireless technology hasn't yet reached us," Iain said, lifting his voice as if to explain to the entire room. "Cell phones don't work up here."

It was a rotary phone. The whir and clicks of the dial rattled the air.

"Oh," said Iain, almost as an afterthought, the receiver to his ear. "Gentlemen, ladies. May I introduce Ms. Ruriko Kell. Aye, that Kell. Ms. Kell, the good people of Lir Haven." He turned back to the phone.

"Hello," said Ruri.

A few throats cleared; someone's chair scraped the wood floor. No one else spoke.

She felt a bead of water slide from her temple to her cheek, suspend at the curve of her jaw, and she wiped it away nervously. Still no one stirred. Across the room, the fire in the fireplace settled lower with a flourish of pops and crackles.

Iain spoke a few words, hung up the phone. He crossed back to her, his face closed.

"I should call my aunt," she said quietly, when he was near enough.

"You can call from the house. A car will be here soon. In the meanwhile, shall we sit? We'll have a drink while we wait."

Her gaze flicked back to the room, the tables of people staring.

"Better in here than out there," Iain said, reasonable. "I'm sure these fine folk would agree."

"Aye," said Mab suddenly, coming around the bar. "Sit down, the both of ye. Have a dram on the house."

Iain's palm became a subtle coercion at the small of her back, directing Ruri to a table miraculously cleared of liquor and men. Outside, the wind shifted and rain began to pepper the tavern windows; it was an oddly lonely sound for such a crowded space.

She thought she heard the people come to life as they passed. She thought she heard them shift and whisper behind her, hands to lips, lips to ears, elusive words. An odd fragment of speech caught at her, snared in her thoughts:

*She's come, she's come, she's here. . . .*

But when she looked around, no one was speaking.

Iain held out her chair. She sat, damply, and watched the woman named Mab hasten forward. As Ruri struggled out of her coat, Iain ordered whiskey for them both.

She didn't usually drink in the middle of the day, but she had the feeling that to refuse their hostess's hospitality would be a profound social gaffe.

Mab poured at the table, two glasses that seemed rather larger than the usual shot.

"Aught to eat?" she asked, her eyes on Ruri, but it was Iain who answered.

"Nay, this will do."

"Thank you," Ruri added.

Mab gave a nod—her smile fleet—and backed away, sweeping Ruri with one final, swift inspection before returning to the bar.

"Ho there, Dùghall MacGaw," she said loudly. "Ye'll be having another pint?"

There was a lingering silence, and then, "Aye," came the response, grudging.

Ruri lifted her whiskey to her lips, let it touch her tongue. Flame and spice; she tried a careful sip and managed not to cough.

"It's the local label," Iain offered, tasting his own. "Single malt, forty years. Mab honors us."

Gradually the folk around the room began to resume their conversations, although most of the voices remained muted. Iain seemed content not to speak any longer. He savored his drink and gazed into the changing light of the fire, by all appearances a man lost in heavy thought.

Ruri didn't buy it. The bar, the phone, the languid, indifferent way he handled the whiskey—all of it was quite conscious, she was certain. Even how he had guided her to the table, his open hand across her back, had been a message of sorts, a calculated proclamation. It was possible what he had said about the cell reception was true, but there was a public phone just across the street. She could see it from here.

He had wanted to bring her to this place. He had wanted her to be seen in this village. With him.

It had been a very, very long day. Perhaps it was only that she was so drenched and weary, that after the plane and the sea and the storm, and Kell, her nerves were frayed—but the thought of Iain MacInnes publicly using her to suit his own needs sent a rush of hot resentment through her. Ruri scanned the room anew, meeting only hastily averted glances, men and women dropping their eyes and their whispers while Iain mulled on.

She set her glass aside with a thump. Iain's languid air vanished in a flash; his focus on her was immediate and piercing.

"I'm going to comb my hair," she announced, and stood.

He stood with her, opened his mouth to speak—then looked past her, to the window.

"Our ride is here. Can it wait a few minutes more?"

Long and silent, a sedan pulled up outside the pub, windshield wipers batting raindrops back and forth.

The roomful of faces now watched them more openly, countenances ranging from somber to reserved to plainly curious.

"Fine." She didn't wait for him to touch her again, but grabbed her coat and walked away, her eyes resolutely on the door. She was nearly there when the corner shadows came to life; a hand reached out and seized her wrist.

Ruri jerked back, instinctive, and a woman was pulled from the dark, blond-haired, aged, and thin, her fingers still curved into Ruri's flesh.

The woman inched closer, breathing heavily through her nose. Her voice throbbed low, a guttural hiss.

"I know what ye are."

"Excuse me?"

Iain was there, warm against her shoulder. "Let her go, Aileen."

The woman ignored him, staring up at Ruri with a dark and hostile gaze, her lips drawn back. She smelled musty, like old clothes left too long in a closet. There was lipstick on her teeth.

Ruri twisted her arm over and down, breaking the hold, feeling the scrape of fingernails against her skin.

"Aileen." It was Mab, at Ruri's other side. "Have a seat now, dearie. They're on their way out."

"I *know*," the woman repeated, never looking away from Ruri's face. "*I know.*"

Iain's arm wrapped around Ruri's shoulders; with a graceful turn he merely slipped around the other woman, taking Ruri with him out into the rain. The pub door hitched closed behind them.

Ruri took in a lungful of cold, wet air. "Who was *that*?"

"Aileen Lamont." He ushered her into the car. "Never mind her. Just the local eccentric. Every village in Scotland seems to have one."

As the sedan began to bump up the lane, Ruri looked back to The Syren, discovered a line of faces gathered to stare back at her through the windows.

"Just one?" she asked, and beside her, Iain chuckled.

# CHAPTER EIGHT

✦

Kell desired a garden by our palace.

As far as I was concerned, it was only another device of man, but he was persistent about wanting it, and in the end I told him to do as he wished, if it would gratify him.

So he did. It was small and, I fear, ragged at first, with wildflowers wilting in amphorae, and saplings rescued from shipwrecks struggling to anchor their roots to life. Soon our children were eager to help him, hiking the isle to unearth intriguing new flora, swimming out to the reef to search the wrecks for any plants that had not yet succumbed to the saltwater.

Kell was especially fond of those, the plants rescued from the reef.

And in a few years, I had to admit it exceeded my expectations; his garden became a place of halcyon luxury, with exotic trees dripping fruit in jeweled clusters, herbs and flowers fanning colors along the narrow paths.

I made him a gift of a bench I had found at the bottom

of the sea, solid alabaster, unbroken, only gently worn from the currents. In daylight it looked very fine, especially beneath the shade of the pomegranate tree. Often we would sit there together, just the two of us, looking out at the bend of land below, the wide blue sea. Peace flowed around us like the dreams of the gods.

The single failure of the garden was the plum tree, salvaged too late from the reef to ever thrive again. Kell kept it in a large clay pot and gave it the best space in the garden, right next to my bench. Many of the leaves had withered, but he would not abandon hope. When the wind spoke, the purple branches swayed, sending the remaining leaves at their ends fluttering with alarm.

But gradually, to my surprise, my husband's dedication yielded results. The plum tree began to bud and spread new leaves.

"Thou hast done well here," I told him one day as we sat close, leaning my head upon his bronzed shoulder.

"It pleases thee?" he asked, stroking my arm.

"Aye."

"That was all I wished."

I smiled, charmed. "Truly?"

"Aye." The stroking slowed, then stopped. "My mother . . ."

I waited, with his hand paused at my elbow.

"Aye, thy mother," I prompted.

"She had such a place. Not so fine as this, of course. She had not . . ." His voice faded, and his hand fell completely from me. I lifted my head.

He was staring at the horizon, his gaze lost. There was a memory there on his face, a memory that did not include me. I reached up, ran my fingers through his dark hair. After all this while it was threaded with gray, but his features, when he looked back at me, were as warm and comely as ever.

"Thy mother had a garden," I said. "But thine is the better. She would be jealous?"

"Nay." He shook his head, his lips lifting. "She would be . . . surprised."

"And proud."

"Mayhap."

A peal of laughter reached us from the cove below; four of our children played in the water, splashing each other as they romped through the waves. Eos swam up behind her youngest brother, scooped him up in her arms and rolled them both underwater with just the flick of her tail. They emerged as one a few minutes later, sputtering with glee, two golden creatures with hair that floated and gleamed.

"Betimes I worry," Kell said, almost to himself. "What will become of them?"

"Of whom? Our children?"

He looked at me again, not quite so warm as before. "They live here with us, they thrive and they grow—but what of the future? What does the island hold for them then? In my time—in my world—Eos is of an age to wed. Yet she stays here a maiden, forever young. Is this to be her fate?"

He had never spoken so before, separating our lives into two different realms. His. Mine. I sat up straighter and curled my fingers into my palms to hide my sudden dread.

"She will leave when the time is ripe," I told him. "When the song of the ocean becomes too sweet to resist, she will go. And she will find love."

"How dost thou know?"

"Because I know," I answered, impatient. "It is the way of us all."

His smile stretched thin. "The way of siren."

"Aye," I said, after a moment.

He was silent, watching the children. Someone shouted a challenge; more splashing ensued. Eos hung apart from this new game. She had a sister in her arms now, their heads close together. They would be trading secrets, I knew.

"Shall she ever return to us?" Kell asked quietly.

"Aye. She shall return. This is her home. *Our* home," I emphasized, and he rewarded me with a truer smile than before. My relief felt like tears; I blinked and turned to the little potted tree at my side.

I said, "Mayhap I'll grow plums for her children."

"Nay, for me," he teased, and when I glanced up at him the smile had reached his eyes.

"Aye, beloved, for thee. My plums, my heart . . ." I put my hands behind his neck and brought his face to mine, "all and always for thee."

# CHAPTER NINE

❦

House, he'd called it, and as Kelmere manifested, rising up from the pleated knolls, Ruri felt an astonished laugh catch in her throat. This was no house. It was an estate, a manor. A mansion.

She'd seen such places only in guidebooks or movies, a wide opulence of stone, curving archways, fanciful cupolas streaked in mist. She was no expert on architecture—most of what she knew had been absorbed from casual reading—but even Ruri could see that Iain's residence was unique, an example of no particular style and many, from the lead-filigreed windows to the stately balustrades to the medieval—or older—tower house bracing the western wing. A lawn of perfectly trimmed grass unfurled as they approached; it spread and vanished into the woods beyond, supple green fading into the black forest of the hills.

Even the fog was richer here, aloft in the Scottish mountains. It drifted in slow passage across the road, seizing and then freeing them in long white fingers. The car never lost its steady pace.

"You live here?" Ruri asked, as at last they rolled to a halt in front of the horseshoe stairway of the main entrance.

"I do."

"Alone?"

"More or less."

The driver of the sedan opened her door, stood ready with an umbrella.

"It doesn't get any smaller, the longer you wait," Iain murmured in her ear.

Ruri climbed out and he followed, accepting the umbrella from the chauffeur with a short nod of dismissal.

She didn't overlook it, that nod, nor the way the other man bowed and backed away, throwing Ruri one briefly avid glance—although she should be getting used to that, she thought wryly—before returning to the sedan. The car eased down the driveway once more, a dragon's puff of exhaust tailing behind.

Iain leaned closer to hold the umbrella just over her head; all the world outside their little shelter lay frosted in vapor and rain. They stood there awhile in silence, breathing the same mountain air, before Ruri tucked her hands beneath her arms and spoke.

"Nice place. What is it, exactly, that you do, Dr. MacInnes?"

His smile was faint. "You mean, what is it, exactly, that I do that allows me to live here, Ms. Kell?"

"You're *not* a professor."

"Not full time, no."

She waited, water sheering off the umbrella in platinum ribbons.

Iain said, "I'm a hunter," and gave her a sidelong look,

correctly interpreting her expression. "Not that sort. I hunt the oceans."

"For what?"

"Treasure."

Her brows raised, and he smiled again, looking ahead.

"I've a gift," he said mildly, "for finding sunken ships."

She surveyed the looming mansion. "That must be quite a gift."

"Aye. I admit it's a handy thing."

They began to walk, measured steps not quite kept within the umbrella's protective circle, crossing the slate-paved drive. At the foot of the stairway a new thought struck her, and she turned to him, so close their breath mingled into clouds.

"My attorney said there were shipwrecks around Kell. Is that why you want it? For treasure?"

"No." For a long moment he held her eyes, his gaze almost searching; then his lashes lowered, sending gold to dusk. "Kell is simply . . . a place I've admired for many, many years."

Doubt crept into her tone. "You're saying there's no treasure there?"

His eyes flashed to hers and he grinned, roguish again. "I confess I intend to find out." He nodded toward the stairs and they began to ascend, splashing in tandem through clear thin puddles. "The currents surrounding Kell are notorious for both their strength and their devastation, but there hasn't been a ship lost there since the second World War. Previous wrecks have long since eroded, or scattered. There might be pottery shards left, ballast stones, anchors, cannons, even a hull or two preserved in sand, if we're fortunate. But if you mean fantastic riches—chests of doubloons and ropes of pearls, that sort of thing—no. Of course not. That's the stuff of fantasy, lass."

"Fantasy. But you're willing to pay twelve million for it."

"I'll spend half that just in the preliminary surveys. Nautical archaeology is not for the faint of heart."

"Or wallet," she said, shocked.

Another grin. "Aye."

They had reached the double doors of the entrance, dark, steel-studded oak. His hand grazed the latch; some hidden sorcery had the doors swing open at just this whispered touch.

Ruri watched him turn to shake out the umbrella to the stairs, wet-haired and fascinating, a practical pirate with the home of a king.

She said slowly, "You're a very interesting man, Dr. MacInnes."

"I was hoping you'd think so." He motioned for her to walk ahead.

The entrance hall was vast. She paused a few steps in, feeling too small in the tall, dim space, imposing granite columns flanking the walls, spreading arches like creased scythes into the vaulted ceiling. The air in here was near as cold as outdoors, but thinner, paler, lacking the tang of ocean and pine.

Iain came just behind her. His hands met her shoulders; with the lightest of pressure he tugged her into a turn, so that she faced him again.

If there was a chandelier in the hallway, it remained dark. The only illumination came from the windows of the room ahead of them, an eerie gray brilliance, finely misted, that softened his features and lent silver smoke to his eyes.

"I've welcomed you to Scotland already," he said gravely. "Now I bid you welcome to my home, Ruriko."

His head tipped to hers. Before she could shift away, his lips brushed her left cheek, then her right. It was a sensation invitingly like silk, like thistledown, smooth and warm and barely there. With his hands still at her shoulders, his head lifted; his mouth lingered over hers, not touching, not retreating. She was staring, fascinated, into those silver-gold eyes, realized his intent only just before they swept closed. All her will fled. Ruri couldn't move, couldn't stop him: He kissed her fully on the mouth, a sweet, erotic meeting of lips that clung and parted—heat, taste—leisurely withdrew.

His eyes opened.

"Thank you."

It flustered her, his solemn gratitude, nearly more than his kiss had, and she pulled back to find a row of people now watching them from the gray-lit end of the hall, men and women both, uniformed, faces drawn thin with silence.

"Ah, Niall, there you are," said Iain impassively, from over her shoulder. "Kindly show Ms. Kell to her room."

She followed the man named Niall in a daze, kept pressing her fingertips to her mouth. Marveling.

Corridors, turns, a spiraled staircase with paintings and statues and great Chinese urns—but all Ruri could take in was that moment in the entrance hall. The brief, burning eternity when Iain had stolen through her defenses with just the drowsy smoke of his eyes and the urgent softness of his lips.

God, it had been like—like sinking into an abyss both wondrous and darkly frightening; like drifting blind through the tail of a comet, no light but everything heat and sensation, silent glitter across her skin.

Niall stopped, his hand on the golden latch of a high white door. He opened it without comment, stood waiting as Ruri came back to the moment and entered the room.

Cool elegance, a true haven for a princess, she first thought, and then revised it: an enchanted princess, more like, bespelled in some winter woods. She'd been expecting something grandiose, something more in line with the exterior of the mansion. This was no room of frills and fussy baubles, however, but rather one of gently graceful form and function, soothing colors, classical lines.

"If ye need aught, miss, there's the bell by the bed."

She turned, but before she could respond, Niall was gone, the open door revealing nothing but the dusky blank hallway beyond.

Ruri's sense of being stranded in a fairy tale abruptly increased.

She stood uncertain in the middle of the chamber and took it all in, the ivory-and-sage silk striped walls, the gossamer crush of organza drapery that fell like waterfalls from ceiling to floor. Everything was polished and perfect, gleaming marble, ebony furniture set like artwork against the high walls. The bed alone—four posts but no canopy, ocean-pale covers—seemed nearly the size of her apartment.

And everywhere—on tables, on nightstands, nodding in vases by the door—were flowers.

Roses, mostly, massed in dense pastel bunches, the most dreamy hues she'd ever imagined, cream and pink and peach and coral, snow and magical lavender. She crossed to a vase of translucent jade, cupped her hand near the blooms and caught the scent of heaven.

"Do you like them?"

His voice was smooth and deep, as cool as the room. She didn't turn around.

"They're incredible." And then, with nervous honesty: "I'm afraid to touch anything."

"Don't be." Iain's footsteps were hardly audible across the floor. "They're only things."

"Very *nice* things."

"I'm glad they please you."

She wasn't ready to look at him yet. Instead, she let the flat of her hand skim the petals, ruffled resistance against her palm. "It wasn't pottery shards that got you all this, I think."

"No." He sounded amused. "Rather not."

Her suitcase had somehow preceded her; it stood propped next to the armoire, small and shabby against burnished wood.

"If you like," said Iain, "I'll have the maid unpack for you."

"No." She found her fingers pressed again to her lips, and quickly lowered her hand. "No, um . . . I'll do it. It's not much."

"Ruriko."

There was an invitation to her name, an unhurried command. She straightened her shoulders and looked round, finding him standing near the bed. He held a stem of starry white flowers in his hands, she guessed plucked from the vase on the dresser beside him. He was gazing down at the flowers, twirling the stem lazily between his fingers.

"I meant to ask you. What did you think of Kell?"

She grappled for an answer to that, found nothing she could articulate or even wished to share; too many emotions rose through her, strange and potent.

*Yearning, foreboding.*

"It was beautiful."

"Aye." He looked up. "Did it—remind you of aught?"

"Remind me?"

*Home.*

"Of anything. I'm only curious."

*Sanctuary.*

"No," she lied. "I don't think so."

His mouth tightened. For some reason it irked her, his grim-faced disapproval, as though she had failed a test she'd never meant to take. His kiss, his expectations: all beyond her, all part and parcel of this odd and mysterious place, wreathed with clouds, encircled with water, woods and legends and secrets hiding around corners. She was goaded into speech.

"Have I satisfied your condition yet?" His eyes glanced to hers, guarded, narrowed topaz in the winter-cool room. "To buy the island," she clarified, deliberate. "You wanted me to see it, and I have. So is your condition fulfilled?"

"No," he answered, just as deliberate. "It is not."

"But I saw it."

"You must go there, I said."

She opened her hand to the windows, rain pebbling the glass. "When?"

"When we can." He was impassive again, closed. He turned and dropped the stem of flowers back into its vase. "Dinner's not for an hour at least, later if you wish. If you'd like a bath to warm up, I'll ring for it."

"My, you have maids for everything."

His smile came, instantly sardonic. "Not everything."

Ah, not quite impassive. Ruri inhaled too sharply, seeing the smile, with a peculiar skip of her heart knowing exactly what it meant. It seemed to her she had seen that barbed lift of his lips before—it wasn't true, it couldn't be—but in that moment the slow freefall took her again;

she was sinking into the abyss, with only the cold, searing glint of his eyes to hold her.

She became excruciatingly aware of his presence, the raven mess of his hair, the soaked cling of his sweater to broad shoulders. The lines of his legs, his thighs, encased in water-black jeans. A ferocious heat began to suffuse her. She wrenched her gaze back up to his, the blood rising in her cheeks.

He noticed. His head tilted slightly; the barbed smile did not waver.

Iain said pleasantly, "There are salts, I believe. For the bath."

She found her voice. "Thank you. An hour should be fine."

His footsteps as he left were much louder than before.

There wasn't a lock on the door. She checked.

The bathroom was enormous, and the tub could fit four people. She preferred showers, usually, but the claw-foot bathtub was really so outrageously big. . . .

Ruri carried the vase of white flowers into the bathroom with her, set them carefully near the tub's edge. As water rushed against porcelain, the fragrance of orange blossoms lifted to wrap around her with the rising steam.

She did not use the salts.


He waited for her in the portrait gallery. They were dining in the great room tonight; he'd never been truly comfortable eating there by himself, and it had settled, by idle days and vast hollow nights, into a museumlike gravitas, seldom used. Iain was far more at ease on the balcony outside his bedroom, dining without a roof or rules, but today, tonight—for Ruriko—he would abide by the ways of civilization. He'd ordered the candelabras lit, the formal china unpacked. After years of Iain's casual repasts, Kelmere's chef was in ecstasy.

Everything was set; all he needed now was his guest. He wouldn't go to her door again. He didn't quite trust himself that far. The portrait gallery was the logical compromise, an impressive corridor that ran from her room to the main stairs. She'd have to come by soon.

To wile the time he paced, and then caught himself pacing. Iain paused in front of the doe-blue eyes of a long-ago siren, her powdered hair done up in ringlets, her gown ornately cinched. She gazed down at him with the impression of genteel serenity; only the slight, whimsical crook of her smile offered any hint of the lady's true spirit.

He did not need to look at the name on the etched plate beneath the painting. He knew them all by now, lairds and ladies, the faces of his own children forming a visual ladder through time.

Lady Serafina Adelina MacMhuirich. Daughter of Ronan, son of Coinneach, son of Deirdre, daughter of Uisdean . . .

The sound of the rain was distant here, a ghostly patter that rolled along the floor and walls, trembled lightly against stretched canvas, from old to new.

He hadn't meant to kiss her so soon. He hadn't meant to, but even as Iain had watched Ruriko walk into his home he had known he was going to. He'd managed to let her pass the entry, beguiled by the pale flash of her hands, the sway of her hair. She moved with watchful curiosity, wary of everything new, he supposed; yet when he reached for her she hadn't resisted in the least. She'd met his touch with such flowing compliance, and he wanted her so badly, and it had been so damned long. . . .

In the gloom of the vestibule she'd been nearly swallowed in shadow, but even then he could see her. The last scrap of his vow to wait had been flattened by just the faint, silvery throw of light across her face.

Her skin had been perfect ice. Her kiss had been honey-eyed flame.

He thought of it and felt a rising of pure lust come up through him again; endless black and aching, midnight shorn of stars. Just that one kiss, the caress of her lips, and the years fell away and the pain of her loss was fresh renewed—he wanted her almost to a frenzy—

God help him, how was he going to curb himself now?

She entered the gallery silently. Iain had the sense of her first, before he even turned to see her, a lithe ripple of electricity encompassing him, his body responding with instinctive fervor. To contain it he stood very still, let the air flow around and through him. He was empty, he was a vessel. He could restrain the need.

Ruriko came to stand beside him, unaware, undaunted. It seemed inconceivable that she didn't feel it too—she had stood so still for his kiss, so still and willing—but she was studying the painting with an open gaze, nothing to hide, no primitive urgent passions sending her blood to a heated peak; no spark of hunger and pain and craving lit in her lovely eyes.

Or did it? She noticed his stare, at least; she threw him a glance from beneath long lashes, there and gone. He might have imagined that demure, enticing look.

He wanted to take her here, right now. He wanted to lower her to the checker-tiled floor and press his body over hers. He wanted to unbutton the prim white blouse she wore—prim and not, for beneath the filmy fabric he could see the outline of her bra—and taste her, his tongue on her skin, between the valley of her breasts. Push up her tailored skirt and run his hands along her legs, her hair chocolate satin against his cheek—

"Serafina," Ruriko read aloud, her voice gliding into echo down the hall. "How pretty she was."

He could not even reply, his jaw locked too tight. He was undone, his body and mind beyond him. It took all his will to drag himself back from the dark precipice of fantasy.

He could make it real, though. He knew that he could.

She glanced up at him again, a more fixed regard than before. The blue of her eyes was an exact match to the painted girl's.

"Was she a lady of the manor?"

"A daughter," he managed, and focused on the portrait, concentrating on each careful brush stroke, each skillful line, until his heart and his blood were once more under his command, and the gilded frame held an image instead of a flat collection of colors and shapes.

When he looked back at Ruriko she was examining him still, her gaze shadowed now, cryptic. He found his eyes falling, inevitable, to the open fold of her collar, the thrumming pulse at her throat.

Iain said roughly, "You don't wear it. The locket."

"I don't wear jewelry."

"Why not?"

"I find it—troublesome."

He scowled. "You did bring it, though?"

She strolled a few steps from him, crossing to the opposite wall; her hair made a dark smooth comma down her back. "You know, I read every offer for the island. Yours was the only one mentioning the Soul of Kell, making it part of the sale. But in your final bid, that paragraph had been deleted."

"I changed my mind," he said, into the silence. "I don't want it now."

There was more than a suggestion of skepticism in the line of her lips; in spite of his disquiet, it nearly brought him to smile.

"It belongs with you. I knew that from the moment I first saw you." And then, when her mouth only flattened further, "You should wear it. There's no reason why you shouldn't."

She considered him a moment, then drifted closer. "Do you have a watch?"

"Aye."

"May I see it?"

He raised his wrist, allowed the starched cuff of his shirt to inch back. Her hand lifted, then paused.

"Do you like it?"

"Would I wear it if I didn't?"

Her lips pressed thinner still, a fleet vexation, then relaxed. She covered his watch with curved fingers, a feathery touch that lit through him like fox fire—a cold, luminous tremor to his soul. Iain tried to jerk away but she held fast, a new light to her eyes.

"What's this about?" he demanded.

She let go. "Wait."

"For what?"

"What time is it now?"

He drew in air past his teeth, unsettled, then glanced grudgingly at the timepiece. Iain shook his wrist. Generations of Swiss ingenuity had been rendered moot: His watch was dead. He lifted his head and sent her a long, appraising look.

"Clever trick."

She clasped her hands behind her back. "Merely an expensive one, I'm afraid. Metal acts . . . oddly around me.

Almost like I'm a conductor. I've always been this way, but I stopped wearing jewelry four years ago, after my microwave blew up." She sidled back a step. "Your watch probably isn't permanently damaged. If I stay away, it'll start again."

He released the clasp, shook the piece again, then slipped it into his pocket. "Ah, well, who wants to be a slave to time?"

For a second he thought she might return his smile; instead, she only ducked back another step, a sudden diffidence in the slope of her shoulders, turning to the next painting.

Iain remained where he was, still holding the watch, rubbing his thumb over the warm glass face.

Ruriko stooped to make out the portrait title, retreated to take in the entire scene. It was one of the grander portrayals, floor-length, a Regency family fetchingly arranged around an alabaster bench in a lush, lofty green garden.

He knew the bench. He knew the garden. He was watching Ruriko, the frown that came to her, her instant, arrested attention. She stood on her toes to examine some higher detail, balancing with her arms held out, a ballerina in a chaste wool skirt and her hair wanton free.

She made a soft sound, hushed revelation. Every inch of him tensed.

"What is it?"

"I just noticed—the lady—the mother—she's wearing the locket."

Hope was a terrible thing. He didn't want it, he had never asked for it, yet it kept returning to him again and again. Iain had to look away from her before he could answer, and even still his tone was too harsh. "Aye. Those people were your kin."

"What?" She sank back to her heels, facing him.

He walked to the portrait, pointed to the lace-bedecked baby dangled on her father's knee. "Genevieve Christine. Your . . . great-great-great-grandmother, I believe. The youngest daughter. She married a local squire. Their . . . son's son sought a new life, in America."

Ruriko was silent, her face pensive, gazing at the father and child.

"But Kelmere was her home," Iain finished, forcing himself to examine the picture. "And it would have been yours as well, if so many of your ancestors had not been quite so extraordinarily bad with investments."

It was an unworthy strike; he regretted it as soon as he said it, but she didn't seem to notice. Her chin lowered and brows lifted, a look of perplexed incredulity.

"You bought this place from—my relatives?"

"From the last earl."

He led her down the hall, all the way to the end, where the portrait of Eric, twelfth Earl of Kell, glared down at them. Shade and light, thick with paint, the unique strokes of Sargent brought the earl to vivid life. It had been done in the twenties; even then Eric had been an old man, with abundant white hair and a penetrating stare. He had never wed, never sired a child. Perhaps no woman would have him—despite the innate magnetism that was his birthright, he'd been stiff-rumped, exceedingly pompous, as much a throwback to any nonsiren lineage as Iain could imagine. Even here, in this small, informal likeness, audacity shone from those eyes; discontent lined his mouth.

By the time Eric had inherited the earldom, the unpaid taxes on the estate were already crippling. By the time Iain had come along, the earl had shaved off and sold as much of the land as legally possible, and still it was not enough. He'd been reduced to pawning antiques from the manor.

Perhaps there'd been some just cause for the old man's discontent.

Iain had always thought it brash conceit that had the earl hang his portrait so conspicuously, for so long—a simpleton could have done the math—but now that he was gone, Iain didn't have the heart to move it. Eric MacMhuirich had been, in his way, the last of the line.

Almost.

Ruriko reached up, touched delicate fingers to the frame. "Where did he go, after you bought his home?"

Her tone was curiously empty; he slanted her a look.

"Don't worry. I didn't boot him out, if that's what you're thinking. He went to Kell." Iain shrugged. "He wanted to go there, anyway."

"But—is there a house there?"

"Of sorts."

Her expression turned severe. "Of sorts? An elderly man, by himself on an island—"

"Ruriko, listen to me. He went there well content. And, eventually, he died a satisfied man."

"How do you know?"

"I was his friend," he said simply. "And I made certain of it."

"Oh." Her chin dropped; she tucked her hair behind an ear, a feminine, self-conscious gesture. "I'm sorry. I guess I got carried away. I thought—" Her head lifted. She razed him with melting blue eyes. "I just thought of how awful it would be to die alone, in exile."

"Aye," he agreed, dispassionate.

Outside, the wind gave a treble moan.

Ruriko studied him, her head tilted, her gaze roaming his face. Whatever she saw didn't satisfy her; the frown returned, an endearing little wrinkle between her brows. He had to stuff his hands into his pockets to keep from smoothing it away.

"But, to be frank, I doubt the earl would have been gratified by your concern," Iain said, putting a careful distance between them. "He was a very independent man. Proud of his life, and of his heritage."

"And of his family," she said, not making it a question.

"Of course."

Ruriko glanced down the long shadowed hallway, painting after painting fading into the rainy-day gloom.

"There certainly were a lot of them."

He had recovered enough to offer her his arm. "Aye. There were."

# CHAPTER TEN

❧

he children made up a game. They called it Fisherman, and when nothing else would cajole the
young ones from their tempers, Fisherman
would draw them back into smiles and mirth. I never
knew which of them first created it; it became a diversion
that belonged to them all.

Fisherman was played on land, not water. One child
would be the mortal man, sitting in the sand, shells or
driftwood or flotsam arranged around him in a studious
imitation of a boat. At times they had true rowboats—sad
husks discarded from the reef—but they were not careful
with them, and the tide usually carried them off again in
days.

Around the Fisherman swam the Fish, kicking sand
with pretend tails, rolling, wriggling in laughing circles.
The Fisherman would throw his net, and the sibling who
wasn't swift enough to avoid it was captured. In this way,
the last free Fish would win the game.

They had a series of rules, devoutly obeyed: Fish may use their feet but not hands; Fish may speak but the Fisherman will not hear; Fish may escape the boat but only if the Fisherman looks away. Fish may be recaptured. Fish may not sing.

Eos made a tenderhearted Fisherman. She would always look to the sky while the littlest ones squirmed to freedom.

I sat on the beach watching them one gray cloudy day, holding my infant in my arms. She was old enough to open her eyes and smile, young enough to screech when left alone. As the others frolicked, I crooned her a soft lullaby, thinking sliding, melancholy thoughts . . . of the tender curve of her cheek . . . of when she might be weaned. Of the promise of her new life, and what she might find awaiting her in the human world. I think I knew even then that she would be the last of my children.

She watched me sing with wide blue eyes, her little mouth a puckered *O* around her thumb.

I don't know why I looked up just then. Perhaps one of the others laughed especially loud, but look up I did, finding Kell standing across from me, on the other side of the game.

He was not watching me. Stone-still, he was watching the Fisherman, our eldest son, toss his net over a sister. Her shrieking cries, as she thrashed and fought with her hands pinned to her sides.

My song perished in my throat.

I was standing before I knew it. I was moving toward him, hurrying, and his gaze shifted, finding me, freezing my feet.

The clouds bubbled low behind him, the surf writhed. He stood alone with his legs braced, his arms clenched to rigid muscle, a mortal man cast dark against the tear of the sea. But it was his eyes that frightened me. Feral and hopeless, they held the dying light of a wild creature trapped without recourse.

Without a word, he turned and walked away from us all.

# CHAPTER ELEVEN

*

Dinner was a success. At least, Iain thought it a
success. The food was exceptional and Ruriko
glowed like the heavens they could not see,
seated and nearly silent in her chair, tasting each dish in
small, dainty bites that almost shamed his own appetite;
he must have eaten thrice what she did.

But it didn't matter. She was here, at his table, in his
home. That was all that mattered.

He'd had the electric lights turned off, so the chande-
liers hung like prismatic specters above them, cobwebs of
crystal. True flame lit the hall instead. He wanted to
watch her by candlelight, because that was more natural
to him, and because that was how he remembered her
best: by gold and smoke and dancing fire.

Yet the past was not always his ally. He said something
once, pointed out some minutia of the room—the
hammered-silver chalice on the mantel over the hearth—
and just the way she turned in her chair to see it—the
shadowed brilliance of her skin, the shine of her hair, the

slope of her cheekbone—clicked in his mind, was enough to send him drowning in memories.

She wasn't much like before. But enough. Just enough.

He had to stop talking. His throat tightened, his body ached with a bitter longing; when she looked back at him, he was pretending to taste the pinot blanc, mastering himself again.

But apparently he wasn't as good as he thought.

"Iain? Is something wrong?"

When he glanced at her she was simply Ruriko, fair and dark and bonny as the night.

"I was thinking of your job," he said, a reckless shot at diversion. She angled her head and sent him a look he couldn't interpret.

"Do you enjoy it?" he asked, setting the wine aside. "Being a—what do you call it?"

"Telephone psychic."

"Aye."

There was rose on her cheeks, firelight or blush, he couldn't tell, but her response came perfectly composed. "I suppose you think it's ridiculous."

"I have no opinion of it."

She hid her smile behind her own wineglass. "How refreshing."

"Do you enjoy it?" he persisted, when it seemed she would not speak again.

"Yes. No. It . . . accommodates me."

"There are other things you could do. You have a degree."

Her eyes met his. "For now, I do this. I'm not ashamed of it."

"No. I never thought you should be. I'm sure you're very good."

"I am."

It was the most she had spoken the entire meal. He was about to respond when Niall and Duncan appeared with the third course, filos of mushrooms and pine nuts, roasted shallots, sweet pepper rice. Polished lids were whisked from silver platters; steam spun and twirled into the high gloom of the ceiling.

Iain waited until his men finished serving before taking up the subject again.

" 'Tis said there's more than a touch of the sight in the clan family." He sliced into his filo. "A fey bit of blood married into the line, generations back."

"Gypsy?" she inquired, smiling again.

"Spanish," he replied, serious. "Can you read me now?"

Her eyes widened. "What?"

"Can you read me now? Tell me what I'm thinking?"

She looked, very quickly, at the two men still standing in the shadows of the room, hands locked behind their backs. "No. It doesn't work like that."

"How, then?"

She let out a little laugh, frustration, embarrassment. "I can't say."

"I see. Can't—but truly won't."

Her knife and fork clattered a trifle louder against her plate. "I don't know why you'd care."

"Call it idle curiosity. But . . . perhaps you don't have the sight, after all. Perhaps the Spanish blood's run too thin. Still, it's a fine excuse for the job, isn't it?"

Ruriko set her utensils aside. "Was that a dare?"

He shrugged, looking away.

"All right."

She pushed back her chair. Niall rushed forward to help but was too late; with a subtle, pointed look from Iain, he disappeared back into his unlit corner.

She came to him with easy elegance, right up to where

he waited at the head of the table. Light spilled from the hearth behind her, granting the gauzy blouse a fiery halo, betraying the slender lines of her torso, the dip of her waist. Iain kept his focus fixed ruthlessly on her face.

"I can't control what comes," she warned.

"I'll take my chances."

"Are you sure?"

"I *did* remove my watch."

She studied him a moment longer with those blue storm eyes. "Your hand, then," she said finally, raising her own.

He smiled and lifted his palm. Her fingers wrapped hard around his.

Ah. No fox fire now to frost through his heart, only Ruriko, a true touch, a tempting connection. He wanted, very much, to feel what she did. He wanted to know what she might see. He wanted her to understand it all—his passion, his newfound hope—and at the same time he didn't. But for all his unspoken wishes, Iain saw only his siren's fathomless face, wiser than the ages, painted by the gods. Her lashes swept down and then he couldn't even see her eyes; firelight burned and sparked around her, a flowering of flames.

When she spoke again, her voice was a velvet murmur. "You're not what you seem."

He held silent at that, carefully detached.

"You have secrets."

"Don't you?" he asked, and she looked up at him again, releasing his hand.

"And you tend to counter anything uncomfortable with a question."

"I beg your pardon."

One shoulder lifted; a fall of hair slipped silkily down her arm. "That wasn't a supernatural observation."

"Anything else?"

The French lyre clock on the mantel struck nine in a cascade of chimes. Ruriko backed away from him, out of the light.

"You really want to go to Kell. With me. But I knew that already, so I suppose it doesn't count."

"I suppose not."

She walked to her seat. This time Niall stood ready, holding out the chair, sliding her in. She accepted her napkin, picked up her fork, and added, very poised, "You had a dog named Auger as a boy. You rode a horse named Sol. The dog has died, but the horse . . . lives here, in the stables."

From the corner of the room came a pair of gasps, quickly stifled.

"Were you thinking of the horse?" she asked, piercing a shallot.

"No," Iain said. But he had been thinking about the corona around her as she held his hand in hers, all heat and brightness, her figure lit in flame. He had been thinking about the sun.

*The storm had died. She was on an island, a teardrop of paradise set upon the blanket of the sea. The sand was staggering soft. It shifted between her toes, melted to the soles of her feet, liquid gold that gave and reformed.*

*She was alone here. She was not alone. She searched but saw no one else, only water, trees. The thunderclouds of before—so violent, so enraged—had wisped thin and feather-light; they stretched across the heavens in milk-white farewell.*

*She was walking up the beach, slow steps. A voice called out behind her and she looked back—*

Ruri's eyes were open. It took a while to understand that, that she wasn't on the beach, any beach, but in a place of darkness. And comfort. Pillows, not sand. Quilts, not clouds.

She stretched in the sheets, and then stretched again: The old restlessness itched through her, waking her fully, sending her upright in the bed. Crazy-bones. She felt like she could run for miles, just to get rid of this ache.

Iain's winter room kept its spellbound cast even in the deep of night. Black shadow draped the furniture and walls, pewtered light from the windows fell to the floor in rainwater squares. The curtains stirred with an unseen draft, stiff pale fabric sifting, swelling, like the folds of a lady's skirt.

She had always been able to see well in the dark, even as a little girl. She'd never been afraid of the night. Perhaps that was why she stole so readily to her feet, flexing her toes, her calves, as the organza rustled and sighed.

The faintest sound came from her left, deft and small as a mouse. A click. The bedroom door had just closed.

Ruri stood there, her senses raw, wondering if she'd imagined that. She had shut the door before going to bed, of that she was absolutely certain. But just seconds ago—hadn't there been a narrow gap in that dark, a long splinter of gray against the pitch that her eye had passed over?

She grabbed a sweater from her open suitcase, didn't bother looking for shoes. On bare feet she ran lightly to the door, put her hand on the golden latch. It eased open with only a silent stroke of air.

The corridor beyond lay empty, murky as the bottom of the sea. With the door now cracked, the draft found its mate; a ghost of a breeze swept over her shoulders into the night, lifting strands of her hair into a still floating.

She pulled back to tug the sweater over her head, then listened hard again. All she heard was rainfall.

Who would be up so late? Who would be at her door?

No one, Ruri told herself firmly. It was the draft.

But she stepped out into the hall.

It was easy to move without noise. Her only accompaniment was the dull lamentation of the storm and the shadow of her shadow, pressing ahead. She passed a statue of Diana, posed with her bow in the air, and then one of Psyche and Eros, spread wings and a stone kiss. In the arched recess of an alcove a bronze mermaid was tucked, arms aloft, rising from the waves.

She paused at the entrance to the portrait gallery, looking around, still seeing nothing unusual.

No—there—at the other end of the gallery. A flicker of life from the corner of her eye, gone by the time she turned. She was frozen, breathing through her mouth, but it didn't happen again. It had not been the draft, or her imagination.

She should go back to her room, drag one of those exquisite pieces of furniture in front of the door and return to bed to wait for morning. She should not, *not* walk forward into the corridor as she was doing, drawn by a force she couldn't even define, an urging deeper than curiosity, calmer than fear.

Against a high, rounded skylight, the downpour became a rippling resonance, a hint of some long-forgotten song that stirred in her ears.

Something lay waiting ahead. Ruri needed to know what it was.

Perhaps she was still dreaming. Perhaps this was all part of a dream, with the rain gently singing, and the air comforting and warm.

She passed the paintings of long-dead kin, looked up

CHE LAST MERMAID • 525

without qualm into rows of watching eyes. Now that she knew who they were, she recognized them in fragments: her father's chin on a Restoration gentleman, his tawny hair on an Edwardian other. Her own nose on a redheaded damsel, but little else, until she found a lady—medieval? Elizabethan?—with a gemmed headdress and a solemn face, and Ruri's hands folded in her lap.

And nearly every one of them had her father's—her own—lapis blue eyes. How curious she hadn't noted it before.

At the end of the hall, the passageway divided around a landing and a window of long panes that spread a phantom light. When she looked out, only watered mist greeted her, pressing hard against the glass. There might not have been anything else beyond the manor house; all the world was gone, swallowed in fog and witchery.

For the first time, Ruri felt a chill. She hugged her arms to her chest, glancing round, but she was still alone. Even the draft had vanished.

Softly, unmistakably, there came another *click* in the dark, down the hallway to her right.

Her feet began without her; she was walking toward it even as her mind processed the sound. The shadows grew ever thicker. She moved on instinct as her eyes adapted— marble floors, baroque tables, closed doors. Once a mirror framed in teak, showing the astral glance of a woman as she slipped by, tilted cat eyes, rumpled smoke hair.

In the exact middle of the corridor it happened. Ruri came to a new door, barely open—and as she hesitated, it swung on soundless hinges, revealing the room beyond.

It was another bedroom. A bedchamber, more like, even larger than her own. And this bed had a canopy, and heavy rich curtains.

The door held open in mute invitation; as she peered

in, the dark began to dissolve into dusk. From the balcony doors beside the bed more mist light stretched, lifting black to gray, and gray to near light.

The air parted so smoothly as she crossed to the bed.

Wrapped in the covers was Iain. Asleep. Sound asleep on his side, with his hair mussed and one arm flung out to the pillows.

The world seemed to slide into a slow spin. It was so familiar. Even the way he slept was familiar, the curve of his body beneath the sheets, the arc of his arm.

She'd had boyfriends, teenagers in school and then grown men, but some quirk in her nature had her gone before every dawn. She'd never stayed awake to admire a lover by the grace of the moon or in the morning's new light. She'd never felt sure enough or safe enough to sleep beside them through the night. She had never felt that kind of love.

Yet here, in this dream moment, Ruri thought she had seen this man, in this pose, a hundred times before, a thousand. She knew every wayward lock of his hair, the way his fingers crushed into the sheets. How he'd toss swift and settle deep again, never waking.

A new draft swept through, gave the bed curtains a little flutter, a push against her back. Iain turned against it, and the covers dragged down his chest. Bare skin and sculpted glory: He wasn't wearing a shirt.

It was much cooler in here than in the rest of the mansion. Ruri leaned over him, tugged the blanket back to his shoulders. A dim wonder took her—was she really here? was he?—but it was as dreamlike as the room. When her hand brushed his forearm, she did not jerk away, only paused in place, guilty pleasure blooming through her with just this small discovery of him. He didn't feel like a dream, but warm and tangible, living flesh against the backs of her fingers.

She remembered, with stark clarity, an instant from yesterday on the boat. His face with the lowered sky behind him, sea spray beading his hair.

Iain's arm tensed; her hand lifted. He rolled again in his sleep, brought his other hand over, and rubbed the place where they had touched. His lips curved in smile.

Ruri took in a breath of cold air and backed quietly out of his room.


The rain had ceased. He came awake knowing it; he'd slept and dreamed by the sound of it, and when the storm tapered off in the hours before sunrise, his body roused to alertness. By its utter silence the day woke him. When Iain went to the balcony, all the hills and trees were steaming great curls of smoke. The sky was clearing.

Today, then. He'd take her today.

He broke an early fast, up before anyone, before even his most efficient servants. In the tidy kitchens of Kelmere he scrambled eggs and brewed a pot of very strong tea. He managed toast and butter as well, was pleased to find a jar of ruby-red jam hidden in a pantry. Strawberry was his favorite.

He thought of eating alone there over the sink, watching the morning rise and chase the clouds. But Ruriko might wake at any time. She'd look for breakfast in the great hall, no doubt.

He carried his meal there.

But he wasn't expecting her yet, not truly, and certainly as the sun spread fevered rays across the horizon she did not come. Iain knew the time change could be an issue. He decided, in a generous mood, to let her sleep as long as she required.

He wanted her refreshed for Kell. He wanted her mind sharp, the better to see and hear and step with him into her destiny.

He finished the eggs, ate two slices of toast thick with jam. He wanted more but also wanted to wait for her; his fingers began to tap the table, a nervous rhythm all their own. The sky past the fluted windows shifted from vermilion into orange.

But he would wait.

When movement came at the entrance to the hall, he looked up too quickly and then gave a short bark of laughter.

"Great God. How much did you pay Angus Drummann to sail out so early?"

Rupert slouched in, pulling off his hat, beating it idly against his legs as he walked. He moved more stiffly than usual, his face scored with fatigue, but his response was lively enough. "Sweet Jesus, I'll tell ye aught. That thief of a seaman an' his slag-bottomed rust bucket, with a slow leak in the stern for a fortnight now. I had to leave the car behind. Shamed Angus should be, to charge an auld man for such."

"You must have left in the middle of the night."

"Aye. When the storm was off, so were we."

"She would have still been here, you know."

He had said it mildly, but Rupert shot him a too keen glance. "Would she, now? I wonder why I had it in me head ye'd have her to Kell as soon as physically possible?"

Iain laughed again, surrendering, and gestured him into a chair. "I have no idea."

He felt some of the tension of before begin to filter away, watching Rupert sigh and settle in, grabbing the teapot and the spare cup he'd set out for Ruriko, mixing and pouring, hot ceylon and great dollops of cream.

"And did she change her mind about the isle, as ye said?" the other man asked, not looking up from his work.

"Not yet. But she will."

"As soon as she sees it, said ye. Has she no' seen it?"

Iain flicked a toast crumb from the table, not answering.

"Thought ye'd pass close enough yesterday morn. Thought ye'd have time enough to fly by in that fine new boat of yers afore the storm."

"She will change her mind." He said the words again, stubbornly, as if with just his tone he could make it true.

"But no' yet."

His fingers commenced a new tapping; he stilled them. "Nay."

Against the great room walls, medieval tapestries still hung, protected now behind glass but still clear, colorful, their timeless beauty undimmed.

Iain stared at a unicorn prancing through a glen, purple flowers at its feet, its sharp twisting horn a brazen challenge to the sky.

"Ye know the siren curse," said Rupert, in his aged and sonorous voice.

His reply was curt. "I know it."

" 'Twin spirits lost, returned.' " Rupert slurped at his tea. "What would happen, I wonder, if one of them souls didn't come back as told? Or—if it wanted naught of the other?"

Iain watched the unicorn, alone in its glen, rare and exotic and alone.

"Uncommon churlish are curses, especially one so recklessly thrown. I'd hate me to see it turned wrong. All the good that come before, all the lovers joined, wiped away like they never was."

"It's just a story, Rupert."

"Mayhap the ocean'd swallow the wee isle."

"Don't be daft."

"Mayhap that's what's meant to be, anyway."

"Leave off." He was angry now, and tried to quell it. "It's just a story."

Rupert smiled benignly into his cup. "Aye, so ye said. But I wonder now. I do."

# CHAPTER TWELVE

The villagers began to arrive just after breakfast. They came to Kelmere in cars and on foot, but most rode bicycles, mud caking the wheels, tinny bells and baskets and baskets of gifts.

For Ruriko, the heir of Kell.

Iain greeted them cordially, ordered up tea and scones and sent a maid to wake her, wondering inwardly how long this was going to take. He had wanted to catch the morning tide out, but the lioned knocker just kept sounding. . . .

The maid crept back to him and whispered, into the interested lull of the great hall, that Miz Kell was not abed, nor in her room a'tall.

Rupert sent him a look of unmistakable wit. Iain nodded to the maid and dispatched her for more scones—these island folk were a hungry lot—then excused himself from the chamber. He left to the rising hum of country gossip and a great racket of spoons against imported china. No doubt Rupert would keep them entertained.

The maid had been perfectly correct: Ruriko was not in her room. Not in the gallery, or the drawing room, or any of the parlors. Not in the ballroom, with its haunted, empty extravagance. Not in the armory, admiring Roman shields. Not in the auld tower, or—God forbid—the dungeon. Out of habit he tested the padlock on the cover of the black Celtic well. Still firmly fastened.

Hell. Where had she gone?

Iain discovered her outside, standing by herself at the hushed edge of the forest, intent on something he could not see. He had been searching for half an hour already, was nearly ready to summon help; only pride and the remembrance of Rupert's face kept him going alone. In the end he had found her by nothing more than the bent stems of the grass she had tread, new green pliant with water, a wandering trail from the rear lawn to the brink of the woods.

Her back was to him. Brown hair that matched the stillness, shadowed by the trees; she seemed elvish slight, shaped by the mist, half there, half not . . . perched between worlds.

The notion held an uneasy charm. Not in the thicket nor out of it, not of the grass nor the heather, not his and yet—his own. His heart. His lost soul.

Highland mist rolled in loops between them, vanished up into the sky.

He approached her quietly but she heard him anyway; the tilt of her cheek flashed to cream as she turned her head and took him in. She was standing just behind a heavy beech, her arms wrapped around herself, the hem of her jeans indigo with dew.

Iain came up beside her, stopped close enough to touch. She greeted him with the faintest whisper.

"Look."

He followed her eyes, saw bracken and shaggy moss, peat littered with pine needles and the fallen hearts of aspen leaves.

"Just there." Her arm lifted a fraction.

Beneath the fronds of a fern there was a rustle, wee and furtive and then gone. He angled closer. A trio of rabbit kits was curled in the leaves, eyes closed, ears folded, dundrab as the earth. The one in the middle twitched and settled down again, tucking its nose beneath the flank of its brother.

"They're abandoned," Ruriko murmured. "No mother."

"No." He matched her pitch. "She's around."

The lift of her brows told him what she thought of that. He put his hand on her arm, drew her back with him to another tree, farther away.

"She won't come to them but once a day. The rest of the time, they're alone."

"But they're so small."

"Aye. That's the way of it."

His hand rested still on her arm. She wore a sweater this morn, simple and soft, a warm hazy color reminding him of cinnamon. His fingers lay in the crook of her elbow in stolen rapport, finding the strength of her, slender resistance to the weight of his hand.

He thought of all the people back in the mansion, waiting for them. He thought of Rupert, and of Kell, and the siren curse that hung like a sword over his head. In the tapering fog and the thrall of her proximity, a mad tumble of ideas seemed to swim at him:

He would steal her away to the fell glens and falls, where it would be just the two of them, together alone. He would take her into his arms and soothe her and kiss her beneath the aspens and shivering pines. He would breathe her and taste her and tell her who she was, and who he was, and what was meant to be—

Ruriko's arm relaxed to her side. Iain's hand fell away.

"Have you ever noticed how in fairy tales, there's never a mother?" She rested her cheek against the gnarled trunk of a pine. "No father either."

"Not especially."

She gave a muffled laugh. "No. I guess fairy tales are more of a girl thing." One arm lifted lazily again, embracing the tree for balance. "Where are your parents?"

"I don't know."

She straightened, turning.

"I never knew them." He stared hard into the laced thicket of the woods. "They gave me up as a babe." At her silence his eyes slanted to hers; he could read nothing in her steady look.

"I'm sorry," she said at last.

"Don't be. I never missed them." Which was a lie, but she didn't need to know it. He wanted to tell her how he had found his true family after all, not of blood but of spirit, of karma and destiny—but the words would not come.

"Are you close to your adoptive parents?"

"I wasn't adopted. I—remained in foster care."

She looked down at her feet, scuffed a bit of spongy dirt from her shoe.

"Who gave you the dog? Auger?"

"He was a stray." He took a breath; the air tasted like damp spring. "Followed me home one day, just like the story goes. A mongrel, torn ears, a balding tail. Ugly as they come. I kept him hidden in the woodshed when I was at school. We shared suppers."

A smile pressed against the corners of her lips. "And the horse?"

"I stole him."

She laughed at that, a clear silvery sound, prettier and sweeter than bells. "Saved him from a terrible fate?"

"Naturally." In spite of himself, Iain felt himself grin. "He was a discarded carriage horse—the kind that hauls tourists around parks—sold for glue. I broke the lock of the slaughterhouse pen and rode him out. He was fast enough to save us both."

"Kept him in the woodshed?"

"I had a house by then, close to my university campus. The neighbors weren't pleased."

She reached over, still smiling, and took up his hand. "Why, Dr. MacInnes, I do believe you're a hero."

Sincere words, but Ruri had said them teasingly, enjoying his smile, the crinkling little lines that narrowed his eyes to glinting gold. When he smiled like that, he seemed nearly a different man, not the sober Scot who lived in this time-frozen place, but someone generous and warm, with sunlit looks and a pirate's clever charm.

She had hoped to make him laugh, to watch his face light with humor. But his gaze dropped from hers; even the boyish grin faded. He watched their hands instead, his fingers gently flexed in her grip. Then his mouth curled, not humor at all but something more acrid.

"Am I?"

"Another deflecting question. You're very good at that."

His fingers tightened through hers, and he raised his eyes.

"May I meet him?" she asked, before he could speak. "Your valiant Sol?"

"Not today. Tomorrow, mayhap. Today . . ." He sighed. "There are some people come to see you."

"Really? I thought today you'd want to go to Kell."

"Aye. I do. And we might yet, if we hurry." He loosened their hands. "Will you come?"

"Yes."

She threw a last look over her shoulder as they headed back to the mansion, but the bunnies were well hidden in the ferns. "Who are the people?"

"Your own," he said, and left it at that.

The massive chamber that was the great hall was speckled with people, some sitting, many standing, grouped in brown-hatted clusters or circles of teacups and skirts. Mab was there, her red hair a beacon; Ruri fixed on her first, the one familiar face.

"There she is!" said that woman, with a bright, happy smile. "How fare ye, dearie?"

"Well, thank you." Ruri found herself cushioned in a hug, freed again to reel in a cloud of perfume. "How are you?"

"Bonny, bonny. I've brought me niece up. She wanted to meet ye. Laurie! Come over, lass, and say how do."

A yellow-haired girl approached, no more than sixteen, and she had brought her boyfriend—tall, freckled—who had invited his mother, a lady with four sisters and a dog, but the dog was outside, scratching at fleas—who would let a muddy dog into a grand place such as this!—but here was a husband to meet, as well. . . .

There were so many of them. She tried to keep names and faces straight and then gave it up; they were Maggies and Bridgets and Hughs, a few with names so rich and dark she could not wrap her tongue around them. That bought her more smiles, and a slower stream of words to follow. Listening to them was like listening to spoken music—Iain's brogue, but ever thicker—a lilting pattern that both tickled and pleased.

Someone bade her to sit; Ruri did so, surrounded again at once. Through the press of bodies she caught a glimpse of Iain leaning back in his chair, apart from everyone else, his arms behind his head and his feet propped against a corner of the table. He wasn't looking at her but at the high, narrow windows above them. For all the time and place, he might well have been the lone aristocrat at a provincial hunt, sophistication and restless languor, a hint of taut impatience around his mouth. The muddy dog would have suited him as well: His crossed boots were dripping muck all along the table.

"And I hope ye dinna mind, dearie, but I've a wee present for ye."

Ruri turned back to Mab, who was pressing a hard something wrapped in cheesecloth into her hands.

"Oh—that's very kind of you, but I really couldn't—"

"No, no, naught of that! 'Tis only to say hello, like, is all."

"A custom," offered one of the other ladies.

"Aye, a custom. One of the auld ways of the isles."

Ruri lifted the bundle, peeled back the cloth. It was a jar of marmalade.

"Made it over Christmas, I did, with the last of the bitter oranges," said Mab. "A fine batch it was. I was saving this for May Day, but now ye've come, and I knew . . ." Her smile faltered a bit, but she recovered and nodded her head. "I knew I had saved it for ye instead."

"Thank you." Ruri cradled the jar in her palms. "I'm sure it's delicious."

"And here." A man came forward—Camdin? Cameron?—carrying a whittled stick. "From the woodland. Good rowan, that is." He turned it in her palms, showing a line of carefully drilled holes. "A pipe, d'ye see? Song from the wood, to complement the sea."

They were all like that, simple gifts, most handmade, a plate of shortbread, a lace kerchief. A large tasseled shawl done in the tartan they assured her was her family's—their own—the pure, deep colors of the ocean and the trees and the setting sun.

A rounded seashell, striped with beige, given to her by a brown-eyed little girl.

"What d'ye say, Marsaili?" whispered her mother.

"It's from the shore here, Miss," said the girl dutifully. "So ye might remember us by when ye'r off to Kell."

"I will keep it safe," Ruri vowed, and the girl dashed a bashful curtsy.

"Ah, but didn't ye hear?" came a new voice, light and sly. "She'll be selling the isle."

The effect was instantaneous, a bomb that smashed and scattered into silence and shocked, frozen looks. Only Iain moved, sitting up straight again, watchful in his chair.

"Ain't that right, lass?" It was the chauffeur of before, the man with the iron hair and surly manners. He was standing near the hearth, a cup in his hands, watching her with clear-eyed devilment.

Ruri turned her gaze slowly around the room. "I am thinking of selling it, yes."

"To our good professor here. To Iain MacInnes."

"Dr. MacInnes—has made an offer."

"But ye *can't*," burst out Mab, and then clapped her hand over her mouth. "I mean," she said, calmer, lowering her hand, "why would ye? It's been in the family forever and a day. It's our heritage."

"Our history," said another.

Ruri stood to face them better. "I mean you no offense,

none of you. No doubt it's a wonderful place." She set Marsaili's seashell on the table. "But that is why I've come."

One of the men spoke with rasping disbelief. "He brought ye here—just to sell him the isle?"

From across the room Iain's eyes held hers, pale, unfathomable. "He is my host," Ruri said finally, in the strangled quiet unable to summon anything better.

He released her from his look, turning his head to meet the stares of the others with level indifference. A column of sunlight sliced the air behind him, darkening his face and form. The was an emptiness around him, a space no one touched; alone in his circle, he might have been shadow instead of man.

The chauffeur came forward, his words rolling baritone against the paneled walls. "A thousand, thousand years it's been our isle. Our kings shed blood for it, our lairds have died upon it. We've kith and kin buried in Kell's soil. Ye think to take that away from us?"

"I don't want to take away anything. Look, I haven't *said* I'm going to sell it. I came to . . . see."

The green-eyed chauffeur stopped a pace away. "And do ye?" His voice dropped. "Do ye see, lass?"

As everyone watched, he lifted his hands to her, held them out between them with his palms flat down, expectant. Ruri looked down at them, veined and knotted, reddened knuckles and bony fingers that did not tremble by even a hairbreadth.

She opened her own palms faceup, a remembrance of a childhood game, and lifted them to his.

A strange warmth where their hands met; a throbbing ache in her joints. But Ruri didn't pull away, and neither did he: Their gazes clashed. She saw, in green diminutive, her own reflection in his eyes.

The aching swelled and then dimmed. She'd heard of

people who shared energy like this. She knew witches who claimed to channel power through palms, and, true or not, in these remote foggy hills and isles Ruri believed anything was possible. But the pain was so distant. And then it didn't hurt at all. If it was a test, she wasn't going to fail, not to this man. Not to anyone.

The chauffeur leaned close, his voice sunk to a whisper. "Ye dinna even know yerself."

He stepped back and raised his hands to the room, opening and closing his fingers in a show of rapid victory. Ruri looked around at the marveling faces, then again to Iain. He was gazing idly at a point beyond them both.

"I think our lady Kell is in need of a lesson," declared the chauffeur, with a bow in her direction. "It seems she knows naught of the honor of the clan. And who kens our history better than ourselves, I ask ye?" He glanced to her, a little of the mischief gone from his eyes. "Sit down, lass. Listen to the story of Kell." He grabbed the nearest chair, rubbed his hands together in something like glee. "And then we'll see who'll be buyin' what."


They were marvelous tales, terrible tales, dreamy, mysterious, heartbreaking tales. She listened and sipped tea and tried the marmalade on a raisin-studded scone, as the villagers gathered close and took turns speaking. They told her of mermaids and kings as if they knew them by heart, as if they swam the seas beside them and fought their battles and felt their dear true love.

She did listen. And though they spoke of myth, she saw in their eyes that they held it much deeper than that, that myth had changed and mingled in their blood by Highland magic, and now every tale, every character was as true to them as Mab or Laurie or Hugh.

Platters of crumpets and then sandwiches appeared and disappeared; more tea was poured and then red ale. At one point when Ruri scanned the earnest faces she discovered Iain's servants loitering behind the chairs, listening and nodding to the legends of her family.

But the sun rose and rose, and a few men—farmers, fishermen—began to glance more frequently at the windows, until one stood, and another, and announced matter-of-factly that they'd best be gettin' on. And so did they all.

At the entrance to the mansion, the clog of people slowed, stilled, claiming bicycles and car keys on their way back to their days, voices carrying in the crisp, thin air. The infamous dog leapt and barked among them with frenzied joy.

Ruri walked down the stairs with Marsaili clutching her hand, the child's initial reluctance to speak long gone. Ruri heard breathless more about sirens and duels and was questioned very intently about cowboys. In time even the child's mother was ready to depart, throwing Ruri a look of sheepish apology as she tried to tug her daughter away.

"But where is the soul?" Marsaili asked, her eyes wide as Ruri leaned down for a last embrace.

She pulled back. "The . . . what?"

"The Soul of Kell," said the girl, sounding distressed. "Ye dinna wear it?"

"Oh—the locket. No, I don't."

In a breath all the villagers fell quiet, exchanging fresh looks. Ruri braced herself.

"Why not?" piped Marsaili.

"Has anyone a watch?" drawled Iain, from up by the doors.

# CHAPTER THIRTEEN

❦

Father has changed," said my eldest daughter, with an unhappy, shielded look. She sat before my chamber window, leaning her cheek to her fist. Blue sky made a stained-glass contrast against her honey-blond hair.

"Men do," I answered, short. I could not tell her more than that; varying and uncertain, mortal men's desires seemed to shift like the errant rainbow. I had no explanation for it.

"He speaks of his village. He speaks of leaving." Eos lifted her head. "Does he love us not?"

"Whence this talk? Forsooth he loves thee. He loves us all."

"He desires to leave."

"But he will not."

"Mother," she said, rising, putting her hand on my arm. "If he craves it so, and if it harms none . . ."

"Heed me, Eos. Men oft speak of things they do not nor cannot understand. I have told him true of his childhood lands, all charred ruins. His mortal kin are long fallen dead. We are his family now. Thy father has a goodly wit, he fathoms me full well. To leave our home would mean his death. There lies naught for him beyond our isle but misery and cold company."

I moved to the window myself, glanced out to the wild open beach and sky, as empty and fierce as the gods designed. "Naught," I said again, firmly.

But Eos only turned her comely face away.

# CHAPTER FOURTEEN

୬ଟ

S he wore the plaid shawl on the speedboat. In her
pocket was the necklace, a hard warmth next to
her thigh; Iain had asked her to bring it and so she
had, although she kept a careful distance from the
switches and knobs of the helm.

They did not tear along quite so swiftly as the first
time she had ridden with him. But it was fast enough to
send the land into a thin gray band behind them and the
close water to a green-blue slur. Above them the sun
shone at last, a pale heat so high and distant the Scottish
air consumed it; she felt only the cold of the ocean against
her cheeks and hands and ears. Long, sloping rays of light
lit fire across the sea, dazzling copper that shattered and
faded as the boat howled on. Ruri drew the shawl a little
closer to her chest.

She thought it late in the day to be going to the island.
By the time the last villager had straggled away from
Kelmere it was past two. But Iain insisted they go; the
weather was fine and the sea steel-calm.

A corner of the shawl flipped up into her face with the wind, snapping hard against her nose. Ruri pulled it down again. She'd been hoping for the yacht. She'd had enough of the damned speedboat for a good while.

In the distance rose other islands, slinging low on the polished line of the horizon, blue whales of land that sank again to nothing as Iain passed them by.

The air seemed to grow a little warmer. She sat up straighter, found herself searching the waters. Once, far off, she spotted a family of dolphins, dark magic against the light, but they were headed the other way. She looked up at Iain and got only a short, negative shake of his head.

"You'll see more," he said.

She settled back into her seat with the shawl held over her mouth, feeling sullen and then ridiculous.

There were dolphins in the Pacific. She could see them there, if she wished.

But he wouldn't be there. She'd see them alone.

Ruri bowed her head against the wind and took a deep breath, wondering why that thought made her glum. She barely even knew Iain MacInnes, after all. And she wouldn't truly be alone; she had her family, she had friends. . . .

She took another deep breath into the shawl. It smelled of wool and apples, of smoky winter.

"It suits you."

She glanced up at him again, her face still half covered in plaid. He had a slight smile.

"The tartan," he said, with a gesture. "The colors look good on you."

She nodded her thanks, but this time he didn't look away. He wore a fisherman's sweater for the ride, cabled cream against the swarthy tan of his skin. His hair was a black tangle, his eyes tearing a little in the full force of the wind. He was staring down at her, then, gradually, through her, a faint, distracted crease between his brows.

The boat soared high and shuddered. Iain turned instantly back to the wheel.

Softer air, a lower sun; Kell was coming nearer. She felt it. Her heart began to quicken.

The boat slowed, and slowed, and soon it seemed only the wind moved them. Kell rose in full pageantry directly ahead, first a crest, then a hill, then mountains. A strand of clouds was caught at the highest peak, streaming out over the sea in a lacy white flag.

She thought they were drifting now, their boat sliding in gentle concourse toward the black fringe of trees that bristled above the shore. There was a buoy bobbing to their right, wavering in a drunken circle. Ruri leaned over the side of the boat to stare straight down. The water was inky deep, churning bubbles in ice-blue patches, rolling over and swallowing them to back to azure.

"Go ahead," Iain said, behind her. "Touch it."

The corner of the shawl danced free as she reached down. She saw her hand and the whipping colors of the plaid, and then her fingers dipped into the sea.

Warm, very warm, and slippery smooth like heated oil. She pulled back, startled, then tried it again.

"I thought it would be cold!"

"Only sometimes." He came beside her, his legs brushing hers. She felt his touch on her shoulder. "Come back, lass. I've got to steer us in. It's a tricky bit."

He didn't bring them straight to shore, like she thought he would. Instead, the boat began a sideways curl around the isle, coming closer in bare degrees. In their circling path and the isolation of the vessel, it seemed that Kell was revolving and they were still, trees and beach and a wedge of cliffs that widened into crevices and shade. They weren't merely cliffs, though. An artist had come to Kell, once upon a time: In faded relief she saw dragons, sea monsters carved haphazard into the stone . . . and then a face, clearer than the rest. A woman, lovely, wistful, with long waving hair and a Mona Lisa smile.

"I suppose that's the siren," Ruri said, twisting in place to see her better.

"No. 'Tis what's said, but that's not what she looked like."

Ruri gave a muted laugh. "How do you know?"

He didn't answer for a while. "I don't. Just a feeling."

The engines were a hollow cadence beneath her feet, tamed now, a fraction of the power that had lifted them from Kelmere to here. She felt it when he began to increase speed, maneuvering cannily through the frothing waters on a course she could not follow, left and right and left and sharp left again. He followed an invisible maze, every line of him focused on the job with tight, rock-jawed attention. But the sea looked just the same to her as it had before, shifting colors like a strutting peacock, turquoise and green and teal and royal blue.

They were headed for a sharp thrust of reef jutting from the waves. Foam stressed and hissed around it; the serrated edges shone like a handful of knives. She held her breath, speechless, as the boat revved nearer. The engines fought the currents, whining higher and higher while they still crept so slow.

Iain slid them past the reef so close she could count the woolly crabs clinging to the sides.

Kell hung both near and far, a new, milder beach slipping into view. The nose of the boat swung toward it.

"There's no dock," Ruri said suddenly, rising from her seat.

"Nay." He did not look away from his task.

"How will we land?"

"You'll see." The powerboat made another groaning turn.

More reef was visible above these waves, much of it sprouting marine life and coral. A nest of seabirds had colonized the largest outcrop; as they skidded by, the birds rushed the air in a chorus of affronted squawks.

The boat dipped to the left, hard, and Ruri's legs buckled, jolting her back into her seat. With a sick reel of her stomach, she comprehended that they might not actually make it to the beach. She tore her gaze from the jagged surf, started to question Iain—but his teeth were bared and his fingers were nearly bloodless with brute force. Despite his grip, the wheel began to turn beneath him. He threw his full weight against it, and they glided into a spin.

Kell whirled behind them. Ahead. In a careening white wheel above, the gulls were screeching. Ruri squeezed her eyes shut and got a spatter of foam across the face; the boat had tipped low again.

They hit the reef. It wasn't a violent collision or even a very loud one, but it ripped through the belly of the powerboat with a harrowing, grinding moan. The engines began to sputter.

"Aw, hell," said Iain. "Hold on."

And she did—she had to, because all at once he opened the throttle and sent the vessel surging forward, a lurching skip across the water that rattled and crashed as they struck more of the razored stone. Someone was screaming. Ruri realized that it was she, and then she simply ran out of air, her mouth still open and her arms wrapped around the seat, and Kell racing toward them like a great blurred wall. The boat tipped high and then higher still. They were sinking by the stern, and her grip on her seat became the only thing that kept her from toppling back into the water.

A rock, a wave, monstrous foam and thunder in her ears. The plaid shawl ripped from her fingers and flung itself up into the sky, a flash of blue and green, winging off with the gulls.

"Hold on!" Iain shouted again. With a final, bone-rattling squeal, the powerboat leapt and then rolled, spilling them both out into the sea.

She felt herself falling, weightless, her arms spread and her hair in her eyes. Warm water sucked at her; the boat was a colossal shadow that hung over her and pressed down, down, the propellers spinning by her head with deadly vehemence.

She gulped water, felt it burning in her lungs. She kicked and twisted and the boat sifted away but tugged her along, pulling her deeper into the blank blue depths. She was caught in silent undertow, flailing, dying. The ocean began to turn to acid, eating at her blood.

Something grabbed her hand. Something yanked her up, snapping back her head, a man surrounded in light. They were lifting together, sloshing, and Ruri broke the surface and still couldn't breathe. Seawater filled her. Her heart throbbed with panic.

They were on sand. She was on her hands and knees, retching, and then collapsed to her side with a gasping, squeaky sob.

Iain dragged her into his arms. They sat with his face pressed to her hair, rocking, entangled, and Ruri's fingers curled into the wet nap of his sweater. She was weeping small, hiccuping tears, until she ran out of breath again and had to stop.

"Well," he murmured, his lips to her temple. "That wasn't so bad."

She pushed away, hard enough to send him sprawling back to the ground.

"How could you?" She got to her knees and wiped a hand across her eyes, smearing more grit into them. "How could you *do* that?"

"I got us ashore." He sat up, dusted the sand from his chest.

"You sank the boat! You nearly killed us! There's no dock and no"—her voice cracked; she wheezed for air— "no place to *go*, and you sit there and you *smile*—"

He slanted her a look that definitely wasn't a smile, then climbed to his feet. He leaned down and held out his hand to her; she ignored it with savage dignity, managing to get one foot beneath her, and then the other, standing by herself in a drizzle of sand.

"It *was* my first time," he pointed out, watching her shove back her dripping hair.

Her spine stiffened. "You—you've never even been here before?"

"Oh, aye, I have. Just not in a very long while."

"You mean you brought me here, and you didn't even—" Her arm swept out to the surf, the lost boat. "Did you *plan* this?"

He lifted his shoulders. "I admit I was hoping to get us a bit closer in."

"You bastard! You know I can't swim!"

"But I can, Ruriko. And we're here, and we're fine— judging by your temper."

"Oh my God." She brought her hands to her head, turning a crooked ellipse in the sand, too dazed to do more than that: trees and pebbles and a great pile of rocks above them. Surrounded by the ocean. Shipwrecked.

"Ruriko—"

"No." She lifted a hand to him, still glaring at the sea. "Don't talk to me. Don't say anything. Just—just stay away."

She started hiking up the beach.


Eric had lived well in the ruins. Iain was glad of that; he'd seen the earl once a month for just over the ten years they'd known each other, when Eric would come to shore to take care of whatever human business needed to be done. At six o'clock every fourth Wednesday, they would meet in the village pub, share a drink in stilted silence and a few vague comments on the weather and the state of the world. Iain had never mentioned aught of the earl's heritage and Eric himself certainly never discussed it, guarding his privacy with the stiff vigilance of an aged bulldog. Yet never once had he declined to sit with the man who had acquired his ancestral home.

Each time they met, Iain had brought his distant son tokens, singular trifles meant to please him in the autumn of his life—a case of his favorite Bordeaux, volumes of Voltaire and Marlowe, tobacco, candlesticks of silver gilt—and betimes a few things more practical than that, batteries, blankets, a radio, and matches. Iain knew even those of siren blood could not conjure fire from thin air.

It seemed like so long ago now. For all of Iain's gifts, the tower chamber appeared quite deserted. There was a fine, granular layer of dust on the furnishings; the bed was stripped of linens; the chest of blankets and quilts remained untouched.

He lowered the lid of the chest, rising to take a heavy breath with his palm pressed flat against the wall.

This had been their room, this old-fashioned square chamber. The first completed, the largest. In its plain corners and gray-shadowed space he could summon ghosts immeasurable. Three perfect windows let in the light; he walked to the one in the center, leaned out, and let the wind steal his senses.

Ruriko was nearby. He felt her, her righteous wrath, but more obvious than that he could track her—she'd left a line of footprints in the sand that wavered up into the coppice woods.

She'd be safe, no matter where she went. This was her island, whether she wanted it or not.

But he would go find her soon. He could not wait much longer.


Ruri sat with her knees hugged to her chest, her back against a tree, watching the afternoon sun plop down into a hazy sky. The shadows grew longer, the light more mellowed. When she looked up she could see the daytime moon riding above her, bone-white, half a button against the middle blue.

Wind flirted with the trees. A pair of crinkled leaves in the sand lifted to their points, went twirling by her feet.

How long before rescue came? How long would she have to stay here?

She thought mournfully of her snug little apartment, of Setsu and Toshio and Molly. Of never seeing them again. Of staying here forever.

With *him.*

*Snap out of it,* she thought sternly. Someone would miss them. Someone would come. All she had to do was wait.

Her clothes were drying at last. She'd stripped off her

sweater and hung it over a bush. She thought of doing the same for her jeans and couldn't summon enough nerve. She'd endure damp jeans. At least her camisole was blowing dry, if gritty.

The beach was just below her, a pretty strand of color and stone. If she hadn't been so wretched—so furious—she might have enjoyed the view.

Behind her was more of the woods, too thin here to be a true forest, with bent pines and rambling ground cover that traced through the dunes. She'd walked until she could not see the ocean anymore, got as far as a little round meadow carpeted in bluebells and red clover, then turned back. God help her if she got lost here.

Once, as she walked, the breeze lifted and encircled her in an eerie acoustic ruse. Instead of leaves whispering, it sounded like children, like laughter. She'd swung around sharply, but of course there was no one else there. Still, Ruri was more than a little glad to stumble upon the familiar beach again.

Iain had granted her her privacy and disappeared into what she had thought was just an odd mountain of rubble; the afternoon's sliding light, however, helped her pick out order from chaos. It wasn't just rubble but a ruin. It had an entrance, and stairs. From here she could see the dark slit of a window.

The wind whistled harder; her sweater curled and then rolled to the ground. She regarded it without moving. One sleeve rippled up in a floppy scarecrow wave.

The light lowered still more, clear and candescent, gradually suffusing the heavens with violet. A bird began a song in the woods behind her, and then two, a duet of sweet, piercing notes. The ocean kept up its soothing rumble.

Iain came up the path she had made, his feet trudging

through her own ragged marks. In spite of the sand he moved gracefully, broad shoulders, muscled legs, a white T-shirt that molded to him with the breeze.

He stopped just before her.

"I've made a fire," he said, and once more held out his hand. This time, she accepted it.

The fire was on the beach, not in the ruins. He'd dug a pit and found wood and even a log to sit on. The wind shifted and a spiraling updraft of sparks floated like fairies into the gloaming sky.

"Are you hungry?" he asked, as she perched upon the log.

"No."

"There's food—not much. Rather more wine, if you'd like."

"No, thank you."

He sat beside her, propped his elbows on his knees, and bent his head to inspect the backs of his hands.

"Are you still angry, lass?"

She considered it. She wanted to be . . . but the firelight played off his hair, stroked color down the hard pure lines of his nose and mouth and chin. He looked at her without turning his head, thick eyelashes still dusted with sand. There might have been the faintest shade of regret to his lips. Or not.

"I've lost the locket," she said, and his lashes lifted. "It must have fallen in the water when we crashed."

He straightened, staring away from her, past the flames to the sea. She could not see his face.

"Good riddance," she added sulkily. "I knew that thing was bad luck the moment I saw it."

Some nameless emotion seemed to fill him; she heard his breath pulling deep, watched the wind persuade a lock

of hair to his forehead. She was sorry for losing the necklace and she wasn't. She'd never wanted it, never liked it.
But he held so terribly still.

"Maybe it'll wash to shore," she said.

He shook his head, silent. The fire popped, throwing
embers that flashed and died in midair. Iain's fingers
flexed and closed as he gazed into the purpled distance.
The moon had already set; just beyond him, a dull silvery
rope of stars began to stripe the sky.

"I found something of yours," he said finally, and
reached behind the log, holding up a fold of cloth. Her
shawl. She took it gingerly, shook it out, and let it settle
on her lap.

"How long before anyone notices we're missing?" she
asked.

"Tonight."

"Will they look for us at night?"

His shoulders hunched, a shrug or just disinterest.
"Perhaps not."

She looked down at the material across her legs,
smoothed out a pucker near her knees. The dangling tas-
sels traced perfect circles in the sand.

They would have to spend the night here. It was what
he wasn't saying, what she understood nonetheless, very
clear. She would have to sleep with him near, out here in
the open by his fire. Just the two of them, and the arctic,
infinite beauty of the northern skies.

She remembered, suddenly, the ruin behind her. The
trace of window.

"Is this where the last earl came to live?" Ruri glanced
at it over her shoulder, pressed up against the trees. "Isn't
that what you said?"

"This is where all the members of your family have

come, for untold generations, save those who traveled to the New World. Kell was always their final home."

She blinked at that, turning it over in her mind. "But . . . how did they actually get here? How could anyone ever land?"

Iain only looked at her, night falling over his shoulders.

"No," she said, and started to laugh. "Not you too."

He did not smile in return. He did not move. He had eyes that matched the fire.

"Stop it." Ruri pushed off the log. "It's not funny."

"No. It's not."

She felt her breath shorten, staring down at him. She felt a strange, anxious tension in her chest. The plaid had fallen to a jumble at her feet; she felt trapped, ensnared, and didn't even know why.

"How is it," he asked softly, "that you understand nothing of yourself?" And he rose.

"Stop," she whispered, but he didn't. He lifted his hand to her cheek, his gaze following the movement with absolute concentration, his handsome mouth somber, the black line of his brows drawn down. In the flickering light—against the open arch of the twilight—his face held an edged golden glamour that struck straight through her heart.

"My God," she breathed, shaken. "I know you. I do."

His touch was so gentle, a glide down her cheek to her throat, his fingers resting in her hair. His voice was a husky murmur between them.

"You cannot change fate, Ruriko, any more than you can change the stars. You may only change yourself. If you wish it."

Fire and night, gold and black, and her body trembling with something close to fear. She caught his wrist. "I don't know what you want of me."

"Everything." He smiled at her then, slow and wicked dark. "I want everything."

The pressure of his fingers behind her neck became an unsubtle urging; he brought his lips to hers and kissed her, and all the glory of the sunken sun lifted and sparkled down into her bones.

# CHAPTER FIFTEEN

ain drew back and studied her with hooded eyes, still somber, still golden, a man of stark splendor and impressive breadth, who skimmed his palms down her shoulders until his fingers meshed with her own.

"Come," he said, only that, and Ruri found herself following him, away from the fire, toward the stairs to the pale stone ruin. He made no sound either in the sand or upon the steps, an apparition that cast a starshadow before them, lifting and stretching up the earth.

She knew these stairs. She knew their uneven curve, the way they looped around a granite boulder, turned and met at its top, a flat resting ledge before the graven steps wound on.

The entrance to the ruin—*palace*, sang her mind—was a balanced arch, a black waiting. She passed through it with Iain's hand firm over hers.

No light, but it hardly mattered. He moved forward as if he could see through the night too, his stride confident, the white of his shirt a shaped echo of his form. She felt

as if she had plunged into a new vivid dream, some ancient clan memory—but oh, his hand was so strong and
so real.

More stairs, shorter, wider. They led to room of fine-set
stone, four walls and three windows, and a view she could
close her eyes to see.

"This place," Ruri whispered, a shiver in her voice. She
pulled her hand from his. "What's happening to me?"

He was the starlight and the dark, large and tall, standing apart from her.

"Don't you know?"

She didn't, she didn't, she was afraid to. Yet he held
fixed, his head cocked, as if he listened for her response.
She tried to search his face and found the stone ruin deceived her; in here, all nuance was gone. His eyes were
masked. She caught only the set of his mouth, the rough
tumble of his hair. Behind him, the windows revealed a
gathering of diamonds and soft dusky hills.

Ruri felt her heart turn. She felt things she had never
known beating through her, yearning and memory and
sharp, willful hunger. She couldn't see him—she couldn't
understand herself—but somehow she knew that all the
answers stood before her, this man, his welcome body, his
urgent touch. She said his name and like a key it freed
him; Iain came to her with his arms closing hard around
her and his mouth over hers in hot instant pleasure.

Ruri gave into it, melting, and felt the stars began to
fall.

She tasted like salt, bittersweet and dear, a taste he
knew and still savored, stroking her lips. When she drew
breath he took it back from her; when she turned her head
he followed, running his mouth along the curve of her
jaw, finding the silken column of her throat, tracing her
with his tongue. Her hands grazed his arms, his own

tightened, bringing her body to his. Her gasp sounded through him like quicksilver, sensual anticipation.

The bed was old and wooden and not very far. He used will and motion, brought them both to its edge. In slow, sinking motion they lowered to the blankets.

He had prepared the room, his heart, for this moment, yet still it rose to overwhelm him. She held her fingers to his cheek and he turned his face into her palm, closing his eyes against her cool skin, struggling for control.

He wanted to cover her, to devour her. But she was precious to him, beyond measure or pain or hope. In the throes of his desire Iain let her set the pace, holding himself hushed and as much apart as he could stand, only the lightest, most agonizing connection of their chests and loins and thighs.

"Ruriko. I . . ."

He didn't finish his sentence, or couldn't. He found her mouth again and told her that way how he felt, that she was wine and wonder to him, that she drove him to the wild aching brink with just the shy, lovely brush of her tongue to his.

It was too much, too soon. He had waited his whole life for her—longer—but never truly expected her to happen, never thought to be so lucky. He wasn't a man who had denied himself gratification when it beckoned; no celibate, no sinner, only human. But fate had laughed and spun his life around: He had the only woman who ever mattered open and supple beneath him, and her every touch was like a splinter to his soul.

Iain pulled back, panting, Ruriko's breath a broken percussion of his. She stared up at him in the half light, more captivating than pearls or jewels or the sun, her lips moist and gleaming. With every lift of her chest, the straps of her little shirt pulled taut over her shoulders, lustrous thin ribbons that pressed into her flesh, ivory and cream. He found the sight so erotic he had to swallow and close his eyes, bury his face in her throat.

*Remember me.*

He meant to say it aloud, but his mind was thick and drowning, he had no idea if he had spoken. She didn't answer him either, not in words, but her jaw pressed against his temple and her fingers found his hair. She drew him back to her with a fervent sound, and then a soft willing moan with their new kiss.

*Remember me.*

He eased the ribbons from her shoulders, ran his palms up her sides and pushed the camisole away. She wore nothing beneath it. Her arms lifted above her head; the scrap of cloth melted into the dark. He found her breasts, alluring curves and delectable weight. He rubbed his thumbs over her nipples, over and around, and her fingers knotted in his hair in a sensuous tug.

He smiled down at her, lowered his eyes and then his mouth, and the tug tightened into a moan.

Oh, and she was salt there too, sugar and salt, and he teased and suckled until her legs lifted to cradle him and her hips rocked against his. Her hands fell back to the rumpled blankets, her fingers spread.

He had made the bed a pillowed richness, napped silk, plush down. But her skin proved the softest favor of all, polished satin beneath his hands and tongue. The cotton of his shirt seemed unbearable against her, a scratchy barrier that rucked between them. He yanked it off impatiently, lowered himself back to her with an inward grown. God, she was lush and firm and ocean cool, her belly to his, her chest, her arms around his back.

If there was magic in this night, he commanded it. If

there was hope in this world, he drew it into him, channeled it from his body into hers, to weave her closer, to bind her and bring her to him and let them join in age-old bliss.

*Remember me.* With every kiss, every motion, it was a spell he cast, an enchantment, a demand.

*Remember.*

Her hands fumbled at the waist of his jeans; she worked the buttons, pulling hard. Like her, he hadn't bothered with undergarments. The caress of her fingers over his bare, rigid flesh tore a gasp from his throat.

Her own jeans were simpler, a single button, a short zipper. He peeled them down her hips.

They rolled together, lips mating, parting, as their hands explored. Her hair turned the pillows to velvet and her eyes held his, the deepest blue, the longest lashes, love-play tinting her cheeks. Iain pressed a finger inside her, caught her tongue as she licked her lips.

Her chest rose and fell against him. Their heartbeats combined.

Ruri felt the shifting of his muscles, lean and spare, burning warmth that covered her, that promised untold revelations. She wanted what he offered her, grasped his shoulders and bit her lip as his hand wrought mindless rapture, gliding in and out of her, a rising, desperate elation.

She sparkled, she glittered, she was made of stars. She quivered with his touch. He said her name on a deep-voiced note, shifting over her, spreading her legs. Her heels pressed to the bed, her body arched. He pushed into her with a long, luxurious stroke, and the light inside her threatened to come apart.

His breath was a song; it matched the sea and the sliding rhythm of his body over hers, consuming her. Her hands smoothed the contours of his back, light circles that deepened; her nails dragged across his skin. He whispered encouragement as he filled her, his arms braced near her head.

His chin grazed hers, his mouth traced words over her lips she did not hear; the very shape of them bewitched her, enraptured her. She met his words with ardent kisses, stealing them for her own as their bodies strained and met and she brought him back to her.

There was a storm in her heart that swelled like the black clouds, that flashed and spread in something like torment. It stretched and stretched until she couldn't bear it any longer, and then the flash turned to blinding fire, to the stars again. Ruri cried out at its peak, as the storm and stars sank through her and swept her into the dark-edged night.

Iain groaned and shuddered; she felt the storm take him too, and as it happened she curled her arms around him and kept him close.

He nuzzled her neck, teased breathless kisses down her throat. His body relaxed to heavy stillness; he sighed and held his lips to her hair.

*Remember me. Because I have always loved you.*


She watched him sleep. She sat up in the wood-slatted bed with her legs folded beneath her and the counterpane puffed between them. She was nude and uncovered but not cold; when she touched his skin he still seemed a little like fire to her, elusive flame contained in the shape of a well-made man.

Ruri glanced around the room. It was barely furnished, the bed and a desk and chair, something that looked like a treasure chest against the far wall.

There should be banners upon the walls. The thought came to her, rambling from nowhere, and she shook her head. But in her mind the vision stayed clear: banners, plain vibrant colors, to shield the chamber from the cool nip of bare stone.

She got out of the bed, moving soundlessly. She walked to the windows, restive, and then to the door.

Past the inner stairs, past the rounded entry, out to the sand-scrubbed mystery of the night. Her hair lashed with the wind, stinging her face and then her back. She made her way down the steep, worn path as the ocean boomed and settled, and she ended up skipping the last few stairs, landing in the sand at half a run.

*Liquid gold that gave and reformed—*

She was running, after all. She ran down to the crescent of the beach, where seaweed and pebbles marked the tideline, and then lower, to where the water reached and fell back and left glassy bubbles to pop in the sand.

*She was alone here. She was not alone.*

Even the clouds were distant, skating the upper atmosphere in jetty sheets. No birds stirred. No seals. Only the ocean lived before her.

Ruri walked closer to the surf. Water frothed over her toes, the arch of her foot. She stopped, feeling it—so oddly, improbably warm—and then it rushed to her ankles.

A voice *called out* spoke behind her.

"It's going to hurt."

She looked back at him. The ocean dragged up to her shins.

"Only at first," Iain said, coming closer. He was unclad as well; she saw him better out here than in the silent shelter of his ruin. He moved easily through the heavy sand, all elegance and sinewy grace, his arms swinging free, his hair windblown and blacker than the clouds. His face had that hard, severe aspect that made him both beautiful and aloof, a stranger with a body she knew now near as well as her own.

At her feet, the ocean began to boil. Her bones began to ache.

"Go on," he said roughly. "Go. For God's sake, you've never been afraid of anything."

She looked back at the water, the pale marbled foam that pulsed and drew around her.

She was floating, sailing, at the edge of a high dark descent. She was a sand castle dissolving with the tide.

"Ruriko."

She did not answer. She took three splashing steps into the sea and then threw her body into the waves.

# CHAPTER SIXTEEN

❦

In the hills I searched for him, in the woods, in the meadows. Kell had gone from me a day and a night, never before so long, never without word. Over the years I had come to grant him his peace alone, but it was winter, and the island was powdered in snow. Protected he was from most dangers, but not the cold. Even I could not subdue the seasons.

I hid my fears from the children and combed the isle alone until, on the eve of the second day, I found him. He sat at the edge of the cliffs that breached the sea, staring out. Bedraggled grass blew flat around him; a waterfall erupting from the bluffs below sent crystal-bit billows up into the sky.

I realized how old he had become, despite my magic. His hair was gray and his figure was gaunt, and still I loved him more than my own self.

I approached him warily; I did not know if he could hear me over the wind. I wore sandals and a long white

THE LAST MERMAID · 567

chiton wrapped as a skirt, gifts he had presented to me ages past. Frost crackled beneath my feet as I walked.

He made no indication he noticed me. His head was bowed as he stared down, past the ice cloud, to the sea. I came beside him and stood, then sat, throwing my legs over the cliff just as he had done.

His hands were clasped before him. My hair blew between us and caught on his rings. Gradually, his fingers loosened. He turned a palm up, a skim of yellow across his skin—then his hand closed again to a fist upon his lap.

"A view of emperors," he remarked, in a voice dry as parchment. "If ever an emperor should see it."

"I cannot live without thee," I said. "I cannot be."

His face creased in smile, neither mirthful nor tart, betwixt and between. "Canst thou not? Even so, my lady, I think thou shalt survive me."

"Everything I have," I told him fiercely, "everything I am, is for thee. The island, the palace, our children— naught but for thee. If thou goest, what have I left?"

He looked at me full on. "Thyself."

The ice cloud pricked my cheeks, pierced my skin. I was frozen inside. I was dying. He looked away again.

"I was a man, once."

"Thou art yet."

"A free man, with a free soul. Where bides it now?" He shook his head, his grizzled hair matted with the wind. "I am . . . ashamed."

I placed my hand on his leg and said it once more, softly, grieving:

"I cannot be without thee."

The air flashed before us in a haze of rainbowed white. He did not speak. But slowly his arm lifted to my shoulders, and pulled me close.

# CHAPTER SEVENTEEN

For an instant she floated. She felt herself floating, with the water beneath her and the air on her back, and Ruri thought, *Why, this is easy*, and then the pain came. It racked through her with sudden ferocity; she tried to kick against it, to fight free, but instead the ocean took her in and she sank deeper into the waves.

Fire, fury, her blood. It was like being dropped into a black savage sun, an inferno seething and dark. God, how stupid she had been—she was about to die here—after all her fears, she was going to drown anyway—

But she did not.

Iain watched her glide under the surf, a kick of her heels and then nothing but breakers. For a long while, he kept his eyes trained on the spot where she had gone under, but she didn't arise again.

He walked back to his fire—cinders now, charcoaled

wood—found her plaid shawl and wrapped it into a makeshift kilt. Then he sat down, and he waited.

In time, the sun began to rise.

She could breathe. She could swim. The pain had stopped and Ruri felt unfettered, liberated. She was an arrow shot from a bow, a bullet, speeding through light. In the ocean's silky suspension she turned her body and looked up at the surface of the sea, and saw the black sky shimmering.

She was a mermaid. She was.

She laughed at that. She turned a loop and caught a glimpse of her fish tail, tiny scales the color of coral, fins like dawn mist. She found a forest of kelp and threaded through it, let the leaves brush her face, let the currents sway her back and forth. How strangely intimate it was, to feel the life of the sea against her. How right.

She had not known who she was. She had never guessed. And all those people at Kelmere—the chauffeur, Mab—even the madwoman in the bar. Iain. They knew. And she had not.

Ruri found the reef, that stony protective circle. She found hulls of ships snared in its merciless arms. In the long rocky slope that was Kell, she found a sunken portal and swam through it to discover an empty grotto, a slick marble platform she could not climb.

She tried twice before giving up, staring down, confounded, at the pretty shimmer of her tail in the water.

Ruri slid back into the sea.

He saw her first as a mirage, as fair and far as an angel might be, a dark fleck against the twinkle of the ocean. But he knew it was she, he knew it, and the fleck vanished to reappear, closer; he could make out her slick hair, and the next time, her face. He stood and walked to the edge of the shore.

She rolled in with the waves, slipped a little, and then found her balance. He splashed out to her without waiting, the shock of the frigid water crawling up his skin, but Iain ignored that. He was looking at Ruriko, seated in the sand with her arms supporting her and latticed foam riffling at her waist. He felt his heart constrict in his chest.

She was bright with saltwater, black starry lashes and shining lips. Her tail—delicate pink, a shell touched by the sun—was coiled behind her in the sand. She kept her gaze below his, somewhere in the vicinity of his chest. He could not read her face.

Iain knelt before her, caught her chin with his fingers. The ocean lapped at the knotted plaid.

"Ruriko."

"When did you know?" She looked up at him.

"From the moment I first saw you." He wanted to smile, but his mouth couldn't manage it. "From the first instant."

She turned her face away, and he dropped his hand.

"How?" she asked, low.

He caught his breath. "Don't you remember?"

"No." But she shifted on her hands, foam dappling her arms.

He couldn't believe it—after all this, after all his hopes, all his work, it came to this moment when she'd found her true form, when she reflected glory like a damned mirror to eternity, and she *refused* to remember—

Her arm lifted, wet and gleaming. She held something in her fist.

"Here." Her fingers opened, and the silver locket flipped

down. He caught it as it fell, the chain slapping into his palm. "I found it after all."

"It's yours," Iain said.

"I don't want it."

"It doesn't matter if you *want* it," he said, rising. "You have to have it."

She glanced away, down to the swelling water and froth. Her tail made an angry little swish in the sand. "Why?"

"Because—" He laughed, an awful sound, bitter and irate and despairing. "Because, Ruriko, it carries your soul."

Her eyes raised to his.

"Don't you remember?" he asked again, helpless. "By the gods, lass. How could you truly forget?" He went back to his knees, gestured to the crested sea. "There, out there, I saved you, and you gave me your vow." He pointed to the beach. "There, we first made love." To the palace. "There—I built you a home."

Her face was pale, her eyes bruised. He took up her sanded hand, the locket cold between them, and the last of his hope fell through him like rain through a dark sky, washing away all that he was to reveal a great void, the absence of self.

"All my life, it's haunted me, these memories, like a dream or—sometimes—a mad delusion. As a child, they could comfort me. As a man—" His voice turned ragged. "God, these thoughts, these images, burned into my head—they seemed so incredible. But I could never escape the call of the ocean. I went to school, and I studied, and I learned. I discovered ancient ships that I knew, sunk in places that I knew, miles deep in the sea. I made my fortune reliving my past. I even found Kelmere, and Kell. And then I found our family. But I never found you."

He looked at her fingers, so slender over his own. "I've

been a man missing half himself, walking around, talking, existing . . . incomplete. No one seemed to notice. But a half life is no way to be."

Iain turned his face to the sky, a stone in his throat that he fought to contain, and then, when he could, looked back at her again. She was ice and impossible radiance, blue storms in her eyes.

"Ah, Ruriko," he said, with a sound caught between a laugh and a groan, "you don't remember." Slowly, slowly, he brought his forehead to rest on their clasped hands. "But everything I was, everything I am—was for you. Ever you."

Ruri felt the tremor of his fingers, the rush of his breath over her wrist. He had wrapped the shawl around him but the knot had loosened; the cloth began to float free, pushing against her. The sun carved sharp shadows around them both, throwing gold along his shoulders, the proud bend of his back.

And all at once, by the gleam of his bowed head and the numbed, imperfect flowering of her mind, a single memory broke through.

*Her hand, tearing the locket from a white throat. Opening it, and hearing a voice—dulcet, ravaged—cry out. Darkness falling up to meet her.*

Pain cut through her body, an unexpected rising that tore into her bones. She jerked away from him, anguished, nearly falling back, but Iain had her again by the waist.

"Stand up! You've legs again. Stand up." Together they staggered to their knees and then their feet. He steadied her until she found sure footing, then drew her close. "I love you." He pressed salt kisses to her cheek. "I love you. I've waited so long."

*Live thee with me, my hand, my heart.*

She raised her face to his—and remembered.

*Thy soul.*

He claimed her mouth, his hands skimming her back, then harder, a deeper stroking.

And she remembered.

*Always and for always.*

Ruri pulled from his embrace, panting. "I can't. I can't stay here."

He didn't reach for her again, only looked at her with a taut strain around his eyes, his arms falling to his sides.

"I can't," she repeated, desperate, as if he argued. "I have a family now. I have people who love me."

"I love you," he said, very quiet.

"I have a life! And—a job! And I can't spend it just here, on this island." She felt vulnerable suddenly, aware of her body, and his, shining bare in the surf. She bent down to scoop the shawl from the water and clutched it to her chest. "Please—don't ask me to do that."

"I won't."

Her hands and wrists were twined at her throat. "What?"

"I won't keep you, Ruriko. I ask nothing of you. You're not a prisoner here." He began to walk back up the beach, a spreading wake behind him. She looked blankly at the colors he had stirred from the sea, then at his retreating shape. With the shawl still held to her chest, she followed.

Iain went to the fire, picked up a stick of driftwood and gave the charred ash a vicious poke. Ruri stood apart, dripping.

"You—won't make me stay?"

He laughed once more, deep in his throat. "And how might I accomplish that, I ask you? Look around you. This is your world. You may swim all the way back to America, if you wish. I wouldn't stop you, even if I could."

One of the burned logs fell apart in a rustle of red-fringed coals. He sent her a defiant look.

"Don't mistake me. You belong to me. You belonged to me then, and you belong to me now. When you died, I—" He glared down at the coals, his jaw clenching, then went on in a grimmer tone. "But I'd like to think I learned something from that life." He poked the cinders again. "I can damned well hope so, in any case."

She stood there, hearing his words, watching the bare, muscular contours of him against the rugged outline of Kell.

Iain against forest.

Iain against sand, and ruins.

And for a second, with the cool breath of the northern wind, she saw—someone else. A different face. The same wild, wild heart—

*No.*

He looked up at her once more, a lone man by a dying fire; his voice dropped soft. "*You* are my soul, Ruriko Kell. And all my faith. My good hope. I was flawed then, fatally so. I loved too much, I feared too much. But through it all—through all my mistakes—I always knew that you were the finest part of me. Perhaps that's why I held on to you so tight." He kicked sand at a glowing ember, sending it to dust. "I'll not do it again. If you don't want to stay, then go."

The wind returned, lifted the wet shawl from her arms. She released it and it flopped down into the sand.

"I'm going to get dressed," Ruri said.

The refuge of the ruin was like a balm over her skin, flushed from the sun and from him. She walked to their room without thinking, went to the chest of her clothing and only stopped when she realized she had no clothing in there. It was on the floor. On the bed. She thought her sweater might still be by the bush outside.

Ruri found her camisole, pressed her face into its stiff folds. It smelled of the ocean. It reminded her of him.

She did not know him; he was a stranger to her heart. But at the same time . . .

She raised her head, looked guardedly around the chamber. And in her mind's eye the tower transformed:

The bed used to be over there, closer to the windows. They would lie together at night, heads together, and count the constellations.

The banners had been in her favorite colors. The chest had been covered in leather.

There had been a starling that sang from the eaves, that every spring offered a pure descant to the dark evening winds.

She went to her knees on the stone floor. She lost her breath. She felt her heart hammering and a strange, dry panic in her blood. Years of accumulated sand and grit scratched into her legs.

Ruri thought of Iain and saw again that someone else, someone with dark blue eyes and a blinding smile, who had laughed with her and lived with her and made her feel truly whole. Cherished.

Her face was hot and stinging; she made a sound into the camisole. When it rose again into her throat, she pinched her lips tight against it and felt her world begin to pull apart.

She was the night sky, shattered. She had monsters, memories, tugging at her depths, and they roiled and turned and became his face, nothing monstrous at all, but something beloved and worn, and more dear than her own life.

She had thought herself so alone after her parents had

died. She thought she had understood the word—but the look in Iain's eyes just now . . .

A man without family, but who had lived to claim his own. A man without history, who had wrenched it from the past. Who lived in a mansion with echoing rooms; who possessed paintings and mountains, and slept alone in his bed.

A man without love, but who had found that too—who had waited for her with golden glances and hard-tempered patience—

*If you don't want to stay, then go.*

Ruri pulled the camisole over her shoulders, looked around until she found her panties at the foot of the bed and then her jeans—dried stiff as well—in a petrified heap beside the desk. She began to work them up her legs.

She wanted, absurdly, to comb her damp hair, and made do with quickly braiding it instead. She stood before the windows as her hands worked, taking in the clean span of sky and hills, a single gannet soaring by.

Ruri moved closer and looked down to the beach below. Iain wasn't there.

She took another step, frowning, and leaned out. He wasn't anywhere that she could see, not by the shore or in the woods. Not climbing the stairs.

She left the chamber swiftly, went down to the beach, and stood by his fire. The sand spread in hillocks, and the trees nodded, and spray washed off the sea. And Iain was not there.

She closed her eyes and lifted her arms to the heavens and knew where she would find him.

The garden was a patchwork of foliage now, the fruit trees she had once prized—*plums, apples, pears*—long gone, the careful paths winding in different directions, wild roses and brambles strewn like tattered lace across everything familiar and not.

The alabaster bench was broken into pieces. Iain sat on the ground with his back propped against what used to be the base, staring out at the view of the sea. He still wore no clothes. One knee was drawn up, his arm slung across it. The locket dangled from his fingers.

She came to stand near him, facing the ocean as he did. From here she could see three tiny red specks that were buoys, evenly spaced in greenish waters.

"Aren't you cold?" she asked, curling her toes in gravel and moss.

His fine shoulders made a shrug. "A bit."

Ruri sat beside him on the ground. Even now, hard-planed and brusque, he was beautiful, posed for a perfect picture: the majesty of man against the sea. She inched a little closer to him.

"I could keep you warm," she said. "If you wish."

He gave her a sidelong look. The cautious glint to his eyes seemed to tear at her heart, so she dropped her gaze, then lifted his hand to her lap.

"You know, you told me once that your interest in me was purely professional."

"Aye." He watched her stroke his fingers, aligning hers over his, then sliding them through to join their hands. "I'm a good liar. I usually win at poker too."

"Remind me not to play with you."

His voice tightened. "On the contrary. You may play with me anytime you wish."

Very deliberately, she turned her head, brushed a kiss across the smooth rise of his shoulder.

Iain said her name, a harsh entreaty, but did not move.

"I'm sorry," she whispered, "for what's done. For what

I did back then. I'm sorry for leaving you. I always loved you."

"I know."

"I don't remember everything, but that night, with the locket—I can't explain it. I was so—empty. And alone. Even with you there, I was alone. I think I lost myself here, a little more and a little more every passing year. And then one day I realized there was nothing of me left." She pressed her face into his arm. "I never knew it would hurt so much, to feel this way."

"It doesn't have to hurt, Ruriko."

"I cannot stay."

"I wouldn't keep you, lass. I know you have family, and a home in the States. But—it's a wide, wide world." He touched her cheek with one callused finger. "Mayhap—sometime—you could share some of it with me."

"I don't know." She took a breath, looked up at him from beneath her lashes. "My family's rather strict in a lot of ways. I don't think they'd approve of me living in sin."

He made a faint laugh. "Is this sin?"

She lifted her chin. "I don't know why it has to be."

The cool contact of his skin shifted away from her. He turned, sun-sculpted, and gazed at her with intent amber eyes.

"Would you marry me?"

"Well, I think I already have." And she smiled.

In the poetic tumble of her garden he smiled back at her, and then his hands came to her shoulders, slipped up her neck to the unfinished braid of her hair. She brought her cheek to his chest and closed her eyes.

"I love you," he said to her, combing his fingers through the braid, freeing it to soft waving strands. "Through myth and time. I have always loved you."

"Through myth and time," she murmured, tasting the words. "I still love you."

The wind tossed the leaves above their heads and a spark of silver lit from the gravel. He had let go of the locket. It lay between them, the chain looped to a spiral around a rough white pebble. Iain stiffened slightly, as if he had just noticed it too.

Ruri raised her head. "Does it really hold my soul?" she asked, serious.

"I don't know, lass. I don't know anymore."

"I thought it was gone. I thought—" She paused, awkward. "When I opened it, before—"

His expression was bleak. "So did I." He picked up the locket, sunlight winking across its face. "But even the ancient magics might not have been so strong. A human soul is an imperishable thing. You're here. And so is the necklace. I think mayhap . . . mayhap it never held your soul at all, but only your word. And when that was broken . . ."

The locket swung between them, turning against the green-blue sea.

"Open it," Ruri demanded.

His look to her was incredulous. "Nay."

She reached for it; his fist closed on the links.

"Ruriko—"

"I won't be a prisoner. I love you, and I choose to be with you. But I won't be kept by force."

Iain gazed at her a long moment with that hard, distant look she knew, then lowered his lashes. His fingers worked the metal. The scrolled oval resisted—then eased apart into two hinged pieces. He held them cupped in his palms, his brows drawn into a scowl.

The locket was empty.

Ruri cast a wild look up to the sky—endless, open—then back to him. Iain began to laugh once more, softly.

"What does it mean?"

His grin was jubilant. "We are free." He stood and lifted her in his arms, swinging her into a brisk, breathless whirl. "My love, my eternal heart. We are free."

# · EPILOGUE ·

Once there was an island. . . .

For a thousand, thousand years it lay untouched, alone and apart. But there came lovers, and then a palace, and laughter laced the air, and the moon rose and fell on many blessed lives. Time stretched to claim the isle; the days flashed and faded, and the nights drew out into a dusky string of pearls.

Yet in the ruins of the palace remained a chamber, and in the chamber was a fine bed, and tapestries, a desk and a chair. Atop the desk was a montage of glossy photographs, arranged along the wood.

Each photograph showed a different horizon, a different world, Vienna and Rome, Hobart and Tokyo and Saipan. And in every one stood a couple, dark-haired, handsome, their hands clasped and their faces close, the man tall and smiling, his lady blue-eyed, ethereal.

On the desk before the photos was placed a locket, polished silver that, when the sun turned just so, sent a spray of delicate light across the room to the windows, to join with the sky and the sea.